THE DELTA DECISION

Novels by Wilbur Smith

WILBUR SMITH

The Delta Decision

DOUBLEDAY & COMPANY, INC.
Garden City, New York
1981

Once again this book is for my wife
Danielle Antoinette

THE DELTA DECISION

There were only fifteen joining passengers for the British Airways flight at Victoria Airport on the island of Mahé in the oceanic republic of the Seychelles.

Two couples formed a tight group as they waited their turn for departure formalities. They were all young, all deeply tanned and they seemed still carefree and relaxed by their holiday in that island paradise. However, one of them made her three companions seem insignificant by the sheer splendour of her physical presence.

She was a tall girl, with long limbs and her head set on a proud, shapely neck. Her thick, sun-gilded blonde hair was twisted into a braid and coiled high on top of her head, and the sun had touched her with gold and brought out the bloom of youth and health upon her skin.

As she moved with the undulating grace of one of the big predatory cats, bare feet thrust into open sandals, the big pointed breasts joggled tautly under the thin cotton of her T-shirt and the tight round buttocks strained the faded denim of her hacked-off shorts.

Across the front of her T-shirt was blazoned the legend I AM A LOVE NUT and below it was drawn the suggestive outline of a coco-de-mer.

She smiled brilliantly at the dark-skinned Seychellois immigration officer as she slid the green United States Passport with its golden eagle across the desk to him, but when she turned to her male companion she spoke in quick fluent German. She retrieved her passport and led the others through into the security area.

Again she smiled at the two members of the Seychelles Police Force who were in charge of the weapons search, and she swung the net carry bag off her shoulder.

"You want to check these?" she asked, and they all laughed. The bag contained two huge coco-de-mer; the grotesque fruit, each twice the size of a human head, were the most popular souvenirs of the Islands. Each of her three companions carried similar trophies in net bags, and the police officer ignored such familiar objects and instead ran his metal detector in a perfunctory manner over the canvas flight bags which made up the rest of their hand luggage. It buzzed harshly on one bag and the boy who carried it shamefacedly produced a small Nikkormat camera. More laughter and then the police officer waved the group through into the final Departure Lounge.

It was already crowded with transit passengers who had boarded at Mauritius, and beyond the lounge windows the huge Boeing 747 Jumbo squatted on the tarmac, lit harshly by floodlights as the refuelling tenders fussed about her.

There were no free seats in the lounge and the group of four formed a standing circle under one of the big revolving punkah fans, for the night was close and humid—and the mass of humanity in the closed room sullied the air with tobacco smoke and the smell of hot bodies.

The blonde girl led the gay chatter and sudden bursts of laughter, standing inches above her two male companions and a full head above the other girl, so that they were a focus of attention for the hundreds of other passengers. Their manner had changed subtly since they entered the lounge, there was a sense of relief as though a serious obstacle had been negotiated, and an almost feverish excitement in the timbre of their laughter. They were never still, shifting restlessly from foot to foot, hands fiddling with hair or clothing.

Although they were clearly a closed group, quarantined by an almost conspiratorial air of camaraderie, one of the transit passengers left his wife sitting and stood up from his seat across the lounge.

"Say, do you speak English?" he asked, as he approached the group.

He was a heavy man in his middle fifties with a thick thatch of steel-grey hair, dark horn-rimmed spectacles, and the easy confident manner of success and wealth.

Reluctantly the group opened for him, and it was the tall blonde girl who answered, as if by right.

"Sure, I'm American also."

"No kidding?" The man chuckled. "Well, what do you know." And he was studying her with open admiration. "I just wanted to know what those things are." He pointed to the net bag of nuts that lay at her feet.

"They are coco-de-mer," the blonde answered.

"Oh yeah, I've heard of them."

"They call them 'love nuts,'" the girl went on, stooping to open the heavy bag at her feet. "And you can see why." She displayed one of the fruit for him.

The double globes were joined in an exact replica of a pair of human buttocks.

"Back end." She smiled, and her teeth were so white they appeared as translucent as fine bone china.

"Front end." She turned the nut, and offered for his inspection the perfect *mons veneris* complete with a feminine gash and a tuft of coarse curls, and now it was clear she was flirting and teasing; she altered her stance, thrusting her hips forward slightly, and the man glanced down involuntarily at her own plump *mons* beneath the tight blue denim, its deep triangle bisected by the fold of material which had rucked up into the cleft.

He flushed slightly and his lips parted with a small involuntary intake of breath.

"The male tree has a stamen as thick and as long as your arm." She widened her eyes to the size and colour of blue pansies, and across the lounge the man's wife stood up and came towards them, warned by some feminine instinct. She was much younger than her husband and very heavy and awkward with child.

"The Seychellois will tell you that in the full moon the male pulls up its roots and walks around to mate with the females—"

"As long and as thick as your arm"—smiled the pretty little dark-haired girl beside her—"wow!" She was also teasing now, and both girls dropped their gaze deliberately down the front of the man's body. He squirmed slightly, and the two young men who flanked him grinned at his discomfort.

His wife reached him and tugged at his arm. There was a red angry rash of prickly heat on her throat and little beads of perspiration across her upper lip, like transparent blisters.

"Harry, I'm not feeling well," she whined softly.

"I've got to go now," he mumbled with relief, his poise and confidence shaken, and he took his wife's arm and led her away.

"Did you recognize him?" asked the dark-haired girl in German, still smiling, her voice pitched very low.

"Harold McKevitt," the blonde replied softly in the same language. "Neuro-surgeon from Fort Worth. He read the closing paper to the convention on Saturday morning." She explained. "Big fish—very big fish," and like a cat she ran the pink tip of her tongue across her lips.

Of the four hundred and one passengers in the final Departure Lounge that Monday evening three hundred and sixty were surgeons, or their wives. The surgeons, including some of the most eminent in the world of medicine, had come from Europe and England and the United States, from Japan and South America and Asia, for the convention that had ended twenty-four hours previously on the island of Mauritius, five hundred miles to the south of Mahé island. This was one of the first flights out since then and it had been fully booked ever since the convention had been convoked.

"British Airways announces the departure of Flight BA 070 for Nairobi and London; will transit passengers please board now through the main gate." The announcement was in the soft singsong of the Creole accent, and there was a massed movement towards the exit.

"Victoria Control this is Speedbird Zero Seven Zero request push back and start clearance."

"Zero Seven Zero you are cleared to start and taxi to holding point for runway Zero One."

"Please copy amendment to our flight plan for Nairobi. Number of Pax aboard should be 401. We have a full house."

"Roger, Speedbird, your flight plan is amended."

The gigantic aircraft was still in its nose-high climb configuration and the seat belt and no-smoking lights burned brightly down the length of the first-class cabin. The blonde girl and her companion sat side by side in the roomy seats 1A and 1B directly behind the forward bulkhead that partitioned off the command area and the first-class galley. The seats that the young couple occupied had been reserved many months previously.

The blonde nodded and the young man leaned forward to screen her from the passengers across the aisle while she slipped one of the coco-de-mer from its net bag and held it in her lap.

Through its natural division the nut had been carefully sawn into two sections to allow removal of the milk and the white flesh, then the two sections had been glued together again just as neatly. The joint was only apparent after close inspection.

The girl inserted a small metal instrument into the joint and twisted it sharply, and with a soft click the two sections fell apart like an Easter egg.

In the nests formed by the double husk of the shells, padded with strips of plastic foam, were two smooth, grey, egg-like objects —each the size of a baseball.

They were grenades of East German manufacture, with the Warsaw Pact command designation MK IV (C). The outer layer of each grenade was armoured plastic, the type used in landmines to prevent discovery by electronic metal detectors. The yellow stripe around each grenade indicated that it was not a fragmentation type, but was designed for high impact concussion.

The blonde girl took a grenade in her left hand, unlatched her lap belt and slipped quietly from her seat. The other passengers paid her only passing interest as she ducked through the curtains into the galley area. However, the purser and the two stewardesses, still strapped into their fold-down seats, looked up sharply as she entered the service area.

"I'm sorry, madam, but I must ask you to return to your seat until the Captain extinguishes the seat-belt lights."

The blonde girl held up her left hand and showed him the shiny grey egg.

"This is a special grenade, designed for killing the occupants of a battle tank," she said quietly. "It could blow the fuselage of this aircraft open like a paper bag or kill by concussion any human being within fifty yards."

She watched their faces, saw the fear bloom like an evil flower.

"It is fused to explode three seconds after it leaves my hand." She paused again, and her eyes glittered with excitement and her breath was quick and shallow.

"You"—she selected the purser—"take me to the flight deck; you others stay where you are. Do nothing, say nothing."

When she ducked into the tiny cockpit, hardly large enough to contain the members of the flight crew and its massed banks of instruments and electronic equipment, all three men turned to look back at her in mild surprise—and she lifted her hand and showed them what she carried.

They understood instantly.

"I am taking command of this aircraft," she said, and then, to the flight engineer, "Switch off all communications equipment."

The engineer glanced quickly at his captain, and when he nodded curtly, began obediently to shut down his radios—the very high frequency sets, then the high frequency, and the ultra high frequency.

"And the satellite relay," the girl commanded. He glanced up at her, surprised by her knowledge.

"And don't touch the bug." He blinked at that. Nobody, but nobody, outside the company should have known about the special relay which, when activated by the button beside his right knee, would instantly alert Heathrow Control to an emergency and allow them to monitor any conversation on the flight deck. He lifted his hand away.

"Remove the fuse to the bug circuit." She indicated the correct box above his head, and he glanced at the captain again, but her voice stung like the tail of a scorpion.

"Do what I tell you."

Carefully he removed the fuse and she relaxed slightly.

"Read your departure clearance," she instructed.

"We are cleared to radar departure on track for Nairobi and an unrestricted climb to cruise altitude of thirty-nine thousand feet."

"When is your next 'operations normal' due?"

Operations normal was the routine report to Nairobi Control to assure them that the flight was proceeding as planned.

"In eleven minutes and thirty-five seconds." The engineer was a young, dark-haired, rather handsome man with a deep forehead, pale skin and the quick, efficient manner instilled by his training.

The girl turned to the captain of the Boeing and their gazes locked as they measured each other. The captain's hair was more grey than black and cropped close to his big rounded skull. He was bull-necked, and had the beefy, ruddy face of a farmer or of a butcher—but his eyes were steady and his manner calm and unshakeable. He was a man to watch, the girl recognized instantly.

"I want you to believe that I am committed entirely to this operation," she said slowly, "and that I would welcome the opportunity to sacrifice my life to my cause." Her dark blue eyes held his without fear, and she read the first growth of respect in him. That was good, all part of her careful calculations.

"I believe that," said the pilot, and nodded once.

"Your duty is to the four hundred and seventeen lives aboard this aircraft," she went on. He did not have to reply. "They will be safe, just as long as you follow my commands implicitly. That I promise you."

"Very well."

"Here is our new destination." She handed him a small white typewritten card. "I want a new course with forecast winds, and a time of arrival. Your turn onto the new heading to commence immediately after your next 'operations normal' report in—" She glanced back at the engineer for the time.

"Nine minutes fifty-eight seconds," he said promptly.

"And I want your turn to the new heading to be very gentle, very balanced. We don't want any of the passengers to spill their champagne—do we?"

In the few minutes that she had been on the flight deck she had already established a bizarre rapport with the captain; it was a blend of reluctant respect and overt hostility and of sexual awareness. She had dressed deliberately to reveal her body, and in her excitement her nipples had hardened and darkened, pushing out through the thin cotton shirt with its suggestive legend, and the musky woman's smell of her body again intensified by her excitement filled the confined cockpit.

Nobody spoke again for many minutes, then the flight engineer broke the silence.

"Thirty seconds to 'operations normal.'"

"All right, switch on the H F and make the report."

"Nairobi Approach this is Speedbird 070."

"Go ahead Speedbird 070."

"Operations normal," said the engineer into his headset.

"Roger, 070. Report again in forty minutes."

"070."

The blonde girl sighed with relief. "All right, shut down the set." Then to the captain, "Disengage the flight director and make the turn to the new heading by hand. Let's see how gentle you can be."

The turn was a beautiful exhibition of flying, two minutes to make a change of 76° of heading, the needles of the turn-and-balance indicator never deviating a hair's breadth, and when it was completed, the girl smiled for the first time.

It was a gorgeous sunny flash of very white teeth.

"Good," she said, smiling directly into the captain's face. "What is your name?"

"Cyril," he replied after a moment's hesitation.

"You can call me Ingrid."

There was no set routine to the days in this new command of Peter Stride's, except the obligatory hour on the range with pistol and automatic weapons. No member of Thor Command—not even the technicians—was spared daily range practice.

The rest of Peter's day had been filled with unrelenting activity, beginning with a briefing on the new electronic communications equipment that had just been installed in his command aircraft. This had taken half the morning, and he had been only just in time to join his striker force in the main cabin of the Hercules transport for the day's exercise.

Peter jumped with the first stick of ten men. They jumped from five hundred feet, the parachutes seeming to snap open only seconds before they hit the ground. However, the crosswind had been strong enough to spread them out a little even from that height. The first landing had not been tight enough for Peter. They had taken two minutes fifty-eight seconds from jump to penetration of the deserted administration block standing forlornly in one of the military zones of Salisbury plain.

"If they had been holding hostages in here, we'd have arrived just in time to start mopping up the blood," Peter told his men grimly. "We'll do it again!"

This time they had cut one minute fifty seconds off their time, falling in a tightly steered pattern about the building—beating the time of Colin Noble's No. 2 striker team by ten seconds.

To celebrate Peter had scorned the military transports and they had run the five miles to the airstrip, each man in full combat kit and carrying the enormous bundle of his used parachute silk.

The Hercules was waiting to fly them back to base, but it was after dark before they landed and taxied into Thor Command's security compound at the end of the main runway.

For Peter the temptation to leave the de-briefing to Colin Noble had been strong indeed. His driver would have picked up Melissa-Jane at East Croydon Station and she would already be waiting alone in the new cottage, only half a mile from the base gates.

He had not seen her for six weeks, not since he had taken command of Thor, for in all that time he had not allowed himself a single day's respite. He felt a tickle of guilt now, that he should be allowing himself this indulgence, and so he lingered a few minutes after the briefing to transfer command to Colin Noble.

"Where are you going for the weekend?" Colin demanded.

"She's taking me to a pop concert tomorrow night—The Living Dead, no less," Peter chuckled. "Seems I haven't lived until I hear the Dead."

"Give M.J. my love, and a kiss," Colin told him.

Peter placed high value on his new-found privacy. He had lived most of his adult life in officers' quarters and messes, constantly surrounded by other human beings. However, this command had given him the opportunity to escape.

The cottage was only four and a half minutes' drive from the compound, but it might have been an island. It had come furnished and at a rental that surprised him pleasantly. Behind a high hedge of dog rose, off a quiet lane, and set in a sprawling rather unkempt garden, it had become home in a few weeks. He had even been able to unpack his books at last. Books accumulated over twenty years, and stored against such an opportunity. It was a comfort to have them piled around his desk in the small front room or stacked on the tables beside his bed, even though there had been little opportunity to read much of them yet. The new job was a tough one.

Melissa-Jane must have heard the crunch of gravel under the Rover's tyres, and she would certainly have been waiting for it. She came running out of the front door into the driveway, directly into the beam of the headlights, and Peter had forgotten how lovely she was. He felt his heart squeeze.

When he stepped out of the car she launched herself at him and clung with both arms around his chest. He held her for a long moment, neither of them able to speak. She was so slim and warm, her body seeming to throb with life and vitality.

At last he lifted her chin and studied her face. The huge violet eyes swam with happy tears, and she sniffed loudly. Already she had that old-fashioned English porcelain beauty, there would never be the acne and the agony of puberty for Melissa-Jane.

Peter kissed her solemnly on the forehead. "You'll catch your death," he scolded fondly.

"Oh Daddy, you are a real fusspot." She smiled through the tears and on tip-toe she reached up to kiss him full on the mouth.

They ate lasagne and cassata at an Italian restaurant in Croydon, and Melissa-Jane did most of the talking. Peter watched and listened, revelling in her freshness and youth. It was hard to believe she was not yet fourteen, for physically she was almost fully developed, the breasts under the white turtle-neck sweater no longer merely buds; and she conducted herself like a woman ten years older, only the occasional gleeful giggle betraying her or the lapse as she used some ghastly piece of Roedean slang—"grotty" was one of these.

Back at the cottage she made them Ovaltine and they drank it beside the fire, planning every minute of the weekend ahead of them and skirting carefully around the pitfalls, the unwritten taboos of their relationship which centred mostly on "Mother."

When it was time for bed she came and sat in his lap and traced the lines of his face with her fingertip.

"Do you know who you remind me of?"

"Tell me," he invited.

"Gary Cooper—only much younger, of course," she added hurriedly.

"Of course," Peter chuckled. "But where did you ever hear of Gary Cooper?"

"They had *High Noon* as the Sunday movie on telly last week."

She kissed him again and her lips tasted of sugar and Ovaltine, and her hair smelled sweet and clean.

"How old are you, anyway, Daddy?"

"I'm thirty-nine."

"That isn't really so terribly old." She comforted him uncertainly.

"Sometimes it's as old as the dinosaurs—" and at that moment the bleeper beside his empty cup began its strident, irritating electronic tone, and Peter felt the slide of dread in his stomach.

Not now, he thought. Not on this day when I have been so long without her.

The bleeper was the size of a cigarette pack, the globe of its single eye glared redly, insistent as the audio-signal. Reluctantly Peter picked it up and, with his daughter still in his lap, he switched in the miniature two-way radio and depressed the send button.

"Thor One," he said.

The reply was tinny and distorted, the set near the limit of its range.

"General Stride, Atlas has ordered condition Alpha."

Another false alarm, Peter thought bitterly. There had been a dozen Alphas in the last month, but why on this night. Alpha was the first stage of alert with the teams embarked and ready for condition Bravo which was the GO.

"Inform Atlas we are seven minutes from Bravo."

Four and a half of those would be needed for him to reach the compound, and suddenly the decision to rent the cottage was shown up as dangerous self-indulgence. In four and a half minutes innocent lives can be lost.

"Darling," he hugged Melissa-Jane swiftly, "I'm sorry."

"That's all right." She was stiff and resentful.

"There will be another time soon, I promise."

"You always promise," she whispered, but she saw he was no longer listening. He dislodged her and stood up, the heavy jawline clenched and thick dark brows almost meeting above the narrow, straight, aristocratic nose.

"Lock the door when I'm gone, darling. I'll send the driver for you if it's Bravo. He will drive you back to Cambridge, and I will let your mother know to expect you."

He stepped out into the night, still shrugging into his duffle coat, and she listened to the whirl of the starter, the rush of tyres over gravel and the dwindling note of the engine.

The controller in Nairobi tower allowed the British Airways flight from Seychelles to run fifteen seconds past its reporting time. Then he called once, twice and a third time without reply. He switched frequencies to the channels reserved for information, approach, tower and, finally, emergency, on one at least of which 070 should have been maintaining listening watch. There was still no reply.

Speedbird 070 was forty-five seconds past "operations normal" before he removed the yellow slip from his approach rack and placed it in the emergency "lost contact" slot, and immediately search and rescue procedures were in force.

Speedbird 070 was two minutes and thirteen seconds past "operations normal" when the telex pull sheet landed on the British Airways desk at Heathrow Control, and sixteen seconds later Atlas had been informed and had placed Thor Command on condition Alpha.

The moon was three days short of full, its upper rim only slightly indented by the earth's shadow. However, at this altitude it seemed almost as big as the sun itself and its golden light was certainly more beautiful.

In the tropical summer night great silver cloud ranges towered into the sky, and mushroomed into majestic thunder heads, and the moonlight dressed them in splendour.

The aircraft fled swiftly between the peaks of cloud, like a monstrous black bat on back-swept wings it bored into the west.

Under the port-side wing a sudden dark chasm opened in the clouds like the mouth of hell itself, and deep in its maw there was the faint twinkle of far light, like a dying star.

"That will be Madagascar," said the captain, his voice overly loud in the quiet cockpit. "We are on track." And behind his shoulder the girl stirred and carefully transferred the grenade into her other hand before she spoke for the first time in half an hour.

"Some of our passengers might still be awake and notice that." She glanced at her wristwatch. "It's time to wake up the others and let them know the good news." She turned back to the flight engineer. "Please switch on all the cabin lights and the seat-belt lights and let me have the microphone."

Cyril Watkins, the captain, was reminded once again that this was a carefully planned operation. The girl was timing her announcement to the passengers when their resistance would be at its lowest possible ebb; at two o'clock in the morning after having been awoken from the disturbed rest of intercontinental flight their immediate reaction was likely to be glum resignation.

"Cabin and seat-belt lights are on," the engineer told her, and handed her the microphone.

"Good morning, ladies and gentlemen." Her voice was warm, clear and bright. "I regret having to waken you at such an inconvenient hour. However, I have a very important announcement to make and I want all of you to pay the most careful attention." She paused, and in the cavernous and crowded cabins there was a general stir and heads began to lift, hair tousled and eyes unfocused and blinking away the cobwebs of sleep. "You will notice that the seat-belt lights are on. Will you all check that the persons beside you are fully awake and that their seat belts are fastened. Cabin staff please make certain that this is done."

She paused again, the belts would inhibit any sudden movement, any spontaneous action at the first shock. Ingrid noted the passage of sixty seconds on the sweep hand of her wristwatch before going on.

"First let me introduce myself. My name is Ingrid. I am a senior officer of the Action Commando for Human Rights"—Captain Watkins curled his lip cynically at the pompous, self-righteous title, but kept silent, staring ahead into the starry, moonlit depths of space—"and this aircraft is under my command. Under no circumstances whatsoever will any of you leave your seats without the express permission of one of my officers—if this order is disobeyed, it will lead directly to the destruction of this aircraft and all aboard by high explosive."

She repeated the announcement immediately in fluent German, and then in less proficient but clearly intelligible French before reverting to English once again.

"Officers of the Action Commando will wear red shirts for immediate identification and they will be armed."

As she spoke her three companions in the front of the first-class cabin were stripping out the false bottoms from their canvas flight bags. The space was only two inches deep by fourteen by eight, but it was sufficient for the broken-down twelve-bore pistols, and ten rounds of buckshot cartridges. The barrels of the pistols were fourteen inches long, the bores were smooth and made of armoured plastic. This material would not have withstood the passage of a solid bullet through rifling or any of the newer explosive propellants but it had been designed for use with the lower velocity and pressures of multiple shot and cordite. The breech piece was of plastic as were the double pistol grips, and these clipped swiftly into position. The only metal in the entire weapon was the case-steel firing pin and spring, no bigger than one of the metal studs in the canvas flight bag, so they would not have activated the metal detectors of the security check at Mahé airport. The ten cartridges contained in each bag had plastic cases and bases, again only the percussion caps were of aluminium foil, which would not disturb an electrical field. The cartridges were packed in looped cartridge belts which buckled around the waist.

The weapons were short, black and ugly, they required reloading like a conventional shotgun, the spent shells were not self-ejecting and the recoil was so vicious that it would break the wrists of the user who did not bear down heavily on the pistol grips. However, at ranges up to thirty feet the destructive power was awesome, at twelve feet it would disembowel a man and at six feet it would blow his head off cleanly—yet it did not have the penetrating power to hole the pressure hull of an intercontinental airliner.

It was the perfect weapon for the job in hand, and within a few seconds three of them had been assembled and loaded and the two men had slipped on the bright scarlet shirts that identified them over their T-shirts and moved to their positions—one in the back of the first-class cabin and one in the back of the tourist cabin, they stood with their grotesque weapons ostentatiously displayed.

The slim, pretty, dark-haired German girl stayed in her seat a little longer, working swiftly and neatly as she opened the remaining coco-de-mer and transferred their contents into two of the net bags. These grenades differed from the one carried by Ingrid only in that they had double red lines painted around the middle. This signified that they were electronically fused.

Now Ingrid's clear young voice resumed over the cabin address system, and the long rows of passengers—all fully awake now—sat rigid and attentive, their faces reflecting an almost uniform expression of shock and trepidation.

"The officer of the Action Commando who is moving down the cabin at this time is placing high explosive grenades." The dark-haired girl started down the aisle, and every fifteen rows she opened one of the overhead lockers and placed a grenade in it, closed the locker and moved on. The passengers' heads revolved slowly in unison as they watched her with the fascination of total horror. "A single one of those grenades has the explosive power to destroy this aircraft—they were designed to kill by concussion the crew of a battle tank protected by six inches of armour. The officer is placing fourteen of these devices along the length of this aircraft. They can be detonated simultaneously by an electronic transmitter under my control"—the voice contained a hint of mischief now, a little undercurrent of laughter—"and if that happened they'd hear the bang at the North Pole!"

The passengers stirred like the leaves of a tree in a vagrant breeze, somewhere a woman began to weep. It was a strangled passionless sound and nobody even looked in her direction.

"But don't worry yourselves. That isn't going to happen. Because everybody is going to do exactly as they are told, and when it's all over you are going to be proud of your part in this operation. We are all partners in a noble and glorious mission, we are all warriors for freedom and for the dignity of man. Today we take a mighty step forward into the new world—a world purged and cleansed of injustice and tyranny and dedicated to the welfare of all its peoples."

The woman was still weeping, and now a child joined her on a higher, more strident note.

The dark-haired girl returned to her seat and retrieved the camera that had activated the metal detector at Mahé airport. She slung it around her neck and crouched again to assemble the two remaining shot pistols. Carrying them and the cartridge belts she hurried forward to the flight deck where the big blonde kissed her delightedly and unashamedly on the lips.

"Karen, *Liebling*, you were wonderful." And then she took the camera from her and slung it around her own neck.

"This," she explained to the captain, "is not what it appears to be. It is the remote radio detonator for the grenades in the fuselage."

He nodded without replying, and with obvious relief Ingrid disarmed the grenade that she had carried for so long by replacing the safety pin. She handed it to the other girl.

"How much longer to the coast?" she asked as she strapped and buckled the cartridge belt around her waist.

"Thirty-two minutes," said the flight engineer, and Ingrid opened the breech of the pistol, checked the load and then snapped it closed again.

"You and Henri can stand down now," she told Karen. "Try and sleep."

The operation might last many days still, and exhaustion would be the most dangerous enemy they would have to contend with. It was for this reason alone that they had employed such a large force. From now on, except in an emergency, two of them would be on duty and two would be resting.

"You have done a very professional job"—said the pilot, Cyril Watkins—"so far."

"Thank you." Ingrid laughed, and over the back of his seat placed a comradely hand on his shoulder. "We have practised very hard for this day."

Peter Stride dipped his lights three times as he raced down the long narrow alley that led to the gates of the compound without slowing the Rover, and the sentry swung the gate open just in time for him to roar through.

There were no floodlights, no bustling activity—just the two aircraft standing together in the echoing cavern of the hangar.

The Lockheed Hercules seemed to fill the entire building, one that had been built to accommodate the smaller bombers of World War II. The tall vertical fin of its epinage reached to within a few feet of the roof girders.

Beside it the Hawker Siddeley HS 125 executive jet seemed dainty and ineffectual. The differing origins of the machines emphasized that this unit was a co-operative venture between two nations.

This was underscored once more when Colin Noble hurried forward to meet Peter as he cut the Rover's engine and lights.

"A great night for it, Peter." There was no mistaking the drawl of Midwestern America, although Colin looked more like a successful used-car salesman than a colonel in the U.S. Marines. In the beginning Peter had believed that this strict apportioning of material and manpower on equal national lines might weaken the effectiveness of Atlas. He no longer had those doubts.

Colin wore the nondescript blue overalls and cloth cap, both embroidered with the legend "THOR COMMUNICATIONS" which deliberately made him look more of a technician than a soldier.

He was Peter's second-in-command. They had known each other only the six weeks since Peter had assumed command of Thor, but after a short period of mutual wariness the two men had formed one of those fast bonds of liking and mutual respect.

Colin was of medium height, but none the less a big man. First glance might have given the impression that he was fat, for his body had a certain toad-like spread to it. There was no fat upon his frame, however, it was all muscle and bone. He had boxed heavyweight for Princeton and the marines, and his nose above the wide laughing mouth had been broken just below the bridge, where it was lumped and twisted slightly.

Colin cultivated the boisterous bluff manner of a career athlete, but his eyes were the colour of burned toffee and were brightly intelligent and all-seeing. He was tough and leery as an old alley cat. It was not easy to earn the respect of Peter Stride. Colin had done so in under six weeks.

He stood now between the two aircraft, while his men went about their Alpha preparation with quick understated efficiency.

Both aircraft were painted in commercial airline style, blue and white and gold, with a stylized portrait of the Thunder God on the tail fin and the "THOR COMMUNICATIONS" title down the fuselage. They could land at any airport in the world without causing undue comment.

"What is the buzz, Colin?" Peter Stride demanded as he slammed the Rover's door and hurried to meet the American. It had taken him some time and conscious effort to adapt his language and mode of address to fit in with his new second-in-command. He had learned very early not to expect that, merely because he was the youngest major-general in the British army, Colonel Colin Noble was going to call him "Sir" every time he spoke.

"Missing Aircraft." It could have been a train, an embassy, even an ocean liner, Peter realized. "British Airways. For Chrissake let's get out of the cold." The wind was flapping the legs of Colin's overalls and tugging at his sleeves.

"Where?"

"Indian Ocean."

"Are we set for Bravo?" Peter asked as they climbed into his command plane.

"All set."

The interior of the Hawker had been re-styled to make it a compact headquarters and communications centre.

There was comfortable seating for four officers directly behind the flight deck. Then the two electronic engineers and their equipment occupied a separate rear compartment, beyond which were the toilet and galley in the extreme rear.

One of the technicians looked through the communicating door as Peter stooped into the cabin. "Good evening, General Stride— we have a direct link with Atlas established."

"Put him on the screen," he ordered as he sank into the padded leather of his chair behind the working desk.

There was a single fourteen-inch main television screen in the panel directly facing Peter, and above it four smaller six-inch screens for conference communication. The main screen came alive, and the image of the big noble leonine head firmed.

"Good afternoon, Peter." The smile was warm, charismatic, compelling.

"Good evening, sir."

And Dr. Kingston Parker tilted his head slightly to acknowledge the reference to the time difference between Washington and England.

"Right at this moment we are completely in the dark. All we have is that BA 070 with four hundred and one passengers and sixteen crew on a flight from Mahé to Nairobi has not reported for thirty-two minutes."

Parker was Chairman of the Intelligence Oversight Board, among other duties, and he reported directly to the President of the United States in that capacity. He was the President's personal and trusted friend. They had been in the same class at Annapolis, both of them had graduated in the top twenty, but unlike the President, Parker had gone directly into government.

Parker was an artist, a talented musician, the author of four scholarly works of philosophy and politics, and a grand master of chess. A man of overwhelming presence, of vast humanity and towering intelligence. Yet also he was a secret man, avoiding the glaring scrutiny of the media, hiding his ambitions, if ambitions he had—although the presidency of the United States would not be an impossible dream to such a man—only taking up with rare skill and strength any burden that was thrust upon him.

Peter Stride had met him personally on half a dozen occasions since being seconded to Thor. He had spent a weekend with Parker at his New York home, and his respect for the man had become boundless. Peter realized that he was the perfect head for such a complex concept as Atlas. It needed the philosopher's tempering influence over trained soldiers, it needed the tact and charisma of the diplomat to deal directly with the heads of two governments, and it needed that steely intellect to make the ultimate decision that could involve hundreds of innocent lives and incur fearsome political consequences.

Now swiftly and incisively he told Peter what little they knew of Flight 070 and what search and rescue routine was already in force, before going on, "Without being alarmist, this does seem to be the perfect target. The flight carries most of the world's leading surgeons, and the convention was public knowledge eighteen months ago. Doctors have the necessary image to appeal to public sentiment and their nationalities are nicely mixed—American, British, French, Scandinavian, German, Italian—three of those countries have notoriously *soft* records with militant activity. It's a British aircraft, and the final destination would probably have been chosen to further complicate the issue and inhibit any counter-action."

Parker paused, and a small crease of worry appeared for a moment in the broad smooth forehead.

"I have put Mercury on condition Alpha as well—if this is a strike the final destination could just as easily be eastwards of the aircraft's last reported position."

Atlas's offensive arm comprised three identical units. Thor would be used only in Europe or Africa. Mercury was based at the American Naval installation in Indonesia and covered Asia and Australasia, while Diana was in Washington itself and ready for counter-action in either of the American continents.

"I have Tanner of Mercury on the other relay now. I will be back to you in a few seconds, Peter."

"Very well, sir."

The screen went blank, and in the chair beside him Colin lit one of his expensive Dutch cheroots and crossed his ankles on the desk in front of him.

"Seems the great god Thor came down to earth for a little poontang. When he'd finished pleasuring one of the vestal virgins he thought he'd let her know the honour she'd been given. 'I'm Thor,' he told her. 'Tho am I,' she agreed, 'but it wath loth of fun.'"

Peter shook his head sorrowfully. "That's funny?" he asked.

"Helps to while away the time." Colin glanced at his wrist-watch. "If this is another false alarm, it's going to make it thirteen straight." He yawned. There was nothing to do. It had all been done before. Everything was in the ultimate state of readiness. In the huge Hercules transport, every item of a comprehensive arsenal of equipment was ready for instant use. The thirty highly trained soldiers were embarked. The flight crews of both aircraft were at their stations, the communications technicians had set up their links with satellites and through them to the available intelligence computers in Washington and London. It remained only to wait—the greater part of a soldier's life was spent waiting, but Peter had never become hardened to it. It helped now to have the companionship of Colin Noble.

In a life spent in the company of many men it was difficult to form close relationships. Here in the smaller closed ranks of Thor in shared endeavour they had achieved that and become friends, and their conversation was relaxed and desultory, moving casually from subject to subject, but without relaxing the undercurrent of alertness that gripped both men.

At one stage Kingston Parker came on the screen again to tell them that search and rescue aircraft had found no indications at the last reported position of 070, and that a photographic run by the "Big Bird" reconnaissance satellite had been made over the same area, but that film would not be ready for appraisal for another fourteen hours. Speedbird 070 was now one hour six minutes past "operations normal" and suddenly Peter remembered Melissa-Jane. He asked communications for a telephone line and dialled the cottage. There was no reply, so the driver would have collected her already. He hung up and rang Cynthia in Cambridge.

"Damn it, Peter. This really is most inconsiderate of you." Freshly aroused from sleep, her voice was petulant, immediately awakening only antipathies. "Melissa has been looking forward to this—"

"Yes, I know, and so have I."

"And George and I had arranged—" George, her new husband, was a political history don; despite himself Peter quite liked the man. He had been very good to Melissa-Jane.

"The exigencies of the service," Peter cut in lightly, and her voice took on a bitter edge.

"How often I had to listen to that—I hoped never to hear it again." They were on the same futile old treadmill, and he had to stop it.

"Look, Cynthia. Melissa is on her way—"

In front of him the big television screen lit and Kingston Parker's eyes were dark with regret, as though he mourned for all mankind.

"I have to go," Peter told the woman whom once he had loved, and broke the connection, leaning forward attentively towards the image on the screen.

"The South African radar defences have painted an unidentified target approaching their airspace," Kingston Parker told him. "Its speed and position correspond with those of 070. They have scrambled a Mirage flight to intercept—but in the meantime I'm assuming that it's a militant strike and we'll go immediately to condition Bravo, if you please, Peter."

"We are on our way, sir."

And beside him Colin Noble took his feet off the desk and thumped them together onto the floor. The cheroot was still clamped between his teeth.

The target was live and the pilot of the leading Mirage F.1 interceptor had his flight computer in "attack" mode and all his weaponry—missiles and cannon—were armed. The computer gave him a time to intercept of thirty-three seconds, and the target's heading was constant at 210° magnetic and its ground speed at 483 knots.

Ahead of him the dawn was rising in wildly theatrical display. Avalanches of silver and pink cloud tumbled down the sky, and the sun, still below the horizon, flung long lances of golden light across the heavens. The pilot leaned forward against his shoulder straps and lifted the Polaroid visor of his helmet with one gloved hand, straining ahead for the first glimpse of the target.

His trained gunfighter's eye picked out the dark speck against the distracting background of cloud and sunlight and he made an almost imperceptible movement of the controls to avoid the direct head-on approach to the target.

The speck swelled in size with disturbing rapidity as they converged at combined speeds of nearly fifteen hundred miles per hour, and at the instant he was certain of his identification the leader took his flight, still in a tight "fingers five," up into a vertical climb from which they rolled out neatly five thousand feet above the target and on the same heading, immediately reducing power to conform in speed to the big aircraft far below.

"Cheetah, this is Diamond Leader—we are visual, and target is a Boeing 747 bearing British Airways markings."

"Diamond Leader, this is Cheetah, conform to target, maintain five thousand feet separation and avoid any threatening attitudes. Report again in sixty seconds."

Major-General Peter Stride's executive jet was arrowing southwards and leaving its enormous protégé lumbering ponderously along in its wake. Every minute increased the distance between the two aircraft, and by the time they reached their ultimate destination—wherever that might be—there would probably be a thousand miles or more separating them.

However, the big Hercules's slow speed became a virtue when the need arose to take its heavy load of men and equipment into short unsurfaced strips in unlikely corners of the earth—perhaps in the "hot and high" conditions that a pilot most dreads.

It was the Hawker's job to get General Stride to the scene of terrorist activity as swiftly as possible, and the General's job once there to stall and procrastinate and bargain until Colin Noble's assault team caught up with him.

The two men were still in contact, however, and the small central television screen in front of Peter was permanently lit with a view of the interior of the Hercules's main hold. When he lifted his head from his work, Peter Stride could see a picture of his troops, all in the casual Thor overalls, lounging or sprawled in abandoned attitudes of relaxation down the central aisle of the Hercules. They also were veterans at the hard game of waiting, while in the foreground Colin sat at his small work desk, going through the voluminous checklist for "condition Charlie" which was the next state of alert when terrorist activity was confirmed.

Watching Colin at work, Peter Stride found a moment to ponder once again the enormous cost of maintaining Atlas, most of it paid by the United States intelligence budget, and the obstacles and resistance that had been overcome to launch the project in the first place. Only the success of the Israelis at Entebbe and of the Germans at Mogadishu had made it possible, but there was still violent opposition in both countries to maintaining a dual national counter-action force.

With a preliminary click and hum the central screen of Peter's communications console came alive and Dr. Parker spoke before his image had properly hardened.

"I'm afraid it's condition Charlie, Peter," he said softly, and Peter was aware of the rush of his blood through his veins. It was natural for a soldier whose entire life had been spent in training for a special moment in time to welcome the arrival of that moment—yet he found contempt for himself in that emotion; no sane man should anticipate violence and death, and all the misery and suffering which attended them.

"The South Africans have intercepted and identified 070. It entered their airspace forty-five seconds ago."

"Radio contact?" Peter asked.

"No." Parker shook his great head. "It is declining contact, and we must assume that it is under the control of militants—so now I'm going to be at this desk until this thing is settled." Kingston Parker never used the emotive word "terrorist" and he did not like to hear it from his subordinates either.

"Never hate your adversary blindly," he had told Peter once. "Understand his motives, recognize and respect his strengths—and you will be better prepared to meet him."

"What co-operation can we expect?" Peter asked.

"All African States that we have so far been able to contact have offered full co-operation, including overflight, landing and refuelling facilities—and the South Africans are being helpful. I have spoken to their defence minister, and he has offered the fullest possible co-operation. They will refuse 070 landing clearance, of course, and I anticipate that it will have to go on to one of the black states farther north, which is probably the militants' intention anyway. I think you know my views about South Africa—but in this instance I must say they are being very good."

Parker brought into the television shot a black briar pipe with a big round bowl, and began to stuff it with tobacco. His hands were large, like the rest of his body, but the fingers were long and supple as those of a pianist—which of course he was. And Peter remembered the scented smell of the tobacco he smoked. Even though he was a non-smoker, Peter had not found the odour offensive. Both men were silent, deep in thought, Parker frowning slightly as he seemed to concentrate on his pipe. Then he sighed and looked up again.

"All right, Peter. Let's hear what you have."

Peter shuffled through the notes he had been making. "I have prepared four tentative scenarios and our responses to each, sir. The most important consideration is whether this is a strike 'à l'allemande' or 'à l'italienne.'"

Parker nodded, listening; although this was well-travelled ground they must go over it again. A strike in the Italian fashion was the easier to resolve, a straight demand for cash. The German tradition involved release of prisoners, social and political demands that crossed national boundaries. They worked on for another hour before they were interrupted again.

"Good God." It was a measure of Kingston Parker's astonishment that he used such strong language. "We have a new development here—"

It was only when 070 joined the eastern airway and began to initiate a standard approach and let down, without however obtaining air traffic control clearance, that South African Airforce Command suddenly realized what was about to happen.

Immediately emergency silence was imposed on all the aviation frequencies while the approaching flight was bombarded by urgent commands to immediately vacate national airspace. There was no response whatsoever, and one hundred and fifty nautical miles out from Jan Smuts International Airport the Boeing reduced power and commenced a sedate descent to enter controlled airspace.

"British Airways 070 this is Jan Smuts Control, you are expressly refused clearance to join the circuit. Do you read me, 070?"

"British Airways 070 this is Airforce Command. You are warned that you are in violation of national airspace. You are ordered to climb immediately to thirty thousand feet and turn on course for Nairobi."

The Boeing was a hundred nautical miles out and descending through fifteen thousand feet.

"Diamond Leader, this is Cheetah. Take the target under command and enforce departure clearance."

The long sleek aircraft in its mottled green and brown battle camouflage dropped like a dart, rapidly overhauling the huge multi-engined giant, diving down just behind the tail and then pulling up steeply in front of the gaily painted red, white and blue nose.

Skilfully the Mirage pilot stationed his nimble little machine one hundred feet ahead of the Boeing and rocked his wings in the "Follow me" command.

The Boeing sailed on serenely as though it had not seen or understood. The Mirage pilot nudged his throttles and the gap between the two aircraft narrowed down to fifty feet. Again he rocked his wings and began a steady rate-one turn onto the northerly heading ordered by Cheetah.

The Boeing held rock steady on its standard approach towards Johannesburg, forcing the Mirage leader to abandon his attempts to lead her away.

He edged back alongside, keeping just above the jet-blast of the Boeing's port engines until he was level with the cockpit and could stare across a gap of merely fifty feet.

"Cheetah, this is Diamond One. I have a good view into target's flight deck. There is a fourth person in the cockpit. It's a woman. She appears to be armed with a machine pistol."

The faces of the two pilots were white as bone as they turned to watch the interceptor. The woman leaned over the back of the left-hand seat, and lifted the clumsy black weapon in an ironic salute. She smiled and the Mirage pilot was close enough to see how white her teeth were.

"A young woman, blonde hair, *mooi, baie mooi,*" the Mirage pilot reported. "Pretty—very pretty."

"Diamond One, this is Cheetah. Position for head-on attack."

The Mirage thundered instantly ahead and climbed away swiftly, the other four aircraft of the flight sweeping in to resume their tight "finger five" formation as they went out in a wide turn ahead of the Boeing.

"Cheetah. We are in position for a head-on attack."

"Diamond Flight. Simulate. Attack in line astern. Five-second intervals. Minimum separation. Do not, I say again, do not open fire. This is a simulated attack. I say again, this is a simulated attack."

"Diamond One—understands simulated attack."

And the Mirage F.1 winged over and dived, its speed rocketing around the mach scale, booming through the sonic barrier in a fearsomely aggressive display.

Cyril Watkins saw him coming from seven miles ahead.

"Jesus," he shouted. "This is real," and he lunged forward to take manual control of the Boeing, to pull her off the automatic approach that the electronic flight director was performing.

"Hold her steady." Ingrid raised her voice for the first time. "Hold it." She swung the gaping double muzzles of the shot pistol onto the flight engineer. "We don't need a navigator now."

The captain froze, and the Mirage howled down on them, seemed to grow until it filled the whole view through the windshield ahead. At the last possible instant of time the nose lifted slightly and it flashed only feet overhead, but the supersonic turbulence of its passage struck and tossed even that huge machine like a piece of thistledown.

"Here comes another," Cyril Watkins shouted.

"I mean it." Ingrid pressed the muzzles so fiercely into the back of the flight engineer's neck that his forehead struck the edge of his computer console, and there was the quick bright rose of blood on the pale skin.

The jet blasts struck the Boeing one after the other as the Mirages attacked. Ingrid clutched wildly for support with her free hand, but kept the pistol jammed into the navigator's neck. "I mean it," she kept shouting. "I'll kill him," and they could hear the screams of the passengers even through the bulkhead of the flight deck.

Then the last Mirage was passed and gone and the Boeing's flight director recovered from the battering of close separation and quickly realigned the aircraft on the radio navigational beacons of Jan Smuts Airport.

"They won't buzz us again." Ingrid stepped back from the flight engineer, allowing him to lift his head and wipe away the trickle of blood on the sleeve of his shirt. "They can't come again. We are into controlled airspace." She pointed ahead. "Look!"

The Boeing was down to five thousand feet, but the horizon was obscured by the haze of smog and summer heat. To the right rose the smooth silhouette of the Kempton Park Power Station cooling towers and, closer at hand, the poisonous yellow tablelands of the mine dumps squatted on the flat and featureless plain of the African highveld. Around them human habitation was so dense that hundreds of windowpanes caught the early morning sun and glittered like beacons.

Closer still was the long, straight, blue streak of the main runway of Jan Smuts Airport.

"Take her straight in on runway 21," Ingrid ordered.

"We can't—"

"Do it," snapped the girl. "Air traffic control will have cleared the circuit. They can't stop us."

"Yes, they can," Cyril Watkins answered. "Just take a look at the runway apron."

They were close enough now to count five fuel tenders, to see the Shell company insignia on the tanks.

"They are going to block the runway."

With the tankers were five brilliant red vehicles of the fire service and two big white ambulances. They bumped wildly over the grass verge of the runway and then, one after the other, tenders and fire control vehicles and ambulances parked at intervals of a few hundred yards down the white-painted centre line of the runway.

"We can't land," said the captain.

"Take her off automatic and fly her in by hand." The girl's voice was different, hard, cruel.

The Boeing was sinking through a thousand feet, lined up for runway 21 and directly ahead the revolving red beacons on top of the fire vehicles seemed to flash a direct challenge.

"I can't pile into them," Cyril Watkins decided, and there was no longer hesitation nor doubt in his tone. "I'm going to overshoot and get out of here."

"Land on the grass," the girl shrieked. "There is open grass on the left of the runway—put her down there."

But Cyril Watkins had leaned forward in his seat and rammed the bank of throttles forward. The engines howled and the Boeing surged into a nose-high climb.

The young flight engineer had swivelled his stool and was staring ahead through the windscreen. His whole body was rigid, his expression intense and the smear of blood across his forehead was in vivid contrast to the pallor of his skin.

With his right hand he gripped the edge of his desk, and the knuckles of his fist were white and shiny as eggshell.

Without seeming to move the blonde girl had pinned the wrist of that rigid right hand, pressing the muzzles of the pistol into it.

There was a crash of sound, so violent in the confines of the cabin that it seemed to beat in their eardrums. The weapon kicked up as high as the girl's golden head, and there was the immediate acrid stench of burned cordite.

The flight engineer stared down incredulously at the desk top. There was a hole blown through the metal as big as a teacup, and the edges were jagged with bright bare metal.

The blast of shot had amputated his hand cleanly at the wrist. The severed member had been thrown forward into the space between the pilots' seats, with the shattered bone protruding from the mangled meat. It twitched like a crushed and maimed insect.

"Land," said the girl. "Land or the next shot is through his head."

"You bloody monster," shouted Cyril Watkins, staring at the severed hand.

"Land or you will be responsible for this man's life."

The flight engineer clutched the stump of his arm against his belly and doubled over it silently, his face contorted by the shock.

Cyril Watkins tore his stricken gaze from the severed hand and looked ahead once more. There was wide open grass between the runway markers and the narrow taxiway. The grass had been mown knee-high, and he knew the ground beneath it would be fairly smooth.

Cyril's hand on the throttle bank pulled back smoothly, almost of its own volition, the engine thunder died away and the nose dropped again.

He held his approach aligned with the main runway until he was well in over the threshold lights. He did not want to alert the drivers of the blocking vehicles to his intention while they still had time to counter it.

"You murderous bitch," he said under his breath. "You filthy murderous bitch."

He banked the Boeing steeply, realigned it with the long strip of open grass and cut the throttles completely, bringing her in nose-high and just a fraction above the stall, flaring out deliberately low and banging the Boeing down into the grass for positive touch down.

The huge machine settled to the rough strip, jolting and lurching wildly as Cyril Watkins fought the rudders to keep them lined up, holding his nose wheel off with the control yoke, while his co-pilot threw all her giant engines into reverse thrust and trod firmly down on the main landing gear brakes.

The fire engines and fuel tankers flashed past the starboard wing tip. The startled faces of their crews seemed very close and white—then 070 was past, her speed bleeding off sharply so her nose wheel dropped and she rocked and swayed gradually to a dead stop just short of the brick building which housed the approach and landing beacons, and the main radar installation.

It was 7:25 A.M. local time and Speedbird 070 was down.

"Well, they are down," intoned Kingston Parker. "And you can well understand the extreme efforts that were made to prevent them. Their choice of final destination settles one of your queries, Peter."

"A l'allemande." Peter nodded. "It's got to be political. I agree, sir."

"And you and I must now face in dreadful reality what we have discussed only in lofty theory"—Parker held a taper to his pipe and puffed twice before going on—"morally justifiable militancy."

"Again we have to differ, sir." Peter cut in swiftly. "There is no such thing."

"Is there not?" Parker asked, shaking his head. "What of the German officers killed in the streets of Paris by the French resistance?"

"That was war," Peter exclaimed.

"Perhaps the group that seized 070 believes that they are at war."

"With innocent victims?" Peter shot back.

"The *Haganah* took innocent victims—yet what they were fighting for was right and just."

"I'm an Englishman, Dr. Parker—you cannot expect me to condone the murder of British women and children." Peter had stiffened in his chair.

"No," Parker agreed. "So let us not speak of the Mau-Mau in Kenya, nor of present-day Ireland then—but what of the French Revolution or the spreading of the Catholic faith by the most terrible persecution and tortures yet devised by man—were those not morally justifiable militancy?"

"I would prefer to call it understandable but reprehensible. Terrorism in any form can never be morally justifiable." Provoked himself, Peter used the word deliberately to provoke and saw the small lift of Parker's thick bushy eyebrows.

"There is terrorism from above—as well as from below." Parker picked up the word and used it deliberately. "If you define terrorism as extreme physical or physiological coercion used to induce others to submit to the will of the terrorist, there is the legal terror threat of the gallows, the religious terror threat of hell fire, the paternal terror threat of the cane. Are those more morally justifiable than the aspiration of the weak, the poor, the politically oppressed, the powerless victims of an unjust society? Is their scream of protest to be strangled—"

Peter shifted uncomfortably in his chair.

"Protest outside the law—"

"Laws are made by man, almost always by the rich and the powerful. Laws are changed by men, usually only after militant action. The women's suffragette movement, the civil rights campaign in this country—" Parker broke off and chuckled. "I'm sorry, Peter. Sometimes I confuse myself. It's often more difficult to be a liberal than it is to be a tyrant. At least the tyrant seldom has doubts." Parker lay back in his chair, a dismissive gesture. "I propose to leave you in peace for an hour or two now. You will want to develop your plans in line with the new developments. But I personally have no doubts now that we are dealing with politically motivated militants, and not merely a gang of old-fashioned kidnappers after a fast buck. Of one other thing I am certain. Before we see this one through we will be forced to examine our own consciences very closely."

"Take the second right," said Ingrid quietly, and the Boeing swung off the grass onto the taxiway. There seemed to be no damage to her landing gear, but now that she had left her natural element, the aircraft had lost grace and beauty and became lumbering and ungainly.

The girl had never been on the flight deck of a grounded Jumbo before, and the height was impressive. It gave her a feeling of detachment, of being invulnerable.

"Now left again," she instructed, and the Boeing turned away from the main airport buildings towards the southern end of the runway. The observation deck of the airport's flat roof was already lined with hundreds of curious spectators, but all activity on the apron was suspended. The waiting machines and tenders were deserted, not a single human figure on the tarmac.

"Park there." She pointed ahead to an open area four hundred yards from the nearest building, midway between the terminal and the cluster of service hangars and the main fuel depot. "Stop on the intersection."

Grimly silent, Cyril Watkins did as he was ordered, and then turned in his seat.

"I must call an ambulance to get him off."

The co-pilot and a stewardess had the flight engineer stretched out on the galley floor, just beyond the door to the flight deck. They were using linen table napkins to bind up the arm and try and staunch the bleeding. The stench of cordite still lingered and mingled with the taint of fresh blood.

"Nobody leaves this aircraft." The girl shook her head. "He knows too much about us already."

"My God, woman. He needs medical attention."

"There are three hundred doctors aboard—" she pointed out indifferently. "The best in the world. Two of them may come forward and attend to him."

She perched sideways on the flight engineer's blood-splattered desk, and thumbed the internal microphone. Cyril Watkins noticed even in his outrage that it needed only a single demonstration and Ingrid was able to work the complicated communications equipment. She was bright and very well trained.

"Ladies and gentlemen, we have landed at Johannesburg Airport. We will be here for a long time—perhaps days, even weeks. All our patience will be tried, so I must warn you that any disobedience will be most severely dealt with. Already one attempt at resistance has been made—and in consequence a member of the crew has been shot and gravely wounded. He may die of this wound. We do not want a repetition of this incident. However, I must again warn you that my officers and I will not hesitate to shoot again, or even to detonate the explosives above your heads— if the need arises."

She paused and watched a moment as two selected doctors came forward and knelt on each side of the flight engineer. He was shaking like a fever victim with shock, his white shirt splashed and daubed with blood. Her expression showed no remorse, no real concern, and her voice was calm and light as she went on.

"Two of my officers will now pass down the aisles and they will collect your passports from you. Please have these documents ready."

Her eyes flicked sideways, as movement caught her eye. From beyond the service hangars a line of four armoured cars emerged in line ahead. They were the locally manufactured version of the French Panhard with heavily lugged tall tyres, a raked turret and the disproportionately long barrels of the cannons trained forward. The armoured vehicles circled cautiously and parked three hundred yards out, at the four points—wing tips, tail and nose—around the aircraft, with the long cannon trained upon her.

The girl watched them disdainfully until one of the doctors pushed himself in front of her. He was a short chubby little man, balding—but brave.

"This man must be taken to a hospital immediately."

"That is out of the question."

"I insist. His life is in danger."

"All our lives are in danger, doctor." She paused and let that make its effect. "Draw up a list of your requirements. I will see that you get them."

"They have been down for sixteen hours now and the only contact has been a request for medical supplies and for a power link-up to the electrical mains." Kingston Parker had removed his jacket and loosened the knot of his tie, but was showing no other ill effects of his vigil.

Peter Stride nodded at the image on the screen. "What have your medics made of the supplies?" he asked.

"Looks like a gunshot casualty. Whole blood type AB Positive, that's rare but one of the crew is cross-matched AB Positive on his service record. Ten litres of plasmalyte B, a blood-giving set and syringes, morphine and intravenous penicillin, tetanus toxoid—all the equipment needed to treat massive physical trauma."

"And they are on mains power?" Peter asked.

"Yes, four hundred people would have suffocated by now without the air-conditioning. The airport authority has laid a cable and plugged it into the external socket. All the aircraft's support system—even the galley heating—will be fully functional."

"So we will be able to throw the switch on them at any time."

Peter made a note on the pad in front of him. "But no demands yet? No negotiator called for?"

"No, nothing. They seem fully aware of the techniques of bargaining in this type of situation—unlike our friends, the host country. I am afraid we are having a great deal of trouble with the Wyatt Earp mentality—" Parker paused. "I'm sorry, Wyatt Earp was one of our frontier marshals."

"I saw the movie, and read the book," Peter answered tartly.

"Well, the South Africans are itching to storm the aircraft, and both our ambassador and yours are hard pressed to restrain them. They are all set to kick the doors of the saloon open and rush in with six-guns glazing. They must also have seen the movie."

Peter felt the crawl of horror down his spine. "That would be a certain disaster," he said quickly. "These people are running a tight operation."

"You don't have to convince me," Parker agreed. "What is your flying time to Jan Smuts now?"

"We crossed the Zambesi River seven minutes ago." Peter glanced sideways through the perspex bubble window, but the ground was obscured by haze and cumulus cloud. "We have another two hours ten minutes to fly—but my support section is three hours forty behind us."

"All right, Peter. I will get back onto them. The South African Government has convened a full cabinet meeting, and both our ambassadors are sitting in as observers and advisers. I think I am going to be obliged to tell them about the existence of Atlas."

He paused a moment. "Here at last we are seeing Atlas justified, Peter. A single unit, cutting across all national considerations, able to act swiftly and independently. I think you should know that I have already obtained the agreement of the President and of your Prime Minister to condition Delta—at my discretion."

Condition Delta was the kill decision.

"But again I emphasize that I will implement Delta only as a last possible resort. I want to hear and consider the demands first, and in that respect we are open to negotiation—fully open—"

Parker went on speaking, and Peter Stride shifted slightly, dropping his chin into the cup of his hand to hide his irritation. They were into an area of dispute now—and once again Peter had to voice disagreement.

"Every time you let a militant walk away from a strike you immediately create the conditions for further strikes, to free the captive."

"I have the clearance for condition Delta," Parker reiterated with a trace of acid in his tone now, "but I am making it clear that it will be used only with the greatest discretion. We are not an assassination unit, General Stride." Parker nodded to an assistant off-screen. "I am going through to the South Africans now to explain Atlas." The image receded into darkness.

Peter Stride leapt up abruptly and tried to pace the narrow aisle between the seats, but there was insufficient headroom for his tall frame and he flung himself angrily into the seat again.

Kingston Parker stood up from his communications desk in the outer office of his suite in the west wing of the Pentagon. The two communications technicians scurried out of his way and his personal secretary opened the door to his inner office.

He moved with peculiar grace for such a large man, and there was no excess weight on his frame, his big heavy bones lean of flesh. His clothes were of fine cloth, well cut—the best that Madison Avenue could offer—but they were worn almost to the point of shoddiness, the button-down collar slightly frayed, the Italian shoes scuffed at the toes as though material trappings counted not at all with him. Nevertheless, he wore them with a certain unconscious panache, and he looked ten years younger than his fifty-three, only a few silver strands in the thick bushy mane of hair.

The inner office was spartan in its furnishings, all of it U.S. Government issue, utilitarian and impersonal; only the books that filled every shelf and the grand piano were his own. The piano was a Bechstein grand and much too large for the room. Parker ran his right hand lightly across the keyboard as he passed it—but went on to the desk.

He dropped into the swivel chair and shuffled through the dozen intelligence folders on his desk. Each of them contained the latest computer print-outs that he had requested. There were personal histories, appraisals, and character studies of all the personalities that had so far become involved in the taking of Speedbird 070.

The names of both the ambassadors were there—their pink files signified the highest security ratings, and were marked "Heads of Departments only." Four other files in lower echelon green were devoted to the South African Government personalities with decision-making capabilities in the emergency. The thickest file was that of the South African Prime Minister—and once again Parker noted wryly that the man had been imprisoned by the pro-British government of General Jan Smuts during World War II as a militant opponent of his country's involvement in that war. He wondered just how much sympathy he would have for other militants now.

There were files for the South African Ministers of Defence and of Justice, and still slimmer green files for the Commissioner of Police and for the Assistant Commissioner who had been given the on-site responsibility of handling the emergency. Of them all, only the Prime Minister emerged as a distinct personality—a powerful bulldog figure, not a man easily influenced or dissuaded, and instinctively Kingston Parker recognized that ultimate authority rested here.

There was one other pink file at the bottom of the considerable stack, so well handled that the cardboard cover was splitting at the hinge. The original print-out in this file had been requisitioned two years previously, with quarterly up-dates since that time.

"STRIDE PETER CHARLES" it was headed—and reclassified "Head of Atlas only."

Kingston Parker could probably have recited its contents by heart—but he untied the ribbons now, and opened it in his lap.

Puffing deliberately at his pipe he began to turn slowly through the loose pages.

There were the bare bones of the subject's life. Born 1939, one of twin war-time babies of a military family, his father killed in action three years later when the armoured brigade of guards he commanded was overrun by one of Erwin Rommel's devastating drives across the deserts of North Africa. The elder twin brother had inherited the baronetcy and Peter followed the well-travelled family course, Harrow and Sandhurst, where he must have disconcerted the family by his academic brilliance and his reluctance to participate in team sports—preferring the loner activities of golf and tennis and long-distance running.

Kingston Parker pondered that a moment. They were pointers to the man's character that had disconcerted him as well. Parker had the intellectual's generalized contempt for the military, and he would have preferred a man who conformed more closely to his ideal of the brass-headed soldier.

Yet when the young Stride had entered his father's regiment, it seemed that the exceptional intelligence had been diverted into conventional channels and the preference for independent thought and action held in check, if not put aside completely—until his regiment was sent to Cyprus at the height of the unrest in that country. Within a week of arrival the young Stride had been seconded, with his commanding officer's enthusiastic approval, to Central Army Intelligence. Perhaps the commanding officer had already become aware of the problems involved in harbouring a wonder-boy in the tradition-bound portals of his officers' mess.

For once the military had made a logical, if not an outright brilliant, choice. Stride in the sixteen years since then had not made a single mistake, apart from the marriage which had ended in divorce within two years. Had he remained with his regiment that might have affected his career—but since Cyprus, Stride's progress had been as unconventional and meteoric as his brain.

In a dozen different and difficult assignments since then, he had honed his gifts and developed new talents; rising against the trend of reduced British expenditure on defence, he had reached staff rank before thirty years of age.

At NATO Headquarters he had made powerful friends and admirers on both sides of the Atlantic, and at the end of his three-year term in Brussels he had been promoted to major-general and transferred to head British Intelligence in Ireland, bringing his own particular dedication and flair to the job.

A great deal of the credit for containing the sweep of Irish terrorism through Britain was his, and his in-depth study of the urban guerrilla and the mind of the militant, although classified departmentally, was probably the definitive work on the subject.

The Atlas concept was first proposed in this study, and so it was that Stride had been on the short list to head the project. It seemed certain the appointment would be made—the Americans had been impressed with his study, and his friends from NATO had not forgotten him. His appointment was approved in principle. Then at the last moment there had developed sudden and intense opposition to the appointment of a professional soldier to head such a sensitive agency. The opposition had come from both Whitehall and Washington simultaneously and had prevailed.

Kingston Parker knocked out his pipe, and carried the file across the room and laid it open on the music rack of the piano. He seated himself at the keyboard and, still studying the print-out sheets, began to play.

The stream of music, the lovely ethereal strains of Liszt, did not interrupt his thoughts but seemed to buoy them brightly upwards.

Parker had not wanted Stride, had considered from the very first that he was dangerous, sensing in him ambitions and motivations which would be difficult to control. Parker would have preferred his own nominees—Tanner, who now commanded the Mercury arm of Atlas, or Colin Noble—and had expected that Stride would have declined a command so far below his capability.

However, Stride had accepted the lesser appointment and headed Thor. Parker suspected that there was unusual motivation in this, and had made every effort to study the man at first hand. On five separate occasions he had ordered Stride to Washington, and focused upon him the full strength of his charisma and personality. He had even invited him to stay with him in his New York home, spending many hours with him in deep far-ranging discussions—from which he had developed a prudent respect for the man's mind, but had been able to reach no firm conclusions as to his future in Atlas.

Parker turned a page of the character appraisal. When he looked for the weakness in an opponent, Parker had long ago learned to start at the groin. With this man there was no evidence of any unnatural sexual leanings. Certainly he was not homosexual, if anything too much the opposite. There had been at least a dozen significant liaisons with the opposite sex since his divorce. However, all of these had been discreet and dignified. Although three of the ladies had been married, none of them were the wives of his subordinates in the armed services, nor of brother officers or of men who might be able to adversely affect his career.

The women he chose all had certain qualities in common—they all tended to be tall, intelligent and successful. One was a journalist who had her own syndicated column, another was a former fashion model who now designed and marketed her clothes through her own prestigious outlets in London and on the continent. Then there was an actress who was a leading female member of the Royal Shakespeare Company—Parker skimmed the list impatiently, for Parker himself had no sympathy or patience with a man who succumbed to the dictates of his body.

Parker had trained himself to be totally celibate, channelling all his sexual energies into pursuits of the mind, while this man Stride, on the other hand, was not above conducting two or three of his liaisons concurrently.

Parker moved on to the second area of weakness. Stride's inheritance had been decimated by the punitive British death duties—yet his private income even after savage taxation was still a little over twenty thousand pounds sterling a year, and when this was added to his salary and privileges as a general officer, it enabled him to live in good style. He could even indulge in the mild extravagance of collecting rare books—along with, Parker observed acidly, the greater extravagance of collecting rare ladies.

However, there was no trace of any illicit hoard—no Swiss bank accounts, no deposits of gold bullion, no foreign properties, no shares in off-share companies held by nominees—and Parker had searched diligently for them, for they would have indicated payments received, perhaps from foreign governments. A man like Stride had much to sell, at prices he could set himself—but it seemed he had not done so.

Stride did not smoke; Parker removed the old black briar from his own mouth, regarded it affectionately for a moment. It was his one indulgence, a harmless one despite what the surgeon-general of the United States had determined, and he took the stem firmly between his teeth again.

Stride took alcohol in moderation and was considered knowledgeable on the subject of wine. He raced occasionally, more as a social outing than as a serious punter, and the odd fifty pounds he could well afford. There was no evidence of other gambling. However, he did not hunt, nor did he shoot—traditional pursuits of the English gentleman. Perhaps he had moral objections to blood sports, Parker thought, though it seemed unlikely, for Stride was a superlative marksman with rifle, shotgun and pistol. He had represented Britain at the Munich Olympics as a pistol shot, winning a gold in the fifty-metre class, and he spent at least an hour every day on the range.

Parker turned to the page of the print-out that gave the man's medical history. He must be superbly fit as well—his body weight at the age of thirty-nine was one pound less than it had been at twenty-one, and he still trained like a front-line soldier. Parker noticed that he had logged sixteen parachute jumps the previous month. Since joining Atlas he had no opportunity or time for golf, though when he was with NATO Stride had played off a handicap of three.

Parker closed the folder and played on softly, but neither the sensual polished feel of cool ivory beneath his fingertips nor the achingly lovely lilt of the music could dispel his sense of disquiet. Exhaustive as the report was, yet it left unanswered questions, like why Stride had downgraded himself to accept the command of Thor—he was not the kind of man who acted ill-advisedly. Yet the most haunting questions that nagged at Parker were just how strong were his qualities of resilience and independent thought, just how strongly was he driven by his ambitions and that penetrating intellect—and just how great a threat such a man would present to the evolution of Atlas into its ultimate role.

"Doctor Parker, sir"—his assistant knocked lightly and entered— "there are new developments."

Parker sighed softly. "I'm coming," he said, and let the last sad and beautiful notes fall from his long, powerful fingers before he stood up.

The Hawker slid almost silently down the sky. The pilot had closed down power at five thousand feet and made his final approach without touching the throttles again. He was ten knots above the stall as he passed over the boundary fence and he touched down twenty feet beyond the chevron markings of the threshold of runway One Fife, instantly applying maximum safe braking. One Fife was the secondary cross-wind runway, and the Hawker's roll-out was so short that every part of the approach and landing had been screened by the buildings of the main airport terminal from where Speedbird 070 stood at the southern intersection of the main taxiway.

The pilot swung the Hawker through 360° and back-tracked sedately up runway 15, using just enough power to keep her rolling.

"Well done," grunted Peter Stride, crouching behind the pilot's seat. He was almost certain that nobody aboard 070 had remarked their arrival.

"They've prepared a slot for us, with hook-up to the electrical mains at the north—" Peter broke off as he saw the apron marshal waving them in with the bats, and beyond him a tight group of four men waiting. Three of them wore camouflage battle dress and the other the trim blue uniform, cap and gold insignia of a senior South African police officer.

The uniformed officer was the first to greet Peter as he came down the Hawker's fold-out air-stairs.

"Prinsloo." He shook hands. "Lieutenant-General."

He ranked Peter, but it was a police, not a military appointment. He was a stocky man, with steel-rimmed spectacles, a little paunchy and not less than fifty-five years of age. He had the rather heavy features, the fleshiness of jowl and lips that Peter had noticed so often in Belgian and Dutch peasants during his NATO tour in the Netherlands. A man of the earth, dour and conservative.

"Let me introduce Commandant Boonzaier." This was a military rank, equivalent to that of colonel, and he was a younger man, but with the same thick accent and his features cast in the same mould. A tall man, however, only an inch or so shorter than Peter—but both of the South Africans were suspicious and resentful, and the reason was immediately apparent.

"I have been instructed to take my orders from you, General," and there was a subtle shift of position, the two officers ranging themselves beside Peter, but facing each other, and he was aware instantly that not all the hostility was directed at him. There had been friction between police and military already—and the basic value of Atlas was underlined yet again.

A single clean-cut line of command and of responsibility was absolutely essential—Peter's mind flicked back to the shoot-out at Larnaca Airport between Egyptian commandos and Cypriot national guardsmen, from which the hijackers of the grounded jet emerged unscathed while the airfield was littered with the burning wreckage of the Egyptian transport aircraft and dozens of dead and dying Cypriots and Egyptians.

The first principle of terrorist strategy was to strike at the point where national responsibilities were blurred. Atlas cut through that.

"Thank you." Peter accepted command without flaunting it. "My back-up team will land in just over three hours' time. We will, of course, use force only as a last resort—but if it comes to that, I will use exclusively Atlas personnel in any counter-strike. I would like to make that quite clear immediately." And he saw the line of the soldier's mouth harden with disappointment.

"My men are the élite—"

"It's a British aircraft, most of the hostages are British or American nationals—it's a political decision, Colonel. But I would value your help in other areas." Peter turned him aside tactfully.

"Firstly, I want you to suggest a position where I can place my surveillance equipment—and then we will go over the ground together."

Peter had no difficulty selecting his forward observation post. The service manager's roomy, sparsely furnished office on the third floor of the terminal building overlooked the entire service area and the southern portion of the taxiway where the Boeing stood.

The windows had been left open when the offices were evacuated, so there was no need to change the external appearance of the room.

The overhang of the observation balcony on the floor above shaded the interior, and the office was deep enough to ensure that an observer out there in the bright glare of sunshine would not be able to see into the room, even with a powerful lens. The militants would expect surveillance from the glass control tower high above—any deception, however trivial, was worth while.

The surveillance equipment was lightweight and compact, the television cameras were neither of them bigger than a Super 8-mm home-movie camera, and a man could carry in one hand both of the aluminium extension tripods. However, the cameras could zoom to 800-mm focal length, and they repeated on the screens of the command console in the cabin of the Hawker, while the image was simultaneously stored on video tape.

The audio intensifier was more bulky, but no heavier. It had a four-foot dish antenna, with the sound collector in the centre. The telescopic sight could aim the intensifier at a sound source with the accuracy of a sniper's rifle—could focus on the lips of a human being at eight hundred yards' distance and clearly record normal conversation at that range, passing sound directly to the command console and at the same time storing it on the big magnetic tape spools.

Two of Peter's communications team were posted here, with a

plentiful supply of coffee and doughnuts, and Peter, accompanied by the South African colonel and his staff, went up in the elevator to the glass house of the control tower.

From the air traffic control tower there was an unobstructed view across the airfield and over the apron and service areas around the terminal. The observation platform below the tower had been cleared of all but military personnel.

"I have road blocks at all the main entrances to the airfield. Only passengers with confirmed reservations and current tickets are being allowed through—no thrill seekers—and we are using only the northern section of the terminal for traffic."

Peter nodded and turned to the senior controller. "What is the state of your traffic pattern?"

"We have refused clearance to all private flights, incoming and departing. All domestic scheduled flights have been re-routed to Lanseria and Germiston airports, and we are landing and despatching only international scheduled flights—but the backlog has delayed departures by three hours."

"What separation are you observing from 070?" Peter asked.

"Fortunately, the international departures terminal is the farthest from the aircraft, and we are not using the taxiways or the apron of the southern section. As you see, we have cleared the entire area—except for those three S.A. Airways aircraft which are undergoing overhaul and servicing, there are no other aircraft within a thousand yards of 070."

"I may have to freeze all traffic, if—" Peter paused, "or should I say, when we have an escalation."

"Very well, sir."

"In the meantime, you may continue as you are at present." Peter lifted his binoculars and once again very carefully examined the huge Boeing.

It stood in stately isolation, silent and seemingly abandoned. The bright, almost gaudy marking gave her a carnival air. Red and blue and crisp sparkling white in the stunning sunlight of the highveld. She was parked fully broadside to the tower, and all her hatches and doors were still armed and locked.

Peter traversed slowly along the line of perspex windows down the length of the fuselage—but in each of them the shades had been firmly closed from the interior, turning them into the multiple eyes of a blinded insect.

Peter lifted his scrutiny slightly onto the windshield and side panels of the flight deck. These again had been screened with blankets, hung over them from inside, completely thwarting any glimpse of the crew or their captors—and certainly preventing a shot into the flight deck, although the range from the nearest corner of the terminal was not more than four hundred yards, and with the new laser sights one of Thor's trained snipers could pick through which eye of the human head he would put a bullet.

Snaking across the open tarmac of the taxiway was the thin black electrical cable that connected the aircraft to the mains supply, a long, vulnerable umbilical cord. Peter studied it thoughtfully, before turning his attention to the four Panhard armoured cars. A little frown of irritation crossed his forehead.

"Colonel, please recall those vehicles." He tried not to let the irritation come through in his tone. "With the turrets battened down, your crews will be roasting like Christmas geese."

"General, I feel it my duty," Boonzaier began, and Peter lowered the glasses and smiled. It was a charming, friendly grin that took the man by surprise, after the previous stern set of features—and yet the eyes were devoid of humour, cracking blue and hard in the craggy granite of the face.

"I want to de-fuse the atmosphere as much as possible." The necessity to explain irked Peter, but he maintained the smile. "Somebody with four great cannons aimed at him is more likely to make a bad decision, and pull the trigger himself. You may keep them in close support, but get them out of sight into the terminal car park, and let your men rest."

With little grace the colonel passed the order over the walkie-talkie on his belt, and as the vehicles started up and slowly pulled away behind the line of hangars, Peter went on remorselessly.

"How many men have you got deployed?" He pointed to the line of soldiers along the parapet of the observation balcony, and then to the heads visible as specks between the soaring blue of the African sky and the silhouette of the service hangars.

"Two hundred and thirty."

"Pull them out," Peter instructed, "and let the occupants of the aircraft see them go."

"All of them?" incredulously.

"All of them," Peter agreed, and now the smile was wolfish, "and quickly, please, Colonel."

The man was learning swiftly, and he lifted the miniaturized walkie-talkie to his mouth again. There were a few moments of scurrying and confusion amongst the troops on the observation deck below before they could be formed up and marched away in file. Their steel helmets, like a bobbing line of button mushrooms, and the muzzles of their slung weapons would show above the parapet, and would be clearly visible to an observer in the Boeing.

"If you treat these people, these animals"—the colonel's voice was choked slightly with frustration—"if you treat them soft—"

Peter knew exactly what was coming, "And if you keep waving guns in their faces, you will keep them alert and on their toes, Colonel. Let them settle down a little and relax, let them get very confident." He spoke without lowering the binoculars. With a soldier's eye for ground he was picking the site for his four snipers. There was little chance that he would be able to use them—they would have to take out every single one of the enemy at the same instant—but a remote chance might just offer itself, and he decided to place one gun on the service hangar roof. There was a large ventilator which could be pierced and would command the port side of the aircraft, two guns to cover the flight deck from both sides—he could use the drainage ditch down the edge of the main runway to get a man into the small hut that housed the approach radar and ILS beacons. The hut was in the enemy's rear. They might not expect fire from that quarter—point by point from his mental checklist Peter planned his dispositions, scribbling his decisions into the small leather-covered notebook, poring over the large-scale map of the airport, converting gradients and angles into fields of fire, measuring "ground to cover" and "time to target" for an assault force launched from the nearest vantage points, twisting each problem and evaluating it, striving for novel solutions to each, trying to think ahead of an enemy that was still faceless and infinitely menacing.

It took him an hour of hard work before he was satisfied. Now he could pass his decisions to Colin Noble on board the incoming Herc, and within four minutes of the big landing wheels hitting tarmac his highly trained team with their complex talents and skills would be in position.

Peter straightened up from the map and tucked the notebook

under the flap of his button-down breast pocket. Once again he scrutinized every inch of the silent, battened-down aircraft through his glasses, but this time he allowed himself the luxury of gut emotion.

He felt the anger and the hatred rise from some hidden depth of his soul and flush his blood and tighten the muscles of his belly and thighs.

Once again he was confronted by the many-headed monster. It crouched out there in ambush, waiting for him as it had so often before.

He remembered suddenly the shards of splintered glass littering the cobbles of a Belfast street and glittering like diamond chips in the arc lamps, the smell of explosives and blood thick in the air.

He remembered the body of a young woman lying in the gutted interior of a fashionable London restaurant. Her lovely young body stripped by the blast of all but a flimsy pearl-coloured pair of French lace panties.

He remembered the smell of a family, father, mother and three small children, burning in the interior of their saloon car, the bodies blackening and twisting in a slow macabre ballet as the flames scorched them. Peter had not been able to eat pork since that day.

He remembered the frightened eyes of a child, through a mask of blood, a dismembered arm lying beside her, the pale fingers still clutching a grubby little rag doll.

The images flashed in disjointed sequences across his memory, feeding his hatred until it pricked and stung behind his eyes and he had to lower the binoculars and wipe his eyes with the back of his hand.

It was the same enemy that he had hunted before, but his instincts warned him that it had grown even stronger and more inhuman since last he had met and fought it. He tried to suppress the hatred now, lest it cloud his judgement, lest it handicap him during the difficult hours and days that he knew lay ahead—but it was too powerful, had been too long nurtured.

He recognized that hatred was the enemy's vice, that from it sprang their twisted philosophy and their monstrous actions, and that to descend to hatred was to descend to their sub-human levels—yet still the hatred persisted.

Peter Stride understood clearly that his hatred was not only for the ghastly death and mutilation that he had witnessed so often.

More it was fostered by the threat that he recognized to an entire society and its civilized rule of law. If this evil should be allowed to triumph, then in the future laws would be made by the wild-eyed revolutionary, with a gun in his fist—the world would be run by the destroyers instead of the builders, and Peter Stride hated that possibility more even than the violence and the blood, and those he hated as a soldier hates. For only a soldier truly knows the horror of war.

His soldier's instinct now was to immediately engage the enemy and destroy him—but the scholar and philosopher in him warned that this was not the moment, and with an enormous effort of will he held that fighting man's instinct in check.

Yet still he was deeply aware that it was for this moment, for this confrontation of the forces of evil, that he had jeopardized his whole career.

When command of Atlas had been plucked away and a political appointee named in his place, Peter should have declined the offer of a lesser position in Atlas. There were other avenues open to him, but instead he had elected to stay with the project—and he hoped that nobody had guessed at the resentment he felt. God knows, Kingston Parker had no cause for complaint since then. There was no harder working officer on Atlas, and his loyalty had been tested more than once.

Now all that seemed worth while, and the moment for which he had worked had arrived. The enemy waited for him out there on the burning tarmac under an African sun, not on a soft green island in the rain nor in the grimy streets of a crowded city—but still it was the same old enemy, and Peter knew his time would come.

His communications technicians had Colin Noble on the main screen as Peter ducked into the Hawker's cabin that was now his command headquarters, and settled into his padded seat. On the top right screen was a panoramic view of the southern terminal area, with the Boeing squatting like a brooding eagle upon its nest in the centre of the shot. On the next screen beside it was a blow-up through the 800-mm zoom lens of the Boeing's flight deck. So crisp was the detail that Peter could read the maker's name on the tab of the blanket that screened the windshield. The third small screen held a full shot of the interior of the air traffic control tower. In the foreground the controllers in shirt sleeves sitting over the radar repeaters, and beyond them through the floor to ceiling windows still another view of the Boeing. All these were being shot through the cameras installed an hour earlier in the terminal building. The remaining small screen was blank, and Colin Noble's homely, humorous face filled the main screen.

"Now if only it had been the cavalry instead of the U.S. Marines," Peter said, "you'd have been here yesterday—"

"What's your hurry, pal. Doesn't look like the party has started yet." Colin grinned at him from the screen and pushed his baseball cap to the back of his head.

"Damned right," Peter agreed. "We don't even know who is throwing the party. What's your latest estimate on arrival time?"

"We've picked up a good wind—one hour twenty-two minutes to fly now," Colin told him.

"Right, let's get down to it," Peter said, and he began his briefing, going carefully over the field notes he had taken. When he wanted to emphasize a point, Peter called for a change of shot from his cameramen, and they zoomed in or panned to his instruction, picking up the radar shed or the service hangar ventilator where Peter was siting his snipers. The image was repeated not only on the command console but in the cavernous body of the approaching Hercules so that the men who would be called to occupy those positions could study them now and prepare themselves thoroughly for the moment. The same images were hurled across the stratosphere to the circling satellite and from there bounced down to appear, only slightly distorted, on the screens of Atlas Command in the west wing of the Pentagon. Sagging like an old lion in his armchair, Kingston Parker followed every word of the briefing, rousing himself only when a long telex message was passed to him by his assistant, then he nodded a command to have his own televised image superimposed on Peter's command console.

"I'm sorry to interrupt you, Peter, but we've got a useful scrap here. Assuming that the militant group boarded 070 at Mahé, we asked the Seychelles Police to run a check on all boarding passengers. There were fifteen of them, ten of whom were Seychelles residents. A local merchant and his wife, and eight unaccompanied children between nine and fourteen years of age. They are the children of expatriate civil servants employed on contract by the

Seychelles Government, returning to schools in England for the new term."

Peter felt the weight of dread bearing down upon him like a heavy burden. Children, the young lives seemed somehow more important, somehow more vulnerable. But Parker was reading from the telex carbon in his left hand, the right scratching the back of his neck with the stem of his pipe.

"There is one British businessman, Shell Oil Company, and well-known on the island, and there are four tourists, an American, a Frenchman and two Germans. These last four appeared to be travelling in a group, the immigration and security officers remember them well. Two women and two men, all young. Names Sally-Anne Taylor, twenty-five years, American, Heidi Hottschauser, twenty-four and Gunther Retz, twenty-five, the two Germans, and Henri Larousse, twenty-six, the Frenchman. The police have run a back check on the four. They stayed two weeks at the Reef Hotel outside Victoria, the women in one double room and the two men in another. They spent most of the time swimming and sunbathing—until five days ago when a small ocean-going yacht called at Victoria. Thirty-five foot, single-hander around the world, skippered by another American. The four spent time on board her every day of her stay, and the yacht sailed twenty-four hours before the departure of 070."

"If the yacht delivered their arms and munitions, then this operation has been planned for a long time," Peter pondered, "and damn well planned."

Peter felt the tingling flush of his blood again, the form of the enemy was taking shape now, the outline of the beast becoming clearer, and always it was uglier and more menacing.

"You have run the names through the computer?" he asked.

"Nothing." Parker nodded. "Either there is no intelligence record of them, or the names and passports are false—"

He broke off as there was sudden activity on the screen that monitored the air traffic control tower, and another voice boomed out of the secondary speaker; the volume was set too high, and the technician at the control board adjusted it swiftly. It was a female voice, a fresh, clear young voice speaking English with the lilt and inflexion of the west coast of America in it.

"Jan Smuts tower, this is the officer commanding the task force of the Action Commando for Human Rights that has control of Speedbird 070. Stand by to copy a message."

"Contact!" Peter breathed. "Contact at last."

On the small screen Colin Noble grinned and rolled his cheroot expertly from one side of his mouth to the other. "The party has begun," he announced, but there was the razor edge in his voice not entirely concealed by his jocular tone.

The three-man crew had been moved back from the flight deck, and were held in the first-class seats vacated by the group of four.

Ingrid had made the cockpit of the Boeing her headquarters, and she worked swiftly through the pile of passports, filling in the name and nationality of each passenger on the seating plan spread before her.

The door to the galley was open, and except for the hum of the air-conditioning, the huge aircraft was peculiarly silent. Conversation in the cabins was prohibited, and the aisles were patrolled by the red-shirted commandos to enforce this edict.

They also ordered the use of the toilets, a passenger must return to his seat before another was allowed to rise. The toilet doors had to remain open during use, so that the commandos could check at a glance.

Despite the silence, there was a crackling atmosphere of tension down the full length of the cabin. Very few of the passengers, mostly the children, were asleep, but the others sat in rigid rows, their faces taut and strained—watching their captors with a mixture of hatred and of fear.

Henri, the Frenchman, slipped into the cockpit.

"They are pulling back the armoured cars," he said. He was slim, with a very youthful face and dreaming poet's eyes. He had grown a drooping blond gunfighter's moustache, but the effect was incongruous.

Ingrid looked up at him. "You are so nervous, chéri." She shook her head. "It will all be all right."

"I am not nervous," he answered her stiffly.

She chuckled fondly, and reached up to touch his face. "I did not mean it as an insult." She pulled his face down and kissed him, thrusting her tongue deeply into his mouth. "You have proved your courage—often," she murmured.

He dropped his pistol onto the desk with a clatter and reached for her. The top three buttons of her red cotton shirt were unfastened, and she let him grope and find her breasts.

They were heavy and pointed and his breathing went ragged as he teased out her nipples. They hardened erect like jelly beans—but when he reached down with his free hand for the zipper of her shorts, she pushed him away roughly.

"Later," she told him brusquely, "when this is over. Now get back into the cabin." And she leaned forward and lifted a corner of the blanket that screened the side window of the cockpit. The sunlight was very bright but her eyes adjusted swiftly and she saw the row of helmeted heads above the parapet of the observation deck. So they were pulling back the troops as well. It was nearly time to begin talking—but she would let them stew in their own juice just a little longer.

She stood up, buttoned her shirt and adjusted the camera on its strap around her neck, paused in the galley to rearrange the shiny mass of golden hair, and then walked slowly back down the full length of the central aisle, pausing to adjust the blanket over a sleeping child, to listen attentively to the complaints of the pregnant wife of the Texan neuro-surgeon.

"You and the children will be the first off this plane, I promise you."

When she reached the prone body of the flight engineer, she knelt beside him.

"How is he?"

"He is sleeping now. I shot him full of morphine." The fat little doctor muttered, not looking at her, so she could not read the hatred in his expression. The injured arm was elevated to control the bleeding, sticking up stiffly in its cocoon of pressure bandages. Oddly foreshortened with the bright ooze of blood through the dressing.

"You are doing good." She touched his arm. "Thank you." And now he glanced at her startled, and she smiled—such a radiant lovely smile, that he began to melt.

"Is that your wife?" Ingrid dropped her voice, so that he alone could hear, and he nodded, glancing at the plump little Jewish woman in the nearest seat. "I will see she is among the first to leave," she murmured, and his gratitude was pathetic. She stood and went on down the aircraft.

The red-shirted German stood at the head of the tourist cabin, beside the curtained entrance to the second galley. He had the intense drawn face of a religious zealot, dark burning eyes, long black hair falling almost to his shoulders—a white scar twisted the corner of his upper lip into a perpetual smirk.

"Kurt, everything is all right?" she asked in German.

"They are complaining of hunger."

"We will feed them in another two hours—but not as much as they expect," and she ran a contemptuous glance down the cabin. "Fat," she said quietly, "big, fat, bourgeoisie pigs," and she stepped through the curtains into the galley and looked at him in invitation. He followed her immediately, drawing the curtains behind them.

"Where is Karen?" Ingrid asked, as he unbuckled his belt. She needed it very badly, the excitement and the blood had inflamed her.

"She is resting—at the back of the cabin."

Ingrid slipped the button that held the front of her shorts together and drew down the zipper. "All right, Kurt," she whispered huskily, "but quickly, very quickly."

Ingrid sat in the flight engineer's seat, at her shoulder stood the dark-haired girl. She wore the cartridge belt across the shoulder of her bright red shirt, like a bandolier—and she carried the big ugly pistol on her hip.

Ingrid held the microphone to her lips, and combed the fingers of her other hand through the thick golden tangle of her tresses as she spoke.

"One hundred and ninety-eight British subjects. One hundred and forty-six American nationals." She was reading the list of her captives. "There are one hundred and twenty-two women on board, and twenty-six children under the age of sixteen years." She had been speaking for nearly five minutes and now she broke off and shifted in her seat, turning to smile at Karen over her shoulder. The dark-haired girl smiled in return and reached across to caress the fine mass of golden hair with a narrow bony hand, before letting it drop back to her side.

"We have copied your last transmission."

"Call me Ingrid." She spoke into the mike with the smile turning into a wicked grin. There was a moment's silence as the controller in the tower recovered from his shock.

"Roger, Ingrid. Do you have any further messages for us?"

"Affirmative, Tower. As this is a British aircraft and as three hundred and forty-four of my passengers are either British or American, I want a spokesman, representing the embassies of those countries. I want him here in two hours' time to hear my terms for the release of passengers."

"Stand by, Ingrid. We will be back to you immediately we have been able to contact the ambassadors."

"Don't horse around, Tower." Ingrid's voice snapped. "We both know damned well they are breathing down your neck. Tell them I want a man here in two hours—otherwise I am going to be forced to put down the first hostage."

Peter Stride was stripped down to a pair of bathing trunks, and he wore only canvas sneakers on his feet. Ingrid had insisted on a face-to-face meeting, and Peter had welcomed the opportunity to assess at close range.

"We'll be covering you every inch of the way there and back," Colin Noble told Peter, fussing over him like a coach over his fighter before the gong. "I'm handling the gunners, personally."

The snipers were armed with specially hand-built .22 magnums with accurized barrels that threw small light bullets with tremendous velocity and striking power. The ammunition was match-grade, each round lovingly hand finished and polished. The infra-red telescopic sights were readily interchangeable with the laser sights, making the weapon deadly accurate either in daylight or at night. The bullet had a clean, flat trajectory up to seven hundred yards. They were perfectly designed man-killers, precision weapons that reduced the danger to bystanders or hostages. The light bullet would slam a man down with savage force, as though he had been hit by a charging rhinoceros, but it would break up in his body, and not over-penetrate to kill beyond the target.

"You're getting into a lather," Peter grunted. "They want to talk, not shoot—not yet, anyway."

"The female of the species," Colin warned, "that one is real poison."

"More important than the guns are the cameras, and sound equipment."

"I went up there and kicked a few asses. You'll get pictures that will win you an Oscar—my personal guarantee." Colin checked his wristwatch. "Time to go. Don't keep the lady waiting." He punched Peter's shoulder lightly. "Hang loose," he said, and Peter walked out in the sunshine, lifting both hands above his shoulders, palms open, fingers extended.

The silence was as oppressive as the dry fierce heat, but it was intentional. Peter had frozen all air traffic, and had ordered the shut down of all machinery in the entire terminal area. He did not want any interference with his sound equipment.

There was only the sound of his own footfalls, and he stepped out briskly—but still it was the longest walk of his life, and the closer he got to the aircraft, the higher it towered above him. He knew that he had been required to strip almost naked, not only to ensure that he carried no weapons, but to place him at a disadvantage—to make him feel ill at ease, vulnerable. It was an old trick— the Gestapo always stripped the victim of an interrogation—so he held himself proud and tall, pleased that his body was so lean and hard and muscled like an athlete's. He would have hated to drag a big, pendulous gut and sagging old-man's tits across those four hundred yards.

He was half-way there when the forward door, just behind the cockpit, slid back and a group of figures appeared in the square opening. He narrowed his eyes, there were two uniformed figures, no three—British Airways uniforms, the two pilots and between them the shorter slimmer feminine figure of a stewardess.

They stood shoulder to shoulder, but beyond them he could make out another head, a blonde head—but the angle and the light were against him.

Closer, he saw that the older pilot was on the right, short-cropped grey curls, ruddy round face—that would be Watkins, the commander. He was a good man, Peter had studied his service record. He ignored the co-pilot and stewardess and strained for a glimpse of the figure beyond them, but it was only when he stopped directly below the open hatch that she moved to let him get a clear view of her face.

Peter was startled by the loveliness of that golden head, by the smooth gloss of young sun-polished skin and the thundering innocence of wide-set, steady, green eyes—for a moment he could not believe she was one of them, then she spoke.

"I am Ingrid," she said. Some of the most poisonous flowers are the loveliest, he thought.

"I am the accredited negotiator for the British and American governments," he said, and switched his gaze to the beefy red face of Watkins. "How many members of your commando are aboard?" he asked.

"No questions!" Ingrid snapped fiercely, and Cyril Watkins extended four fingers of his right hand down his thigh without a change of expression.

It was vital confirmation of what they already suspected, and Peter felt a rush of gratitude towards the pilot.

"Before we discuss your terms," Peter said, "and out of common humanity, I would like to arrange for the well being and comfort of your hostages."

"They are well cared for."

"Do you need food or drinking water?"

The girl threw back her head and laughed delightedly. "So you can dope it with laxative—and have us knee deep in shit? Stink us out, hey?"

Peter did not pursue it. The doped trays had already been prepared by his doctor.

"You have a gunshot casualty on board?"

"There are no wounded aboard," the girl denied flatly, cutting her laughter short—but Watkins made the circular affirmative sign of thumb and forefinger, effectively contradicting her, and Peter noticed the spots of dried blood on the sleeves of his white shirt. "That's enough," Ingrid warned Peter. "Ask one more question and we'll break off—"

"All right," Peter agreed quickly. "No more questions."

"The objective of this commando is the ultimate downfall of the brutally fascist, inhuman, neo-imperialistic regime that holds this land in abject slavery and misery—denying the great majority of the workers and the proletariat their basic rights as human beings."

"And that," thought Peter bitterly, "even though it's couched in the garbled jargon of the lunatic left, is every bit as bad as it can be." Around the world hundreds of millions would have immediate sympathy, making Peter's task just that little bit more difficult. The hijackers had picked a soft target.

The girl was still speaking, with an intense, almost religious fervour, and as he listened Peter faced the growing certainty that the girl was a fanatic, treading the thin line which divided sanity from madness. Her voice became a harsh screech as she mouthed her hatred and condemnation, and when she had finished he knew that she was capable of anything—no cruelty, no baseness was beyond her. He knew that she would not stop even at suicide, the final act of destroying the Boeing, its passengers and herself—he suspected she might even welcome the opportunity of martyrdom, and he felt the chill of it tickle up along his spine.

They were silent now, staring at each other, while the hectic flush of fanaticism receded from the girl's face and she regained her breath, and Peter waited, controlling his own misgivings, waiting for her to calm herself and continue.

"Our first demand"—the girl had steadied and was watching Peter shrewdly now—"is that the statement I have just made be read on every television network in Britain and the United States, and also here upon the South African network." Peter felt his loathing of that terrible little box rise to the surface of his emotions. That mind-bending electronic substitute for thought, that deadly device for freezing, packaging and distributing opinion. He hated it, almost as much as the violence and sensation it purveyed so effectively. "It must be read at the next occurrence of 7 P.M. local time in Los Angeles, New York, London and Johannesburg." Prime time, of course, and the media would gobble it up hungrily, for this was their meat and their drink—the pornographers of violence!

High above him in the open hatch the girl brandished a thick buff envelope. "This contains a copy of that statement for transmission—it contains also a list of names. One hundred and twenty-nine names, all of them either imprisoned or placed under banning orders by this monstrous police regime. The names on this list are the true leaders of South Africa." She flung the envelope, and it landed at Peter's feet.

"Our second demand is that every person on that list be placed aboard an aircraft provided by the South African Government. Aboard the same aircraft there will be one million gold Kruger Rand coins also provided by the same government. The aircraft will fly to a country chosen by the freed political leaders. The gold will be used by them to establish a government in exile, until such time as they return to this country as the true leaders of the people."

Peter stooped and picked up the envelope, calculating swiftly.

A single Kruger Rand coin was worth $170 at the very least. The ransom demand was, therefore, one hundred and seventy million dollars.

There was another calculation. "One million Krugers will weigh well over forty tons," he told the girl. "How are they going to get all that on one aircraft?"

The girl faltered. It was a little comfort to Peter to realize that they hadn't thought out everything perfectly. If they made one small mistake, then they were capable of making others.

"The government will provide sufficient transport for all the gold and all the prisoners," the girl said sharply. The hesitation had been momentary only.

"Is that all?" Peter asked; the sun was stinging his naked shoulders and a cold drop of sweat trickled down his flank. He had never guessed it could be this bad.

"The aircraft will depart before noon tomorrow, or the execution of hostages will begin then." Peter felt the crawl of horror. "Execution." She was using the jargon of legality, and he realized at that moment that what she promised she would deliver.

"When those aircraft arrive at the destination chosen by the occupants, a pre-arranged code will be flashed to us, and all women and children aboard this aircraft will immediately be released."

"And the men?" Peter asked.

"On Monday the sixth—three days from now, a resolution is to be tabled before the General Assembly of the United Nations in New York. It will call for immediate total mandatory economic sanctions on South Africa—including withdrawal of all foreign capital, total oil and trade embargoes, severance of all transport and communications links, blockade of all ports and air borders by a UN peace-keeping force—pending free elections under universal suffrage supervised by UN inspectors—"

Peter's mind was racing to keep ahead of the girl's demands. He knew of the UN motion, of course, it had been tabled by Sri Lanka and Tanzania. It would be vetoed in the Security Council. That was a certainty—but the girl's timing brought forward new and frightening considerations. The beast had changed shape again, and what he had heard sickened him. It surely could not be merely coincidence that the resolution was to be tabled within three days of this strike—the implications were too horrible to contemplate. The connivance, if not the direct involvement, of world leaders and governments in the strategy of terror.

The girl spoke again deliberately. "If any member of the Security Council of the UN—America, Britain or France—uses the veto to block the resolution of this General Assembly, this aircraft and all aboard her will be destroyed by high explosive."

Peter had lost the power of speech. He stood gaping up at the lovely blonde child, for child she still seemed, so young and fresh.

When he found voice again, it croaked hoarsely. "I don't believe you could have got high explosive aboard this aircraft to carry out that threat," he challenged her.

The blonde girl said something to somebody who was out of sight, and then a few moments later she tossed a dark round object down to Peter.

"Catch!" she shouted, and he was surprised by the weight of it in his hands. It took only a moment to recognize it.

"Electronically fused!" The girl laughed. "And we have so many I can afford to give you a sample."

The pilot, Cyril Watkins, was trying to tell him something, touching his own chest—but Peter was occupied with the explosive in his hands. He knew that a single one of these would be fully capable of destroying the Boeing and all aboard her.

What was Watkins trying to tell him? Touching his neck again. Peter transferred his attention to the girl's neck. She wore a small camera slung around her neck. Something connecting camera and grenade—perhaps? Is that what the pilot was trying to tell him?

But now the girl was speaking again. "Take that to your masters, and let them tremble. The wrath of the masses is upon them. The revolution is here and now," she said, and the door of the hatchway was swung closed. He heard the lock fall into place.

Peter turned and began the long walk back, carrying an envelope in one hand, a grenade in the other, and sick loathing in his guts.

Colin Noble's rugged frame almost filled the hatchway of the Hawker, and for once his expression was deadly serious, no trace of laughter in his eyes or at the corners of the wide friendly mouth.

"Doctor Parker is on the screen." He greeted Peter who was

still buttoning his overalls as he hurried to the command plane. "We copied every word, and he was hooked into the system."

"Christ, it's bad, Colin," Peter grunted.

"That was the good news," Colin told him. "When you have finished with Parker, I've got the bad news for you."

"Thanks, pal." Peter shouldered his way past him into the cabin, and dropped into his leather command chair.

On the screen Kingston Parker was hunched over his desk, poring over the teleprinter sheet on which the entire conversation between Ingrid and Peter had been recorded, the cold empty pipe gripped between his teeth, the broad brow creased with the weight of his responsibility as he studied the demands of the terrorist commando.

The communications director's voice from off-screen alerted Parker.

"General Stride, sir." And Parker looked up at the camera.

"Peter. This is you and me alone. I have closed the circuit and we will restrict to single tape recording. I want your first reaction, before we relay to Sir William and Constable—" Sir William Davies was the British Ambassador and Kelly Constable was the United States Ambassador to Pretoria.

"I want your first reaction."

"We are in serious trouble, sir," Peter said, and the big head nodded.

"What is the militant capability?"

"I am having my explosives team take down the grenade—but I have no doubt that they have the physical capability to destroy 070, and all aboard. I reckon they have an overkill potential of at least ten."

"And the psychological capability."

"In my view, she is the child of Bakunin and Jean Paul Sartre—" again Parker nodded heavily and Peter went on. "The anarchist conception that destruction is the only truly creative act, that violence is man re-creating himself. You know Sartre said that when the revolutionary kills, a tyrant dies and a free man emerges."

"Will she go all the way?" Parker insisted.

"Yes, sir." Peter answered without hesitation. "If she is pressed she'll go all the way—you know the reasoning. If destruction is beautiful, then self-destruction is immortality. In my view, she'll go all the way."

Parker sighed and knocked the stem of his pipe against his big white teeth.

"Yes, it squares with what we have on her."

"You have read her?" Peter asked eagerly.

"We got a first-class voice print, and the computer cross-matched with her facial structure print."

"Who is she?" Peter cut in impatiently; he did not have to be told that the sound intensifier and the zoom video cameras had been feeding her voice and image into the intelligence computer even as she issued her demands.

"Her born name is Hilda Becker. She is a third-generation American of German extraction. Her father is a successful dentist widowed in 1959. The girl is thirty-one years old"—Peter had thought her younger, that fresh young skin had misled him—"I.Q. 138. Columbia University, 1965–68, Master's degree in Modern Political History. Member of SDS—that's Students for a Democratic Society—"

"Yes." Peter was impatient. "I know."

"Activist in Vietnam War protests. Worker for the draft evasion pipeline to Canada. One arrest for possession of marijuana 1967, not convicted. Implicated with Weathermen—and one of the leaders of on-campus rioting in the spring of 1968. Arrested for bombing of Butler and released. Left America in 1970 for further study at Düsseldorf. Doctorate in Political Economics 1972. Known association with Gudrun Ensslin and Horst Mahler of the Baader-Meinhof. Went underground in 1976 after suspicion of implication in the abduction and murder of Heinrich Kohler, the West German industrialist." Her personal history was an almost classical development of the modern revolutionary, Peter reflected bitterly, a perfect picture of the beast. "Believed to have received advanced training from the PFLP in Syria during 1976 and 1977. No recorded contact since then. She is a habitual user of cannabis-based drugs, reported voracious sexual activity with members of both sexes." Parker looked up. "That's all we have," he said.

"Yes," Peter repeated softly. "She'll go all the way."

"What is your further assessment?"

"I believe that this is an operation organized at high level—possibly governmental—"

"Substantiate!" Parker snapped.

"The co-ordination with UN proposals sponsored by the una-ligned nations points that way."

"All right, go on."

"For the first time we have a highly organized and heavily sup-ported strike that is not seeking some obscure, partisan object. We've got demands here about which a hundred million Ameri-cans and fifty million Englishmen are going to say in unison, 'Hell, these aren't unreasonable.' "

"Go on," said Parker.

"The militants have picked a soft target which is the outcast pariah of Western civilization. That UN resolution is going to be passed a hundred to nil, and those millions of Americans and Englishmen are going to have to ask themselves if they are going to sacrifice the lives of four hundred of their most prominent citi-zens to support a government whose racial policies they abhor."

"Yes?" Parker was leaning forward to stare into the screen. "Do you think they'll do a deal?"

"The militants? They might." Peter paused a moment and then went on. "You know my views, sir. I oppose absolutely dealing with these people."

"Even in these circumstances?" Parker demanded.

"Especially now. My views of the host country's policies are in accord with yours, Doctor Parker. This is the test. No matter how much we personally feel the demands are just, we must oppose to the death the manner in which they are presented. If these people win their objects, it is a victory for the gun—and we place all man-kind in jeopardy."

"What is your estimate for a successful counter-strike?" Parker demanded suddenly, and even though he had known the question must come, Peter hesitated a long moment.

"Half an hour ago I would have put the odds at ten to one in our favour that I could pull off condition Delta with only militant casualties."

"And now?"

"Now I know that these are not fuddle-headed fanatics. They are probably as well trained and equipped as we are, and they have had years to set this operation up."

"And now?" Parker insisted.

"We have a four to one in our favour of getting them out with a Delta strike, with say less than ten casualties."

"What is the next best chance?"

"I would say there is no middle ground. If we failed, we would be into a situation with one hundred per cent casualties—we would lose the aircraft and all aboard, including all Thor personnel involved."

"All right then, Peter." Parker leaned back in his chair, the gesture of dismissal. "I am going to speak with the President and the Prime Minister, they are setting up the link now. Then I will brief the ambassadors—and be back to you within the hour."

His image flickered into darkness, and Peter realized that all his hatred was suppressed. He felt cold and functional as the surgeon's blade. Ready to do the job for which he had trained so assiduously, and yet able to assess and evaluate the enemy and the odds against success.

He pressed the call button. Colin had been waiting beyond the sound-proof doors of the command cabin, and he came through immediately.

"The explosives boys have taken down the grenade. It's a dandy. The explosive is the new Soviet CJ composition, and the fusing is factory manufacture. Professional stuff—and it will work. Oh, baby, will it ever work."

Peter hardly needed this confirmation, and Colin went on as he flung himself untidily in the chair opposite Peter.

"We put the list of names and the text of the militant statement on the teleprinter for Washington"—he leaned forward and spoke into the cabin intercom—"Run that loop—without sound first." Then he told Peter grimly, "Here's the bad news I promised."

The loop of video tape began to run on the central screen. It had clearly been shot from the observation post in the office overlooking the service area.

It was a full shot of the Boeing, the background flattened by the magnification of the lens and swimming and wavering with heat mirage rising from the tarmac of the main runway beyond the aircraft.

In the foreground were Peter's own naked back and shoulders as he strode out towards the aircraft. The lens had again flattened the action so that Peter appeared to be marking time on the same spot without advancing at all.

Suddenly the forward hatch of the Boeing changed shape as the door was slid aside, and the cameraman instantly zoomed in for the closer shot.

The two pilots and the air hostess in the doorway, the camera checked for a few frames and then zoomed closer. The aperture of the lens adjusted swiftly, compensating for the gloom of the interior, and the shot was close and tight on the blonde girl's head for a heart beat, then the head turned slightly and the lovely line of her lips moved as she spoke—it seemed like three words—before she turned back full face to the camera.

"Okay," Colin said. "Run it again—with neutral balance on the sound."

The entire loop re-ran, the cabin door opened, there were the three hostages, the fine golden head turned, and then the words "Let's slide," from Ingrid, but there was background hiss and clutter.

" 'Let's slide?' " Peter asked.

"Run it again with the bass density filter on the sound," Colin ordered.

The same images on the screen, the golden head turning on the long neck.

" 'It's slide.' " Peter could not quite catch it.

"Okay," Colin told the technician. "Now with full filter and resonance modulation."

The repetitive images, the girl's head, the full lips parting, speaking to somebody out of sight in the body of the aircraft.

Very clearly, unmistakably, she said, "It's Stride." And Peter felt it jolt in his belly like a fist.

"She recognized you," said Colin. "No, hell, she was expecting you!"

The two men stared at each other, Peter's handsome craggy features heavy with foreboding. Atlas had one of the highest security classifications. Only twenty men outside the close ranks of Atlas itself were privy to its secrets. One of those was the President of the United States—another was the Prime Minister of Great Britain.

Certainly only four or five men knew who commanded the Thor arm of Atlas—and yet there was no mistaking those words the girl had spoken.

"Run it again," Peter ordered brusquely.

And they waited tensely for those two words, and when they came they were in the clear lilt of that fresh young voice.

"It's Stride," said Ingrid, and the screen went blank.

Peter massaged his closed eyelids with thumb and forefinger. He realized with mild surprise that he had not slept for nearly forty-eight hours, but it was not physical weariness that assailed him now but the suddenly overwhelming knowledge of treason and betrayal and of undreamed-of evil.

"Somebody has blown Atlas," said Colin softly. "This is going to be a living and breathing bastard. They'll be waiting for us at every turn of the track."

Peter dropped his hand and opened his eyes. "I must speak to Kingston Parker again," he said. And when Parker's image reappeared on the main screen he was clearly agitated and angry.

"You have interrupted the President."

"Doctor Parker," Peter spoke quickly, "circumstances have altered. In my opinion the chances of a successful Delta strike have dropped. We have no better than an even chance."

"I see." Parker checked the anger. "That's important. I will inform the President."

The lavatories were all blocked by this time, the bowls almost filled, and the stench permeated all the cabins despite the air-conditioning.

Under the strict rationing of food and water most of the passengers were suffering from the lethargy of hunger, and the children were petulant and weepy.

The terrible strain was beginning to show on the hijackers themselves. They were standing a virtually continuous watch—four hours of broken rest followed by four of ceaseless vigil and activity. The red cotton shirts were rumpled and sweat-stained at the armpits, the sweat of nervous and physical strain, eyes bloodshot and tempers uncertain.

Just before nightfall, the dark-haired girl, Karen, had lost her temper with an elderly passenger who had been slow to respond to her command to return to his seat after using the toilet. She had worked herself up into an hysterical shrieking rage, and repeatedly struck the old man in the face with the short barrel of her shot pistol, laying his cheek open to the bone. Only Ingrid had been able to calm her, leading her away to the curtained tourist galley where she pampered and hugged her.

"It will be all right, *Liebchen*." She stroked her hair. "Only a little longer now. You have been so strong. In a few more hours we will all take the pills. Not long now." And within minutes Karen had controlled the violent trembling of her hands, and although she was pale, she was able to take her position at the rear of the tourist cabin again.

Only Ingrid's strength seemed without limits. During the night she passed slowly down the aisles, pausing to talk quietly with a sleepless passenger, comforting them with the promise of imminent release.

"Tomorrow morning we will have an answer to our demands, and all the women and children will be free—it's going to be all right, you just wait and see."

A little after midnight the little roly-poly doctor sought her out in the cockpit.

"The navigator is very ill," he told her. "Unless we get him to a hospital immediately we will lose him."

Ingrid went back and knelt beside the flight engineer. His skin was dry and burning hot and his breathing rasped and sawed.

"It's renal failure," said the doctor, hovering over them. "Breakdown of the kidneys from delayed shock. We cannot treat him here. He must be taken to hospital."

Ingrid took the semi-conscious flight engineer's uninjured hand. "I'm sorry, but that's impossible."

She went on holding his hand for another minute.

"Don't you feel anything?" the doctor demanded of her bitterly.

"I feel pity for him—as I do for all mankind," she answered quietly. "But he is only one. Out there are millions."

The towering flat-topped mountain was lit by floodlights. It was high holiday season and the fairest cape in all the world was showing her beauty to the tens of thousands of tourists and holiday-makers.

On the penthouse deck of the tall building, named for a political mediocrity as are so many buildings and public works in South Africa, the cabinet and its special advisers had been in session for most of the night.

At the head of the long table brooded the heavily built figure of the Prime Minister, bulldog-headed, powerful and unmovable as one of the granite kopjes of the African veld. He dominated the large panelled room, although he had hardly spoken, except to encourage the others with a nod or a few gruff words.

At the far end of the long table sat the two ambassadors, shoulder to shoulder, to emphasize their solidarity. At short intervals the telephones in front of them would ring, and they would listen to the latest reports from their embassies or instructions from the heads of their governments.

On the Prime Minister's right hand sat the handsome moustached Minister of Foreign Affairs, a man with enormous charisma and a reputation for moderation and common sense—but now he was grim and hard faced.

"Your own governments have both pioneered the policy of non-negotiation, of total resistance to the demands of terrorists—why now do you insist that we take the soft line?"

"We do not insist, Minister, we have merely pointed out the enormous public interest that this affair is generating in both the United Kingdom and in my own country." Kelly Constable was a slim, handsome man, intelligent and persuasive, a Democratic appointee of the new American administration. "It is in your government's interest even more than ours to see this through to a satisfactory conclusion. We merely suggest that some accommodation to the demands might bring that about."

"The Atlas Commander on the spot has assessed the chances of a successful counter-strike as low as fifty-fifty. My government considers that risk unacceptable." Sir William Davies was a career diplomat approaching retirement age, a grey, sere man with gold-rimmed spectacles, his voice high pitched and querulous.

"My men think we can do better than that ourselves," said the Minister of Defence, also bespectacled, but he spoke in the thick blunt accent of the Afrikaaner.

"Atlas is probably the best equipped and most highly trained anti-terrorist group in the world," Kelly Constable said, and the Prime Minister interrupted harshly.

"At this stage, gentlemen, let us confine ourselves to finding a peaceful solution."

"I agree, Prime Minister." Sir William nodded briskly.

"However, I think I should point out that most of the demands made by the terrorists are directly in line with the representations made by the government of the United States—"

"Sir, are you expressing sympathy with these demands?" the Prime Minister asked heavily, but without visible emotion.

"I am merely pointing out that the demands will find sympathy in my country, and that my government will find it easier to exercise its veto on the extreme motion of the General Assembly on Monday if some concessions are made in other directions."

"Is that a threat, sir?" the Prime Minister asked, a small humourless smile hardly softening the question.

"No, Prime Minister, it's common sense. If that UN motion was carried and implemented, it would mean the economic ruin of this country. It would be plunged into anarchy and political chaos, a ripe fruit for further Soviet encroachment. My government does not desire that—however, nor does it wish to endanger the lives of four hundred of its citizens." Kelly Constable smiled. "We have to find a way out of our mutual predicament, I'm afraid."

"My Minister of Defence has suggested a way out."

"Prime Minister, if your military attack the aircraft without the prior agreement of both the British and American heads of state, then the veto will be withheld in the Security Council and regretfully we will allow the majority proposal to prevail."

"Even if the attack is successful?"

"Even if the attack is successful. We insist that military decisions are made by Atlas only," Constable told him solemnly; and then, more cheerfully, "Let us examine the minimum concessions that your government would be prepared to make. The longer we can keep open the lines of communication with the terrorists, the better our chances of a peaceful solution. Can we offer to fulfil even one small item on the list of demands?"

Ingrid supervised the serving of breakfast personally. Each passenger was allowed one slice of bread and one biscuit with a cup of heavily sweetened coffee. Hunger had lowered the general resistance of the passengers, they were apathetic and listless once they had gobbled their meagre meal.

Ingrid went amongst them again, passing out cigarettes from the duty-free store. Talking gently to the children, stopping to sympathize with a mother—smiling and calm. Already the passengers were calling her "the nice one."

When Ingrid reached the first-class galley she called her companions to her one at a time, and they each ate a full breakfast of eggs and buttered toast and kippers. She wanted them as strong and alert as the arduous ordeal would allow. She could not begin to use the stimulants until midday. The use of drugs could only be continued for seventy-two hours with the desired effects. After that the subject would become unpredictable in his actions and decisions. Ratification of the sanctions vote by the Security Council of the United Nations would take place at noon New York time on the following Monday—that was 7 P.M. local time on Monday night.

Ingrid had to keep all her officers alert and active until then, she dared not use the stimulants too early and risk physical disintegration before the decisive hour, and yet she realized that lack of sleep and tension were corroding even her physical reserves; she was jumpy and nervous, and when she examined her face in the mirror of the stinking first-class toilets, she saw how inflamed her eyes were, and for the first time noticed the tiny lines of ageing at the corners of her mouth and eyes. This angered her unreasonably. She hated the thought of growing old, and she could smell her own unwashed body even in the overpowering stench from the lavatory.

The German, Kurt, was slumped in the pilot's seat, his pistol in his lap, snoring softly, his red shirt unbuttoned to the waist and his muscular hairy chest rising and falling with each breath. He was unshaven and the lank, black hair fell over his eyes. She could smell his sweat, and somehow that excited her, and she studied him carefully. There was an air of cruelty and brutality about him, the machismo of the revolutionary, which always attracted her strongly—had perhaps been the original reason for her radical leanings so many years ago. Suddenly she wanted him very badly. However, when she woke him with a hand down the front of his thin linen slacks, he was bleary-eyed and foul-breathed, not even her skilful kneading could arouse him, and in a minute she turned away with an exclamation of disgust.

As a displacement activity, she picked up the microphone, switched on the loudspeakers of the passenger cabins. She knew she was acting irrationally, but she began to speak.

"Now listen to me everybody, I have something very important to tell you." Suddenly she was angry with them. They were of the class that had devised and instituted the manifestly unjust and sick society against which she was in total rebellion. They were the fat, complacent bourgeoisie. They were like her father, and she hated them as she hated her father. As she began to speak she realized that they would not even understand the language she was using, the language of the new political order, and her anger and frustration against them and their society mounted. She did not realize she was raving, until suddenly she heard as from afar the shriek of outrage in her own voice, like the death wail of a mortally wounded animal—and she stopped abruptly.

She felt giddy and light-headed, so she had to clutch at the desk top for support and her heart banged wildly against her ribs. She was panting as though she had run a long way, and it took nearly a full minute for her to bring herself under control.

When she spoke again, her tone was still ragged and breathless.

"It is now nine o'clock," she said. "If we do not hear from the tyrant within three hours I shall be forced to begin executing hostages. Three hours," she repeated ominously, "only three hours."

Now she prowled the aircraft like a big cat paces along the bars of its cage as feeding time approaches.

"Two hours," she told them later, and the passengers shrank away from her as she passed.

"One hour." There was a bright sadistic splinter of anticipation in her voice. "We will choose the first hostages now."

"But you promised," pleaded the fat little doctor as Ingrid pulled his wife out of her seat and the Frenchman hustled her forward towards the flight deck.

Ingrid ignored him, and turned to Karen. "Get children, a boy and a girl," she instructed. "Oh yes, and the pregnant one. Let them see her big belly. They won't be able to resist that."

Karen herded the hostages into the forward galley and forced them at pistol point to sit in a row upon the fold-down air-crew seats.

The door to the flight deck was open and Ingrid's voice carried clearly to the galley, as she explained to the Frenchman Henri, speaking in English.

"It is of the utmost importance that we do not allow a deadline to pass without retaliating strongly. If we miss one deadline, then our credibility is destroyed. It will only be necessary once, we must show the steel at least once. They must learn that every one of our deadlines is irrevocable, not negotiable—"

The girl began to cry. She was thirteen years old, able to understand the danger. The plump doctor's wife put her arm around her shoulders and hugged her gently.

"Speedbird 070," the radio squawked suddenly, "we have a message for Ingrid."

"Go ahead, Tower, this is Ingrid." She had jumped up to take the microphone, pushing the door to the flight deck closed.

"The negotiator for the British and American governments has proposals for your consideration. Are you ready to copy?"

"Negative." Ingrid's voice was flat and emphatic. "I say again negative. Tell the negotiator I will talk only face to face—and tell him we are only forty minutes to the noon deadline. He had better get out here fast," she warned. She hooked the microphone and turned to Henri.

"All right. We will take the pills now—it has truly begun at last."

It was another cloudless day, with brilliant sunlight flung back in piercing darts of light from the bare metal parts of the aircraft. The heat came up through the soles of his shoes and burned down upon Peter's bare neck.

The forward hatch opened, as it had before, when Peter Stride was half-way across the tarmac.

This time there were no hostages on display, the hatchway was a black empty square. Suppressing the urge to hurry, Peter carried himself with dignity, head up, jaw clenched firmly.

He was fifty yards from the aircraft when the girl stepped into the opening. She stood with indolent grace, her weight all on one leg, the other cocked slightly, long, bare, brown legs. She carried the big shot pistol on one hip, and the cartridge belt emphasized the narrow waist.

She watched Peter come on, with a half smile on her lips. Suddenly a medallion of light appeared on her chest, a dazzling speck like a brilliant insect and she glanced down at it contemptuously.

"This is provocation," she called. Clearly she knew that the bright speck was the beam thrown by the laser sight of one of the marksmen covering her from the airport building. A few ounces more of pressure on the trigger would send a .22 bullet crashing precisely into that spot, tearing her heart and lungs to bloody shreds.

Peter felt a flare of anger at the sniper who had activated his laser sight without the order, but his anger was tempered by reluctant admiration for the girl's courage. She could sneer at that mark of certain death upon her breast.

Peter made a cut out sign with his right hand, and almost immediately the speck of light disappeared as the gunner switched off his laser sight.

"That's better," the girl said, and she smiled, running her gaze appraisingly down Peter's body.

"You've a good shape, baby," she said, and Peter's anger flared again under her scrutiny.

"Nice flat belly," she said, "good legs, and you didn't get those muscles sitting at a desk and pushing a pen." She pursed her lips thoughtfully. "You know I think you're a cop or a soldier. That's what I think, baby. I think you're a goddamned pig." Her voice had a new harsh quality, and the skin seemed drier and drawn— older than it had been before.

He was close enough now to see the peculiar diamantine glitter in her eyes, and he recognized the tension that seemed to rack her body, the abrupt restless gestures. She was onto drugs now. He was certain of it. He was dealing with a political fanatic, with a long history of violence and death, whose remaining humane traits would be now entirely suppressed by the high of stimulant drugs. He knew she was more dangerous now than a wounded wild animal, a cornered leopard, a man-eating shark with the taste of blood exciting it to the killing frenzy.

He did not reply, but held her gaze steadily, keeping his hands in view, coming to a halt below the open hatchway.

He waited quietly for her to begin, but the itch of the drug in her blood would not allow her to stand still. She fidgeted with the weapon in her hands, touched the camera still hanging from around her neck. Cyril Watkins had tried to tell him something about that camera—and suddenly Peter realized what it was. "The trigger for the fuses?" he pondered, as he waited. "Almost certainly," he decided, that was why it was with her every moment. She saw the direction of his eyes, and dropped her hand guiltily, confirming his conclusion.

"Are the prisoners ready to leave?" she demanded. "Is the gold packed? Is the statement ready for transmission?"

"The South African Government has acceded to urgent representations by the governments of Great Britain and the United States of America."

"Good." She nodded.

"As an act of common humanity the South Africans have agreed to release all the persons on your list of detainees and banned persons—"

"Yes."

"They will be flown to any country of their choice."

"And the gold?"

"The South African Government refuses categorically to finance or to arm an unconstitutional foreign-based opposition. They refuse to provide funds for the persons freed under this agreement."

"The television transmission?"

"The South African Government considers the statement to be untrue in substance and in fact and to be extremely prejudicial to the maintenance of law and order in this country. It refuses to allow transmission of the statement."

"They have accepted only one of our demands—" The girl's voice took on an even more strident tone, and her shoulders jerked in an uncontrolled spasm.

"The release of political detainees and banned persons is subject to one further condition," Peter cut in swiftly.

"And what is that?" the girl demanded, two livid burning spots of colour had appeared in her cheeks.

"In return for the release of political prisoners, they demand the release of all hostages, not only the women and children, all persons aboard the aircraft—and they will guarantee safe passage for you and all members of your party to leave the country with the released detainees."

The girl flung back her head, the thick golden mane flying wildly about her head as she screeched with laughter. The laughter was a wild, almost maniacal sound, and though it went on and on, there was no echo of mirth in her eyes. They were fierce as eagles' eyes, as she laughed. The laughter was cut off abruptly, and her voice was suddenly flat and level.

"So they think they can make demands, do they? They think

they can draw the teeth from the UN proposals, do they? They think that without hostages to account for, the fascist governments of Britain and America can again cast their veto with impunity?"

Peter made no reply.

"Answer me!" she screamed suddenly. "They do not believe we are serious, do they?"

"I am a messenger only," he said.

"You're not," she screamed in accusation. "You're a trained killer. You're a pig!" She lifted the pistol and aimed with both hands at Peter's face.

"What answer must I take back?" Peter asked, without in any way acknowledging the aim of the weapon.

"An answer—" Her voice dropped again to an almost conversational level. "Of course, an answer." She lowered the pistol and consulted the stainless steel Japanese watch on her wrist. "It's three minutes past noon—three minutes past the deadline, and they are entitled to an answer, of course."

She looked around her with an almost bewildered expression. The drug was having side effects, Peter guessed. Perhaps she had overdosed herself, perhaps whoever had prescribed it had not taken into account the forty-eight sleepless hours of strain that preceded its use.

"The answer," he prodded her gently, not wanting to provoke another outburst.

"Yes. Wait," she said, and disappeared abruptly into the gloom of the interior.

Karen was standing over the four hostages on the fold-down seats. She looked around at Ingrid with smouldering dark eyes. Ingrid nodded once curtly, and Karen turned back to her prisoners.

"Come," she said softly, "we are going to let you go now." Almost gently she lifted the pregnant woman to her feet with a hand on her shoulder.

Ingrid left her and passed swiftly into the rear cabins. She nodded again to Kurt, and with a toss of his head he flicked the lank locks of hair from his eyes and thrust the pistol into his belt.

From the locker above his head he brought down two of the plastic grenades. Holding one in each fist he pulled the pins with his teeth and held the rings hooked over his little fingers.

With his arms spread like a crucifix, he ran lightly down the aisle.

"These grenades are primed. Nobody must move, nobody must leave their seats—no matter whatever happens. Stay where you are."

The fourth hijacker took up the cry from him, holding primed grenades in both hands above his head.

"Nobody move. No talking. Sit still. Everybody still." He repeated in German and in French and his eyes had the same hard, glossy glitter of the drug high.

Ingrid turned back towards the flight deck.

"Come, sweetheart." She placed an arm round the girl's shoulder, shepherding her towards the open hatchway—but the child shrank away from her with dread.

"Don't touch me," she whispered, and her eyes were huge with terror. The boy was younger, more trusting. He took Ingrid's hand readily.

He had thick curly hair, and honey brown eyes as he looked up at her. "Is my daddy here?" he asked.

"Yes, darling." Ingrid squeezed his hand. "You be a good boy now, and you'll see your daddy very soon."

She led him to the open hatchway. "Stand there," she said.

Peter Stride was uncertain what to expect, as the boy stepped into the open hatchway high above him. Then next to him appeared a plump middle-aged woman in an expensive but rumpled, high-fashion silk dress, probably a Nina Ricci, Peter decided irrelevantly. The woman's elaborate lacquered hair style was coming down in wisps around her ears, but she had a kindly humorous face and she placed a protective arm about the boy-child's shoulders.

The next person was a taller and younger woman, with a pale sensitive skin; her nostrils and eyelids were inflamed pink from weeping or from some allergy and there were blotches of angry prickly heat on her throat and upper arms. Under the loose cotton maternity dress her huge belly bulged grotesquely, throwing her off balance; she stood with her thin white legs knock-kneed awkwardly—and blinked in the sparkling sunshine, her eyes still attuned to the shaded gloom of the cabin.

The fourth and last person was a young girl, and with a sudden blinding stab of agony below the ribs Peter thought it was Melissa-Jane. It took a dozen racing beats of his heart before he realized it was not her—but she had the same sweet Victorian face, the classical English skin of rose petals, the finely bred body of almost woman with delicate breast-buds and long coltish legs below narrow boyish hips.

There was naked terror in her huge eyes, and almost instantly she seemed to realize that Peter was her hope of salvation. The eyes turned on him pleading, hope starting to awaken.

"Please," she whispered, "don't let them hurt us." So softly that Peter could hardly catch the words. "Please, sir. Please help us."

But Ingrid was there, her voice rising stridently.

"You must believe that what we promise, we mean. You and your evil capitalist masters must understand completely that we will not let a single deadline pass without executions. We have to prove that for the revolution we are without mercy. You must be made to understand that our demands must be met in full, that they are not negotiable. We must demonstrate the price for missing a deadline." She paused. "The next deadline is midnight tonight. If our demands are not met in full by then—you must know the price you will be made to pay." She halted again, and then her voice rose into that hysterical shriek. "This is the price!" and she stepped back out of sight.

Helpless with dread, Peter Stride tried to think of some way to prevent the inevitable.

"Jump!" he shouted, lifting both hands towards the girl. "Jump, quickly. I will catch you!"

But the child hesitated, the drop was almost thirty feet, and she teetered uncertainly.

Behind her, ten paces back, the dark-haired Karen and the blonde lion-maned girl stood side by side, and in unison they lifted the short, big-bored pistols, holding them in the low double-handed grip, positioning themselves at the angle and range which would allow the mass of soft heavy lead beads with which the cartridges were packed to spread sufficiently to sweep the backs of the four hostages.

"Jump!" Peter's voice carried clearly into the cabin, and Ingrid's mouth convulsed in a nervous rictus, an awful parody of a smile.

"Now!" she said, and the two women fired together. The two shots blended in a thunderous burst of sound, a mind-stopping roar, and blue powder smoke burst from the gaping muzzles, flying specks of burning wadding hurled across the cabin, and the impact of lead shot into living flesh sounded like a handful of watermelon pips thrown against a wall.

Ingrid fired the second barrel a moment before Karen, so this time the two shots were distinct stunning blurts of sound, and in the dreadful silence that followed the two men in the passenger cabins were screaming wildly.

"Nobody move! Everybody freeze!"

For Peter Stride those fractional seconds seemed to last for long hours. They seemed to play on endlessly through his brain, like a series of frozen frames in a grotesque movie. Image after image seemed separated from the whole, so that forever afterwards he would be able to re-create each of them entire and undistorted and to experience again undiluted the paralysing nausea of those moments.

The pregnant woman took the full blast of one of the first shots. She burst open like an overripe fruit, her swollen body pulled out of shape by the passage of shot from spine to navel, and she was flung forward so she somersaulted out into space. She hit the tarmac in a loose tangle of pale thin limbs, and was completely still, no flicker of life remaining.

The plump woman clung to the boy beside her, and they teetered in the open doorway—around them swirled pale blue wisps of gunsmoke. Though she kept her balance, the tightly stretched beige silk of her dress was speckled with dozens of tiny wounds, as though she had been stabbed repeatedly with a sharpened knitting needle. The same wounds were torn through the boy's white school shirt, and little scarlet flowers bloomed swiftly around each wound, spreading to stain the cloth. Neither of them made any sound, and their expressions were startled and uncomprehending. The next blasts of sound and shot struck them solidly, and they seemed boneless and without substance as they tumbled forward, still locked together. Their fall seemed to continue for a very long time, and then they sprawled together over the pregnant woman's body.

Peter ran forward to catch the girl-child as she fell, and her weight bore him to his knees on the tarmac. He came to his feet running, carrying her like a sleepy baby, one arm under her knees and the other around her shoulders. Her lovely head bumped against his shoulder, and the fine silken hair blew into his face, half blinding him.

"Don't die," he found himself grunting the words in time to his pounding feet. "Please don't die." But he could feel the warm wet leak of blood down his belly, soaking into his shorts, and dribbling down the front of his thighs.

At the entrance to the terminal buildings Colin ran out a dozen paces and tried to take the child from his arms, but Peter resisted him fiercely.

Peter relinquished the frail, completely relaxed body to the Thor doctor, and he stood by without word or expression of regret as the doctor worked swiftly over her. Peter's face was stony and his wide mouth clamped in a hard line when the doctor looked up at last.

"I'm afraid she's dead, sir."

Peter nodded curtly and turned away. His heels cracked on the echoing marble of the deserted terminal hall and Colin fell in silently beside him. His face was as bleak and expressionless as Peter's, as they climbed into the cabin of the Hawker command aircraft.

"Sir William, you point at us for holding enemies of the State without trial." The Foreign Minister leaned forward to point the accuser's finger. "But you British discarded the citizen's right of Habeas Corpus when you passed the Prevention of Terrorism Act, and in Cyprus and Palestine you were holding prisoners without trial long before that. Now your H block in Ulster—is that any better than what we are forced to do here?"

Sir William, the British Ambassador, gobbled indignantly, while he collected his thoughts.

Kelly Constable intervened smoothly. "Gentlemen, we are trying to find common ground here—not areas of dispute. There are hundreds of lives at stake—"

A telephone shrilled in the air-conditioned hush of the room and Sir William lifted the receiver to his ear with patent relief, but as he listened, all blood drained from his face, leaving it a jaundiced, putty colour.

"I see," he said once, and then, "very well, thank you," and replaced the receiver. He looked down the length of the long polished imbuia wood table to the imposing figure at the end.

"Prime Minister," his voice quavered a little, "I regret to inform you that the terrorists have rejected the compromise proposals offered by your government, and that ten minutes ago they murdered four hostages—"

There was a gasp of disbelief from the attentive circle of listening men.

"The hostages were two women and two children—a boy and a girl—they were shot in the back and their bodies thrown from the aircraft. The terrorists have set a new deadline—midnight tonight —for the acceptance of their terms. Failing which there will be further shootings."

The silence lasted for almost a minute as head after head turned slowly, until they were all staring at the big hunched figure at the head of the table.

"I appeal to you in the name of humanity, sir." It was Kelly Constable who broke the silence. "We must save the women and children at least. The world will not allow us to sit by as they are murdered."

"We will have to attack the aircraft and free the prisoners," said the Prime Minister heavily.

But the American Ambassador shook his head. "My government is adamant, sir—as is that of my British colleague"—he glanced at Sir William, who nodded support. "We cannot and will not risk a massacre. Attack the aircraft and our governments will make no attempt to moderate the terms of the UN proposals, nor will we intervene in the Security Council to exercise the veto."

"Yet, if we agree to the demands of these—these animals"—the last words were said fiercely—"we place our nation in terrible danger."

"Prime Minister, we have only hours to find a solution—then the killing will begin again."

"You yourself have placed the success chances of a Delta strike as low as even," Kingston Parker pointed out, staring grimly at Peter Stride out of the little square screen. "Neither the President nor I find those odds acceptable."

"Doctor Parker, they are murdering women and children out

there on the tarmac." Peter tried to keep his tone neutral, his reasoning balanced.

"Very strong pressure is being brought to bear on the South African Government to accede to the terms for release of the women and children."

"That will solve nothing." Peter could not restrain himself. "It will leave us with exactly the same situation tomorrow night."

"If we can secure the release of the women and children, the number of lives at risk will be reduced, and in forty hours the situation might have changed—we are buying time, Peter, even if we have to pay for it with a heavy coin."

"And if the South Africans do not agree? If we come to the midnight deadline without an agreement with the hijackers, what happens then, Doctor Parker?"

"This is a difficult thing to say, Peter, but if that happens"—Parker spread those long graceful hands in a gesture of resignation—"we may lose another four lives, but that is better than precipitating the massacre of four hundred. And after that the South Africans will not be able to hold out. They will have to agree to free the women and children—at any cost."

Peter could not truly believe what he had heard. He knew he was on the very brink of losing his temper completely, and he had to give himself a few seconds to steady himself. He dropped his eyes to his own hands that were interlocked on the desk top in front of him. Under the fingernails of his right hand were black half moons, the dried blood of the child he had carried back from the aircraft. Abruptly he unlocked his fingers and thrust both hands deeply into the pockets of his blue Thor overalls. He took a long deep breath, held it a moment, then let it out slowly.

"If that was difficult to say, Doctor Parker, console yourself that it was a bloody sight harder to listen to."

"I understand how you feel, Peter."

"I don't think you do, sir." Peter shook his head slowly.

"You are a soldier—"

"—and only a soldier knows how to really hate violence," Peter finished for him.

"Our personal feelings must not be allowed to intrude in this." Kingston Parker's voice had a sharp edge to it now. "I must once again forcibly remind you that the decision for condition Delta has been delegated to me by the President and your Prime Minister. No strike will be made without my express orders. Do you understand that, General Stride?"

"I understand, Doctor Parker," Peter said flatly. "And we hope to get some really good video tapes of the next murders. I'll let you have copies for your personal collection."

The other 747 had been grounded for servicing when the emergency began, and it was parked in the assembly area only a thousand yards from where Speedbird 070 stood, but the main service hangars and the corner of the terminal buildings effectively screened it from any observation by the hijackers.

Although it wore the orange and blue of South African Airways with the flying Springbok on the tail, it was an almost identical model to its sister ship. Even the cabin configurations were very close to the plans of Speedbird 070, which had been teleprinted from British Airways Headquarters at Heathrow. It was a fortunate coincidence, and an opportunity that Colin Noble had seized immediately. He had already run seven mock Deltas on the empty hull.

"All right, you guys, let's try and get our asses out of low gear on this run. I want to better fourteen seconds from the 'go' to penetration." His strike team glanced at one another as they squatted in a circle on the tarmac, and there were a few theatrical rollings of eyes. Colin ignored them. "Let's go for nine seconds, gang," he said and stood up.

There were sixteen men in the actual assault group—seventeen when Peter Stride joined them. The other members of Thor were technical experts—electronics and communications, four marksmen snipers, a weapons quartermaster, and a bomb disposal and explosives sergeant, doctor, cook, three engineering N.C.O.s under a lieutenant, the pilots and other flight personnel—a big team, but every man was indispensable.

The assault group wore single-piece uniforms of close fitting black nylon, for low night visibility. They wore their gas masks loosely around their necks, ready for instant use. Their boots were black canvas lace-ups, with soft rubber soles for silence. Each man wore his specialized weapons and equipment either in a back pack or on his black webbing belt. No bulky bullet-proof flak jackets to impede mobility or to snag on obstacles, no hard helmets to tap against metal and tell tales to a wary adversary.

Nearly all the group were young men, in their early twenties, hand picked from the U.S. Marine Corps or from the British 22.SAS regiment that Peter Stride had once commanded. They were superbly fit, and honed to a razor's edge.

Colin Noble watched them carefully as they assembled silently on the marks he had chalked on the tarmac, representing the entrances to the air terminal and the service hangars nearest to 070. He was searching for any sign of slackness, any deviation from the almost impossible standards he had set for Thor. He could find none. "All right, ten seconds—to flares," he called. A Delta strike began with the launching of phosphorus flares across the nose of the target aircraft. They would float down on their tiny parachutes, causing a diversion which would hopefully bunch the terrorists in the flight deck of the target aircraft as they tried to figure out the reason for the lights. The brilliance of the flares would also sear the retina of the terrorists' eyes and destroy night vision for many minutes afterwards.

"Flares!" shouted Colin, and the assault group went into action. The two "stick" men led them, sprinting out directly under the gigantic tail of the deserted aircraft. Each of them carried a gas cylinder strapped across his shoulder, to which the long stainless steel probes were attached by flexible armoured couplings—these were the "sticks" that gave them their name.

The leader carried compressed air in the tank upon his back at a pressure of 250 atmospheres, and on the tip of his twenty-foot probe was the diamond cutting bit of the air-drill. He dropped on one knee under the belly of the aircraft ten feet behind the landing gear and reached up to press the point of the air-drill against the exact spot, carefully plotted from the manufacturer's drawing, where the pressure hull was thinnest and where direct access to the passenger cabins lay just beyond the skin of alloy metal.

The whine of the cutting drill would be covered by the revving of the jet engines of aircraft parked in the southern terminal. Three seconds to pierce the hull, and the second stick man was ready to insert the tip of his probe into the drill hole.

"Power off," Colin grunted; at that moment electrical power from the mains to the aircraft would be cut to kill the air-conditioning.

The second man simulated the act of releasing the gas from the bottle on his back through the probe and saturating the air in the aircraft's cabins. The gas was known simply as Factor V. It smelled faintly of newly dug truffles, and when breathed as a five per cent concentration in air would partially paralyse a man in under ten seconds—loss of motor control of the muscles, unco-ordinated movement, slurred speech and distorted vision, were initial symptoms.

Breathed for twenty seconds the symptoms were total paralysis, for thirty seconds loss of consciousness; breathed for two minutes, pulmonary failure and death. The antidote was fresh air or, better still, pure oxygen, and recovery was rapid with no long-term after-effects.

The rest of the assault group had followed the "stick" men and split into four teams. They waited poised, squatting under the wings, gas masks in place, equipment and weapons ready for instant use.

Colin was watching his stop-watch. He could not chance exposing the passengers to more than ten seconds of Factor V. There would be elderly people, infants, asthma sufferers aboard; as the needle reached the ten-second mark, he snapped, "Power on."

Air-conditioning would immediately begin washing the gas out of the cabins again, and now it was "Go!"

Two assault teams poured up the aluminium scaling ladders onto the wing roots, and knocked out the emergency window panels. The other two teams went for the main doors, but they could only simulate the use of slap-hammers to tear through the metal and reach the locking device on the interior—nor could they detonate the stun grenades.

"Penetration." The assault leader standing in for Peter Stride on this exercise signalled entry of the cabins, and Colin clicked his stop-watch.

"Time?" asked a quiet voice at his shoulder, and he turned quickly. So intent on his task, Colin had not heard Peter Stride come up behind him.

"Eleven seconds, sir." The courteous form of address was proof of Colonel Colin Noble's surprise. "Not bad—but sure as hell not good either. We'll run it again."

"Rest them," Peter ordered. "I want to talk it out a bit."

They stood together at the full windows in the south wall of the air traffic control tower, and studied the big red, white and blue aircraft for the hundredth time that day.

The heat of the afternoon had raised thunderheads, great purple and silver mushroom bursts of cloud that reached to the heavens. Trailing grey skirts of torrential rain they marched across the horizon, forming a majestic backdrop that was almost too theatrical to be real, while the lowering sun found the gaps in the cloud and shot long groping fingers of golden light through them, heightening the illusion of theatre.

"Six hours to deadline," Colin Noble grunted, and groped for one of his scented black cheroots. "Any news of concessions by the locals?"

"Nothing. I don't think they will buy it."

"Not until the next batch of executions." Colin bit the end from the cheroot and spat it angrily into a corner. "For two years I break my balls training for this, and now they tie our hands behind our backs."

"If they gave you Delta, when would you make your run?" Peter asked.

"As soon as it was dark," Colin answered promptly.

"No. They are still revved up high on drugs," Peter demurred. "We should give them time to go over the top, and start downing. My guess is they will dope again just before the next deadline. I would hit them just before that—" he paused to calculate. "I'd hit them at fifteen minutes before eleven—seventy-five minutes before the deadline."

"If we had Delta," Colin grunted.

"If we had Delta," Peter agreed, and they were silent a moment. "Listen, Colin, this has been wearing me down. If they know my name, what else does that gang of freaks know about Thor? Do they know our contingency planning for taking an aircraft?"

"God, I hadn't worked it out that far."

"I have been looking for a twist, a change from the model, something that will give us the jump even if they know what to expect."

"We've taken two years to set it up tightly—" Colin looked dubious. "There is nothing we can change."

"The flares," said Peter. "If we went, we would not signal the Delta with the flares, we would go in cold."

"The uglies would be scattered all through the cabins, mixed up with passengers and crew—"

"The red shirt Ingrid was wearing. My guess is, all four of them will be uniformed to impress their hostages. We would hose anything and everybody in red. If my guess is wrong, then we would have to do it Israeli style."

Israeli style was the shouted command to lie down, and to kill anyone who disobeyed or who made an aggressive move.

"The truly important one is the girl. The girl with the camera. Have your boys studied the video tapes of her?"

"They know her face better than they do Farrah Fawcett's," Colin grunted, and then, "the bitch is so goddamned lovely—I had to run the video of the executions three times for them, twice in slow motion, to wipe out a little of the old chivalry bit." It is difficult to get a man to kill a pretty girl, and a moment of hesitation would be critical with a trained fanatic like Ingrid. "I also made them take a look at the little girl before they put her in a basket and took her down to the morgue. They're in the right mood." Colin shrugged. "But what the hell, Atlas isn't going to call Delta. We're wasting our time."

"Do you want to play make believe?" Peter asked, and then without waiting for an answer, "Let's make believe we have a Delta approval from Atlas. I want you to set up a strike timed to 'go' at exactly 10:45 local time tonight. Do it as though it was the real thing—get it right in every detail."

Colin turned slowly and studied his commander's face, but the eyes were level and without guile and the strong lines of jaw and mouth were unwavering.

"Make believe?" Colin Noble asked quietly.

"Of course," Peter Stride's tone was curt and impatient, and Colin shrugged.

"Hell, I only work here," and he turned away.

Peter lifted the binoculars and slowly traversed the length of the big machine from tail to nose, but there was no sign of life, every port and window still carefully covered—and reluctantly he let his binoculars sink slightly until he was staring at the pitiful pile of bodies that still lay on the tarmac below the forward hatch.

Except for the electrical mains hook-up, the delivery of medicines and the two occasions when Peter himself had made the long trip out there, nobody else had been allowed to approach the machine. No refuelling, no refuse nor sanitary removals, no catering—not even the removal of the corpses of the murdered hostages. The hijackers had learned the lesson of previous hijacking attempts when vital information had been smuggled off the aircraft in refuse and sewerage at Mogadishu, and at Lod where the storming party had come disguised as caterers.

Peter was still gazing at the bodies, and though he was accustomed to death in its most obscene forms, these bodies offended him more deeply than any in his life before. This was a contemptuous flaunting of all the deepest rooted taboos of society. Peter was grimly content now with the decision of the South African police not to allow any television teams or press photographers through the main gates of the airport.

Peter knew that the world media were howling outrage and threats, protesting in the most extreme terms against the infringement of their God-given rights to bring into the homes of all civilized people images of dreadful death and mutilation, lovingly photographed in gorgeous colour with meticulous professional attention to all the macabre details.

Without this enthusiastic chronicling of their deeds, international terrorism would lose most of its impetus and his job would be a lot easier. For sneaking moments he envied the local police the powers they had to force irresponsibles to act in the best interests of society, then as he carried the thought a step further, he came up hard once again against the question of who was qualified to make such decisions on behalf of society. If the police made that decision and exerted it, was it not just another form of the terrorism it was seeking to suppress? "Christ," thought Peter angrily, "I'm going to drive myself mad."

He stepped up beside the senior air traffic controller.

"I want to try again," Peter said, and the man handed him the microphone.

"Speedbird 070 this is the tower. Ingrid, do you read me? Come in, Ingrid."

He had tried a dozen times to make contact in the last few hours, but the hijackers had maintained an ominous silence.

"Ingrid, come in please." Peter kept trying, and suddenly there was the clear fresh voice.

"This is Ingrid. What do you want?"

"Ingrid, we request your clearance to have an ambulance remove the bodies," Peter asked.

"Negative, Tower. I say again, negative. No one is to approach this aircraft." There was a pause. "We will wait until we have a round dozen bodies for you to remove"—the girl giggled, still on the drug high—"wait until midnight, and we'll make it really worth your while." And the radio clicked into silence.

"We are going to give you dinner now," Ingrid shouted cheerfully, and there was a stir of interest down the length of the cabin. "And it's my birthday today. So you're going to have champagne —isn't that great!"

But the plump little Jewish doctor rose suddenly to his feet. His grey sparse hair stood up in comical wisps, and his face seemed to have collapsed, like melting candle wax, ravaged and destroyed by grief. He no longer seemed to be aware of what had been said or what was happening. "You had no right to kill her." His voice sounded like a very old man. "She was a good person. She never hurt anyone—" He looked about him with a confused, unfocused look, and ran the fingers of one hand through his disordered hair. "You should not have killed her," he repeated.

"She was guilty," Ingrid called back at him. "Nobody is innocent—you are all the cringing tools of international capitalism." Her face twisted, in an ugly spasm of hatred. "You are guilty, all of you, and you deserve to die—" She stopped short, controlled herself with an obvious effort of will, and then smiled again; going forward to the little doctor, she put an arm around his shoulders. "Sit down," she said, almost tenderly, "I know just how you feel, please believe me, I wish there had been another way."

He sank down slowly, his eyes vacant with sorrow and his fingers plucking numbly at themselves.

"You just sit there quietly," Ingrid said gently. "I'm going to bring you a glass of champagne now."

"Prime Minister," Kelly Constable's voice was husky with almost two days and nights of unceasing tension, "it's after ten o'clock already. We must have a decision soon, in less than two hours—"

The Prime Minister lifted one hand to silence the rest of it.

"Yes, we all know what will happen then."

An air force jet had delivered a copy of the video tape from Johannesburg, a thousand miles away, and the cabinet and the ambassadors had watched the atrocity in detail, recorded by an 800-mm lens. There was not a man at the table who did not have children of his own. The toughest right-wingers amongst them wavered uncertainly, even the puckish little Minister of Police could not meet the ambassador's eyes as he swept the table with a compelling gaze.

"And we all know that no compromise is possible, we must meet the demands in full or not at all."

"Mister Ambassador," the Prime Minister broke the silence at last, "if we agree to the terms, it will be only as an act of humanity. We will be paying a very high price indeed for the lives of your people. But if we agree to that price, can we be absolutely assured of your support—the support of both Britain and the United States—in the Security Council the day after tomorrow at noon?"

"The President of the United States has empowered me to pledge his support in return for your co-operation," said Kelly Constable.

"Her Britannic Majesty's Government has asked me to assure you of the same support," intoned Sir William. "And our governments will make good the 170 million dollars demanded by the hijackers."

"Still I cannot make the decision on my own. It is too onerous for one man," the Prime Minister sighed. "I am going to ask my ministers, the full cabinet"—he indicated the tense, grim faces around him—"to vote. I am going to ask you gentlemen to leave us alone now for a few minutes while we decide."

And the two ambassadors rose together and bowed slightly to the brooding, troubled figure before leaving the room.

"Where is Colonel Noble?" Kingston Parker asked.

"He is waiting," Peter indicated with a jerk of his head the sound-proof door of the Hawker's command cabin.

"I want him in on this, please," Parker said from the screen, and Peter pressed the call button.

Colin Noble came in immediately, stooping slightly under the low roof, a chunky powerful figure with the blue Thor cap pulled low over his eyes.

"Good evening, sir." He greeted the image on the screen and squeezed into the seat beside Peter.

"I'm glad Colonel Noble is here." Peter's voice was crisp and businesslike. "I think he will support my contention that the chances of a successful Delta counter-strike will be greatly enhanced if we can launch our attack not later than ten minutes before eleven o'clock." He tugged back the cuff of his sleeve, and glanced at his watch. "That is forty minutes from now. We reckon to catch the militants at the moment when the drug cycle is at its lowest, before they take more pills and begin to arouse themselves to meet their deadline. I believe that if we strike then, we will have an acceptable risk—"

"Thank you, General Stride," Parker interrupted him smoothly, "but I wanted Colonel Noble present so there could be no misunderstanding of my orders. Colonel Noble"—Parker's eyes shifted slightly as he changed the object of his attention—"Commander of Thor has requested an immediate Delta strike against Speedbird 070. I am now, in your presence, disapproving that request. Negotiations with the South African Government are at a critical state, and under no circumstances must there be either overt or covert hostile moves towards the militants. Do I make myself entirely clear?"

"Yes, sir." Colin Noble's expression was stony.

"General Stride?"

"I understand, sir."

"Very well. I want you to stand by, please. I am going to confer with the ambassadors. I will re-establish contact as soon as I have further concrete indications."

The image receded rapidly, and the screen went dark. Colonel Colin Noble turned slowly and looked at Peter Stride, his expression changed slightly at what he saw, and quickly he pressed the censor button on the command console, stopping all recording tapes, killing the video cameras so there would be no record of his words now.

"Listen, Peter, you're in line for that NATO command, everybody knows that. From there the sky is the limit, pal. Right up there to the joint chiefs—just as far as you want to go."

Peter said nothing, but glanced once more at the gold Rolex wristwatch. It was seventeen minutes past ten o'clock.

"Think, Peter. For God's sake, man. It's taken you twenty heartbreaking years of hard work to get where you are. They would never forgive you, buddy. You'd better believe it. They'll break you and your career. Don't do it, Peter. Don't do it. You're too good to waste yourself. Just stop and think for one minute."

"I'm thinking," said Peter quietly. "I haven't stopped thinking since—" he checked. "Always it comes back to this. If I let them die—then I am as guilty as that woman who pulls the trigger."

"Peter, you don't have to beat your head in. The decision is made by someone else—"

"It would be easier to believe that, wouldn't it," Peter snapped, "but it won't save those people out there."

Colin leaned across and placed a large hairy paw on Peter's upper arm. He squeezed slightly. "I know, but it eats me to see you have to throw it all away. In my book, you're one of the tops, buddy." It was the first time he had made any such declaration, and Peter was fleetingly moved by it.

"You can duck this one, Colin. It doesn't have to touch you or your career."

"I never was very hot at ducking." Colin dropped his hand away. "I think I'll go along for the ride—"

"I want you to record a protest—no sense us all getting ourselves fired," said Peter, as he switched on the recording equipment, both audio and video; now every word would be recorded.

"Colonel Noble," he said distinctly, "I am about to lead an immediate Delta assault on Flight 070. Please make the arrangements."

Colin turned to face the camera. "General Stride, I must formally protest at any order to initiate condition Delta without express approval from Atlas Command."

"Colonel Noble, your protest is noted," Peter told the camera gravely, and Colin Noble hit the censor button once again, cutting tapes and camera.

"Okay, that's enough crap for one day." He came nimbly to his feet. "Let's get out there and take the bastards."

Ingrid sat at the flight engineer's desk, and held the microphone of the on-board loudspeaker system to her lips. There was a greyish tone beneath the sun-gilded skin, she frowned a little at the throbbing pulse of pain behind her eyes and the hand that held the microphone trembled slightly. She knew these were all symptoms of the drug hang-over. She regretted now having increased the initial dosage beyond that recommended on the typed label of the tablet phial—but she had needed that extra lift to be able to carry out the first executions. Now she and her officers were paying the price, but in another twenty minutes she would be able to issue another round of tablets. This time she would stay exactly within the recommended dosage, and she anticipated the rush of it through her blood, the heightened vision and energy, the tingling exhilaration of the drug. She even anticipated the thought of what lay ahead; to be able to wield absolute power, the power of death itself, was one of life's most worthwhile experiences. Sartre and Bakunin and Most had discovered one of the great truths of life—that the act of destruction, of total destruction, was a catharsis, a creation, a re-awakening of the soul. She looked forward, even through the staleness and ache of the drug let down, she looked forward to the next executions.

"My friends," she spoke into the microphone, "we have not heard from the tyrant. His lack of concern for your lives is typical of the fascist imperialist. He does not concern himself with the safety of the people, though he sucks and bloats himself on the blood and sweat—"

Outside the aircraft the night was black and close. Thunderheads blotted out half the sky, and every few minutes lightning lit the clouds internally. Twice since sundown abrupt fierce downpours of torrential rain had hammered briefly against the Boeing hull, and now the airport lights glinted on the puddled tarmac.

"We have to show the face of unrelenting courage and iron purpose to the tyrant. We cannot afford to show even a moment's hesitation. We must now choose four more hostages. It will be done with the utmost impartiality—and I want you all to realize that we are now all part of the revolution together, you can be proud of that—"

Lightning exploded suddenly, much closer, a crackling greenish, iridescent flaming of the heavens that lit the field in merciless light, and then the flail of the thunder beat down upon the aircraft. The girl Karen exclaimed involuntarily and sprang nervously to her feet and crossed quickly to stand beside Ingrid. Her eyes were now heavily underscored by the dark kohl of fatigue and drug withdrawal, she trembled violently, and Ingrid caressed her absently the way she might calm a frightened kitten as she went on speaking into the microphone.

"We must all of us learn to welcome death, to welcome the opportunity to take our place and add our contribution, no matter how humble it might be, to man's great re-awakening."

Lightning burst in fierce splendour once again, but Ingrid went on talking into the microphone, the senseless words somehow hypnotic and lulling so that her captives sat in quietly lethargic rows, not speaking, unmoving, seeming no longer capable of independent thought.

"I have drawn lots to choose the next martyrs of the revolution. I will call out the seat numbers and my officers will come to fetch you. Please co-operate by moving quickly forward to the first-class galley." There was a pause, and then Ingrid's voice again. "Seat number 63B. Please stand up."

The scarred German in the red shirt and with the lank black hair hanging over his eyes had to force the thin, middle-aged man to his feet, twisting his wrist up between his shoulder blades. The man's white shirt was crumpled and he wore elastic braces over his shoulders and old-fashioned narrow trousers.

"You can't let them," the man pleaded with his fellow passengers, as Henri pushed him up the aisle. "You can't let them kill me, please." And they looked down at their laps. Nobody moved, nobody spoke.

"Seat number 43F." It was a handsome brunette woman in her middle thirties, and her face seemed to dissolve slowly as she read the number above her seat, and she covered her mouth with one hand to prevent herself crying out—but from the seat exactly across the aisle from her a sprightly old gentleman with a magnificent mane of silver-grey hair rose swiftly to his feet and adjusted his tie.

"Would you care to change seats with me, madam?" he said softly in a clipped English accent, and strode down the aisle, on long, thin, stork-like legs, contemptuously brushing past the blond moustached Frenchman who came hurrying forward to escort him. Without a glance to either side, and with thin shoulders thrown back, he disappeared through the curtains into the forward galley.

The Boeing had a blind spot that extended back from the side windows of the flight deck at an angle of 20° to the tail, but the hijackers were so well equipped and seemed to have considered every eventuality in such detail that there was reason to fear that they had worked out some arrangement to keep the blind spot under surveillance.

Peter and Colin discussed the possibility quietly as they stood in the angle of the main service hangar, and both of them carefully studied the soaring shape of the Boeing tailplane and the sagging underbelly of the fuselage for the glint of a mirror or some other device. They were directly behind the aircraft and there was a little over four hundred yards to cover, half of that through knee-high grass and the rest over tarmac.

The field was lit only by the blue periphery lights of the taxiway, and the glow of the airport buildings.

Peter had considered dousing all the airport lights, but discarded the idea as self-defeating. It would certainly alert the hijackers, and would slow the crossing of the assault team.

"I can't see anything," Colin murmured.

"No," agreed Peter and they both handed their night glasses to a hovering NCO—they wouldn't need them again. The assault team had stripped all equipment down to absolute essentials.

All that Peter carried was a lightweight eleven-ounce VHF transceiver for communicating with his men in the terminal building —and in a quick-release holster on his right hip a Walther P.38. Automatic pistol.

Each member of the assault team carried the weapon of his choice. Colin Noble, the only fickle one amongst them, vacillated between the Browning Hi-power 9mm. parabellum which he liked for its 13 shot magazine and the Colt Commander .45 ACP for its lighter weight and massive killing power—Peter on the other hand favoured the pinpoint accuracy and light recoil of the Walther with which he could be sure of a snap head-shot at twenty metres.

One item was standard equipment for all members of the assault team. Every one of their weapons was loaded with Super Velex explosive bullets which trebled the knock-down power at impact, breaking up in the human body and thereby reducing the risk of over-penetration and with it the danger to innocents. Peter never let them forget they would nearly always be working with terrorist and victim closely involved.

Beside Peter, Colin Noble unclipped the thin gold chain from around his neck which held the tiny Star of David, twinkling gold on the black bush of his chest hair. He slipped the ornament into his pocket and buttoned down the flap.

"I say, old chap"—Colin Noble gave an atrocious imitation of a Sandhurst accent—"shall we toddle along then?"

Peter glanced at the luminous dial of his Rolex. It was sixteen minutes to eleven o'clock. The exact moment at which my career ends, he thought grimly, and raised his right arm with clenched fist, then pumped it up and down twice, the old cavalry signal to advance.

Swiftly the two stick men raced out ahead, absolutely silent on soft rubber soles, carrying their probes at high port to prevent them clattering against tarmac or against the metal parts of the aircraft, black hunch-backed figures under the burden of the gas cylinders they carried.

Peter gave them a slow count of five, and while he waited he felt the adrenalin charge his blood, every nerve and muscle of his body coming under tension, and he heard his own words to Kingston Parker echo in his ears like the prophecy of doom.

"There is no middle ground. The alternative is one hundred per cent casualties. We lose the aircraft, the passengers and all the Thor personnel aboard her."

He thrust the the thought aside, and repeated the signal to advance. In two neat files, bunched up close and well in hand, the assault teams went out, at the run. Three men carrying each of the aluminium alloy scaling ladders, four with the sling bags of stun grenades, others with the slap hammers to tear out the door locks, and each with his chosen weapon—always a big calibre handgun—for Peter Stride would trust nobody with an automatic weapon in the crowded interior of a hijacked aircraft, and the minimum requirement for every member of the assault teams was marksmanship with a pistol that would enable him to pick a small moving target and hit it repeatedly and quickly without endangering innocents.

They ran in almost total silence; the loudest sound was Peter's breathing in his own ears, and he had time now for a moment's regret. It was a gamble which he could never win, the best that could happen was the utter ruin of his life's work, but he steeled himself brutally and thrust aside the thought. He ran on into the night.

Just ahead of him now, silhouetted by the lights of the terminal building, the figures of the stick men were in position under the bulging silver belly; and lightning flared suddenly, so that the tall silver thunderheads rippled with intense white fire, and the field was starkly lit, the double column of black-clad figures standing out clearly against the paler grass. If they were observed, it would come now, and the crash of thunder made Peter's nerves jump, expecting detonation and flame of a dozen percussion grenades.

Then it was dark again, and the sponginess of wet grass beneath his feet gave way to flat hard tarmac. Suddenly they were under the Boeing fuselage, like chickens under the protective belly of the hen, and the two columns split neatly into four separate groups and still in tight order every man dropped onto his left knee, and at the same moment, with the precision of repeated rehearsals, every member of the team lifted his gas mask to cover his nose and mouth.

Peter swept one quick glance back at them, and then depressed the transmit button on his transceiver. He would not speak a word from now until it was over, there was always a remote possibility that the hijackers were monitoring this frequency.

The click of the button was the signal to the members of his team in the terminal—and almost immediately, there was a rising whistling howl of jet engines running up.

Even though the aircraft were parked up in the northern international departures area, they had been turned so the jet exhausts were pointed at the service area, and there were five intercontinental jet liners co-operating. The combined sound output of twenty big jet engines was deafening even at that range—and Peter gave the open hand signal.

The stick man was waiting poised, and at the signal he reached up and placed the drill bit against the belly of the fuselage. Any sound of the compressed air spinning the drill was effectively drowned, and there was only the slight jerk of the long probe as it went through the pressure hull. Instantly the second stick man placed the tip of his probe into the tiny hole, and glanced at Peter. Again the open hand signal, and the gas was spurting into the hull. Peter was watching the sweep hand of his watch.

Two clicks on the transmit button, and the lights behind the row of shaded portholes blinked out simultaneously as the mains power was cut—and the air-conditioning in the Boeing's cabins with it.

The howl of combined jet engines continued a few seconds longer and Peter signalled the ladder men forward.

Gently the rubber padded tops of the ladders were hooked onto the leading edges of the wings and into the door sills high above them by black-costumed, grotesquely masked figures working with deceptively casual speed.

Ten seconds from discharge of the Factor V gas into the hull, and Peter clicked thrice. Instantly mains power to the Boeing was resumed and the lights flicked on. Now the air-conditioning was running again, washing the gas swiftly from the cabins and flight deck.

Peter drew one long, slow, deep breath and tapped Colin's shoulder. They were up the ladders in a concerted silent rush, Peter and Colin leading the teams to each wing surface.

"Nine minutes to eleven," said Ingrid to Karen. She lifted her voice slightly above the din of jet engines howling somewhere out there in the night. Her throat was dry and sore from the drug withdrawal and a nerve jumped involuntarily in the corner of her eye. Her headache felt as though a knotted rope was being twisted slowly tighter around her forehead. "It looks as though Caliph miscalculated. The South Africans aren't going to give in—" She glanced with a small anticipatory twist of her lips back through the open door of the flight deck at the four hostages sitting in a row on the fold-down seats. The silver-haired Englishman was smoking a Virginia cigarette in a long amber and ivory holder, and he returned her gaze with disdain, so that Ingrid felt a prickle of annoyance and raised her voice so he could hear her next words. "It's going to be necessary to shoot this batch also."

"Caliph has never been wrong before." Karen shook her head vehemently. "There is still an hour to deadline—" and at that instant the lights flickered once and then went out. With all the portholes shaded the darkness was complete, and the hiss of the air-conditioning faded into silence before there was a murmur of surprised comment.

Ingrid groped across the control panel for the switch which transferred the flight deck onto the power from the aircraft's own batteries, and as the soft ruddy glow of the panel lights came on her expression was tense and worried.

"They've switched off the mains," she exclaimed. "The air-conditioning—this could be Delta."

"No." Karen's voice was shrill. "There are no flares."

"We could be—" Ingrid started but she could hear the drunken slur in her own voice. Her tongue felt too large for her mouth, and Karen's face started to distort before her eyes, the edges blurring out of focus.

"Karen—" she said, and now in her nostrils the unmistakable aroma of truffles and on her tongue the taste of raw mushrooms.

"Christ!" she screamed wildly and lunged for the manual oxygen release. Above each seat the panels dropped open and the emergency oxygen masks dangled down into the cabins on their corrugated hoses.

"Kurt! Henri!" Ingrid shrieked into the cabin intercom. "Oxygen! Take oxygen! It's Delta. They are going to Delta."

She grabbed one of the dangling oxygen masks and sucked in deep pumping breaths, cleansing the numbing paralysing gas from her system. In the first-class galley one of the hostages collapsed slowly forward and tumbled onto the deck, another slumped sideways.

Still breathing oxygen, Ingrid unslung the camera from around her neck, and Karen watched her with huge terrified eyes, lifted the oxygen mask from her face to ask,

"You're not going to blow, Ingrid?"

Ingrid ignored her and used the oxygen in her lungs to shout into the microphone.

"Kurt! Henri! They will come as soon as the mains are switched on again. Cover your eyes and ears for the stun grenades and watch the doors and wing windows." Ingrid slapped the oxygen mask back over her mouth and panted wildly.

"Don't blow us up, Ingrid," Karen pleaded around her mask. "Please, if we surrender Caliph will have us free in a month. We don't have to die."

At that moment the lights of the cabin came on brightly, and there was the hiss of the air-conditioning. Ingrid took one last breath of oxygen and ran back into the first-class cabin, jumping over the unconscious figures of the hostages and of two air hostesses. She grabbed another of the dangling oxygen masks above a passenger seat and looked down the long fuselage.

Kurt and Henri had obeyed her orders. They were breathing oxygen from the roof panels. The German was ready at the port wing panel, and Henri waited at the rear doorway hatch—both of them had the short big-mouthed shot pistols ready, but their faces were covered with the yellow oxygen masks, so Ingrid could not see nor judge their expressions.

Only a small number of the passengers had been quick enough and sensible enough to grab the dangling oxygen masks and remain conscious—but hundreds of others slumped in their seats or had fallen sideways into the aisles.

A thicket of dangling, twisting, swinging oxygen hoses filled the cabin like a forest of lianas, obscuring and confusing the scene, and after the darkness the cabin lights were painfully bright.

Ingrid held the camera in her free hand, for she knew that they must continue breathing oxygen. It would take the air-conditioning many minutes longer to cleanse the air of all trace of Factor V, and she held a mask over her mouth and waited.

Karen was beside her, with her shot pistol dangling from one hand and the other pressing a mask to her mouth.

"Go back and cover the front hatch," Ingrid snapped at her. "There will be—"

"Ingrid, we don't have to die," Karen pleaded, and with a crash the emergency exit panel over the port wing burst inward, and at the same instant two small objects flew through the opening into the cabin.

"Stun grenades!" Ingrid howled. "Get down!"

Peter Stride was light and jubilant as an eagle in flight. His feet and hands hardly seemed to touch the rungs of the ladder, now in the swift all-engulfing rush of action there were no longer doubts, no more hesitations—he was committed, and it was a tremendous soaring relief.

He went up over the smooth curved leading edge of the wing with a roll of his shoulders and hips, and in the same movement was on his feet, padding silently down the broad glistening metal pathway. The raindrops glittered like diamonds under his feet, and a fresh wind tugged at his hair as he ran.

He reached the main hull, and dropped into position at the side of the panel, his fingertips finding the razor-tight joint while his number-two man knelt swiftly opposite him. The grenade men were ready facing the panel, balanced like acrobats on the curved slippery upper surface of the great wing.

"Under six seconds." Peter guessed at the time it had taken them to reach this stage from the "go." It was as swift and neat as it had never been in training, all of them armed by the knowledge of waiting death and horror.

In unison Peter and his number two hurled their combined strength and weight onto the releases of the emergency escape hatch, and it flew inwards readily, for there was no pressurization to resist, and at exactly the same instant the stun grenades went in cleanly, thrown by the waiting grenade men, and all four members of Peter's team bowed like Mohammedans in prayer to Mecca, covering eyes and ears.

Even outside the cabin, and even with ears and eyes covered, the thunder of the explosions was appalling, seeming to beat in upon the brain with oppressive physical force, and the glare of burning phosphorus powder painted an X-ray picture of Peter's own fingers on the fleshy red of his closed eyelids. Then the grenade men were shouting into the interior, "Lie down! Everybody down!" They would keep repeating that order Israeli style as long as it lasted.

Peter was a hundredth of a second slow, numbed by the blast, fumbling slightly at the butt of the Walther, thumbing the hammer as it snapped out of the quick-release holster, and then he went in—feet first through the hatch, like a runner sliding for home base. He was still in the air when he saw the girl in the red shirt running forward brandishing the camera, and screaming something that made no sense, though his brain registered it even in that unholy moment. He fired as his feet touched the deck and his first shot hit the girl in the mouth, punching a red hole through the rows of white teeth and snapping her head back so viciously that he heard the small delicate bones of her neck crackle as they broke.

Ingrid used both arms to cover eyes and ears, crouching forward into the appalling blast of sound and light that swept through the crowded cabins like a hurricane wind, and even when it had passed she was reeling wildly clutching for support at a seat back, trying to steady herself and judge the moment when the attackers were into the hull.

Those outside the hull would escape the direct force of the explosives she was about to detonate, there was a high survival chance for them. She wanted to judge the moment when the entire assault team penetrated the hull, she wanted maximum casualties, she wanted to take as many with her as possible, and she lifted the camera above her head with both hands.

"Come on!" she shrieked, but the cabin was thick with swirling clouds of white acrid smoke, and the dangling hoses twisted and writhed like the head of the Medusa. She heard the thunder of a shot pistol and somebody screamed, voices were chanting, "Lie down! Everybody down!"

It was all smoke and sound and confusion, but she watched the opening of the emergency hatchway, waiting for it, finger on the detonator button of the camera. A supple black-clad figure in a grotesque face mask torpedoed feet first into the cabin, and at that same instant Karen shrieked beside her.

"No, don't kill us," and snatched the camera from Ingrid's raised hands, jerking it away by the strap, leaving Ingrid weaponless. Karen ran down the aisle through the smoke, still screaming, "Don't kill us!" holding the camera like a peace offering. "Caliph said we would not die." She ran forward screaming frantically. "Caliph—" and the black-clad and masked figure twisted lithely in the air, arching his back to land feet first in the centre of the aisle; as his feet touched the deck so the pistol in his right hand jerked up sharply but the shot seemed muted and unwarlike after the concussion of the stun grenades.

Karen was running down the aisle towards him, screaming and brandishing the camera, when the bullet took her in the mouth and wrenched her head backwards at an impossible angle. The next two shots blended into a single blurt of sound, fired so swiftly as to cheat the hearing, and from such close range that even the Velex explosive bullets ripped the back out of Karen's shirt and flooded it with a brighter wetter scarlet as they erupted from between her shoulder blades. The camera went spinning high across the cabin, landing in the lap of an unconscious passenger slumped in one of the central seats between the aisles.

Ingrid reacted with the instinctive speed of a jungle cat, diving forward, flat on the carpet aisle below the line of fire; shrouded by the sinking white smoke of the grenades she wriggled forward on her belly to reach the camera.

It was twenty feet to where the camera had landed, but Ingrid moved with the speed of a serpent; she knew that the smoke was hiding her, but she knew also that to reach the camera she would have to come to her feet again and reach across two seats and two unconscious bodies.

Peter landed in balance on the carpeted aisle, and he killed the girl swiftly, and danced aside, clearing space for his number two to land.

The next man in landed lightly in the space Peter had made for him, and the German in the red shirt jumped out from the angle of the rear galley and hit him in the small of the back with a full charge of buckshot. It almost blew his body into two separate parts, and he seemed to break in the middle like a folding penknife as he collapsed against Peter's legs.

Peter whirled at the shot, turning his back on Ingrid as she crawled forward through the phosphorus smoke.

Kurt was desperately trying to pull down the short, thick barrel of the pistol, for the recoil had thrown it high above his head. His scarlet shirt was open to the navel, shiny hard brown muscle and thick whorls of black body hair, mad glaring eyes through a greasy fringe of black hair, the scarred lip curled in a fixed snarl.

Peter hit him in the chest, taking no chance, and as he reeled backwards still fighting to aim the pistol, Peter hit again, in the head through the temple just in front of the left ear; the eyelids closed tightly over those wild eyes, his features twisted out of shape like a rubber mask and he went down face first into the aisle.

"Two." Peter found that, as always in these desperate moments, he was functioning very coldly, very efficiently. His shooting had been as reflexively perfect as if he were walking a combat shoot with jump-up cardboard targets.

He had even counted his shots, there were four left in the Walther.

"And two more of them," he thought, but the smoke was still so thick that his visibility was down to under fifteen feet, and the swirling forest of dangling oxygen hose still agitated by the grenade blasts cut down his visibility further.

He jumped over the broken body of his number two, the blood squelching under his rubber soles, and suddenly the chunky black figure of Colin Noble loomed across the cabin. He was in the far aisle, having come in over the starboard wing. In the writhing smoke he looked like some demon from the pit, hideous and menacing in his gas mask. He dropped into the marksman's crouch, holding the big Browning in a double-handed grip, and the clangour of the gun beat upon the air like one of the great bronze bells of Notre Dame.

He was shooting at another scarlet-shirted figure, half seen through the smoke and the dangling hoses, a man with a round boyish face and drooping sandy moustache. The big Velex bullets tore the hijacker to pieces with the savagery of a predator's claws. They seemed to pin him like an insect to the central bulkhead, and they smashed chunks of living flesh from his chest and splinters of white bone from his skull.

"Three," thought Peter. "One left now—and I must get the camera."

He had seen the black camera in the hands of the girl he had killed, had seen it fall, and he knew how deadly important it was to secure the detonator before it fell into the hands of the other girl, the blonde one, the dangerous one.

It had been only four seconds since he had penetrated the hull, yet it seemed like a dragging eternity. He could hear the crash of the slap-hammers tearing out the door locks, both fore and aft, within seconds there would be Thor assault teams pouring into the Boeing through every opening, and he had not yet located the fourth hijacker, the truly dangerous one.

"Get down! Everybody down!" chanted the grenade men, and Peter spun lightly, and ran for the flight deck. He was certain the blonde girl would be there at the control centre.

Then, in front of him lay the girl he had shot down, the long, dark hair spread out around her pale, still terrified face. Her hair was already sodden with dark blood, and the black gap in her white teeth made her look like an old woman. She blocked the aisle with a tangle of slim boneless limbs.

The forward hatch crashed open as the lock gave way, but there were still solid curtains of white smoke ahead of him. Peter gathered himself to jump over the girl's body, and at that instant the other girl, the blonde girl, bounded up from the deck, seeming to appear miraculously from the smoke, like some beautiful but evil apparition.

She dived half across the block of central seating, groping for the camera, and Peter was slightly off balance, blocking himself in the turn to bring his gun hand on to her. He changed hands smoothly, for he was equally accurate with either, but it cost him the tenth part of a second, and the girl had the strap of the camera now and was tugging desperately at it. The camera seemed to be snagged, and Peter swung on her, taking the head shot for she was less than ten paces away, and even in the smoke and confusion he could not miss.

One of the few passengers who had been breathing oxygen from his hanging mask, and was still conscious, ignored the chanted orders "Get down! Stay down!" and suddenly stumbled to his feet, screaming, "Don't shoot! Get me out of here! Don't shoot!" in a rising hysterical scream. He was directly between Peter and the red-shirted girl, blocking Peter's field of fire, and Peter wrenched the gun off him at the moment that he fired. The bullet slammed into the roof, and the passenger barged into Peter, still screaming.

"Get me out! I want to get out!"

Peter tried desperately to clear his gun hand, for the girl had broken the strap of the camera and was fumbling with the black box. The passenger had an arm around Peter's gun arm, was shaking him wildly, weeping and screaming.

From across the central block of seats, Colin Noble fired once. He was still in the starboard aisle and the angle was almost impossible, for he had to shoot nine inches past Peter's shoulder, and through the forest of dangling hose.

His first shot missed, but it was close enough to flinch the girl's head violently, the golden hair flickered with the passage of shot, and she stumbled backwards, groping with clumsy fingers for the detonator.

Peter chopped the hysterical passenger in the throat with the stiffened fingers of his right hand and hurled him back into his seat, trying desperately to line up for a shot at the girl—knowing he must get the brain and still her fingers instantly.

Colin fired his second shot, one hundredth of a second before Peter, and the big bullet flung the girl aside, jerking her head out of the track of Peter's shot.

Peter saw the strike of Colin's bullet, it hit her high in the right shoulder, almost in the joint of the scapula and the humerus, shattering the bone with such force that her arm was flung upwards in a parody of a communist salute, twisting unnaturally and whipping above her head; once again the camera was flung aside and the girl's body was thrown violently backwards down the aisle as though she had been hit by a speeding automobile.

Peter picked his shot, waiting for a clean killing hit in the head as the girl tried to drag herself upright—but before he could fire a mass of black-costumed figures swarmed out of the smoke, and covered the girl, pinning her kicking and screaming on the carpet of the aisle. The Thor team had come in through the forward hatch, just in time to save her life, and Peter clipped the Walther into his holster and stooped to pick up the camera gingerly. Then he pulled off his mask with his other hand.

"That's it. That's all of them," he shouted. "We got them all. Cease fire. It's all over." Then into the microphone of the transceiver. "Touch down! Touch down!" The code for total success. Three of his men were holding the girl down, and despite the massive spurting wound in her shoulder, she fought like a leopard in a trap.

"Get the emergency chutes down," Peter ordered, and from each exit the long plastic slides inflated and drooped to the tarmac—already his men were leading the conscious passengers to the exits and helping them into the slide.

From the terminal building a dozen ambulances with sirens howling, gunned out across the tarmac. The back-up members of Thor were running out under the glare of the floodlights, cheering thinly. "Touch down! Touch down!"

Like prehistoric monsters the mechanical stairways lumbered down from the northern apron, to give access to the body of the Boeing.

Peter stepped up to the girl, still holding the camera in his hands, and he stood looking down at her. The icy coldness of battle still gripped him, his mind felt needle sharp and his vision clear, every sense enhanced.

The girl stopped struggling, and looked back at him. The image of a trapped leopard was perfect. Peter had never seen eyes so fierce and merciless, as she glared at him. Then she drew her head back like a cobra about to strike, and spat at him. White frothy spittle splattered down the front of Peter's legs.

Colin Noble was beside Peter now, pulling off his gas mask.

"I'm sorry, Peter. I was going for the heart."

"You'll never hold me," shrieked the girl suddenly. "I'll be free before Thanksgiving!"

And Peter knew she was right. The punishment that a befuddled world society meted out to these people was usually only a few months' imprisonment, and that often suspended. He remembered the feel of the dying child in his arms, the warm trickle of her blood running over his belly and legs.

"My people will come for me," the girl spat again, this time into the face of one of the men who held her down. "You will never hold me. My people will force you to free me."

Again she was right, her capture was a direct invitation for further atrocity, the wheel of vengeance and retribution was set in motion. For the life of this trapped and vicious predator, hundreds more would suffer, and dozens more would die.

The reaction was setting in now, the battle rage abating, and Peter felt the nausea cloying his bowels. It had been in vain, he thought, he had thrown away a lifetime's strivings and endeavour to win only a temporary victory. He had checked the forces of evil, not beaten them—and they would regroup and attack again, stronger and more cunning than ever, and this woman would lead them again.

"We are the revolution." The girl lifted her uninjured arm in the clenched fist salute. "We are the power. Nothing, nobody can stop us."

When this woman had fired a load of buckshot through the swollen body of the pregnant woman it had distorted her shape completely. The image was recaptured entire and whole in Peter's memory, the way she had burst open like the pod of a ripe fruit.

The blonde woman shook the clenched fist into Peter's face.

"This is only the beginning—the new era has begun."

There was a taunt and a sneering threat in her voice, uttered in complete confidence—and Peter knew it was not misplaced. There was a new force unleashed in the world, something more deadly than he had believed possible, and Peter had no illusion as to the role that blind fortune had played in his small triumph. He had no illusion either that the beast was more than barely wounded, next time it would be more powerful, more cunning, having learned from this inconsequential failure—and with the reaction from battle came a powerful wave of dread and despair that seemed to overwhelm his soul. It had all been in vain.

"You can never win," taunted the woman, splattered with her own blood, but undaunted and unrepentant, seeming to read his very thoughts.

"And we can never lose," she shrieked.

"Gentlemen." The South African Prime Minister spoke with painful deliberation. "My cabinet and I are firmly of the opinion that to accede to the terrorists' demands is to take a seat on the back of the tiger, from which we will never be able to dismount." He stopped, hung his great granite-hewn head for a moment and then looked up at the two ambassadors. "However, such is the duty we owe to humanity and the dignity of human life, and such is the pressure which two great nations can bring to bear upon one much smaller, that we have decided unanimously to agree in full to all the conditions necessary for the release of the women and children—"

A telephone on the tabletop in front of the American Ambassador began to shrill irritatingly, and the Prime Minister paused, frowned slightly.

"However, we place complete faith in the undertaking given by your governments—" He stopped again for the telephone insisted. "You had best answer that, sir," he told Kelly Constable.

"Excuse me, Prime Minister." The American lifted the receiver, and as he listened an expression of utter disbelief slowly changed his features. "Hold the line," he said into the receiver, and then, covering the mouthpiece with his hand, he looked up. "Prime Minister—it is a very great pleasure to inform you that three minutes ago the Thor assault team broke into Flight 070 and killed three of the terrorists—they wounded and captured a fourth terrorist, but there were no casualties amongst the passengers. They got them all out, every last one of them. Safe and sound."

The big man at the head of the table sagged with relief in his seat, and as the storm of jubilation and self-congratulation broke about him, he started to smile. It was a smile that transformed his forbidding features, the smile of an essentially fatherly and kindly man. "Thank you, sir," he said, still smiling. "Thank you very much."

"You are guilty of blatant dereliction of your duty, General Stride," Kingston Parker accused grimly.

"My concern was entirely with the lives of hostages and the force of moral law." Peter answered him quietly, it was less than fifteen minutes since he had penetrated the hull of the Boeing in a blaze of fire and fury. His hands were still shaking slightly and the nausea still lay heavily on his guts.

"You deliberately disobeyed my specific orders." Parker was an enraged lion, the mane of thick shot-silver hair seemed to bristle, and he glowered from the screen; the vast power of his personality seemed to fill the command cabin of the Hawker. "I have always had grave reservations as to your suitability for the high command with which you have been entrusted. I have already expressed those reservations in writing to your superiors, and they have been fully justified."

"I understand by all this that I have been removed from command of Thor," Peter cut in brusquely, his anger seething to the surface, and Parker checked slightly.

Peter knew that even Kingston Parker could not immediately fire the hero of such a successful counter-strike. It would take time, a matter of days, perhaps, but Peter's fate was sealed. There could be no doubt of that, and Parker went on to confirm this.

"You will continue to exercise command under my direct surveillance. You will make no decision without referring directly back to me, no decision whatsoever. Do you understand that, General Stride?"

Peter did not bother to reply, he felt a wildly reckless mood starting to buoy his sagging spirits, a sense of freedom and choice of action such as he had never known before. For the first time in his career he had deliberately disobeyed a superior officer, and luck or not, the outcome had been a brilliant success.

"Your first duty now will be to withdraw all Thor units, and swiftly and in as good an order as possible. The militant you have taken will be returned to London for questioning and trial—"

"Her crimes were committed here. She should be tried here for murder. I have already had demands from the local—"

"Arrangements are being made with the South African authorities." Parker's anger had not abated, but he had it better under control. "She will return to Britain aboard your command aircraft, with the Thor doctor in attendance."

Peter remembered what had happened to the terrorist Leila Khaled, dragged from the El Al airliner where she was being held by Israeli security agents. As a guest of the British police, she had spent six short days in captivity, and then been released in a blaze of publicity and glory, heroine of the communications media, Joan of Arc of terror—released to plan and execute the death and destruction of hundreds more innocents, to lead the attack on the foundations of civilization, to shake the columns that held aloft the rule of law and society.

"I want this woman in London within twenty-four hours. She is to be strictly guarded at all times against retaliation. We cannot afford another bloodbath—like the one you led on o70."

Peter Stride walked very erect, very tall into the echoing, marble-columned domestic departures hall of the airport, and his men called to him as he came.

"Well done, sir."

"Great stuff, General."

"Way to go—"

They were tending the released passengers, re-assembling their scattered gear, dismantling the security and communications equipment and packing it away—within the hour they would be ready to pull out—but now they left their tasks to crowd about him, competing to shake his hand.

The passengers realized that this must be the architect of their salvation and they cheered him as he passed slowly through the hall, and now he was smiling, acknowledging their pitiful gratitude, stopping to talk with an old lady, and submitting to her tearful embrace.

"God bless you, my boy. God bless you." And her body trembled against him. Gently Peter set her aside and went on, and though he smiled it was with his lips only, for there was steel in his heart.

There were Thor guards on the main administrative offices on the mezzanine floor armed with submachine guns, but they stood aside for him and Peter went through.

Colin Noble was still in his black skin-tight assault suit with the big .45 on his hip, and a cheroot clamped between his teeth.

"Take a look at this," he called to Peter. The desk was covered with explosives and weapons. "Most of it's iron-curtain stuff— but God alone knows where they got these." He indicated the double-barrelled shot pistols. "If they had these custom built, it would have cost them plenty."

"They have got plenty," Peter answered drily. "The ransom for the OPEC ministers was one hundred and fifty million dollars, for the Braun brothers twenty-five million, for Baron Altmann another twenty million—that's the defence budget for a nation." He picked up one of the shot pistols and opened the breech. It had been unloaded.

"Is this the one she used to gun down the hostages?"

Colin shrugged. "Probably, it's been fired through both barrels." Colin was right, there were specks of burned powder down the short smooth bores.

Peter loaded it with buckshot cartridges from the pile on the desk, and walked on down the long office with the covered typewriters on the deserted desks and the airline travel posters decorating the wall.

Along one wall the three bodies of the hijackers were laid out in a neat row, each encapsuled in its separate translucent plastic envelope.

Two Thor men were assembling the contents of their pockets—personal jewellery, meagre personal effects—and they were packing them into labelled plastic bags.

The body of Peter's number two was against the far wall, also in his plastic body-bag, and Peter stooped over him. Through the plastic he could make out the features of the dead man's face. The eyes were wide and the jaw hung open slackly. Death is always so undignified, Peter thought, and straightened up.

Still carrying the shot pistol, Peter went on into the inner office, and Colin Noble followed him.

They had the girl on another stretcher, a plasma drip suspended above her, and the Thor doctor and his two orderlies were working over her quietly, but the young doctor looked up irritably as Peter pushed open the door, then his expression changed as he recognized Peter.

"General, if we are going to save this arm, I have to get her into theatre pretty damned quickly. The joint of the shoulder is shattered—"

The girl rolled the lovely head towards Peter. The thick springing golden hair was matted with drying blood, and there was a smear of it across one cheek.

Now her face was completely drained of all colour, like the head of an angel carved out of white marble. The skin had a waxen, almost translucent, lustre and only the eyes were still fierce, not dulled by the pain-killing drugs that they had injected into her.

"I have asked the South Africans for co-operation," the doctor went on. "They have two top orthopaedic surgeons standing by, and they have offered a helicopter to fly her into the Central Hospital at Edenvale."

Already she was being treated, even by Thor, as the major celebrity she was. She had taken her first step along the rose-strewn pathway to glory, and Peter could imagine how the media would extol her beauty—they had gone berserk with extravagant praise for the swarthy ferrety-eyed Leila Khaled with her fine dark moustache—they would go over the top for this one.

Peter had never known any emotion so powerful as the emotion that gripped him now.

"Get out," he said to the doctor.

"Sir?" The man looked startled.

"Get out," Peter repeated, "all of you." And he waited until the opaque glass door closed behind them, before he spoke to the girl in conversational tones.

"You have made me abandon my own principles, and descend to your level."

The girl watched him uncertainly, her eyes flickered to the shot pistol that Peter held dangling from his right hand.

"You have forced me, a career soldier, to disobey the orders of a superior officer in the face of the enemy." He paused. "I used to be a proud man, but when I have done what I must do now, I will no longer have much of which to be proud."

"I demand to see the American Ambassador," said the girl huskily, still watching the pistol. "I am an American citizen. I demand the protection—"

Peter interrupted her, again speaking quickly. "This is not revenge. I am old and wise enough to know that revenge has the most bitter taste of all human excess."

"You cannot do it—" The girl's voice rose, the same strident tones, but now shriller still with fear. "They will destroy you."

But Peter went on as though she had not spoken. "It is not revenge," he repeated. "You, yourself, gave the reason clearly. If you continue to exist, they will come to get you back. As long as you live, others must die—and they will die stripped of all human dignity. They will die in terror, the same way you murdered—"

"I am a woman. I am wounded. I am a prisoner of war," screamed the girl, trying to struggle upright.

"Those are the old rules," Peter told her. "You tore up the book, and wrote a new one—I am playing to your rules now. I have been reduced to your level."

"You cannot kill me," the girl's voice rang wildly. "I still have work—"

"Colin," Peter said quietly, without looking at the American. "You'd better get out now."

Colin Noble hesitated, his right hand on the butt of the Browning, and the girl rolled her head towards him imploringly.

"You can't let him do it."

"Peter—" Colin said.

"You were right, Colin." Peter spoke quietly. "That kid did look a lot like Melissa-Jane."

Colin Noble dropped his hand from the pistol and turned to the door. Now the girl was shrieking obscenity and threat, her voice incoherent with terror and hatred.

Colin closed the door softly and stood with his back to it. The single crash of shot was shockingly loud, and the stream of filthy abuse was cut off abruptly. The silence was even more appalling than the harrowing sounds which had preceded it. Colin did not move. He waited four, five seconds before the door clicked open and General Peter Stride came out into the main office. He handed the shot pistol to Colin and one barrel was hot in his hand.

Peter's handsome aristocratic features seemed ravaged, as though by a long wasting disease. The face of a man who had leapt into the abyss.

Peter Stride left the glass door open, and walked away without looking back. Despite the terrible expression of despair, he still carried himself like a soldier and his tread was firm.

Colin Noble did not even look through the open door.

"All right," he called to the doctor. "She's all yours now." And he followed Peter down the broad staircase.

There was a long hard gallop over good going and open pasture to the crest of the ridge, with only one gate. Melissa-Jane led on her bay filly, her Christmas gift from Uncle Steven. She was in the midst of the passionate love affair that most pubescent girls have with horses, and she looked truly good astride the glistening thoroughbred. The cold struck high colour into her cheeks and the braid of honey-coloured hair thumped gaily down her back at each stride. She had blossomed even in the few weeks since last Peter had seen her—and he realized with some awe and considerable pride that she was fast becoming a great beauty.

Peter was up on one of Steven's hunters, a big rangy animal with the strength to carry his weight, but the gelding was slogging hard to hold the flying pair that danced ahead of him.

At the hedge, Melissa-Jane scorned the gate, gathered the filly with fine strong hands and took her up and over. Her little round bottom lifted out of the saddle as she leaned into the jump, and clods of black earth flew from the filly's hooves.

As soon as she was over she swivelled in the saddle to watch him, and Peter realized that he was under challenge. The hedge immediately appeared to be head-high and he noticed for the first time how the ground fell away at a steep angle beyond. He had not ridden for almost two years, and it was the first time he had been up on this gelding—but the horse went for the jump gamely, and they brushed the top of the hedge, landed awkwardly, stumbled with Peter up on his neck for an appalling instant of time in which he was convinced he was to take a toss in front of his daughter's critical eye; caught his balance, held the gelding's head up and they came away still together.

"Super-Star!" Melissa-Jane shouted laughing, and by the time he caught her she had dismounted under the yew tree at the crest, and was waiting for him with her breath steaming in the crisp calm air.

"Our land once went right as far as the church"—Peter pointed to the distant grey needle of stone that pricked the belly of the sky—"and there almost to the top of the downs." He turned to point in the opposite direction.

"Yes," Melissa-Jane slipped her arm through his as they stood close together under the yew. "The family had to sell it when grandfather died. You told me. And that's right too. One family shouldn't own so much."

Peter glanced down at her, startled. "My God, a communist in the family. An asp in the bosom."

She squeezed his arm. "Don't worry, Daddy darling. It's Uncle Steven who is the bloated plutocrat. You're not a capitalist—you aren't even employed any more—" And the instant she had said it, her laughter collapsed around her and she looked stricken. "Oh, I didn't mean that. I truly didn't."

It was almost a month now since Peter's resignation had been accepted by the War Office, but the scandal had not yet run out of steam.

The first heady paeans of praise for the success of Thor's Delta strike had lasted only a few days. The glowing editorials, the full front pages, the lead news item on every television channel, the effusive messages of congratulations from the leaders of the Western governments, the impromptu triumph for Peter Stride and his little band of heroes, had quickly struck an odd note, a sudden souring of the ecstasies.

The racist Government of South Africa had actually agreed to the release of political prisoners *before* the assault, one of the hijackers had been taken alive, and died of gunshot wounds received in the terminal buildings. Then one of the released hostages, a freelance journalist who had been covering the medical convention in Mauritius and was returning aboard the hijacked aircraft, published a sensational eye-witness account of the entire episode, and a dozen other passengers supported his claims that there had been screams from the fourth hijacker, screams for mercy, before she was shot to death after her capture.

A storm of condemnation and vilification from the extreme left of the British Labour Government had swept through the Westminster parliament, and had been echoed by the Democrats in the American Congress. The very existence of the Thor Comnand had come under scrutiny and been condemned in extravagant terms. The Communist parties of France and Italy had marched, and the detonation of an M.26 hand grenade—one of those stolen by the Baader-Meinhof gang from the American base in Metz—amongst the crowd leaving the Parc des Princes football stadium in Paris had killed one and injured twenty-three. A telephone call to the offices of *France Soir* by a man speaking accented French claimed that this fresh atrocity was revenge for the murder of four hijackers by the Imperialist execution squad.

Pressure for Peter's discharge had come initially from the Pentagon, and there was very little doubt that Dr. Kingston Parker was the accuser, though, as head of Atlas, he was never identified, total secrecy still surrounding the project. The media had begun to demand an investigation of all the circumstances surrounding Thor. "And if it is ascertained that criminal irregularities did indeed exist in the conduct of the operation, then the person or persons responsible be brought to trial either by a military tribunal or the civil courts." Fortunately the media had not yet unravelled the full scope of Atlas Command. Only Thor was under scrutiny; they did not yet suspect the existence of either Mercury or Diana.

Within the War Office and the governments of both America and Britain, there had been much sympathy and support for Peter Stride—but he had made it easier for his friends and for himself by tendering his resignation. The resignation had been accepted, but still the left was clamouring for more. They wanted blood, Peter Stride's blood.

Now Melissa-Jane's huge pansy violet eyes flooded with the tears of mortification. "I didn't mean that. I truly didn't."

"One thing about being out of a job—I have more time to be with my favourite girl." He smiled down at her, but she would not be mollified.

"I don't believe the horrible things they are saying. I know you are a man of honour, Daddy."

"Thank you." And he felt the ache of it, the guilt and the sorrow. They were silent a little longer, still standing close together, and Peter spoke first.

"You are going to be a palaeontologist—" he said.

"No. That was last month. I've changed my mind. I'm not interested in old bones any more. Now I'm going to be a doctor, a child specialist."

"That's good." Peter nodded gravely. "But let's go back to old bones for a moment. The age of the great reptiles. The dinosaurs —why did they fade into extinction?"

"They could not adapt to a changing environment." Melissa-Jane had the answer promptly.

Peter murmured, "A concept like honour. Is it outdated in today's world, I wonder?" Then he saw the puzzlement, the hurt in her eyes, and he knew they had wandered onto dangerous ground. His daughter had a burning love for all living things, particularly human beings. Despite her age, she had a developed political and social conscience, distinguished by total belief in shining ideals and the essential beauty and goodness of mankind. There would be time in the years ahead for the agony of disillusion. The term "man or woman of honour" was Melissa-Jane's ultimate accolade. No matter that it could be applied to any of her current heroes or heroines—the Prince of Wales, or the singer of popular songs with an outrageous name that Peter could never remember, to Virginia Wade, the former Wimbledon champion, or to the Fifth Form science teacher at Roedean who had aroused Melissa-Jane's interest in medicine—Peter knew that he should feel proper gratitude for being included in this exalted company.

"I will try to live up to your opinion of me." He stooped and kissed her, surprised at the strength of his love for this child-woman. "And now it's too cold to stand here any longer, and Pat will never forgive us if we are late for lunch."

They clattered over the stone cobbles of the stable yard, riding knee to knee, and before he dismounted, Peter indulged himself in the pleasure of his favourite view of the house that had always been home, even though it belonged now, together with the title, to Steven, the older brother, older by three hours only, but older none the less.

The house was red brick with a roof that ran at fifty different unlikely angles. It missed being hideous by a subtle margin and achieved a fairytale enchantment. Peter could never grudge it to Steven, who loved the sprawling edifice with something close to passion.

Perhaps the desire to own the house and to restore it to its former magnificence was the goad which had pricked Steven to the super-human effort that a British resident must make against taxation and socialist restrictions in order to amass anything like a fortune.

Steven had made that effort, and now Abbots Yew stood immaculate and well-beloved in glorious gardens, and Sir Steven kept baronial style. His affairs were so complicated, spread over so many continents that even the British tax man must have been daunted. Peter had once skirted this subject with his twin brother, and Steven had replied quietly.

"When a law is patently unjust, such as our tax law is, it's the duty of an honest man to subvert it."

Peter's old-fashioned sense of rightness had balked at such logic, but he let it pass.

It was strange that it had worked this way for the two brothers, for Peter had always been the brilliant one, and the family had always referred to "Poor Steven." Nobody was very surprised when Steven left Sandhurst amid dark whispers half-way through his final year—but two years later Steven was already a millionaire while Peter was a lowly second lieutenant in the British Army. Peter grinned without rancour at the memory. He had always been particularly fond of his elder brother—but at that moment his train of thought was interrupted as his eye caught the mirror-like finish of the silver limousine parked at the end of the stable yard. It was one of those long Mercedes-Benz favoured by pop stars, Arab oil men, or Heads of State. The chauffeur was uniformed in sober navy-blue and was busy burnishing the paintwork to an even higher gloss. Even Steven did not run to that sort of transportation, and Peter felt mildly intrigued. House guests at Abbots Yew were always interesting. Steven Stride did not concern himself with those who did not wield either power, wealth or extraordinary talent. Beyond the Mercedes 600 was parked another smaller model; this one was black and the two men in it had the hard closed faces that marked them as bodyguards.

Melissa-Jane rolled her eyes at the automobile. "Another bloated plutocrat, I expect," she muttered. It was the currently favoured term of extreme disapproval, a great advance on "grotty" which had preceded it, Peter could not help thinking as he helped his daughter unsaddle and then rub down the horses. They went up through the rose garden, arm in arm, and then laughing together into the main drawing-room.

"Peter old boy!" Steven came to meet him, as tall as his brother, and once he had been as lean, but good living had thickened his body while at the same time the strains of being a professional deal maker had greyed his hair at the temples and laced his moustache with silver bristles. His face was not quite a mirror image of Peter's, slightly more fleshy and florid—but the twin resemblance was still strongly marked, and now his face was alive with pleasure.

"Thought you'd broken your bloody neck, what!" Steven carefully cultivated the bluff manner of the country squire to shield his quick and shrewd intelligence.

Now he turned to Melissa-Jane and hugged her with barely a touch of incestuous pleasure. "How did Florence Nightingale go?"

"She's a darling, Uncle Steven. I will never be able to thank you."

"Peter, I would like you to meet a very charming lady—"

She had been talking to Patricia Stride, Steven's wife, and now as she turned, the winter sunshine through the bay windows behind lit her with a soft romantic aura.

Peter felt as though the earth had tilted under his feet, and a fist closed around his ribs constricting his breathing and inhibiting the action of his heart.

He recognized her immediately from the photographs in the official file during the long-drawn-out kidnapping and subsequent murder of her husband. At one stage it had seemed that the kidnappers had crossed the Channel with their victim, and Thor had gone to condition Alpha for almost a week. Peter had studied the photographs that had been assembled from a dozen sources, but even the glossy coloured portraits from *Vogue* and *Jours de France* had not been able to capture the magnificence of the woman.

Surprisingly, he saw his own immediate recognition reflected. There was no change in her expression, but it flared briefly like deep-green emerald fire in her eyes. There was no question in Peter's mind but that she had recognized him, and as he stepped towards her he realized she was tall, but the fine proportion of her body had not made that immediately apparent. Her skirt was of a fine wool crêpe which moulded the long, stately legs of a dancer.

"Baroness, may I present my brother, General Stride."

"How do you do, General." Her English was almost perfect, a low husky voice, the slight accent very attractive, but she pronounced his rank as three distinct syllables.

"Peter, this is Baroness Altmann."

Her thick glossy black hair was scraped back severely from the forehead with a perfect arrowhead of widow's peak at the centre, emphasizing the high Slavic cheekbones and the unblemished perfection of her skin—but her jawline was too square and strong for beauty, and the mouth had an arrogant determined line to it. Magnificent, but not beautiful—and Peter found himself violently attracted. The breathless wholesale feeling he had not experienced for twenty years.

She seemed to epitomize everything he admired in a woman.

Her body was in the condition of a trained athlete. Beneath the oyster silk of her blouse her arms were delicately sculpted from toned muscle, the waist narrow, the breasts very small and unfettered, their lovely shape pressing clearly through fine material, her clean lightly tanned skin glowed with health and careful grooming. All this contributed to his attraction.

However, the greater part was in Peter's own mind. He knew she was a woman of extraordinary strength and achievement, that was pure aphrodisiac for him, and she exuded also the challenging air of being unattainable. The regal eyes mocked his evident masculinity with the untouchable aloofness of a queen or a goddess. She seemed to be smiling inwardly, a cool patronizing smile at his admiration, which she realized was no more than her due. Quickly Peter reviewed what he knew of her.

She had begun her association with the Baron as his private secretary, and in five years had become indispensable to him. The Baron had recognized her ability by rapidly elevating her to the boards of directors, first of some of the group's lesser subsidiaries, and finally to that of the central holding company. When the Baron's physical strength had begun to decline in his losing battle with an inexorable cancer, he came to rely more upon her, trust well placed as it soon turned out. For she ran the complex empire of heavy industrial companies, of electronics and armaments corporations, of banking and shipping and property developments, like the son he never had. When he married her he was fifty-eight years of age, almost thirty years her senior, and she had been a perfect wife as she had been a perfect business partner.

She had assembled and personally delivered the massive ransom demanded by his abductors, against the advice of the French police, going alone and unguarded to a meeting with merciless killers, and when they had returned the Baron's fearfully mutilated corpse to her, she had mourned him and buried him and continued to run the empire she had inherited with vision and strength so far beyond her years.

She was twenty-nine years old. No, that had been two years ago, Peter realized, as he bowed over her hand, not quite touching the smooth cool fingers with his lips. She would be thirty-one years old now. She wore a single ring on her wedding finger, a solitaire diamond, not a particularly large diamond, not more than six carats but of such a perfect whiteness and fire that it seemed to be endowed with its own life. It was the choice of a woman of immense wealth and even greater style.

As Peter straightened, he realized that she was appraising him as carefully as he was her. It seemed that he would be unable to conceal anything from those slanted emerald eyes, but he returned her gaze steadily, knowing without conceit that he could withstand any such scrutiny; still intrigued, however, with the certainty that she had known him.

"Your name has been much in the news recently," she said, as if in explanation.

There were sixteen for lunch, including Steven and Pat's three children and Melissa-Jane. It was a happy, relaxed meal, but the Baroness was seated at a distance that made it impossible for Peter to speak directly to her, and though he strained to follow her conversation, her voice was low and addressed mostly to Steven and the editor of one of the national daily newspapers who flanked her. Peter found himself fully occupied in fending off the breathless attention of the pretty but featherbrained blonde on his left. She was a starlet who had married well and divorced even better. She had been hand-picked by Pat Stride. Peter's sister-in-law was indefatigable in her efforts to find him a suitable replacement for Cynthia. Twelve years of straight failures had not daunted her in the least.

There was still time for Peter to notice that though the Baroness sipped once or twice at her wine, the level in the glass never fell, and she picked only lightly at her plate.

Though Peter watched her covertly, the Baroness never glanced once in his direction. It was only as they went through for coffee that she came directly and unaffectedly to his side.

"Steven tells me there are Roman ruins on the estate," she said.

"I could show them to you. It is a lovely walk up through the woods."

"Thank you. I do have some business to discuss with Steven before that; shall we meet at three o'clock?"

She had changed into a loose tweed skirt and jacket that would have looked bulky on a shorter or plumper woman, and high boots in the same lavender tinted brown. Under it she wore a cashmere roll-neck jersey, and a scarf of the same fine wool hung down her back. A wide-brimmed hat with a bright feather in the band was pulled down over her eyes.

She walked in silence, hands thrust deeply into the big pockets of her jacket, making no effort to protect the expensive boots from mud, thorns or damp bracken. She moved with a flowing, long-legged grace, swinging from the hips so that her shoulder and head seemed to float beside Peter, at not much lower level than his own. Had she not been a world leader in finance and industry, she might have made a great model, he decided. She had a talent for making clothes look important and elegant, while treating them with indifference.

Peter respected her silence, pleased to be able to step out to match her pace, as they went up through the dripping woods that smelt of leaf mould and cold rain, the oaks bare and moss-pelted, seeming to beseech a purple-grey sky with arthritic limbs held high.

They came out on the higher open ground without having stopped once, although the path had been steep and the ground soft underfoot.

She was breathing deeply but evenly, and she had coloured just sufficiently to flatter the high Slavic cheeks. She must be in peak physical condition, he thought.

"Here they are." Peter indicated the barely discernible grass-covered ditch that circled the hill top. "They are not very impressive, but I didn't want to warn you in advance."

She smiled now. "I have been here before," she said in that intriguing husky accent.

"Well, we are off to a flying start. We have both deceived each other at our first meeting." Peter chuckled.

"I came all the way from Paris," she explained. "It was most inconvenient really—the business I had to discuss with Sir Steven could have been completed by telephone in five minutes. What I had to discuss with you could only be done face by face"—she corrected herself immediately—"I am sorry, face to face." It was a rare slip. Steven had been strangely insistent that Peter spend this particular weekend at Abbots Yew, and was certainly party to this encounter.

"I am flattered by the interest of such a beautiful lady—"

Instantly she frowned, and with a gesture of irritation cut short the compliment as frivolous.

"Very recently you were approached by the Narmco section of Seddler Steel with an offer to head their Sales Division," she said, and Peter nodded. Since his resignation had been accepted by the War Office, there had been many offers. "The terms of employment offered were extraordinarily generous."

"That is true."

"You prefer the cloistered academic life, perhaps?" she asked, and though Peter's expression did not change, he was taken off balance. It seemed impossible that she could know of the offer of the Chair of Modern Military History that he had been offered by a leading American university, an offer with which he was still toying idly.

"There are some books I want to read and write," Peter said.

"Books. You have an important collection, and I have read those you have written. You are an interesting contradiction, General Stride. The man of direct action, and at the same time of deep political and social thought."

"I confuse myself at times," Peter smiled. "So what chance do you have to understand me?"

She did not rise to the smile. "A great deal of your writing coincides with my own conviction. As for your action, if I had been a man and in your position, I might have acted as you did."

Peter stiffened, resenting any allusion to the taking of Flight 070, and again she seemed to understand instinctively.

"I refer to your entire career, General. From Cyprus to Johannesburg—and including Ireland." And he relaxed slightly.

"Why did you refuse the Narmco offer?" she asked.

"Because it was presented with the unstated conviction that I could not refuse. Because the terms were so generous that they left a strange unsatisfying odour in my nostrils. Because I believe that I would have been required to perform duties in line with the reputation I seem to have acquired since the taking of Flight 070."

"What reputation is that?" She leaned slightly towards him, and he smelled her particular aroma. The way perfume reacted upon that petally-smooth skin, heated by the exertion of the climb up the hill. She smelled faintly of crushed lemon blossom and clean healthy mature woman. He felt himself physically aroused by it, and had an almost irrepressible impulse to reach out and touch her, to feel the warmth and glossiness of her skin.

"A man who makes accommodations, perhaps," he answered her.

"What did you think you might have been asked to do?"

This time he shrugged. "Perhaps carry bribes to my one-time colleagues in NATO Command, to induce them to consider favourably the products of Narmco."

"Why would you believe that?"

"I was once a decision-making officer in that Command."

She turned away from him and looked out across the special greens of an English winter landscape, the orderly fields and pastures, the dark wedges and geometrical shapes of the woods and copses.

"Do you know that through Altmann Industries and other companies I control a majority shareholding in Seddler Steel, and naturally in Narmco?"

"No," Peter admitted. "But I cannot say I am surprised."

"Did you know that the offer from Narmco was in reality from me personally?"

This time he said nothing.

"You are quite right, of course, your contacts with the upper echelon of NATO and with the British and American high commands would have been worth every centime of the extravagant salary you were offered. As for bribes"—she smiled then suddenly, and it altered her face entirely, making her seem many years younger, and there was a warmth and a sense of fun that he would not have suspected—"this is a capitalist society, General. We prefer to talk about commissions and introducer's fees."

He found himself smiling back at her, not because of what she had said, but simply because her smile was irresistible.

"However, I give you my solemn word that you would never have been expected to offer or carry—no, since Lockheed was indiscreet, it has changed. Nothing disreputable could ever be traced back to Narmco, and certainly not to the top men there. Certainly not to you."

"It's all academic now," Peter pointed out. "I've refused the offer."

"I disagree, General Stride." The brim of the hat covered her eyes as she looked down. "I hope that when you hear what I had hoped to achieve you may reconsider. I made the error of trying to keep us at arms' length to begin with. I relied on the generosity of the offer to sway you. I do not usually misjudge people so dismally," and she looked up and smiled again, and this time reached out and touched his arm. Her fingers were like her limbs, long and slim, but they were delicately tapered, and the nails were shaped and lacquered to a glossy fleshy pink. She left them on his arm as she went on speaking.

"My husband was an extraordinary man. A man of vast vision and strength and compassion. Because of that they tortured and killed him"—her voice had sunk to a hoarse catchy whisper— "they killed him in the most vile manner." She stopped, but made no attempt to turn her head away, she was unashamed of the tears that filled her eyes but did not break over the lower lids. She did not even blink, and it was Peter who looked away first. Only then she moved her hand, slipping it lightly into the crook of Peter's elbow and coming beside him so her hip almost touched his.

"It will rain soon," she said, her voice level and controlled. "We should go down." And as they started, she went on talking.

"The butchers who did that to Aaron went free, while an impotent society looked on. A society which has systematically stripped itself of defence against the next attack. America has virtually disbanded its intelligence system, and so shackled and exposed what is left that it is powerless. Your own country is concerned only with its own particular problems, as are we in the rest of Europe— there is no international approach to a problem that is international in scope. Atlas was a fine concept, limited as it was by the fact that it was a force that could be used only in retaliation and then only in special circumstances. However, if they ever suspect that it exists, the denizens of the left will mass to tear it down like a hunting pack of hyena." She squeezed his arm lightly, and looked sideways at him with a solemn slant of the emerald eyes. "Yes, General, I do know about Atlas—but do not ask me how."

Peter said nothing, and they entered the forest, stepping carefully, for the path was slick and steep.

"After the death of my husband, I began to think a great deal about how we could protect the world that we know, while still remaining within the laws which were first designed to do that. With Altmann Industries I had inherited a comprehensive system of international information-gathering. Naturally, it was attuned almost entirely to commercial and industrial considerations—" She went on talking in that low intense voice that Peter found mesmeric, describing how she had gradually used her massive fortune and influence to reach across borders closed to most to gain the overall view of the new world of violence and intimidation. "I was not tied by considerations such as that of Interpol, forbidden by suicidal laws to involve itself in any crime that has political motivation. It was only when I was able to pass on what I had learned that I found myself coming up against the same self-destructive state of mind that masquerades as democracy and individual freedom. Twice I was able to anticipate a terrorist strike and to warn the authorities, but intention is not a crime, I was told, and both the culprits were quietly escorted to the border and turned free to prepare themselves almost openly for the next outrage. The world must wait and cringe for the next stroke, prohibited from making any pre-emptive strike to prevent it, and when it comes they are hampered by confused national responsibilities and by the complicated concept of minimum force—" The Baroness broke off. "But you know all this! You have written in depth of the same subject."

"It's interesting to hear it repeated."

"I will come soon enough to the interesting part—but we are almost back at the house."

"Come," Peter told her, and led her past the stables to the swimming pool pavilion. The surface of the heated pool steamed softly, and lush tropical plants were in odd contrast to the wintry scene beyond the glass walls.

They sat side by side on a swing seat, close enough to be able to talk in subdued tones, but the intense mood was broken for the moment. She took off her hat, scarf and jacket, and tossed them onto the cane chair opposite, and she sighed as she settled back against the cushions.

"I understand from Sir Steven that he wants you to go into the bank." She slanted her eyes at him. "It must be difficult to be so sought after."

"I don't think I have Steven's reverence for money."

"It's a readily acquired taste, General Stride," she assured him. "One that can become an addiction."

At that moment the children of both Stride brothers arrived in a storm of shouted repartee and laughter, which moderated only marginally when they realized that Peter and the Baroness were in the swing seat.

Steven's youngest son, bulging over the top of his jacket with puppy-fat and with silver braces on his front teeth, rolled his eyes in their direction and in a stage whisper told Melissa-Jane,

"*Je t'aime, ma chérie*, Swoon! Swoon!" His accent was frighteningly bad and he received a hissed rebuke and a shove in the small of the back that hurled him into the deep end of the pool.

The Baroness smiled. "Your daughter is very protective"—she turned slightly to examine Peter's face again—"or is it merely jealousy?" Without waiting for an answer she went straight on to ask another question. Against the background of shouts and splashes, Peter thought he had misheard.

"What did you say?" he asked carefully, certain that his expression had revealed nothing, and she repeated.

"Does the name Caliph mean anything to you?"

He frowned slightly, pretending to consider, while his memory darted back to the terrible micro-seconds of mortal combat, of smoke and flame and gunfire and a dark-haired girl in a scarlet shirt screaming:

"Don't kill us! Caliph said we would not die. Caliph—" And his own bullets stopping the rest of it, smashing into the open mouth. The word had haunted him since then, and he had tried a thousand variations, looking for sense and meaning, considering the possibility that he had misheard. Now he knew he had not.

"Caliph?" he asked, not knowing why he was going to deny it, merely because it seemed vital that he keep something in reserve, that he were not carried headlong on the torrent of this woman's presence and personality. "It's a Mohammedan title—I think it literally means the heir of Mohammed, the successor to the prophet."

"Yes." She nodded impatiently. "It's the title of a civil and religious leader—but have you heard it used as a code name?"

"No. I am sorry, I have not. What is the significance?"

"I am not sure, even my own sources are obscure and confused." She sighed, and they watched Melissa-Jane in silence. The child had been waiting for Peter's attention, and when she had it she ran lightly out along the springboard and launched herself, light as a swallow in flight, into a clean one-and-a-half somersault, entering the water with hardly a ripple and surfacing immediately with fine pale hair slick down across her face, immediately looking again for Peter's approval.

"She's a lovely child," said the Baroness. "I have no children. Aaron wanted a son—but there was not one." And there was real sorrow in the green eyes that she masked quickly. Across the pool Melissa-Jane climbed from the pool and quickly draped a towel around her shoulders, covering her bosom which was now large enough and yet so novel as to provide her with a constant source of embarrassment and shy pride.

"Caliph," Peter reminded the Baroness quietly, and she turned back to him.

"I first heard the name two years ago, in circumstances I shall never forget—" She hesitated. "May I take it that you are fully aware of the circumstances surrounding my husband's kidnapping and murder? I do not wish to repeat the whole harrowing story—unless it is necessary."

"I know it," Peter assured her.

"You know that I delivered the ransom, personally."

"Yes."

"The rendezvous was a deserted airfield near the East German border. They were waiting with a light twin-engined aircraft, a Russian-built reconnaissance machine with its markings sprayed over." Peter remembered the meticulous planning and the special equipment used in the hijacking of 070. It all tallied. "There were four men, masked. They spoke Russian, or rather two of them spoke Russian. The other two never spoke at all. It was bad Russian." Peter remembered now that the Baroness spoke Russian and five other languages. She had a Middle European background, Peter wished he had studied her intelligence file thoroughly. Her father had escaped with her from her native Poland when she was a small child. "Almost certainly, the aircraft and the Russian were intended to cover their real identity," she mused. "I was with them for some little time. I had forty-five million Swiss francs to deliver and even in notes of large denomination it was a bulky and heavy cargo to load aboard the aircraft. After the first few minutes, when they realized that I had no police escort, they relaxed and joked amongst themselves as they worked at loading the money. The word 'Caliph' was used in the English version, in a Russian exchange that roughly translates as 'He was right again,' and the reply 'Caliph is always right.' Perhaps the use of the English word made me remember it so clearly." She stopped again, grief naked and bleak in the green eyes.

"You told the police?" Peter asked gently, and she shook her head.

"No. I don't know why not. They had been so ineffectual up to that time. I was very angry and sad and confused. Perhaps even then I had already decided that I would hunt them myself—and this was all I had."

"That was the only time you heard the name?" he asked, and she did not reply immediately. They watched the children at play —and it seemed fantasy to be discussing the source of evil in such surroundings, against a background of laughter and innocent high spirits.

When the Baroness answered, she seemed to have changed direction completely.

"There had been that hiatus in international terrorism. The Americans seemed to have beaten the hijacking problem with their Cuban agreement and the rigorous airport searches. Your own successful campaign against the Provisional wing of the IRA in this country, the Entebbe raid and the German action at Mogadishu were all hailed as break-through victories. Everybody was beginning to congratulate themselves that it was beaten. The Arabs were too busy with the war in the Lebanon and with inter-group rivalries. It had been a passing thing." She shook her head again. "But terrorism is a growth industry—the risks are less than those of financing a major movie. There is a proven sixty-seven per cent chance of success, the capital outlay is minimal, with outrageous profits in cash and publicity, with instant results—and potential power not even calculable. Even in the event of total failure, there is still a better than fifty per cent survival rate for the participants." She smiled again, but now there was no joy and no warmth in it. "Any businessman will tell you it's better than the commodity markets."

"The only thing against it is that the business is run by amateurs," Peter said, "or by professionals blinded by hatred or crippled by parochial interests and limited goals."

And now she turned to him, wriggling around in the canvas swing seat, curling those long legs up under her in that double-jointed woman's manner, impossible for a man.

"You are ahead of me, Peter." She caught herself. "I am sorry, but General Stride is much to say, and I have the feeling I have known you so long." The smile now was fleeting but warm. "My name is Magda," she went on simply. "Will you use it?"

"Thank you, Magda."

"Yes." She picked up the thread of conversation again. "The business is in the hands of amateurs, but it is too good to stay that way."

"Enter Caliph," Peter guessed.

"That is the whisper that I have heard; usually there is no name. Just that there was a meeting in Athens, or Amsterdam or East Berlin or Aden—only once have I heard the name Caliph again. But if he exists already, he must be one of the richest men in the world, and soon he will be the most powerful."

"One man?" Peter asked.

"I do not know. Perhaps a group of men—perhaps even a government. Russia, Cuba, an Arab country? Who knows yet?"

"And the goals?"

"Money, firstly. Wealth to tackle the political objectives—and finally power, raw power." Magda Altmann stopped herself, and made a self-deprecating gesture. "This is guesswork again, my own guessing—based only on past performance. They have the wealth now, provided by OPEC and—myself amongst others. Now he or they have started on the political objectives, a soft target first. An African racist minority government unprotected by powerful allies. It should have succeeded. They should have won an entire nation—a mineral-rich nation—for the price of a dozen lives. Even had they failed to gain the main prize, the consolation prize was forty tons of pure gold. That's good business, Peter. It should have succeeded. It *had* succeeded. The Western nations actually put pressure on the victims, and forced them to accede to the demands—it was a trial run, and it worked perfectly, except for one man."

"I am afraid," said Peter softly, "as afraid as I have ever been in my life."

"Yes. I am also, Peter. I have been afraid ever since that terrible phone call on the night they took Aaron, and the more I learn, the more afraid I become."

"What happens next?"

"I do not know—but the name he has chosen has the hint of megalomania, perhaps a man with visions of godlike domination." She spread her fine narrow hands and the diamond flashed white fire. "We cannot hope to fathom the mind of a man who could embark on such a course. Probably he believes that what he is doing is for the eventual good of mankind. Perhaps he wants to attack the rich by amassing vast wealth, to destroy the tyrant with universal tyranny, to free mankind by making it a slave to terror. Perhaps he seeks to right the wrongs of the world with evil and injustice."

She touched his arm again, and this time the strength of those long fingers startled Peter. "You have to help me find him, Peter. I am going to put everything into the hunt; there will be no reservations. All the wealth and influence that I control will be at your disposal."

"You choose me because you believe that I murdered a wounded woman prisoner?" Peter asked. "Are those my credentials?" And she recoiled from him slightly, and stared at him with the slightly Mongolian slant of eyes, then her shoulders slumped slightly.

"All right, that is part of it, but only a small part of it. You know I have read what you have written, you must know that I have studied you very carefully. You are the best man available to me, and finally, you have proved that your involvement is complete. I know that you have the strength and skill and ruthlessness to find Caliph and destroy him—before he destroys us and the world we know."

Peter was looking inwards. He had believed that the beast had a thousand heads, and for each that was struck off a thousand more would grow. But now for the first time he imagined the full shape of the beast. It was still in ambush, not clear yet, but there was only a single head. Perhaps, after all, it was mortal.

"Will you help me, Peter?" she asked.

"You know I will," he answered quietly. "I do not have any choice."

She flew in the brilliance of high sunlight reflected from snowfields of blazing white, jetting through her turns with flowing elegance, carving each turn with a crisp rush of flying snow, swaying across the fall line of the mountain in an intricate ballet of interlinked movement.

She wore a slim-fitting skin suit of pearly grey, trimmed in black at the shoulders and cuffs, she was shod with gleaming black

Heierling snowbirds, and her skis were long, narrow, black Rossignol professionals.

Peter followed her, pressing hard not to lose too much ground, but his turns were solid Christies without the stylish fallback unweighting of the jet turn which gave her each time a fractional gain.

> The dun he ran like a stag of ten
> But the mare like a new roused fawn.

Kipling might have been describing them, and she was a hundred yards ahead of him as they entered the forest.

The pathway was barred with the shadows of the pines, and sugary ice roared under his skis as he pushed the narrow corners dangerously fast. Always she was farther ahead, flickering like a silver-grey wraith on those long lean legs, her tight round buttocks balancing the narrow waist and swinging rhythmically into the turns, marvellous controlled broadsides where the icy roadway denied purchase, coming out fast and straight, leaning into the rush of the wind, and her faint sweet laughter came back to Peter as he chased. There is an expertise that must be learned in childhood, and he remembered then that she was Polish, would probably have skied before she was weaned, and suppressed the flare of resentment he always felt at being outclassed by another human being, particularly by the woman who was fast becoming his driving obsession.

He came round another steeply banked turn, with the sheer snow wall rising fifteen feet on his right hand and on his left the tops of the nearest pines at his own level, so steep the mountain fell away into the valley.

The ice warning signs flashed past, and there was a wooden bridge, its boards waxen, opalescent with greenish ice. He felt control go as he hit the polished iron-hard surface. The bridge crossed a deep sombre gorge, with a frozen waterfall skewered to the black mountain rock by its own cruel icicles, like crucifixion nails.

To attempt to edge in, or to stem the thundering rush across the treacherous going, would have invited disaster, to lean back defensively would have brought him down instantly and piled him into the sturdy wooden guide rails. At the moment he was lined up for the narrow bridge Peter flung himself forward so that his shins socked into the pads of his boots, and in a swoop of terror and exhilaration he went through, and found that he was laughing aloud though his heart leaped against his ribs and his breathing matched the sound of the wind in his own ears.

She was waiting for him where the path debouched onto the lower slopes. She had pushed her goggles to the top of her head, and stripped off her gloves, both sticks planted in the snow beside her.

"You'll never know how much I needed that." She had flown into Zurich that morning in her personal Lear jet. Peter had come in on the Swissair flight from Brussels, and they had motored up together. "You know what I wish, Peter?"

"Tell me," he invited.

"I wish that I could take a whole month, thirty glorious days, to do what I wish. To be ordinary, to be like other people and not feel a moment's guilt."

He had seen her on only three occasions in the six weeks since their first meeting at Abbots Yew. Three too brief and, for Peter, unsatisfying meetings.

Once in his new office suite at the Narmco headquarters in Brussels, again at La Pierre Bénite, her country home outside Paris, but then there had been twenty other guests for dinner. The third time had been in the panelled and tastefully decorated cabin of her Lear jet on a flight between Brussels and London.

Though they had made little progress as yet in the hunt for Caliph, Peter was still exploring the avenues that had occurred to him and had cast a dozen lines, baited and hooked.

During their third meeting Peter had discussed with her the need to restructure her personal safety arrangements. He had changed her former bodyguards, replacing them with operatives from a discreet agency in Switzerland which trained its own men. The director of the agency was an old and trusted friend.

They had come to this meeting now so that Peter might report back on his progress to Magda. But for a few hours the snow had seduced them both.

"There is still another two hours before the light goes." Peter glanced across the valley at the village church. The gold hands of the clock showed a little after two o'clock. "Do you want to run the Rheinhorn?"

She hesitated only a moment. "The world will keep turning, I'm sure." Her teeth were very white, but one of them was slightly crooked, a blemish that was oddly appealing as she smiled up at him. "Certainly it will wait two hours."

He had learned that she kept unbelievable hours, beginning her day's work when the rest of the world still slept, and still hard at it when the offices of Altmann Industries in Boulevard Capucine were deserted, except her own office suite on the top floor. Even during the drive up from Zurich she had gone through correspondence and dictated quietly to one of her secretaries. He knew that at the chalet across the valley her two secretaries would be waiting already, with a pile of telex copies for her consideration and the line held open for her replies.

"There are better ways to die than working yourself to death." He was suddenly out of patience with her single-mindedness, and she laughed easily with high colour in her cheeks and the sparkle of the last run in the green eyes.

"Yes, you are right, Peter. I should have you near to keep reminding me of that."

"That's the first bit of sense I've had from you in six weeks." He was referring to her opposition to his plans for her security. He had tried to persuade her to change established behaviour-patterns, and though the smile was still on her lips, her eyes were deadly serious as she studied his face.

"My husband left me a trust"—she seemed suddenly sad beneath the laughter—"a duty that I must fulfil. One day I should like to explain that to you—but now we only have two hours."

It was snowing lightly, and the sun had disappeared behind the mountains of rock and snow and cloud as they walked back through the village. The lights were burning in the richly laden shop windows and they were part of the gaily clad stream returning from the slopes, clumping along the frozen sidewalks in their clumsy ski boots, carrying skis and sticks over one shoulder and chattering with the lingering thrill of the high piste that even the lowering snow-filled dusk could not suppress.

"It feels good to be free of my wolves for a while." Magda caught his arm as her snowbirds skidded on dirty ridged ice, and after she had regained her balance she left her gloved hand there.

Her wolves were the bodyguards that Peter had provided, the silent vigilant men who followed her either on foot or in a second car. They waited outside her offices while she worked, and others guarded the house while she slept.

That morning, however, she had told Peter, "Today I have as a companion a gold medal Olympic pistol champion, I don't need my wolves."

Narmco marketed its own version of the .9-mm parabellum pistol. It was called "Cobra," and after a single morning in the underground range Peter had taken a liking to the weapon. It was lighter and flatter than the Walther he was accustomed to, easier to carry and conceal, and the single action merchanism saved a flicker of time with the first shot, for there was no need to cock the action. He had had no trouble obtaining a permit to carry one as a trade sample, although it was necessary to check it before every commercial flight, but it carried neatly in a quick-release shoulder holster.

He had felt theatrical and melodramatic at first, but with a little sober thought had convinced himself that to follow on Caliph's tracks unarmed was shortening the odds against himself.

Now it was becoming habit, and he was barely aware of the comforting shape and weight in his armpit, until Magda spoke.

"I am close to dying from thirst," she went on, and they racked their skis and went into the jovial warmth and clouds of steam that billowed from one of the coffee shops that lined the main street.

They found a seat at a table already crowded with young people, and they ordered glasses of steaming hot *Glühwein*.

Then the four-piece band thumped out a popular dance tune and their table companions swarmed onto the tiny dance floor.

Peter raised a challenging eyebrow at her and she asked with amusement, "Have you ever danced in ski boots?"

"There has to be a first time for everything."

She danced like she did everything else, with complete absorption, and her body was strong and hard and slim against his.

It was completely dark as they climbed the narrow track above the village and went in through the electronically controlled gate in the protective wall around the chalet.

It was somehow typical of her that she had avoided the fashionable resorts, and that externally the chalet seemed not much different from fifty others that huddled in the edge of the pine forest.

There was patent relief amongst her entourage at her return, and she seemed almost defiant at their concern as though she had just proved something to herself. But still she did not change from her sports clothes before disappearing into the office suite on the first floor with her two male secretaries. "I work better with men," she had explained to Peter once. As Peter dressed in slacks, blazer and silk roll-neck after a scalding shower, he could still hear the clatter of the telex machine from the floor below, and it was an hour later when she called him on the house telephone.

The entire top floor was her private domain and she was standing at the windows looking out over the snow-fuzzed lights of the valley as he entered.

She wore green slacks tucked in après-ski boots, and a blouse of the same colour, a perfect match for her eyes. The moment Peter entered, she pressed a concealed switch and the curtains slid silently closed, then she turned to him.

"A drink, Peter?" she asked.

"Not if we are going to talk."

"We are going to talk," she said positively, and indicated the soft squashy leather armchair across from the fireplace. She had resisted the traditional Swiss cuckoo-clock and knotty pine decor, and the carpeting was thick Wilton to match the curtains, the furniture low and comfortable but modern, sporty and good fun, the very best made to appear natural and unaffected, blending easily with the modern art on the walls and abstract sculpture in marble and grained wood.

She smiled suddenly at him. "I had no idea that I had found myself a gifted Sales Director for Narmco. I really am impressed with what you have done in so short a time."

"I had to establish a plausible cover." Peter deprecated the compliment. "And I used to be a soldier. The job interests me."

"You English!" she told him with mock exasperation. "Always so modest." She did not seat herself but moved about the room; although never at rest, neither did she give the feeling of restlessness. "I am informed that there is to be a definite NATO testing of Kestrel—after almost two years of procrastination."

Kestrel was Narmco's medium-range ground-to-ground infantry portable missile.

"I am further informed that the decision was made to test after you had met with some of your former colleagues."

"The whole world runs on the old-boy system," Peter chuckled. "You should know that."

"And you are on old-boy terms with the Iranians?" She cocked her head at him.

"That was a small stroke of luck. Five years ago I was on a staff college course with their new military adviser."

"Luck again." She smiled. "Isn't it strange that luck so often favours those who are clever and dedicated and who move faster than the pack?"

"I have had less luck in other directions," Peter pointed out, and immediately there was no trace of laughter left upon her lips nor in the emerald eyes, but Peter went on. "So far I have been unsuccessful with the contact we spoke about on our last meeting."

They had discussed the possibility of access to the Atlas computer link, of requisitioning a print-out on "Caliph" from the central intelligence bank, if there was one programmed.

"As I explained, there was the one remote possibility of access, somebody who owed me a favour. He was of no help. He believes that if there is a 'Caliph' listing, it's blocked and buzzed." Which meant that any unauthorized requisition would sound an alarm in intelligence control. "We'd trigger a Delta condition in Atlas if we put in a print-out requisition."

"You did not give him the name?" Magda asked sharply.

"No. No names, just a general discussion over dinner at Brooks's—but all the implications were there."

"Do you have any further avenues—?"

"I think so. One more, but it's a last resort," Peter said. "Before we come to that, though, perhaps you can tell me if you have anything further from your sources."

"My sources"—Magda had never made more explicit descriptions, and Peter had instinctively known not to pry. There was a certain finality to the way she said it—"have been mostly negative. The seizure of the Netherlands Embassy in Bonn was unconnected with Caliph. It was exactly what it purported to be—South Moluccan extremists. The hijackers of Cathay Airlines and Transit Airlines were both enthusiastic amateurs, as evidence the methods and the outcome." She smiled drily and drifted back across the room to touch the Hundedwasser collage that hung on the side wall, re-arranging the hang of the frame in an essentially feminine gesture. "There is only one recent act that has the style of Caliph."

"Prince Hassied Abdel Hayek?" Peter asked, and she turned to face him, thrusting out one hip with her hand upon it, the nails very red against the light-green cloth and the marquise-cut diamond sparkling.

"What did you make of it?" she asked. The Prince had been shot dead, three bullets of .22 calibre in the back of the head while asleep in his rooms on the Cambridge campus. A nineteen-year-old grandson of King Khalid of Saudi Arabia, not one of the particular favorites of the King, a bespectacled scholarly youth who seemed content to remain outside the mainstream of palace power and politics. There had been no attempt at abduction, no sign of a struggle, no evidence of robbery—the young Prince had no close friends nor apparent enemies.

"It does not seem to have reason or motive," Peter admitted. "That's why I thought of Caliph."

"The deviousness of Caliph." Magda turned away and her haunches rippled under the elastic of her green slacks. There was no ruck line of panties, and her buttocks were perfect spheres, with the shadow of the deep cleft between them showing through the thin material. Peter watched her legs as she paced, realizing for the first time that her feet were long and narrow as her hands, fine and graceful bones in perfect proportion.

"If I told you that Saudi Arabia last week made clear to the other members of OPEC that, far from supporting a rise in the price of crude, she will press for a *five per cent* reduction in the world price at the organization's next meeting"—Peter straightened up in his chair slowly, and Magda went on softly— "and that she will be supported by Iran in her proposal. If I told you that, what would you think?"

"The King has other, more favoured grandchildren—grandsons and sons as well, brothers, nephews."

"Seven hundred of them," Magda agreed, and then went on musing. "And the King of Saudi Arabia is an Arab. You know how Mohammedans are about sons and grandsons." Magda came to stand so close to him that he could feel the warmth of her flesh through the narrow space between them, and her perfume subtly underlined the ripe sweet woman's smell of her body, disturbing him, but strangely heightening his awareness. "Perhaps King Khalid has also been reminded of his own mortality."

"All right." Peter hunched his shoulders and frowned in concentration. "What are we suggesting? That Caliph has struck another easy formula? Men who control the economic destiny of the

Western world? Men who make decisions at the personal level, who are not answerable to cabinets or causes or governments?"

"Men who are therefore vulnerable to personal terrorism, who have records of appeasement to terrorist pressure." Magda paused. "The old truths are still good. 'Uneasy lies the head that wears a crown.' They will be no strangers to the fear of the assassin's blade. They will understand the law of the knife, because they have always lived by it."

"Hell, you have to admire it." Peter shook his head. "There is no need to take and hold hostages. No need for exposure. You kill one obscure member of a large royal family, and you promise that there will be others, each one more important, closer to the head."

"The King's family has a high profile—any time you want to drop into the Dorchester you'll find one of his sons or grandsons sipping coffee in the public lounge. They are soft targets, and there are plenty of them. You might even have to kill two princelings or three, but secretly the world will feel that they had it coming to them anyway. There will not be oceans wept for men who have themselves held the world to ransom."

Peter's frown smoothed away, and he grinned wryly. "Not only do you have to admire it, you've got to have a sneaking sympathy for the object. A dead brake to the crippling inflation of the world, a slowing of disruptive imbalance in trade."

And Magda's expression was fierce as he had never seen it before. "'That is the trap, Peter. To see the end only, and to harden yourself to the means. That was the trap that Caliph set with the taking of 070. His demands coincided with those of the Western powers, and they placed additional pressure on the victim. Now, if we are correct and Caliph is pressuring the oil dictators for a moderation of their demands, how much more support can he expect from the Western capitalist powers?"

"You are a capitalist," Peter pointed out. "If Caliph succeeds, you will be one of the first to benefit."

"I'm a capitalist, yes. But before that I am a human being, and a thinking human being. Do you really believe that if Caliph succeeds now that this will be the last we hear of him?"

"Of course not." Peter spread his hands in resignation. "Always his demands will be harsher—with each success he must become bolder."

"I think we can have that drink now," Magda said softly, and turned away from him. The black-onyx top of the coffee table slid aside at her touch to reveal the array of bottles and glasses beneath.

"Whisky, isn't it?" she asked, and poured a single malt Glenlivet into one of the cut-glass tumblers. As she handed it to him their fingers touched and he was surprised at how cool and dry her skin felt.

She poured half a flute glass of white wine and filled it with Perrier water. As she replaced the wine bottle in the ice bucket, Peter saw the label. It was le Montrachet 1969. Probably the greatest white wine in the world, and Peter had to protest at the way in which she had desecrated it.

"Alexander Dumas said it should be drunk only on bended knee and with head reverently bared."

"He forgot the mineral water," Magda purred with throaty laughter. "Anyway you can't trust a man who employed other people to write his books for him." She lifted the adulterated wine to him. "Long ago I decided to live my life on my own terms. To hell with Messrs. Dumas and Caliph."

"Shall we drink to that?" Peter asked, and they watched each other over the rims. The level of Magda's glass had not lowered and she set the glass aside, moving across to adjust the bowl of hot-house tulips in the chunky free form crystal bowl.

"If we are right, if this is Caliph at work—then it disturbs the instinctive picture I had formed of him." Peter broke the silence.

"How?" she asked without looking up from the flowers.

"Caliph—it's an Arabic name. He is attacking the leader of the Arab world."

"The deviousness of Caliph. Was the name deliberately chosen to confuse the hunters—or perhaps there are other demands apart from the oil price—perhaps pressure is also being put on Khalid for closer support of the Palestinians, or one of the other extremist Arab movements. We do not know what else Caliph wants from Saudi Arabia."

"But then, the oil price. It is Western orientated. Somehow it has always been accepted that terrorism is a tool of the far left," Peter pointed out, shaking his head. "The hijacking of 070—even the kidnapping of your husband—were both aimed against the capitalist society."

"He kidnapped Aaron for the money, and killed him to protect his identity. The attack on the South African Government, the attack on the oil cartel, the choice of name, all point to a person with godlike pretensions." Magda broke the head off one of the tulips with an abrupt, angry gesture, and crushed it in her fist. She let the petals fall into the deep onyx ashtray. "I feel so helpless, Peter. We seem to be going round in futile circles." She came back to him as he stood by the curtained windows. "You said earlier that there was one sure way to flush out Caliph?"

"Yes," Peter nodded.

"Can you tell me?"

"There was an old trick of the Indian shikari. When he got tired of following the tiger in thick jungle without a sight of the beast, he used to stake out a goat and wait for the tiger to come to it."

"A goat?"

"My zodiacal sign is Capricorn—the goat." Peter smiled slightly.

"I don't understand."

"If I were to put the word out that I was hunting Caliph"—he smiled again. "Caliph knows me. The hijacker spoke my name, clearly, unmistakenly. She had been warned. So I believe that Caliph would take me seriously enough to consider it necessary to come after me."

He saw the lingering colour drain dramatically from her high cheeks, and the sudden shadow in the depths of her eyes.

"Peter—"

"That's the only way I'm going to get close to him."

"Peter—" She placed her hand on his forearm, but then she could not go on. Instead she stared at him silently and her green eyes were dark and unfathomable. He saw there was a pulse that throbbed softly in her long graceful neck, just below the ear. Her lips parted, as though she were about to speak. They were delicately sculptured lips, and she touched them with the pink tip of her tongue, leaving them moist and soft and somehow defenceless. She closed them, without speaking, but the pressure of her fingers on his arm increased, and the carriage of her whole body altered. Her back arched slightly so her lower body swayed towards him and her chin lifted slightly.

"I have been so lonely," she whispered. "So lonely, for so very long. I only knew how lonely today—while I was with you."

Peter felt a choking sensation in his throat, and the prickle of blood behind his eyes.

"I don't want to be lonely again, ever."

She had let her hair come down. It was very thick and long. It fell in a straight rippling curtain shot through with glowing lights, to her waist.

She had parted it in the centre; a thin straight line of white scalp divided the great black wings and they framed her face, making it appear pale and childlike with eyes too large and vulnerable, and as she came towards where Peter lay the glossy sheets of hair slid silently across the brocade of her gown.

The hem of the gown swept the carpet, and her bare toes moved out from under it with each step. Narrow, finely boned feet, the nails trimmed and painted with a colorless lacquer. The sleeves of the gown were wide as batwings and lined with satin, the collar buttoned up in a high Chinese style.

Beside the bed she stopped and her courage and poise seemed to desert her, her shoulders slumped a little and she clasped the long narrow fingers before her in a defensive gesture.

"Peter, I don't think I am going to be very good at this." The throaty whisper was barely audible, and her lips trembled with the strength of her appeal. "And I want so badly to be good."

Silently he reached out one hand to her, palm upwards. The bedclothes covered him to the waist, but his chest and arms were bare. Lightly tanned and patterned with wiry body hair. As he reached for her the muscle bunched and expanded beneath the skin, and she saw that there was no surplus flesh on his waist, nor on his shoulders and upper arms. He looked lean and hard and tempered, yet supple as the lash of a bullwhip, and she did not respond immediately to the invitation, for his masculinity was overpowering.

He folded back the thick down-filled duvet between them, and the sheet was crisp and smooth in the low rosy light.

"Come," he ordered gently, but she turned away and with her back to him she undid the buttons of the embroidered gown, beginning at the throat and working downwards.

She slipped the gown from her shoulders, and held it for a moment in the crook of her elbows. The smooth flesh gleamed through the fall of black hair, and she seemed to steel herself like a diver bracing for the plunge into unknown depths.

She let the gown drop with a rustling slide down the full length of her body, and it lay around her ankles in a shallow puddle of peacock colours.

She heard him gasp aloud, and she threw the hair back from her shoulders with a toss of the long, swan-white neck. The hair hung impenetrably to the small of her back; just above the deep cleft of her lower body it ended in a clean line and her buttocks were round and neat and without blemish. But even as he stared the marble smoothness puckered into a fine rash of gooseflesh as though his eyes had physically caressed her, and she had responded with an appealingly natural awareness that proved how her every sense must be aroused and tingling. At the knowledge Peter felt his heart squeezed. He wanted to rush to her and sweep her into his arms, but instinct warned him that she must close the last gap herself, and he lay quietly propped on one elbow, feeling the deep ache of wanting spread through his entire body.

She stooped to pick up the gown, and for a moment the long legs were at an awkward coltish angle to each other and the spheres of her buttocks altered shape. No longer perfectly symmetrical, but parted slightly, and in the creamy niche they formed with her thighs there was an instant's heart-stopping glimpse of a single dense tight curl of hair and the light from beyond tipped the curl with glowing reddish highlights, then she had straightened again, once more lithe and tall, and she dropped the robe across the low couch and in the same movement turned back to face Peter.

He gasped again and his sense of continuity began to break up into a mosaic of distinct, seemingly unconnected images and sensations:

Her breasts, tiny as those of a pubescent child, but the nipples startlingly prominent, the color and texture of ripening young berries, wine red, already fully erect and hard as pebbles.

The pale plain of her belly, with the deep pit of the navel at its centre, that ended at last on the plump darkly furred mound pressed into the deep wedge between her thighs, like a small frightened living creature crouching from the stoop of the falcon.

The feel of her face pressed to his chest, and the tickle of her quick breath stirring his body hair, the almost painful grip of slim powerful arms locked with desperate strength around his waist.

The taste of her mouth as her lips parted slowly, softly, to his and the uncertain flutter of her tongue becoming bolder, velvety on top and slick and slippery on the underside.

The sound of her breathing changing to a deep sonorous pulse in his ears, seeming to keep perfect time with his own.

The smell of her breath, heavy with the aromatic musk of her arousal, and blending with the orangy fragrance of her perfume and the ripe woman smell of her body.

And always the feel of her—the warmth and the softness, the hardness of toned muscle and the running ripple of long hair about his face and down his body, the crisp electric rasp of tight, dense curls parting to unbearable heat and going on for ever to depths that seemed to reach beyond the frontier of reality and reason.

And then later the stillness of complete peace that reached out from the centre where she lay against his heart and seemed to spread to the farthest corners of his soul.

"I knew that I was lonely," she whispered. "But I did not realize just how terribly deeply." And she held him as though she would never relinquish her grip.

Magda woke him in the cold night three hours before dawn, and it was still dark when they left the chalet. The headlights of the following Mercedes that carried her wolves swept the interior of their saloon through each bend in the steep twisting road down from the mountains.

On take off from Zurich, Magda was in the Lear jet's left-hand seat, flying as pilot-in-command, and she handled the powerful machine with the sedate lack of ostentation which marks the truly competent aviator. Her personal pilot, a grizzled and taciturn Frenchman, who was flying now as her co-pilot, evidently held her skill in high regard and watched over her with an almost fatherly pride and approval as she cleared Zurich controlled airspace and levelled out at cruise altitude for Paris Orly before she left him to monitor the auto-pilot and came back to the main cabin. Though she sat beside Peter in the black calfskin armchairs, her manner was unchanged from the way it had been during their last flight together in this machine—reserved and polite—so that he found it difficult to believe the wonders they had explored together the previous night.

She worked with the two business-suited secretaries opposite her, speaking her fluent rippling French with the same enchanting trace of accent that marked her English. In the short time since he had joined Narmco, Peter had been forced to make a crash revision of his own French. Now once again he could manage, if not with éclat, at least with competence, in technical and financial discussion. Once or twice Magda turned to him for comment or opinion, and her gaze was serious and remote, seeming as impersonal and efficient as an electronic computer—and Peter understood that they were to make no show of their new relationship before employees.

Immediately she proved him wrong, for her co-pilot called her over the cabin speaker.

"We will join the Orly circuit in four minutes, Baroness."

And she turned easily and naturally and kissed Peter's cheek, still speaking French.

"Pardon me, chéri. I will make the landing. I need the flying time in my logbook."

She greased the sleek swift aircraft onto the runway as though spreading butter on hot toast. The co-pilot had radioed ahead so that when she parked in the private hangar there were a uniformed immigration policier and a douanier already waiting.

As they came aboard, they saluted her respectfully and then barely glanced at her red diplomatic passport. They took a little longer with Peter's blue and gold British passport, and Magda murmured to Peter with a trace of a smile.

"I must get you a little red book. It's so much easier." Then to the officials: "It is a cold morning, gentlemen, I hope you will take a glass." And her white-jacketed steward was hovering already. They left the two Frenchmen removing their kepis and pistol belts, settling down comfortably in the leather armchairs to make a leisurely selection of the cigars and cognac that the steward had produced for their approval.

There were three cars waiting for them, parked in the back of the hangar with drivers and guards. Peter's lip curled as he saw the Maserati.

"I told you not to drive that thing," he said gruffly. "It's like having your name in neon lights."

They had argued about this vehicle while Peter was reorganizing her personal security, for the Maserati was an electric silver-grey, one of her favourite colours, a shimmering dart of metal. She swayed against him with that husky little chuckle of hers.

"Oh, that is so very nice to have a man being masterful again. It makes me feel like a woman."

"I have other ways of making you feel like that."

"I know," she agreed, with a wicked flash of green eyes. "And I like those even better, but not now—please! What in the world would my staff think!" Then seriously, "You take the Maserati, I ordered it for you, anyway. Somebody may as well enjoy it. And please do not be late this evening. I have especially made it free for us. Try and be at La Pierre Bénite by eight o'clock—will you please."

By the time Peter had to slow for the traffic along the Pont Neuilly entrance to Paris, he had accustomed himself to the surging power and acceleration of the Maserati, and, as she had suggested, he was enjoying himself. Even in the mad Parisian traffic he used the slick gear box to knife through the merest suspicion of an opening, bulling out of trouble or overtaking with the omnipotent sense of power that control of the magnificent machine bestowed upon its driver.

He knew then why Magda loved it so dearly, and when he parked it at last in the underground garage on the Champs Élysées side of Concorde he grinned at himself in the mirror.

"Bloody cowboy!" he said, and glanced at his Rolex. He had an hour before his first appointment, and as a sudden thought unclipped the holster of the Cobra and, with the pistol still in it, locked it in the glove compartment of the Maserati. He grinned again as he pondered the inadvisability of marching into French Naval Headquarters armed to the teeth.

The drizzle had cleared, and the chestnut trees in the Élysées gardens were popping their first green buds as he came out into Concorde. He used one of the call boxes in the Concorde Metro station to make a call to the British Embassy. He spoke to the Military Attaché for two minutes, and when he hung up he knew the ball was probably already in play. If Caliph had penetrated the Atlas Command deeply enough to know him personally as the commander of Thor—then it would not be too long before he knew that the former commander had picked up the spoor. The

Military Attaché at the Paris Embassy had more clandestine duties than kissing the ladies' hands at diplomatic cocktail parties.

Peter reached the main gates of the Marine Headquarters on the corner of the rue Royale with a few minutes to spare, but already there was a secretary waiting for him below the billowing Tricolour. He smoothed Peter's way past the sentries, and led him to the armaments committee room on the third floor overlooking a misty grey view of the Seine and the gilded arches of the Pont Neuf. Two of Peter's assistants from Narmco were there ahead of him with their briefcases unpacked and the contents spread upon the polished walnut table.

The French Flag Captain had been in Brussels, and on one unforgettable evening he had conducted Peter on a magic-carpet tour of the brothels of that city. He greeted him now with cries of Gallic pleasure and addressed him as *tu* and *toi*—which all boded very well for the meeting ahead.

At noon precisely, the French Captain moved that the meeting adjourn across the street to a private room on the first floor of Maxim's, blissful in the certainty that Narmco would pick up the tab, if they were really serious about selling the Kestrel rocket motors to the French Navy.

It required all Peter's tact not to make it obvious that he was taking less than his share of the Clos de Vougeot or of the Rémy Martin, and more than once he found that he had missed part of the discussion which was being conducted at a steadily increasing volume. He found that he was thinking of emerald eyes and small pert bosoms.

From Maxim's back to the Ministry of Marine, and later it required another major act of diplomacy on Peter's part when the Captain smoothed his moustache and cocked a knowing eye at Peter. "There is a charming little club, very close and wonderfully friendly—"

By six o'clock Peter had disentangled himself from the Frenchman's company, with protestations of friendship and promises to meet again in ten days' time. An hour later Peter left his two sales assistants at the Hôtel Meurice after a quick but thorough summation of the day's achievements. They were, all three, agreed that it was a beginning but a long, long road lay ahead to the ending.

He walked back along Rivoli; despite the frowsiness of a long day of endless talk and the necessity for quick thinking in a language which was still strange on the tongue, despite a slight ache behind the eyes from the wine and cognac and despite the taste of cigar and cigarette smoke he had breathed, he was buoyed by a tingling sense of anticipation, for Magda was waiting, and he stepped out briskly.

As he paused for traffic lights, he caught a glimpse of his own reflection in a shop window. He was smiling without realizing it.

While he waited on the ramp of the parking garage for his turn to pay and enter the traffic stream, with the Maserati engine whispering impatiently, he glanced in the rear view mirror. He had acquired the habit long ago when one of the captured Provo death lists had begun with his name; since then he had learned to look over his shoulder.

He noticed the Citroën two back in the line of vehicles because the windshield was cracked and there was a scrape which had dented the mudguard and exposed a bright strip of bare metal.

He noticed the same black Citroën still two back as he waited for pedestrian lights in the Champs Élysées, and when he ducked his head slightly to try and get a look at the driver, the headlights switched on as though to frustrate him and at that moment the lights changed and he had to drive on.

Going around the Étoile, the Citroën had fallen back four places in the grey drizzling dusk of early autumn, but he spotted it once again when he was half-way down the Avenue de la Grande Armée, for by now he was actively searching for it. This time it changed lanes and slipped off the main thoroughfare to the left. It was immediately lost in the maze of side streets and Peter should have been able to forget it and concentrate on the pleasure of controlling the Maserati, but there lingered a sense of foreboding and even after he had shot the complicated junction of roads that got him onto the periphery route and eventually out on the road to Versailles and Chartres, he found himself changing lanes and speed while he scanned the road behind in the mirror.

Only when he left Versailles and was on the Rambouillet road did he have a clear view back a mile down the straight avenue of plane trees, and he was certain there was no other vehicle on the road. He relaxed completely and began to prepare himself for the final turnoff that would bring him at last to La Pierre Bénite.

The shiny wet black python of road uncoiled ahead of him and then humped abruptly. Peter came over the rise at 150 kilometres an hour and instantly started to dance lightly on brake and clutch, avoiding the temptation of tramping down hard and losing adhesion on the slippery uneven tarmac. Ahead of him there was a gendarme in a shiny white plastic cape, wet with rain, brandishing a torch with a red lens; there were reflective warning triangles bright as rubies, a Peugeot in the ditch beside the road with headlights glaring at the sky, a blue police Kombi van half blocking the road, and in the stage lit by the Kombi's headlights two bodies were laid out neatly, and all of it hazed by the soft insistent mantle of falling rain.

Peter had the Maserati well in hand, bringing her neatly down through the gears to a crawl, and as he was lowering the side window, the electric motor whining softly, the icy night air gusting into the heated interior, the gendarme gestured with the flashlight for him to pull over into the narrow gap between hedge and the parked Kombi, and at that moment unexpected movement caught Peter's eye. It was one of the bodies lying in the roadway under the headlights. The movement was the slight arch of the back that a man makes before rising from the prone position.

Peter watched him lift his arm, not more than a few inches, but it was just enough for Peter to realize he had been holding an object conccaled down the outside of his thigh, and even in the rain and the night Peter's trained eye recognized the perforated air-cooled sleeve enclosing the short barrel of a fold-down machine pistol.

Instantly his brain was racing so that everything about him seemed to be taking place in dreamy slow motion.

The Maserati! he thought. They're after Magda.

The gendarme was coming round to the driver's side of the Maserati, and he had his right hand under the white plastic cape, at the level of his pistol belt.

Peter went flat on the gas pedal, and the Maserati bellowed like a bull buffalo shot through the heart. The rear wheels broke from the wet surface, and with a light touch Peter encouraged the huge silver machine to swing like a scythe at the gendarme. It should have cut him down, but he was too quick. As the man dived for the hedge, Peter saw that he had brought the pistol out from under his cape but was too busy at that moment to use it.

The side of the Maserati touched the hedge with a flutter

of foliage, and Peter lifted his right foot, checked the enraged charge of the machine and swung her the other way. The moment she was lined up he hit the gas again, and the Maserati howled. This time she burned blue rubber smoke off her rear wheels.

There was a driver at the wheel of the blue police Kombi, and he tried to pull across to block the road completely, but he was not fast enough.

The two vehicles touched, with a crackle and scream of metal that jarred Peter's teeth, but what concerned him was that the two bodies showing in the headlights were no longer flat. The nearest was on one knee and was swinging the short stubby machine pistol —it looked like a Czech Skorpion or the German VP.70. burst fire shoulder stock pistol, but he was using the fold-down wire butt, wasting vital fractions of a second to get the weapon to his shoulder. He was also blocking the field of fire of the man who crouched behind him with another machine pistol pinned to his hip, pointing with index finger and forearm, ready to trigger with his second finger. "That's the way it should be done." Peter recognized professional skill, and his brain was running so swiftly that he had time to applaud it.

The Maserati cannoned off the police Kombi, and Peter lifted his right foot to take traction off the rear wheels, and spun the wheel hard to the right. The Maserati swung her tail with a screech of rubber and went into a left side slide towards the two figures in the road, and Peter ducked down below the level of the door. He had deliberately induced the left-hand slide, so that he had some little protection from the engine compartment and bodywork.

As he ducked he heard the familiar sound, like a giant ripping heavyweight canvas, an automatic weapon throwing bullets at a cyclic rate of almost two thousand rounds a minute, and the bullets tore into the side of the Maserati, beating in the metal with an ear-numbing clangor, while glass exploded in upon Peter like the glittering spray as a storm-driven wave strikes a rock. Glass chips pelted across his back, and stung his cheek and the back of his neck. They sparkled like a diamond tiara in his hair.

Whoever was doing the shooting had certainly emptied the magazine in those few seconds, and now Peter bobbed up in his seat, slitting his eyes against the cloud of glass splinters. He saw a looming nightmare of hedges and spun the wheel back to hold the Maserati. She swayed to the limits of her equilibrium and Peter had a glimpse of the two gunmen in the road rolling frantically into the half-filled ditch, but at that moment his off rear wheel hit the lip and he was slammed up short against his safety belt with a force that drove the air from his lungs, and the Maserati reared like a stallion smelling the mare and tail-walked, swinging in short vicious surges back and forth across the road, as he desperately fought for control with gear and brake and wheel. He must have spun full circle, Peter realized, for there was a giddy dazzle of light beams and of running and rolling figures, everything still hazy and indistinct in the rain, then the open road ahead again, and he sent the car at it with a great howling lunge, at the same moment glancing up at his mirror.

In the headlights he saw the burned blue clouds of smoke and steam thrown up by his own tyres, and through it the figure of the second gunman obscured from the waist by the ditch. He had the machine pistol at his waist, and the muzzle flash bloomed about him.

Peter heard the first burst hit the Maserati and he could not duck again, for there was a bend ahead in the rain, coming up at dazzling speed and he clenched his jaws waiting for it.

The next burst hit the car, like the sound of hail on a tin roof, and he felt the rude tugging, numbing jerk in his upper body.

Tagged! he realized. There was no mistaking it, he had been hit before. The first time when he had led a patrol into an EOKA ambush a very long time ago, and at the same moment he was evaluating the hit calmly finding he still had use of both hands and all his senses. Either it was a ricochet, or the bullet had spent most of its force in penetrating the rear windshield and seat back.

The Maserati tracked neatly into the bend, and only then he felt the engine surge and falter. Almost immediately the sharp stink of gasoline filled the cab of the Maserati.

Fuel line, he told himself, and there was the warm, uncomfortable spread of his own blood down his back and side, and he placed his wound low in the left shoulder. If it had penetrated it would be a lung hit, and he waited for the coppery salt taste of blood in his throat or the bubbling froth of escaping air in his chest cavity.

The engine beat checked again, surged and checked, as it starved for fuel. That first traversing burst of automatic fire must have ripped through the engine compartment, and Peter thought wryly that in the movies the Maserati would have immediately erupted in spectacular pyrotechnics like a miniature Vesuvius—though in reality it didn't happen like that, still gasoline from the severed lead would be spraying over plugs and points.

One last glance backwards, before the bend hid it and he saw three men running for the police van—three men and the driver, that was lousy odds. They would be after him immediately, and the crippled machine made a final brave leap forward that carried them five hundred yards more, and then it died.

Ahead of him, at the limits of the headlight beam, Peter saw the white gates of La Pierre Bénite. They had set the ambush at the point where they could screen out most extraneous traffic, and gather only the silver Maserati in their net.

He cast his mind back swiftly, recalling the lie of the land beyond the main gates of the estate. He had been here only once before, and it had been night then also, but he had the soldier's eye for ground, and he remembered thick forest on both sides of the road, down to a low bridge over a narrow fast flowing stream with steep banks, a hard left hander and a climb up to the house. The house was half a mile beyond the gates, a long way to go with a body hit and at least four armed men following, and no guarantee that he would be safe there either.

The Maserati was coasting down the slight incline towards the gates, slowing as it ran out of momentum, and now there was the hot smell of oil and burning rubber. The paintwork of the engine hood began to blister and discolour. Peter switched off the ignition to stop the electric pump spraying more fuel onto the burning engine and he slipped his hand into his jacket. He found the wound where he had expected it—low and left. It was beginning to sting and his hand came away sticky and slick with blood. He wiped it on his thigh.

Behind him was the reflected glow of headlights in the rain, a halo of light growing stronger. At any moment they would come through the bend, and he opened the glove compartment.

The 9-mm Cobra gave some little comfort as he slipped it from its holster and thrust it into the front of his belt. There was no spare magazine and the breech was empty, a safety consideration which he now regretted, for it left him with only nine rounds in the magazine—one more might make a lot of difference.

Pretty little fingers of bright flame were waving at him from under the bonnet of the engine compartment, finding the hinge and joint, probing the ventilation slot on the top surface. Peter released his seat belt, held open the door and steered with his other hand for the verge. Here the road was banked and dropped away steeply.

He flicked the wheel back the opposite way and let the change of direction eject him neatly, throwing him clear, while the Maserati swerved back into the centre of the road and rolled away, slowing gradually.

He landed as though from a parachute drop, feet and knees together cushioning the impact and then rolled into it. Pain flared in his shoulder and he felt something tear. He came up in a crouch and ran doubled over for the edge of the woods, the burning auto lit the trees with flickering orange light.

The fingers of his left hand felt swollen and numb as he pumped a round into the chamber of the Cobra, and at that moment the headlights beyond the bend flared with shocking brilliance and Peter had the illusion of being caught in front stage centre of the Palladium. He went down hard on his belly in the soft rain-sodden earth, but still his wound jarred and he felt the warm trickle of running blood under his shirt as he crawled desperately for the treeline.

The police van roared down the stretch of road. Peter flattened and pressed his face to the earth, and it smelled of leaf mould and fungus. The van roared past where he lay.

Three hundred yards down the road the Maserati had coasted to a halt, two wheels still on the road, the off-side wheels over the verge so she stood at an abandoned angle, burning merrily.

The van pulled up at a respectful distance from it, aware of the danger of explosion, and a single figure, the gendarme in his plastic cape, ran forward, took one look into the cab and shouted something. The language sounded like French, but the flames were beginning to drum fiercely and the range too long to hear clearly.

The van locked into a U turn, bumped over the verge, and then started back slowly. The two erstwhile accident victims, still carrying their machine pistols, running ahead like hounds on leash, one on each side of the road, heads down as they searched for signs in the soft shoulders of the road. The white-caped gendarme rode on the running-board of the van, calling encouragement to the hunters.

Peter was up again, doubled over, heading for the edge of the forest, and he ran into the barbed wire fence at full stretch. It brought him down heavily. He felt the slash of steel through the cloth of his trousers, and as he gathered himself again, he thought bitterly: One hundred and seventy guineas. The suit had been tailored in Savile Row. He crawled between the strands of armed wire, and there was a shout behind him. They had picked up his spoor, and as he dodged across the last few yards of open ground, another sharper, more jubilant shout.

They had spotted him in the towering firelight of the blazing Maserati, and again there was the tearing rip of automatic fire; but it was extreme range for the short barrel and low velocity ammunition. Peter heard passing shot like a whisper of bats' wings in the blackness above him and then he reached the first trees and ducked behind one of them.

He found he was breathing deeply, but with a good easy rhythm. The wound wasn't handicapping him yet, and he was into the cold reasoning rage that combat always instilled in him.

The range to the barbed wire fence was fifty metres, he judged, it was one of his best distances—International pistol standard out-of-hand with a 50-mm X circle—but there were no judges out here and he took a double-handed grip, and let them run into the fence just as he had done.

It brought two of them down, and the cries of angry distress were definitely in French; as they struggled to their feet again they were precisely back-lit by the flames, and the Cobra had a luminous foresight. Peter went for mid-section of one of the machine gunners.

The 9-mm had a vicious whipcrack report, and punched into flesh and bone with 385-foot pounds of energy. The strike of the bullet sounded like a watermelon hit with the full swing of a baseball bat. It lifted the man off his feet, and threw him backwards, and Peter swung onto the next target. But they were pros. Even though the fire from the edge of the woods had come as a complete surprise, they reacted instantly, and disappeared flat against the earth. They gave him no target, and Peter was too low on ammunition to throw down holding fire.

One of them fired a burst of automatic and it tore bark and

wood and leaves along the edge of the trees. Peter fired at the muzzle flash only once as a warning and then he ducked away and, keeping his head down to avoid lucky random fire, sprinted back into the woods.

They would be held up for two or three minutes by the fence and by the threat of coming under fire again, and Peter wanted to open some ground between them during that time.

The glow of the burning Maserati kept him well oriented and he moved quickly towards the river; however, before he had covered two yards he was starting to shiver uncontrollably. His two-piece city suit was soaked by the persistent drizzle and by the shower from each bush he brushed against. His shoes were light calf leather with leather soles and he had stepped in puddles of mud, and the knee-high grass was sodden. The cold struck through his clothing; he could feel his wound stiffening agonizingly and the first nauseating grip of shock tightened his belly, but he paused every fifty yards or so and listened for sounds of pursuit. Once he heard the sound of a car engine from the direction of the road, passing traffic probably, and he wondered what they would make of the abandoned police vehicle and the blazing Maserati. Even if it was reported to the real police, it would be all over before a patrol arrived and Peter discounted the chance of assistance from that quarter.

He was beginning now to be puzzled by the total lack of any sign of further pursuit, and he looked for and found a good stance in which to wait for it. There was a fallen oak tree and he wriggled in under the trunk, with a clear avenue of retreat, good cover and a low position from which any pursuer would be silhouetted against the sky glow of the burning Maserati. There were only three pursuers now, and seven cartridges in the Cobra. If it were not for the cold and the demoralizing ache through his upper body, he might have felt more confident, but the nagging terror of the hunted animal was still on him.

He waited five minutes, lying completely still, every sense tuned to its finest, the Cobra held out in extended double grip, ready to roll left or right and take the shot as it came. There was no sound but the drip and plop of the rain-soaked woods.

Another ten minutes passed before it occurred to him suddenly that the pursuers must now realize that the wrong quarry had sprung their trap. They were setting for Magda Altmann, and it must be clear to them that they had a man, and an armed one at that. He pondered their reaction. Almost certainly they would pull out now, had already done so.

Instead of a lady worth twenty or thirty million dollars in ransom money, they must realize they had one of her employees, probably an armed bodyguard, who was driving the Maserati either as a decoy or merely as delivery driver. Yes, he decided, they would pull out—take their casualty and melt away, and Peter was sure they would leave no clues to their identity. He would have enjoyed the opportunity to question one of them, he thought, and grimaced at a new lance of pain in the shoulder.

He waited another ten minutes, utterly still and alert, controlling the spasms of cold and reaction that shook him, then he rose quietly and moved back towards the river. The Maserati must have burned out completely now for the sky was black again and he had to rely on his own sense of direction to keep oriented. Even though he knew he was alone, he paused every fifty yards to listen and look.

He heard the river at last. It was directly ahead and very close. He moved a little faster and almost walked off the bank in the dark. He squatted to rest for a moment, for the shoulder was very painful now, and the cold was draining his energy.

The prospect of wading the river was particularly uninviting. The rain had fallen without a break for days now, and the water sounded powerful and swift—it would certainly be icy cold, and probably shoulder rather than waist deep. The bridge must be only a few hundred yards downstream, and he stood up and moved along the bank.

Cold and pain can sap concentration swiftly, and Peter had to make a conscious effort to keep himself alert, and he felt for every foothold before transferring his weight forward. He held the Cobra hanging at full stretch of his right arm, but ready for instant use, and he blinked his eyes clear of the fine drizzle of rain and the cold sweat of pain and fear.

Yet it was his sense of smell that alerted him.

The rank smell of stale Turkish tobacco smoke on a human body, it was a smell that had always offended him, and now he picked it up instantly, even though it was just one faint whiff.

Peter froze in mid-stride while his brain raced to adjust to the unexpected. He had almost convinced himself that he was alone.

Now he remembered the sound of a car engine on the main road, and he realized that men who had set up such an elaborate decoy—the faked motor accident, the police van and uniform—would certainly have taken the trouble to plot and study the ground between the ambush point and the victim's intended destination.

They would know better than Peter himself the layout of woods and river and bridge, and would have realized immediately they had taken their first casualty that futility of blundering pursuit through the night. It was the smart thing to circle back and wait again, and they would choose the river bank or the bridge itself.

The only thing that troubled Peter was their persistence. They *must* know it was not Magda Altmann, and then even in this tense moment of discovery he remembered the Citroën that had followed him down the Champs Élysées—nothing was what it appeared to be—and slowly he completed the step in which he had frozen.

He stood utterly still, poised, every muscle and every nerve screwed to its finest pitch, but the night was black and the rush of the river covered all sound. Peter waited. The other man will always move if you wait long enough, and he waited with the patience of the stalking leopard, although the cold struck through to his bones and the rain slid down his cheeks and neck.

The man moved at last. The squelch of mud and the unmistakeable brush of undergrowth against cloth, then silence. He was very close, within ten feet, but there was no glimmer of light, and Peter shifted his weight carefully to face the direction of the sound. The old trick was to fire one shot at the sound and use the muzzle flash to light the target for the second shot which followed it in almost the same instant of time—but there were three of them and at ten feet that machine pistol could cut a man in half. Peter waited.

Then from upstream there was the sound of a car engine again, still faint but fast approaching. Immediately somebody whistled faintly, a rising double note in the night up towards the bridge, clearly some prearranged signal. A car door banged shut, much closer than the sound of the approaching engine, and a starter whirred, another harsher engine roared into life, headlights flared through the rain, and Peter blinked as the whole scene ahead of him lit up.

A hundred yards ahead the bridge crossed the stream. The surface of the water was shiny and black as new-mined coal as it flowed about the supporting piles.

The blue van had parked on the threshold of the bridge, obviously to wait, but now it was pulling out, probably alarmed by the approach of the other more powerful engine from the direction of La Pierre Bénite. The driver was heading back towards the main road, the phoney gendarme scrambling alongside with his cape flapping as he tried to scramble through the open offside door—and out of the darkness, close to Peter, a voice cried out with alarm.

"*Attendez!*" The third man had no desire to be left by his companions, and he ran forward, abandoning all attempt at concealment. He had his back to Peter now, waving the machine pistol frantically, clearly outlined by the headlights of the van, and the range was under ten feet. It was a dead shot, and Peter went for it instinctively—and only at the very instant of trigger pressure that would have sent a 125 grain bullet between his shoulder blades was Peter able to check himself.

The man's back was turned and the range would make it murder, Peter's training should have cured him of such nice gentlemanly distinctions. However, what really held his trigger finger was the need to know. Peter had to know who these people were and who had sent them, and what they had been sent to do, who they were after.

Now that the man was being deserted, he had abandoned all stealth and was running as though he were chasing a bus, and Peter saw the chance to take him. Roles had been exchanged completely, and Peter darted forward, transferring the Cobra to his injured left hand.

He caught the man in four paces, keeping low to avoid his peripheral vision, and he whipped his good right arm around the throat, going for the half-nelson and the spin that would disorient the man before he slammed the barrel of the Cobra against the temple.

The man was quick as a cat, something had warned him—perhaps the squelch of Peter's sodden shoes, and he ducked his chin onto his chest rolling his shoulders and beginning to turn back into the line of Peter's attack.

Peter missed the throat and caught him high, the crook of his elbow locking about the man's mouth, and the unexpected turn had thrown him slightly off balance. If he had had full use of his left arm, he could still have spun his victim, but in an intuitive flash he realized that he had lost the advantage, already the man was twisting his head out of the armlock, bulking his shoulders, and by the feel of him, Peter knew instantly that he was steel-hard with muscle.

The barrel of the machine pistol was short enough to enable him to press the muzzle into Peter's body just as soon as he completed his turn, and it would tear Peter to pieces like a chain saw.

Peter changed his grip slightly, no longer opposing the man's turn, but throwing all his weight and the strength of his right arm into the same direction; they spun together like a pair of waltzing dancers, but Peter knew that the moment they broke apart the man would have the killing advantage again.

The river was his one chance, he realized that instinctively, and before the advantage passed back from him to his adversary, he hurled himself backwards, keeping his grip on the man's head.

They went out into black space, falling together in a short gut-swooping drop with Peter underneath. If there was rock below the steep bank of the river, he realized he would be crushed by the other's weight.

They struck the surface of the fast black water, and freezing cold struck like a club so that Peter almost released the air from his lungs as a reflex.

The shock of cold water seemed to have stunned the man in his grip momentarily, and Peter felt the whoosh of air from his lungs as he let go. Peter changed his grip, wedging his elbow under the chin, but not quite able to get at the throat—immediately the man began the wild panic-stricken struggles of somebody held under icy water with empty lungs.

He had lost the machine pistol, for he was tearing at Peter's arms and face with both hands as the water swirled them both end over end down towards the bridge.

Peter had to keep him from getting air, and as he held his own precious single breath, he tried to get on top and stay there.

Fingers hooked at his closed eyes, and then into his mouth as the man reached back desperately over his own shoulders. Peter opened his mouth slightly and the other man thrust his fingers deeply in, trying to tear at his tongue. Immediately Peter locked his teeth into the fingers with a force that made his jaw ache at the hinges, and his mouth filled with the sickening warm spurt of the other man's blood.

Fighting his own revulsion, he hung on desperately with teeth and arms. He had lost his own weapon, dropping it into the black flood from numbed and crippled fingers, and the man was fighting now with the animal strength of his starved lungs and mutilated fingers; every time he tried to yank his hand out of Peter's mouth the flesh tore audibly in Peter's ears and fresh blood made him gag and choke.

They came out on the surface and through streaming eyes Peter had one glimpse of the bridge looming above him. The blue van had disappeared, but Magda Altmann's Mercedes limousine was parked in the centre of the bridge, and in the wash of its head-lights he recognized her two bodyguards. They were leaning far out over the guardrail, and Peter had a moment's dread that one of them might try a shot—then Peter and the man were flung into the concrete piles of the bridge with such force that they lost the deathlock they had upon each other.

The back eddy beyond the bridge swung them in towards the bank. Gasping and swallowing with cold and exhaustion and pain, Peter fought for footing on gravel and rock. The machine-gunner had found bottom also and was stumbling desperately towards the bank. In the headlights of the limousine Peter saw Magda's two bodyguards racing back across the bridge to head him off.

Peter realized that he would not be able to catch the man before he reached the bank.

"Carl!" he screamed at the bodyguard who was leading. "Stop him. Don't let him get away."

The bodyguard vaulted over the guardrail, landing cat-like in complete balance, with the pistol double-handed at the level of his navel.

Below him the machine-gunner dragged himself waist deep towards the bank. It was only then that Peter realized what was going to happen.

"No!" He choked on blood and water. "Take him alive. Don't kill him, Carl!"

The bodyguard had not heard, or had not understood. The muzzle blast seemed to join him and the wallowing figure in the river below him, a blood-orange rope of flame and thunderous explosion. The bullets smacked into the machine-gunner's chest and belly like an axeman cutting down a tree.

"No!" Peter yelled helplessly. "Oh Jesus, no! No!"

Peter lunged forward and caught the corpse before it slid below the black water, and he dragged it by one arm to the bank. The bodyguards took it from him and hauled it up, the head lolling like an idiot's, and the blood diluted to pale pink in the reflected headlights.

Peter made three attempts to climb the bank, each time slithering back tiredly into the water, then Carl reached down and gripped his wrist.

Peter knelt on the muddy bank, still choking with the water and blood he had swallowed, and he retched weakly.

"Peter!" Magda's voice rang with concern, and he looked up and wiped his mouth on the back of his forearm. She had slipped out of the back door of the limousine and was running back along the bridge, long-legged in black boots and ski-pants, her face dead white with concern and her eyes frantic with worry.

Peter pushed himself onto his feet and swayed drunkenly. She reached him and caught him, steadying him as he teetered.

"Peter, oh God, darling. What happened—"

"This beauty and some of his friends wanted to take you for a ride—and they got the wrong address."

They stared down at the corpse. Carl had used a .357 Magnum and the damage was massive. Magda turned her head away.

"Nice work," Peter told the bodyguard bitterly. "He's not going to answer any questions now, is he?"

"You said to stop him." Carl growled as he reloaded the pistol.

"I wonder what you would have done if I'd said to really clobber him." Peter began to turn away with disgust, and pain checked him. He gasped.

"You're hurt." Magda's concern returned in full strength. "Take his other arm," she ordered Carl, and they helped him over the parapet to the limousine.

Peter stripped off the torn and sodden remains of his clothing and Magda wrapped him in the Angora wool travel rug before examining his wound under the interior light of the cab.

The bullet hole was a perfect little blue puncture in the smooth skin, already surrounded by a halo of inflammation, and the bullet was trapped between his ribs and the sheet of flat, hard trapezial muscles. She could see the outline of it quite clearly, the size of a ripe acorn in his flesh, swollen out angry purple.

"Thank God—" she whispered, and unwound the Jean Patou scarf from her long pale throat. She bound the wound carefully. "We'll take you directly to the hospital at Versailles. Drive fast, Carl."

She opened the walnut-fronted cocktail cabinet in the bodywork beside her and poured half a tumbler of whisky from the crystal decanter.

It washed the taste of blood from Peter's mouth and then went warmly all the way down his throat to soothe the cramps of cold and shock in his belly.

"What made you come?" he asked, his voice still rough with the fierce spirit. The timely arrival nagged at his sense of rightness.

"The police at Rambouillet had a report of a car smash—they knew the Maserati, and the inspector rang La Pierre Bénite immediately. I guessed something bad—"

At that moment they reached the gates at the main road. The remains of the Maserati lay smouldering on the side of the road; around it like Boy Scouts around a campfire were half a dozen gendarmes in their white plastic capes and pillbox kepis. They seemed uncertain of what they should do next.

Carl slowed the limousine and Magda spoke tersely through the window to a sergeant, who treated her with immense respect. "*Oui, madame la Baronne, d'accord. Tout à fait vrai—*" She dismissed him with a final nod, and he and his men saluted the departing limousine.

"They will find the body at the bridge."

"There may be another one on the edge of the forest there."

"You are very good, aren't you?" she slanted her eyes at him.

"The really good ones don't get hit," he said, and smiled. The whisky had taken some of the sting and stiffness out of the wound and unknotted his guts. It was good to still be alive, he started to appreciate that again.

"You were right about the Maserati then—they were waiting for it."

"That's why I burned it," he told her, but she did not answer his smile.

"Oh, Peter. You'll never know how I felt. The police told me that the driver of the Maserati was still in it and had been burned. I thought—I felt as though part of me had been destroyed. It was the most terrifying feeling." She shivered. "I nearly did not come, I didn't want to see it. I nearly sent my wolves, but then I had to know—Carl saw you in the river as we turned onto the bridge. He said it was you, I just couldn't believe it." She stopped herself and shuddered at the memory. "Tell me what happened, tell me all of it," she demanded and poured more whisky into his tumbler.

For some reason that he was not sure of himself, Peter did not mention the Citroën that had followed him out of Paris. He told himself that it could not have been relevant. It must have been a coincidence, for if the driver of the Citroën had been one of them he would have been able to telephone ahead and warn the others that Baroness Magda Altmann was not in the Maserati, so that would have meant that they were not after her—but after him, Peter Stride, and that didn't make sense because he had only set himself up as bait that very morning, and they would not have had time yet. He stopped the giddy carousel of thoughts—shock and whisky, he told himself. There would be time later to think it all out more carefully. Now he would simply believe that they were waiting for Magda, and he had run into their net. He told it that way, beginning from the moment that he had seen the police van parked in the road. Magda listened with complete attention, the huge eyes clinging to his face, and she touched him every few moments as if to reassure herself.

When Carl parked under the portico of the emergency entrance of the hospital, the police had radioed ahead and there were an intern and two nurses waiting for Peter with a stretcher.

Before she opened the door to let them take Peter, Magda leaned to him and kissed him full on the lips.

"I'm so very glad to have you still," she whispered, and then with her lips still very close to his ear she went on. "It was Caliph again, wasn't it?"

He shrugged slightly, grimaced at the stab of pain, and answered,

"I can't think of anyone else off-hand that would do such a professional job."

Magda walked beside the stretcher as far as the theatre doors, and she was beside his bed in the curtained cubicle as he struggled up through the deadening, suffocating false death of anaesthetic.

The French doctor was with her, and he produced the gruesome blood-clotted souvenir with a magician's flourish.

"I did not have to cut," he told Peter proudly. "Probe only." The bullet had mushroomed impressively, had certainly lost much of its velocity in penetrating the bodywork of the Maserati. "You are a very lucky man," the doctor went on. "You are in fine condition, muscles like a race horse that stopped the bullet going deep. You will be well again very soon."

"I have promised to look after you, so he is letting you come home now." Magda hovered over him also. "Aren't you, doctor?"

"You will have one of the world's most beautiful nurses." The doctor bowed gallantly towards Magda with a certain wistfulness in his expression.

The doctor was right, the bullet wound gave him less discomfort than the tears in his thighs from the barbed wire, but Magda Altmann behaved as though he were suffering from an irreversible and terminal disease.

When she did have to go up to her office suite in the Boulevard des Capucines the next day, she telephoned three times for no other reason than to make sure he was still alive and to ask for his size in shoes and clothing. The cavalcade of automobiles carrying her and her entourage were back at La Pierre Bénite while it was still daylight.

"You are keeping civil-service hours," he accused when she came directly to the main guest suite overlooking the terraced lawns and the artificial lake.

"I knew you were missing me," she explained, and kissed him before beginning to scold him. "Roberto tells me you have been wandering around in the rain. The doctor said you were to stay in bed. Tomorrow I will have to stay here to take care of you myself."

"Is that a threat?" he grinned at her. "For that sort of punishment I would let Caliph shoot another hole—"

Swiftly she laid her fingers on his lips. "Peter, *chéri,* don't joke like that." And the shadow that passed across her eyes was touched with fear, then immediately she was smiling again. "Look what I have bought you."

Peter's valise had been in the trunk of the Maserati, and she had replaced it with one in black crocodile from Hermes. To fill it she must have started at the top end of the Faubourg St. Honoré and worked her way down to the Place Vendôme.

"I had forgotten how much fun it is to buy presents for one who you—" She did not finish the sentence, but held up a brocade silk dressing-gown. "Everybody in St. Laurent knew what I was thinking when I chose this."

She had forgotten nothing. Shaving gear, silk handkerchiefs and underwear, a blue blazer, slacks and shoes from Gucci, even cufflinks, in plain gold, each set with a small sapphire.

"You have such blue eyes," she explained. "Now I will go and make myself respectable for dinner. I told Roberto we would eat here, for there are no other guests tonight."

She had changed from the gunmetal business suit and turban into floating cloud-light layers of gossamer silk, and her hair was down to her waist, more lustrous than the cloth.

"I will open the champagne," she said. "It needs two hands."

He wore the brocade gown, with his left arm still in a sling, and they stood and admired each other over the tops of the champagne glasses.

"I was right." She nodded comfortably. "Blue is your colour. You must wear it more often." And he had to smile at the quaint compliment, and touched her glass with his. The crystal pinged musically and they saluted each other before they drank. Immediately she set the glass aside, and her expression became serious.

"I spoke with my friends in the Sûrcté. They agree that it was a kidnap attempt against me, and because I asked it, they will not trouble you to make a statement until you feel better. I told them to send a man tomorrow to speak to you. There was no sign of the second man you shot at on the edge of the woods, he must have been able to walk or been carried by his friends."

"And the other man?" Peter asked. "The dead one."

"They know him well. He had a very ugly past. Algeria with the paras. The mutiny." She spread her hands eloquently. "My friends were very surprised that he had not killed you when he tried to do so. I did not say too much about your own past. It is better, I think?"

"It's better," Peter agreed.

"When I am with you like this, I forget that you also are a very dangerous man." She stopped and examined his face carefully. "Or is it part of the reason I find you so"—she searched for the world—"so compelling? You have such a gentle manner, Peter. Your voice is so soft and—" She shrugged. "But there is something in the way you smile sometimes, and in certain light your eyes are so blue and hard and cruel. Then I remember that you have killed many men. Do you think that is what attracts me?"

"I hope it is not."

"Some women are excited by blood and violence—the bull fight, the prize ring, there are always as many women as men at these, and I have watched their faces. I have thought about myself, and still I do not know it all. I know only that I am attracted by strong men, powerful men. Aaron was such a man. I have not found many others since then."

"Cruelty is not strength," Peter told her.

"No, a truly strong man has that streak of gentleness and compassion. You are so strong, and yet when you make love to me it is with extreme gentleness, though I can always feel the strength and cruelty there, held in bate, like the falcon under the hood."

She moved away across the room furnished in cream and chocolate and gold, and tugged the embroidered bell-pull that dangled from the corniced ceiling with its hand-painted panels, pastoral scenes of the type that Marie Antoinette had so admired. Peter knew that much of the furnishing of La Pierre Bénite had been purchased at the auction sales with which the revolutionary committee dispersed the accumulated treasures of the House of Bourbon. With the other treasures there were flowers; wherever Magda Altmann went there were flowers.

She came back to him as Roberto, the Italian butler, supervised the entry of the dinner cart, and then Roberto filled the wine glasses himself, handling the bottles with white gloves as though they were part of the sacrament, and stationed himself ready to serve the meal. But Magda dismissed him with a curt gesture and he bowed himself out silently.

There was a presentation-wrapped parcel at Peter's place setting, tissue paper and an elaborately tied red ribbon. He looked up at her inquiringly as she served the soup into fragile Limoges bowls.

"Once I began buying presents, I could not stop myself," she explained. "Besides, I kept thinking that bullet might have been in my back." Then she was impatient. "Are you not going to open it?"

He did so carefully, and then was silent.

"Africa, it is your speciality, is it not?" she asked anxiously. "Nineteenth-century Africa?"

He nodded, and reverently opened the cover of the volume in its bed of tissue paper. It was fully bound in maroon leather, and the state of preservation was quite extraordinary. Only the dedication on the fly leaf in the author's handwriting was faded yellow.

"Where on earth did you find this?" he demanded. "It was at Sotheby's in 1971. I bid on it then." He had dropped out of the bidding at five thousand pounds.

"You do not have a first edition of Cornwallis Harris?" she asked again anxiously, and he shook his head, examining one of the perfectly preserved colour plates of African big game.

"No, I do not. But how did you know that?"

"Oh, I know as much about you as you do yourself," she laughed. "Do you like it?"

"It is magnificent. I am speechless." The gift was too extravagant, even for someone of her fortune. It troubled him, and he was reminded of the situation comedy when the husband brings home flowers unexpectedly and is immediately accused by his wife: "Why do you have a guilty conscience?"

"Do you truly like it? I know so little about books."

"It is the one edition I need to complete my major works," he said. "And it is probably the finest specimen left outside the British Museum."

"I'm so glad." She was genuinely relieved. "I was truly worried." And she put down the silver soup ladle and lifted both arms to welcome his embrace.

During the meal she was gay and talkative, and only when Roberto had wheeled away the cart and they settled side by side on the down-filled couch before the fire did her mood change again.

"Peter, today I have been unable to think of anything but this business—you and me and Caliph. I have been afraid, and I am still afraid. I keep thinking of Aaron, what they did to him—and then I think of you and what nearly happened."

They were silent, staring into the flames and sipping coffee from the demi-tasse, when suddenly she had changed direction again. He was growing accustomed to these mercurial switches in thought.

"I have an island—not one island, but nine little islands—and in the centre of them is a lagoon nine kilometres wide. The water is so clear you can see the fish fifty feet down. There is an airstrip on the main atoll. Just under two hours' flying time to Tahiti. Nobody would ever know we were there. We could swim all day, walk in the sand, make love under the stars. You would be king of the islands, and I would be your queen. No more Altmann Industries—I would find somebody as good or better than myself to run it. No more danger. No more fear. No more Caliph—no more—" She stopped abruptly, as though she had been about to commit herself too far, but she went on quickly. "Let's go there, Peter. Let's forget all this. Let's just run away and be happy together, for ever."

"It's a pretty thought." He turned to her, feeling deep and genuine regret.

"It would work for us. We would make it work."

And he said nothing, just watching her eyes, until she looked away and sighed.

"No." She mirrored his regret. "You are right. Neither of us could ever give up and live like that. We have to go on. But, Peter, I am so afraid. I am afraid of what I know about you and of what I do not know. I am afraid of what you do not know about me, and what I never can tell you—but we must go on. You are right. We have to find Caliph, and then destroy him. But, oh God, I pray we do not destroy ourselves, what we have found together—I pray we will be able to keep that intact."

"The best way to conjure up emotional disaster is to talk about it."

"All right, let's play riddles instead. My turn first. What is the most miserable experience known to the human female?"

"I give up."

"Sleeping alone on a winter's night."

"Salvation is at hand," he promised her.

"But what about your poor shoulder?"

"If we combine our vast talents and wisdom, I am sure we will manage something."

"I think you are right," she purred and nestled against him like a sleek and silken cat. "As always."

There is always a delightfully decadent feeling about buying underwear for a beautiful woman, and Peter was amused by the knowing air of the middle-aged sales lady. She clearly had her own ideas about the relationship, and slyly produced a tray filled with filmy lace and iniquitously expensive wisps of silk.

"Yes," Melissa-Jane approved rapturously. "Those are exactly—" She held one of them to her cheek, and the sales lady preened at her own foresight. Peter hated to disillusion her, and he played the role of sugar-daddy a few moments longer as he glanced up at the mirror behind her head.

The tail was still there, a nondescript figure in a grey overcoat, browsing through a display of brassieres across the hall with the avid interest and knowledgeable air of a closet queen.

"I don't really think your mother will approve, darling," Peter said, and the sales woman looked startled.

"Oh, please, Daddy. I will be fourteen next month."

They had had a tail on him since he had arrived at Heathrow the previous afternoon, and Peter could not decide who they were. He began to regret he had not yet replaced the Cobra he had lost in the river.

"I think we'd better play it safe," Peter told his daughter, and both Melissa-Jane and the sales lady looked crestfallen.

"Not bloomers!" Melissa-Jane wailed. "Not elastic legs."

"Compromise," Peter suggested. "No elastic legs, but no lace—not until you're sixteen. I think painted finger nails is enough for right now."

"Daddy, you can be so medieval, honestly!"

He glanced at the mirror again, and they were changing the guard across the sales hall. The man in the shabby grey overcoat and checked woollen scarf drifted away and disappeared into one of the lifts. It would take some little time for Peter to spot his replacement—and then he grinned to himself, no it would not. Here he came now. He wore a tweed sports jacket in a frantic hounds' tooth pattern, above Royal Stewart tartan trews and a grin like an amiable toad.

"Son of a gun. This is a surprise." He came up behind Peter and hit him an open-handed blow between the shoulder blades that made Peter wince. At least he knew who they were at last.

"Colin." He turned and took the massive paw with its covering of wiry black hair across the back. "Yes, it is a surprise. I've been falling over your gorillas since yesterday."

"Oafs," Colin Noble agreed amiably. "All of them, oafs!" And turned to seize Melissa-Jane. "You're beautiful," he told her and kissed her with more than avuncular enthusiasm.

"Uncle Colin. You come straight from heaven." Melissa-Jane broke from the embrace and displayed the transparent panties. "What do you think of these?"

"It's you, honey. You've just got to have them."

"Tell my father, won't you."

Colin looked around the Dorchester suite and grunted. "This is really living. You don't get it this good in this man's army."

"Daddy is truly becoming a bloated plutocrat—just like Uncle Steven," Melissa-Jane agreed.

"I notice that you and Vanessa and the other comrades all wear lace panties," Peter counter-attacked his daughter.

"That's different." Melissa-Jane back-tracked swiftly, and hugged the green Harrod's package defensively. "You can have a social conscience without dressing like a peasant, you know."

"Sounds like a good life." Peter threw his overcoat across the couch and crossed to the liquor cabinet. "Bourbon?"

"On the rocks," said Colin.

"Is there a sweet sherry?" Melissa-Jane asked.

"There is Coke," Peter answered. "And you can take it through to your own room, young lady."

"Oh Daddy, I haven't seen Uncle Colin for ages."

"Scat," said Peter, and when she had gone, "sweet sherry, forsooth."

"It's a crying bastard when they start growing up—and they look like that." Colin took the glass from Peter and rattled the ice cubes together as he lay back in the armchair. "Aren't you going to congratulate me?"

"With pleasure." Peter took his own glass and stood at the windows, against the backdrop of bare branches and misty skies over Hyde Park. "What did you do?"

"Come on, Pete! Thor—they gave me your job, after you walked out."

"Before they fired me."

"After you walked out," Colin repeated firmly. He took a sip of the Bourbon and gargled it loudly. "There are a lot of things we don't understand—'Ours not to reason why, ours but to do and die.' Shakespeare."

He was still playing the buffoon, but the small eyes were as honey bright and calculating as those of a brand new Teddy bear on Christmas morning. Now he waved his glass around the suite.

"This is great. Really it's great. You were wasted in Thor—everybody knew that. You must be pulling down more than all the joint-chiefs put together now."

"Seven gets you five that you've already seen a Xerox copy of my contract of employment with Narmco."

"Narmco!" Colin whistled. "Is that you you're working for? No kidding, Pete baby, that's terrific!"

And Peter had to laugh—it was a form of capitulation. He came across and took the seat opposite Colin.

"Who sent you, Colin?"

"That's a lousy question."

"That's just an opener."

"Why should somebody have sent me? Couldn't I just want to chew the fat with an old buddy?"

"He sent you because he worked it out that I might bust the jaw of anybody else."

"Sure now and everybody knows we love each other like brothers."

"What's the message, Colin?"

"Congratulations, Peter baby, I am here to tell you that you have just won yourself a return ticket to the Big Apple." He placed one hand across his heart and sang with a surprisingly mellow baritone. "New York, New York, it's a wonderful town."

Peter sat staring impassively at Colin, but he was thinking swiftly. He knew he had to go. Somehow he was certain that something was surfacing through muddied waters, the parts were beginning to click together. This was the sort of thing he had hoped for when he put the word on the wind.

"When?"

"There is an air force jet at Croydon right now."

"Melissa-Jane?"

"I've got a driver downstairs to take her home."

"She's going to hate you."

"Story of my life," Colin sighed. "Only the dogs love me."

They played gin-rummy and drank teeth-blackening air force coffee all the way across the Atlantic. Colin Noble did most of the talking, around the stub of his cheroot. It was shop, Thor shop, training and personnel details, small anecdotes about men and things they both knew well—and he made no effort to question Peter about his job and Narmco, other than to remark that he would have Peter back in London for the series of Narmco meetings starting on the following Monday. It was a deliberate and not very subtle intimation of just how much Atlas knew about Peter and his new activities.

They landed at Kennedy a little after midnight, and there was an army driver to take them to a local Howard Johnson motel for six hours' sleep, that kind of deep black coma induced by jet-lag.

Peter still felt prickly-eyed and woollen-headed as he watched with a feeling of disbelief Colin devouring one of those amazing American breakfasts of waffles and maple syrup, sausage and bacon and eggs, sugar cakes and sticky buns, washed down with countless draughts of fruit juice and coffee. Then Colin lit his first cheroot and announced,

"Hell, now I know I'm home. Now I realize I've been slowly fading away with malnutrition for two years."

The same army driver was waiting for them at the front entrance of the motel. The Cadillac was an indication of their status in the military hierarchy. Peter looked out with detachment. Their drive caught the junction of Fifth and One Hundred and Eleventh Street, and ran south down the park past the Metropolitan Art Museum in the thickening rush-hour traffic, then slipped off and into the cavernous mouth of a parking garage beneath one of the monolithic structures that seemed to reach to the grey cold heavens.

The garage entrance was posted "Residents Only," but the doorman raised the electronically controlled grid and waved them through. Colin led Peter to the bank of elevators and they rode up with the stomach-dropping swoop while the lights above the elevator door recorded their ascent to the very top of the building.

There they stepped out into a reception area protected by orna-
mental but none the less functional screens.

A guard in military police uniform and wearing a side-arm sur-
veyed them through the grille and checked Colin's Atlas pass
against his register before allowing them through.

The apartment occupied the entire top level of the building, for
there were hanging gardens beyond the sliding glass panels and a
view across the sickening canyons of space to other tall structures farther down Island—the Pan Am Building and the twin
towers of the World Trade Center.

The decor was Oriental, stark interiors in which were displayed
works of art that Peter knew from his previous visit were of incalculable value—antique Japanese brush paintings on silk panels,
carvings in jade and ivory, a display of tiny netsuke—and in an
atrium through which they passed was a miniature forest of Bon-
sai trees in their shallow ceramic bowls, the frozen contortions of
their trunks and branches a sign of their great age.

Incongruously, the exquisite rooms were filled with the thunder
of Von Karajan leading the Berlin Philharmonic Orchestra
through the glories of the "Eroica."

Beyond the atrium was a plain door of white oak. Colin
pressed the buzzer beside the lintel and almost immediately the
door slid open.

Colin led into a long carpeted room, the ceiling of which was
covered with acoustic tiles. The room contained, besides the
crowded bookshelves and work-table, an enormous concert piano,
and down the facing wall an array of hi-fi turntables and loudspeakers that would have been more in place in a commercial
recording studio.

Kingston Parker stood beside the piano, a heroic figure, tall and
heavy in the shoulder, his great shaggy head hanging forward onto
his chest, his eyes closed and an expression of almost religious ec-
stacy glowing upon his face.

The music moved his powerful frame the way the storm wind
sways a giant of the forest. Peter and Colin stopped in the doorway, for it seemed an intrusion on such a private, such an intimate moment, but it was only a few seconds before he became
aware of them and lifted his head. He seemed to shake off the
spell of the music with the shudder that a spaniel uses to shake it-

self free of water when it reaches dry land, and he lifted the arm of the turntable from the spinning black disc.

The silence seemed to tingle after the crashing chords of sound.

"General Stride," Kingston Parker greeted him. "Or may I still call you Peter?"

"Mister Stride will do very nicely," said Peter, and Parker made an eloquent little gesture of regret, and without offering to shake hands indicated the comfortable leather couch across the room.

"At least you came," he said, and as Peter settled into the couch, he nodded.

"I have always had an insatiable curiosity."

"I was relying on that," Kingston Parker smiled. "Have you breakfasted?"

"We've had a snack," Colin cut in but Peter nodded.

"Coffee then," said Parker, and spoke quietly into the intercom set, before turning back to them.

"Where to begin?" Parker combed the thick greying hair back with both hands, leaving it even more tousled than it had been.

"Begin at the beginning," Peter suggested, "as the King of Hearts said to Alice."

"At the beginning." Parker smiled softly. "All right, at the beginning I opposed your involvement with Atlas."

"I know."

"I did not expect that you would accept the Thor command, it was a step backwards in your career. You surprised me there, and not for the first time."

A Chinese manservant in a white jacket with brass buttons carried in a tray. They were silent as he offered coffee and cream and coloured crystal sugar and then, when he had gone, Parker went on.

"At that time, my estimate of you, General Stride, was that although you had a record of brilliance and solid achievement, you were an officer of rigidly old-fashioned thought. The Colonel Blimp mentality more suited to trench warfare than to the exigencies of war from the shadows—the kind of wars that we are fighting now, and will be forced to fight in the future."

He shook the shaggy head and unconsciously his fingers caressed the smooth cool ivory keyboard, and he settled down on the stool before the piano.

"You see, General Stride, I saw the role of Atlas to be too limited by the original terms of reference placed upon it. I did not believe that Atlas could do what it was designed for if it was only an arm of retaliation, if it had to wait for a hostile act before it could react, if it had to rely entirely on other organizations—with all their internecine rivalries and bickerings—for its vital intelligence. I needed officers who were not only brilliant, but who were capable of unconventional thought and independent action. I did not believe you had those qualities, although I studied you very carefully. I was unable to take you fully into my confidence."

Parker's slim fingers evoked a fluent passage from the keyboard as though to punctuate his words, and for a moment he seemed completely enraptured by his own music. Then he lifted his head again.

"If I had done so, then the conduct of your rescue operation of Flight 070 might have been completely different. I have been forced radically to revise my estimate of you, General Stride—and it was a difficult thing to do. For by demonstrating those qualities which I thought you lacked, you upset my judgement. I admit that personal chagrin swayed my reasoned judgement—and by the time I was thinking straight again you had been provoked into offering your resignation—"

"I know that the resignation was referred to you personally, Doctor Parker—and that you recommended that it be accepted." Peter's voice was very cold, the tone clipped with controlled anger —and Parker nodded.

"Yes, you are correct. I endorsed your resignation."

"Then it looks as though we are wasting our time here and now." Peter's lips were compressed into a thin, unforgiving line, and the skin across his cheeks and over the finely chiselled flare of his nostrils seemed tightly drawn and pale as porcelain.

"Please, General Stride—let me explain first." Parker reached out one hand to him as though to physically restrain him from rising, and his expression was earnest, compelling. Peter sank back into the couch, his eyes wary and his lips still tight.

"I have to go back a little first, in order to make any sense at all." Parker stood up from the piano and crossed to the rack of pipes on the work table between the hi-fi equipment. He selected one carefully, a meerschaum mellowed to the colour of precious amber. He blew through the empty pipe and then tramped back across the thick carpet to stand in front of Peter.

"Some months before the hijacking of 070—six months to be precise, I had begun to receive hints that we were entering a new phase in the application of international terrorism. Only hints at first, but these were confirmed and followed by stronger evidence." Parker was stuffing the meerschaum from a leather wallet as he spoke. Now he zipped this closed and tossed it onto the piano top. "What we were looking at was a consolidation of the forces of violence under some sort of centralized control—we were not sure what form this control was taking." He broke off and studied Peter's expression, seemed to misinterpret it for utter disbelief, for he shook his head. "Yes, I know it sounds far-fetched, but I will show you the files. There was evidence of meetings between known militant leaders and some other shadowy figures, perhaps the representatives of an Eastern government. We were not sure then, nor are we now. And immediately after this there was a complete change in the conduct and apparent motivation of militant activity. I do not really have to detail this for you. First, the systematic accumulation of immense financial reserves by the highly organized and carefully planned abduction of prominent figures, starting with the ministers of OPEC, then leading industrialists and financial figures"—Parker struck a match and puffed on his pipe and perfumed smoke billowed around his head—"so that it appeared that the motivation had not really changed and was still entirely self gain or parochial political gain. Then there was the taking of 070. I had not confided in you before, and once you were on your way to Johannesburg it was too late. I could do nothing more than try to control your actions by rather heavy-handed commands. I could not explain to you that we suspected that this was the leading wave of the new militancy, and that we must allow it to reveal as much as possible. It was a terrible decision, but I had to gamble a few human lives for vital information —and then you acted as I had believed you were incapable of acting." Parker removed his pipe from his mouth and he smiled, when he smiled you could believe anything he said and forgive him for it, no matter how outrageous. "I admit, General Stride, that my first reaction was frustrated rage. I wanted your head, and your guts also. Then suddenly I began using my own head instead. You had just proved you were the man I wanted, my soldier capable of unconventional thought and action. If you were discredited and cast adrift, there was just a chance that this new direction of militancy would recognize the same qualities in you that I had been forced to recognize. If I allowed you to ruin your career, and become an outcast—an embittered man, but one with vital skills and invaluable knowledge, a man who had proved he could be ruthless when it was necessary—" Parker broke off and made that gesture of appeal. "I am sorry, General Stride, but I had to recognize the fact that you would be very attractive to"—he made an impatient gesture—"I do not have a name for them, shall we just call them 'the enemy.' I had to recognize the fact that you would be of very great interest to the enemy. I endorsed your resignation." He nodded sombrely. "Yes, I endorsed your resignation, and without your own knowledge you became an Atlas agent at large. It seemed perfect to me. You did not have to act a role— you believed it yourself. You were the outcast, the wronged and discredited man ripe for subversion."

"I don't believe it," Peter said flatly, and Parker went back to the work-table, selected an envelope from a Japanese ceramic tray and brought it back to Peter.

It took Peter a few moments to realize that it was a Bank Statement—Crédit Suisse in Geneva—the account was in his name, and there were a string of deposits. No withdrawals or debits. Each deposit was for exactly the same amount, the net salary of a Major-General in the British Army.

"You see"—Parker smiled—"you are still drawing your Atlas salary. You are still one of us, Peter. And all I can say is that I am very sorry indeed that we had to subject you to the pretence—but it seems it was all worthwhile."

Peter looked up at him again, not entirely convinced, but with the hostility less naked in his expression.

"What do you mean by that, Doctor Parker?"

"It seems that you are very much back in play again."

"I am Sales Director for Northern Armaments Company," he said flatly.

"Yes, of course, and Narmco is part of the Altmann Industrial Empire—and Baron Altmann and his lovely wife are, or rather were, an extraordinarily interesting couple. For instance, did you know that the Baron was one of the top agents of Mossad in Europe?"

"Impossible," Peter shook his head irritably. "He was a Roman

Catholic. Israeli intelligence does not make a habit of recruiting Catholics."

"Yes," Parker agreed. "His grandfather converted to Catholicism—and changed the name of the family home to La Pierre Bénite. It was a business decision, that we are certain of. There was not much profit in being Jewish in nineteenth-century France. However, the young Altmann was much influenced by his grandmother and his own mother. He was a Zionist from a very early age, and he unswervingly used his enormous wealth and influence in that cause—right up until the time of his murder. Yet he did it so cunningly, with such subtlety that very few people were aware of his connections with Judaism and Zionism. He never made the mistake of converting back to his ancestral religion, realizing that he could be more effective as a practising Christian."

Peter was thinking swiftly. If this was true, then it all had changed shape again. It must affect the reasons for the Baron's death—and it would change the role of Magda Altmann in his life.

"The Baroness?" he asked. "Was she aware of this?"

"Ah, the Baroness!" Kingston Parker removed his pipe from between his teeth, and smiled with reluctant admiration. "What a remarkable lady. We are not certain of very much about her—except her beauty and her exceptional talents. We know she was born in Warsaw. Her father was a professor of medicine at the university there, and he escaped to the West when the Baroness was still a child. He was killed a few years later, a traffic accident in Paris. Hit-and-run driver, while the professor was leaving his faculty in the Sorbonne. A small mystery still hangs around his death. The child seems to have drifted from family to family, friends of her father, distant relatives. She already was showing academic leanings, musical talent, at thirteen a chess player of promise. Then for a period there is no record of her. She seems to have disappeared entirely. The only hint is from one of her foster mothers, a very old lady now, with a fading memory. 'I think she went home for a while—she told me she was going home.'" Parker spread his hands. "We do not know what that means. Home? Warsaw? Israel? Somewhere in the East?"

"You have researched her very carefully," Peter said. What he had heard had left him uneasy.

"Of course, we have done so to every contact you have made

since leaving Atlas Command. We would have been negligent not to do so—but especially we have been interested in the Baroness. She has been the most fascinating—you understand that, I am sure."

Peter nodded, and waited. He did not want to ask for more. Somehow it seemed disloyal to Magda, distrustful and petty—but still he waited and Parker went on quietly.

"Then she was back in Paris. Nineteen years of age now—a highly competent private secretary, speaking five languages fluently, beautiful, always dressed in the height of fashion, soon with a string of wealthy, influential and powerful admirers—the last of these was her employer, Baron Aaron Altmann." Parker was silent then, waiting for the question, forcing Peter to come to meet him.

"Is she Mossad also?"

"We do not know. It is possible—but she has covered herself very carefully. We are rather hoping you will be able to find that out for us."

"I see."

"She must have known that her husband was a Zionist. She must have suspected that it had something to do with his abduction and murder. Then there are the missing six years of her life—from thirteen to nineteen, where was she?"

"Is she Jewish?" Peter asked. "Was her father Jewish?"

"We believe so, although the professor showed no interest in religion and did not fill in the question on his employment application to the Sorbonne. His daughter showed the same lack of religious commitment—we know only that her marriage to the Baron was a Catholic ceremony followed by a civil marriage in Rambouillet."

"We have drifted a long way from international terrorism," Peter pointed out.

"I do not think so." Kingston Parker shook his big shaggy head. "The Baron was a victim of it, and almost as soon as you—one of the world's leading experts on militancy and urban warfare—as soon as you are associated with her there is an assassination attempt, or an abduction attempt made on the Baroness."

Peter was not at all surprised that Parker knew of that night on the road to La Pierre Bénite—it was only a few days since Peter's arm had been out of the sling.

"Tell me, Peter. What was your estimate of that affair? I have seen an excerpt of the statement that you made to the French police—but what can you add to that?"

Peter had a vivid cameo memory of the Citroën that had followed him out of Paris, and then almost simultaneously the tearing sound of automatic fire in the night.

"They were after the Baroness," Peter said firmly.

"And you were driving her car?"

"That's right."

"You were at the place at the time that the Baroness usually passed?"

"Right."

"Who suggested that? You?"

"I told her that the car was too conspicuous."

"So you suggested taking it down to La Pierre Bénite that night."

"Yes." Peter lied without knowing why he did so.

"Did anybody else know that the Baroness would not be driving?"

"Nobody." Except her bodyguards, the two chauffeurs who had met them on their return from Switzerland, Peter thought.

"You are certain?" Parker persisted.

"Yes," Peter snapped. "Nobody else." Except Magda, only Magda. He pushed the thought aside angrily.

"All right, so we must accept that the Baroness was the target—but was it an assassination or an abduction attempt? That could be significant. If it was assassination, it would indicate that it was the elimination of a rival agent, that the Baroness was probably also a Mossad agent, recruited by her husband. On the other hand, an abduction would suggest that the object was monetary gain. Which was it, Peter?"

"They had blocked the road," he said, but not completely, he remembered. "And the police impersonator signalled me to stop" —or at least to slow down, he thought, slow down sufficiently to make an easy target before they started shooting—"and they did not open fire until I made it clear that I was not going to stop." But they had been ready to begin shooting at the instant Peter made the decision to send the Maserati through the roadblock. The intention of the two machine-gunners had seemed evident. "I would say the object was to seize the Baroness alive."

"All right," Parker nodded. "We will have to accept that for the time being." He glanced at Colin. "Colonel Noble? You had a question?"

"Thank you, Doctor. We haven't heard from Peter in what terms he was approached by Narmco or the Baroness. Who made the first contact?"

"I was approached by a London firm who specializes in making top executive placements. They came directly from the Narmco Board." And I turned them down flat, he thought. It was only later at Abbots Yew—

"I see." Colin frowned with disappointment. "There was no question of a meeting with the Baroness?"

"Not at that stage."

"You were offered the sales appointment—no mention of any other duties, security, industrial intelligence—"

"No, not then."

"Later?"

"Yes. When I met the Baroness, I realized her personal security arrangements were inadequate. I made changes."

"You never discussed her husband's murder?"

"Yes, we did."

"And?"

"And nothing." Peter was finding it difficult to improvise answers, but he used the old rule of telling as much of the truth as possible.

"There was no mention by the Baroness of a hunt for her husband's murderers? You were not asked to use your special talents to lead a vendetta?"

Peter had to make a swift decision. Parker would know of his leak to the British military attaché in Paris—the bait he had so carefully placed to attract Caliph. Of course Parker would know: he was head of Atlas with access to the Central Intelligence computer. Peter could not afford to deny it.

"Yes, she asked me to relay any information which might point to her husband's murderers. I asked G.2 in Paris for any information he might have. He couldn't help me."

Parker grunted. "Yes. I have a note that G.2 filed a routine report—but I suppose her request was natural enough." He wandered back to his work-table to glance at a pad on which was scribbled some sort of personal shorthand.

"We know of eight sexual liaisons that the Baroness formed prior to her marriage, all with politically powerful or wealthy men. Six of them married men."

Peter found himself trembling with anger so intense that it surprised him. He hated Parker for talking like this of Magda. With a huge effort he kept his expression neutral, the hand in his lap was relaxed and the fingers spread naturally, though he felt a driving desire to bunch it and drive it into Parker's face.

"All these affairs were conducted with utmost discretion. Then during her marriage there is no evidence of any extra-marital activity. Since the Baron's murder there have been three others, a minister in the French Government, an American businessman—head of the world's second largest oil company." He dropped the pad back on the desk and swung back to face Peter. "And recently there has been one other." He stared at Peter with a bright penetrating gaze. "The lady certainly believes in mixing business with pleasure. All her partners have been men who are able to deliver very concrete proof of their affections. I think this rule probably applies to her latest choice of sexual partner."

Colin coughed awkwardly, and shifted in his chair, but Peter did not even glance at him; he went on staring impassively at Kingston Parker. He and Magda had made very little secret of their relationship. Still it was bitterly distasteful to have to discuss it with anybody else.

"I think that you are in a position now to gather vital intelligence. I think that you are very near the centre of this nameless and formless influence—I think that you will be able to make some sort of contact with the enemy, even if it is only another military brush with them. The only question is whether or not you find any reason, emotional or otherwise, that might prevent you fulfilling this duty?" Kingston Parker cocked his head on one side, making the statement into a question.

"I have never let my private life interfere with my duty, Doctor," Peter said quietly.

"No," Kingston Parker agreed. "That is true. And I am sure that now you know a little more about Baroness Altmann you will appreciate just how vital is our interest in that lady."

"Yes, I do." Peter had his anger under control completely. "You want me to use a privileged relationship to spy on her. Is that correct?"

"Just so that we can be sure she is using the same relationship to her own ends—" Parker broke off as an odd thought seemed to occur. "I do hope I have not been too blunt, Peter. I haven't destroyed some cherished illusion." Now Parker's attitude was dismissive. The interview was over.

"At my age, Doctor, a man has no more illusions." Peter rose to his feet. "Do I report to you direct?"

"Colonel Noble will make the arrangements for all communications." Kingston Parker held out his hand. "I would not have asked this of you if I had a choice."

Peter did not hesitate, but took the hand. Parker's hand was cool and dry. Although he made no show of it, Peter could sense the physical power in those hard pianist's fingers.

"I understand, sir," said Peter—and he thought grimly, and even if that is also a lie, I'm going to understand pretty damned soon.

Peter made the excuse of tiredness to avoid the gin-rummy game, and pretended to sleep during most of the long trans-Atlantic flight. With his eyes closed he tried to marshal his thoughts into some sort of pattern, but always they seemed to come around full circle and leave him chasing his tail. He could not even achieve any certainty about his feelings and loyalties to Magda Altmann. They seemed to keep changing shape every time he examined them, and he found himself brooding on irrelevancies. "Sexual liaisons"—what a ridiculously stilted expression Parker had used, and why had it angered Peter so much? Eight liaisons before marriage, six with married men, two others since marriage—all wealthy or powerful. He found himself trying to flesh out these bare statistics, and with a shock of bitter resentment imagined those faceless, formless figures with the slim smooth body, the tiny, perfectly shaped breasts, and the long smoky fall of shimmering hair. He felt somehow betrayed, and immediately scorned himself for this adolescent reaction.

There were other more dire questions and chances that Kingston Parker had raised: the Mossad connection, the six missing years in Magda's life—and yet he came back again to what had happened between them. Was she capable of such skilful deception, or was it not deception? Was he merely suffering from hurt pride now, or somehow unbeknownst to him had she been able to force him into a more vulnerable position? Had she succeeded in making him fall in love with her?

How did he feel about her? At last he had to face that question directly and try to answer it, but when they landed again he still had no answer, except that the prospect of seeing her again pleased him inordinately and the thought that she had deliberately used him to her own ends and was capable of discarding him as she had done those others left him with an aching sense of dismay. He dreaded the answer for which he had to search, and suddenly he remembered her suggestion of an island to which they could escape together. He realized then that she was a victim of the same dread, and with a clairvoyant shudder he wondered if they were somehow preordained to destroy each other.

There were three separate messages from her at the Dorchester. She had left the Rambouillet number, each time. He telephoned immediately he reached the suite.

"Oh Peter. I was so worried. Where were you?" And it was hard to believe her concern was faked, and it was even harder to discount the pleasure when, the following noon, she met him at Charles de Gaulle Airport herself instead of sending a chauffeur.

"I needed to get out of the office for an hour," she explained, and then she tucked her hand into the crook of his elbow and pressed herself against him. "That's a lie, of course. I came because I couldn't wait the extra hour to see you." Then she chuckled huskily. "I am behaving shamelessly. I can't imagine what you must think of me!"

They were with a party of eight that evening, dinner at Le Doyen and then the theatre at the Palais de Chaillot. Peter's French was still not up to Moliére, so he took his pleasure in surreptitiously watching Magda, and for a few hours he succeeded in suppressing all those ugly questions. Only on the midnight drive back to La Pierre Bénite did he begin the next move in the complicated game.

"I couldn't tell you on the telephone," he said in the intimate darkness and warmth of her limousine. "I had an approach from Atlas. The head of Atlas summoned me to New York. That's where I was when you called. They are also onto Caliph."

She sighed then, and her hand stole into his. "I was waiting for you to tell me, Peter," she said simply, and she sighed again. "I knew you'd gone to America, and I had a terrible premonition that you were going to lie to me. I don't know what I would have done then." And Peter felt a lance of conscience driven up under his ribs, and with it the throb of concern—she had known of his journey to New York, but how? Then he remembered her "sources."

"Tell me," she said, and he told her—everything, except the nagging question marks which Kingston Parker had placed after her name. The missing years, the Mossad connection with the Baron, and those ten nameless men.

"They don't seem to know that Caliph uses that name," Peter told her. "But they seem to be pretty certain that you are hunting him, and that you've hired me for that purpose."

They discussed it quietly as the small cavalcade of cars rushed through the night, and later, when she came to his suite, they went on talking, holding each other as they whispered in the night, and Peter was surprised that he could act so naturally, that the doubts seemed to evaporate so easily when he was with her.

"Kingston Parker still has me as a member of Atlas," Peter explained. "And I did not deny it or protest. We want to find Caliph, and if I still have status with Atlas it will be useful, of that I am certain."

"I agree. Atlas can help us—especially now that they are also aware that Caliph exists."

They made love in the dawn, very deeply satisfying love that left bodies and minds replete, and then keeping her discretion she slipped away before it was light, but they met again an hour later for breakfast together in the Garden Room.

She poured coffee for him, and indicated the small parcel beside his plate.

"We aren't quite as discreet as we think we are, chéri." She chuckled. "Somebody seems to know where you are spending your evenings."

He weighed the parcel in his right palm; it was the size of a roll of 35-mm film, wrapped in brown paper, sealed with red wax.

"Apparently it came special delivery yesterday evening." She broke one of the crisp croissants into her plate, and smiled at him with that special slant of her green eyes.

The address was typed on a stick-on label, and the stamps were British, franked in south London the previous morning.

Suddenly Peter was assailed with a terrifying sense of foreboding; the presence of some immense overpowering evil seemed to pervade the gaily furnished room.

"What is it, Peter?" Her voice cracked with alarm.

"Nothing," he said. "It's nothing."

"You suddenly went deadly pale, Peter. Are you sure you are all right?"

"Yes. I'm all right."

He used his table knife to lift the wax seal and then unrolled the brown paper.

It was a small screw-topped bottle of clear glass, and the liquid it contained was clear also. Some sort of preservative, he realized immediately, spirits or formaldehyde.

Hanging suspended in the liquid was a soft white object.

"What is it?" Magda asked.

Peter felt cold tentacles of nausea closing around his stomach.

The object turned slowly, floating free in its bottle, and there was a flash of vivid scarlet.

"Does your mother allow you to wear nail varnish now, Melissa-Jane?" He heard the question echoed in his memory, and saw his daughter flirt her hands, and the scarlet flash of her nails. The same vivid scarlet.

"Oh yes—though not to school, of course. You keep forgetting I'm almost fourteen, Daddy."

The floating white object was a human finger. It had been severed at the first joint, and the preservative had bleached the exposed flesh a sickly white. The skin had puckered and wrinkled like that of a drowned man. Only the painted finger nail was unaltered, pretty and festively gay.

The nausea caught Peter's throat, choking him and he heaved and retched drily as he stared at the tiny bottle.

The telephone rang three times before it was answered.

"Cynthia Barrow." Peter recognized his ex-wife's voice, even though it was ragged with strain and grief.

"Cynthia, it's Peter."

"Oh, thank God, Peter. I have been trying to find you for two days."

"What is it?"

"Is Melissa-Jane with you, Peter?"

"No." He felt as though the earth had lurched under his feet.

"She's gone, Peter. She's been gone for two nights now. I'm going out of my mind."

"Have you informed the police?"

"Yes, of course." The edge of hysteria was in her voice.

"Stay where you are," Peter said. "I'm coming to England right now, but leave any message for me at the Dorchester." He hung up quickly, sensing that her grief would overflow at any moment and knowing that he could not handle it now.

Across the ormolu Louis Quatorze desk Magda was pale, tense, and she did not have to ask the question, it was in the eyes that seemed too large for her face.

He did not have to reply to that question. He nodded once, an abrupt jerky motion, and then he dialled again and while he waited he could not take his eyes from the macabre trophy that stood in its bottle in the centre of the desk.

"Colonel Noble." Peter snapped into the mouthpiece. "Tell him it's General Stride and it's urgent."

Colin came on within the minute. "Peter, is that you?"

"They've taken Melissa-Jane."

"Who? I don't understand."

"The enemy. They've taken her."

"Jesus God! Are you sure?"

"Yes, I'm sure. They sent me her finger in a bottle."

Colin was silent for a few seconds, and then his voice was subdued. "That's sick, Christ that's really sick."

"Get onto the police. Use all your clout. They must be keeping quiet on it. There has been no publicity. I want to be in on the hunt for these animals. Get Thor involved, find out what you can. I'm on my way now. I'll let you know what flight I am on."

"I'll keep a listening watch at this number round the clock," Colin promised. "And I'll have a driver meet you." Colin hesitated. "Peter, I'm sorry. You know that."

"Yes. I know."

"We will all be with you, all the way."

Peter dropped the receiver onto its arm, and across the desk Magda stood up resolutely.

"I'll come with you to London," she said, and Peter reached out and took her hand.

"No," he said gently. "Thank you, but no. There will be nothing for you to do."

"Peter, I want to be with you through this terrible thing. I feel as though it's all my fault."

"That's not true."

"She's such a lovely child."

"You will be more help to me here," said Peter firmly. "Try through all your sources, any little scrap of information."

"Yes, very well." She accepted the decision, without further argument. "Where can I find you if I have anything?"

He gave her Colin Noble's private number at Thor, scribbling it on the pad beside the telephone. "Either there or the Dorchester," he said.

"At least I will come with you as far as Paris," she said.

The news had broken by the time Peter landed at Heathrow Airport. It was on the front page of the *Evening Standard* and Peter snatched a copy off the news stand and read it avidly during the drive up to London.

> The victim was abducted at the front gate of her home in Leaden Street, Cambridge, at eleven o'clock on Thursday. A neighbour saw her speak to the occupants of a maroon Triumph saloon car, and then enter the back door of the vehicle, which drove off immediately.
>
> "I thought there were two people in the car," Mrs. Shirley Callon, 32, the neighbour, told our correspondent, "and Melissa-Jane did not seem alarmed. She appeared to enter the Triumph quite willingly. I know that her father, who is a senior officer in the army, often sends different cars to fetch her or bring her home. So I thought nothing about it."
>
> The alarm was not raised for nearly twenty-four hours, as the missing girl's mother also believed that she might be with her ex-husband.
>
> Only when she was unable to contact Major-General Stride, the girl's father, did she inform the police. The Cambridge police found a maroon Triumph abandoned in the car park at Cambridge railway station. The vehicle had been stolen in London the previous day, and

immediately a nation-wide alert was put in
force for the missing girl.

Chief-Inspector Alan Richards is the police
officer in charge of the investigation and any
person who may be able to provide information should telephone—

There followed a London number and a detailed description of
Melissa-Jane and the clothes she was wearing at the time she
disappeared.

Peter crumpled the newspaper and dropped it on the seat. He
sat staring ahead, cupping his anger to him like a flame, husband-
ing it carefully—because the heat was infinitely more bearable
than the icy despair which waited to engulf him.

Inspector Alan Richards was a wiry little man, more like a jockey
than a policeman. He had a prematurely wizened face, and he had
combed long wisps of hair across his balding pate to disguise it.
Yet his eyes were quick and intelligent, and his manner direct and
decisive.

He shook hands when Colin Noble introduced them. "I must
make it very clear that this is a police matter, General. However,
in these very special circumstances I am prepared to work very
closely with the military."

Swiftly Richards went over the ground he had already covered.
He had mounted the investigation from the two offices set aside
for him on the third floor of Scotland Yard, with a view over
chimney pots of the spires of Westminster Abbey and the Houses
of Parliament.

Richards had two young policewomen answering the telephone
calls coming in through the number they had advertised in the
press and on television. So far they had accepted over four hundred of these. "They range from long shots to the completely
crazy, but we have to investigate all of them." For the first time
his expression softened. "It's going to be a long, slow process,
General Stride, but we have a few more leads to follow—Come
through."

The inner office was furnished in the same nondescript Public
Works Department furniture, solid and characterless, but there
was a kettle boiling on the gas ring, and Richards poured the tea
as he went on.

"Three of my men are taking the kidnap car to pieces. We are sure it is the right car. Your ex-wife has identified a purse found on the floor of the vehicle. It is your daughter's. We have lifted over six hundred finger prints, and these are being processed. It will take some time until we can isolate each and hope for an identification of any alien prints. However, two of these correspond to prints lifted from your daughter's room. Sugar? Milk?"

Richards brought the cup to Peter as he went on.

"The neighbour, Mrs. Callon, who saw the pick-up, is working on an identikit portrait of the driver, but she did not get a very good view of him. That is a very long shot."

Richards sipped his tea. "However, we will show the final picture on television and hope for another lead from it. I am afraid that in cases like this, this is all we can do. Wait for a tip, and wait for the contact from the kidnappers. We do not expect the contact will be made through your ex-wife, but of course we have a tap on her telephone and men watching over her." Richards spread his hands. "That's it, General Stride. Now it's your turn. What can you tell us? Why should anybody want to snatch your daughter?"

Peter exchanged a glance with Colin Noble, and was silent as he collected his thoughts, but Inspector Richards insisted quietly.

"I understand you are not a very wealthy man, General—but your family. Your brother?"

Peter dismissed the idea with a shake of his head. "My brother has children of his own. They would be the more logical targets."

"Vengeance? You were very active against the Provos in Ireland. You commanded the recapture of Flight 070."

"It's possible."

"You are no longer connected with the Army, I understand."

Peter was not going to be drawn further in that direction. "I do not think this type of guesswork will profit us much. We will know the motive as soon as the kidnappers make their demands known."

"That is true." Richards rattled his teacup, a little nervous gesture. "They could not have sent you her—" He broke off as he saw Peter's expression change. "I'm sorry, General. It is horrible and terribly distressing, but we have to accept the finger as proof that your daughter is still alive and that the contact, when it comes, will be made to you. It was an expression of their earnest intention, and a threat—but—"

The telephone on his desk rang shrilly and Richards snatched it up.

"Richards!" he snapped, and then listened at length, occasionally grunting encouragement to the caller. When he hung up the receiver he did not speak immediately, but offered Peter a rumpled pack of cigarettes. When Peter refused, the policeman lit one himself and his voice was diffident.

"That was the laboratory. You know your daughter was a white-cell donor, don't you?"

Peter nodded. It was part of Melissa-Jane's social commitment. If she had not been tactfully dissuaded, she would have donated her blood and marrow by the bucketful.

"We were able to get a tissue typing from the Cambridge hospital. The amputated finger matches your daughter's tissue type. I'm afraid we must accept that it is hers. I cannot imagine that the kidnappers would have gone to the lengths of finding a substitute of the same type."

Peter had been secretly cherishing the belief that it was a bluff. That he had been sent the fingertip from a corpse, from a medical sample, from the casualty ward of a city hospital—and now as that hope died he was assailed by the cold spirit-sapping waves of despair. They sat in silence for fully a minute, and now it was Colin Noble who broke it.

"Inspector, you are aware of the nature of the Thor Command?"

"Yes, of course. There was a great deal of publicity at the time of the Johannesburg hijacking. It is an anti-terrorist unit."

"We are probably the most highly trained specialists in the world at removing hostages safely from the hands of militants—"

"I understand what you are trying to tell me, Colonel," Richards murmured drily. "But let us track down our militants first, and then any rescue attempts will be entirely under the control of the Commissioner of Police."

It was after three o'clock in the morning when Peter Stride checked in with the night receptionist at the Dorchester Hotel in Park Lane.

"We have been holding your suite since midday, General."

"I'm sorry." Peter found himself slurring his words, exhaustion and nervous strain, he realized. He had only left Police Headquarters when he could convince himself that everything possible was being done, and that he could place complete trust in Chief-Inspector Richards and his team. He had Richards' solemn promise that he would be informed, no matter at what time of day or night, as soon as there was any new development.

Now he signed the register, blinking at the gritty swollen feeling of his eyelids.

"There are these messages for you, General."

"Thank you again, and goodnight."

In the elevator he glanced at the mail the clerk had given him. The first was a telephone slip.

"Baroness Altmann asks you to return her call to either Paris or Rambouillet number."

The second was another telephone slip.

"Mrs. Cynthia Barrow called. Please call her at Cambridge 699-313."

The third was a sealed envelope, good-quality white paper, undistinguished by crest or monogram.

His name had been printed in capitals, very regular lettering, an old-fashioned copper-plate script. No stamp, so it would have been delivered by hand.

Peter split the flap with his thumb, and withdrew a single sheet of lined writing paper, again good but undistinguished. There would be a stack of these sheets in any stationery department throughout the United Kingdom.

The writing was the same regular, unnatural script, so that Peter realized that the writer had used a stencil to form each letter, one of those clear plastic cut-out stencils obtainable from any toy store or stationery department. A completely effective method of disguising handwriting.

> A finger you have already, next you will have the hand, then another hand, then a foot, then another foot—and at last the head.
>
> The next package will arrive on April 20th, and there will be another delivery every seven days.
>
> To prevent this you must deliver a life for a life. The day Dr. Kingston Parker dies, your daughter will return to you immediately, alive and suffering no further harm.
>
> Destroy this letter and tell nobody, or the head will be delivered immediately.

The letter was signed with the name which had come to loom so large in Peter's life:

CALIPH

The shock of it seemed to reach to the extremities of his soul. To see the name written. To have complete confirmation of all the evil that they had suspected, to see the mark of the beast deeply printed and unmistakable.

The shock was made greater, almost unbearable, by the contents of the letter. Peter found that such cruelty, such utter ruthlessness, tested his credibility to its limits.

The letter was fluttering in his hands, and he realized with a start of surprise that he was shaking like a man in high fever. The porter carrying his black crocodile valise was staring at him curiously, and it required a huge physical effort to control his hands and fold the sheet of white paper.

He stood rigidly, as though on the parade ground, until the elevator door opened and then he marched stiffly down the passage to his suite. He gave the porter a banknote, without glancing at it, and the moment the latch clicked closed, he unfolded the sheet again, and standing in the centre of the living-room floor scanned the stilted script again, and then again until the words seemed to melt together and lose coherence and meaning.

He realized that for the first time in his life he was in complete panic, that he had lost all resolution and direction.

He took a deep breath and closed his eyes, counting slowly to one hundred, emptying his mind completely, and then giving himself the command:

"Think!"

All right, Caliph knew his movements intimately. Even to when he was expected at the Dorchester. Who knew that? Cynthia, Colin Noble, Magda Altmann and the secretary at Rambouillet who had made the reservation, Colin's secretary at Thor, the Dorchester staff, and anybody else who had made even an idle study of Peter's movements would know he always stayed at the Dorchester. That was a cul-de-sac.

"Think!"

Today was April fourth. There were sixteen days before Caliph sent him Melissa-Jane's severed hand. He felt the panic mounting again, and he forced it back.

"Think!"

Caliph had been watching him, studying him in detail, assessing his value. Peter's value was that he could move unsuspected in high places. He could reach the head of Atlas by simply requesting an audience. More than that, he could probably get access to any head of state if he wanted it badly enough.

For the first time in his life Peter felt the need for liquor. He crossed quickly to the cabinet and fumbled with the key. A stranger's face stared at him out of the gilt-framed mirror above it. The face was pale, haggard, with deep parentheses framing the mouth. There were plum-coloured bruises of fatigue below the eyes, and the gaunt, bony jaw was gun-metal blue with new beard —and the sapphire blue of the eyes had a wild deranged glitter. He looked away from his own image. It only increased his sense of unreality.

He poured half a tumbler of Scotch whisky, and drank half of it straight off. He coughed at the sting of the liquor and a drop of it broke from the corner of his mouth and trickled down his chin. He wiped it away with his thumb, and turned back to study the sheet of white paper again. It was crumpled already, where he had gripped it too hard. He smoothed it carefully.

"Think!" he told himself. This was how Caliph worked, then. Never exposing himself. Picking his agents with incredible attention to detail. Fanatics, like the girl, Ingrid, who had led the taking of Flight 070. Trained assassins, like the man he had killed in the river at La Pierre Bénite. Experts in high places, like General Peter Stride. Studying them, assessing them and their capabilities, and finally finding the pricing formula.

Peter had never believed the old law that every man has his price. He had believed himself above that general rule. Now he knew he was not—and the knowledge sickened him.

Caliph had found his price, found it unerringly. Melissa-Jane. Suddenly Peter had a vivid memory of his daughter on horseback, swivelling in the saddle to laugh and call back to him.

"Super-Star!" And the sound of her laughter on the wind.

Peter shivered, and without realizing it he crumpled the sheet of paper to a ball in his fist.

Ahead of him he saw the road that he was destined to follow. With a new flash of insight, he realized that he had already taken his first steps along the road. He had done so when he had put the gun to the blonde killer in the terminal of Johannesburg Airport, when he had made himself judge and executioner.

Caliph had been responsible for that first step on the road to corruption, and now it was Caliph who was driving him farther along it.

With a sudden prophetic glimpse ahead, Peter knew it would not end with the life of Kingston Parker. Once he was committed to Caliph, it would be for ever—or until one of them, Peter Stride, or the person called Caliph, was completely destroyed.

Peter drank the rest of the whisky in the tumbler.

Yes, Melissa-Jane was his price. Caliph had made the correct bid. Nothing else would have driven him to it.

Peter picked the booklet of matches off the liquor cabinet and like a sleep-walker moved through to the bathroom. He twisted the sheet of paper into a taper and lit the end of it, holding it over the toilet bowl. He held it until the flame scorched his fingers painfully, then dropped it into the bowl and flushed the ash away.

He went back into the lounge, and refilled the glass with whisky. He picked the comfortable armchair below the window and sank into it. Only then did he realize how very weary he was. The nerves in his thighs quivered and twitched uncontrollably.

He thought about Kingston Parker. A man like that had an incalculable amount to offer mankind. It will have to look like an assassination attempt aimed at me, Peter thought. One that finds the wrong victim.

"A bomb," Peter thought. He hated the bomb. Somehow it seemed to be the symbol of the senseless violence which he hated. He had seen it used in Ireland and in London, and he hated it. The undirected destruction, mindless, merciless.

"It will have to be a bomb," he decided, and with surprise he found that his hatred had found a new target. Again for the first time ever, he hated himself for what he was going to do.

Caliph had won. He knew that against an adversary of that calibre there was no chance they would find where Melissa-Jane was hidden. Caliph had won, and Peter Stride sat the rest of the night planning an act which he had dedicated his life, until then, to prevent.

"I cannot understand why we haven't had the demand contact yet." Inspector Richards ran his hand distractedly across his pate, disturbing the feathery wisps that covered it and leaving them standing out at a startled angle. "It's five days now. Still no demands."

"They know where to contact Peter," Colin Noble agreed. "The interview he gave covered that."

Peter Stride had appeared on BBC TV to broadcast an appeal to the kidnappers not to maim his daughter further, and to the general public to offer any information that might lead to her rescue.

On the same programme they had displayed the police identikit portrait of the driver of the maroon Triumph prepared by the one witness.

The response had been overwhelming, jamming the switchboard at Inspector Richards's special headquarters, and a mixed bag had fallen into the net.

A fourteen-year-old runaway had the police barge into the Bournemouth apartment where she was in bed with her thirty-two-year-old lover. She was returned weeping bitterly to the bosom of her family, and had again disappeared within twenty-four hours.

In North Scotland the police sadly bungled a raid on a remote cottage hired by a man with the same lank dark hair and gunfighter's moustache as the identikit portrait. He turned out to be a cottage-industry manufacturer of LSD tablets, and he and his four assistants, one of them a young girl who vaguely fitted the description of Melissa-Jane in that she was female and blonde, had scattered across the Highlands before being overtaken and borne to earth by sweating pounding members of the Scottish Constabulary.

Peter Stride was furious. "If it had been Melissa-Jane, they would have had fifteen minutes in which to put her down," he raged at Richards. "You've got to let Thor go in on the next raid."

Through the Thor communications net he spoke directly to Kingston Parker on the video screens.

"We'll put all our influence into it," Parker agreed, and then with deep compassion in his eyes, "Peter, I'm living every minute of this with you. I cannot escape the knowledge that I have placed you in this terrible situation. I did not expect the attack would come through your daughter. I think you know that you can call on me for any support you need."

"Thank you, sir," said Peter and for a moment felt his resolve weaken. In ten days he would have to execute this man. He steeled himself by thinking of a puckered dead-white finger floating in its tiny bottle.

Kingston Parker's influence worked immediately. Six hours later the order came down from Downing Street via the Commissioner of Police, that the next raid on a suspect hideout would be conducted by Thor Command.

The Royal Air Force placed two helicopters at Thor's disposal for the duration of the operation, and Thor's assault unit went into intensive training for penetration and removal under urban conditions. Peter trained with them, he and Colin swiftly re-establishing the old rapport of concerted action.

When they were not practising and refining the exit and assembly from the hovering helicopters, Peter spent much of his time in the enclosed pistol range, trying to drown his awareness in the crash of gunfire, but the days passed swiftly in a series of false alarms and misleading clues.

Each night when Peter examined his face in the mirror above the liquor cabinet, it was more haggard, the blue eyes muddied by fatigue and terrible gut-eroding terror of what the next day might bring forth.

There were six days left when Peter left the hotel room before breakfast, caught the tube at Green Park and left it again at Finsbury Park. In a garden supplies shop near the station he purchased a twenty-pound plastic bag of ammonium nitrate garden fertilizer. He carried it back to the Dorchester in a locked Samsonite suitcase and stored it in the closet behind his hanging trenchcoat.

That night, when he spoke to Magda Altmann, she pleaded once again to be allowed to come to London.

"Peter, I know I can be of help to you. Even if it's just to stand beside you and hold your hand."

"No. We've been over that." He could hear the brutal tone in his own voice, but could not control it. He knew that he was getting very close to the edge. "Have you heard anything?"

"I'm sorry, Peter. Nothing, absolutely nothing. My sources are doing all that is possible."

Peter bought the dieseline from a pump at the Lex Garage in Brewer Street. He took five litres in a plastic screw-topped container that had contained a household detergent. The pump attendant was a pimply teenager in dirty overalls. He was completely uninterested in the transaction.

In his bathroom Peter worked on the dieseline and the nitrate from the garden shop. He produced twenty-one pounds of savagely weight-efficient high explosive that was, none the less, docile until activated by a blasting cap—such as he had devised with a flashlight bulb.

It would completely devastate the entire suite, utterly destroying everybody and everything in it. However, the damage should be confined to those three rooms.

It would be a simple matter to lure Kingston Parker to the suite under the pretence of having urgent information about Caliph to deliver, information so critical it could only be delivered in person and in private.

That night the face in the mirror above the liquor cabinet was that of a man suffering from a devouring terminal disease, and the whisky bottle was empty. Peter broke the seal on a fresh bottle, it would make it easier to sleep, he told himself.

The wind came off the Irish Sea like the blade of a harvester's scythe, and the low lead-coloured cloud fled up the slopes of the Wicklow hills ahead of it.

There were weak patches in the cloud layer through which a cold and sickly sun beamed swiftly across the green forested slopes. As it passed so the rain followed—icy grey rain slanting in on the wind.

A man came up the deserted street of the village. The tourists had not yet begun the annual invasion, but the "Bed and Breakfast" signs were already out to welcome them on the fronts of the cottages.

The man passed the pub, in its coat of shocking salmon pink paint—and lifted his head to read the bill-board above the empty car park. "Black is Beautiful—drink Guinness" it proclaimed, and the man did not smile but lowered his head and trudged on over the bridge that divided the village in two.

On the stone balustrades of the bridge a midnight artist had used an aerosol paint can to spray political slogans in day-glo colours.

"BRITS OUT" on the left-hand balustrade and "STOP H

BLOCK TORTURE" on the other. This time the man grimaced sourly.

Below him the steely water boiled about the stone piers before hissing on down toward the sea.

The man wore a cyclist's plastic cape and a narrow-brimmed tweed cap pulled down over his eyes. The wind dashed at him, flogging the skirts of the cape against his Wellington boots.

He seemed to cringe to the wind, hunching down against its cold fury, as he trudged on past the few buildings of the village. The street was deserted, though the man knew that he was being watched from curtained windows.

This village on the lower slopes of the Wicklow hills, a mere thirty miles from Dublin, would not have been his choice. Here isolation worked against them, making them conspicuous. He would have preferred the anonymity of the city. However, his preferences had never been asked for.

This was only the third time he had left the house since they had arrived. Each time it had been for some emergency provision, something that a little more forethought might have prevented, which should have been included when the old house was stocked for their stay. That came from having to rely on a drinking man, but here again he had not been consulted.

He was discontented and in a truculent, smouldering mood. It had rained most of the time, and the oil-fired central heating was not working, the only heating was the smoking peat fires in the small fireplaces in each of the two big rooms they were using. The high ceilings and sparse furnishings had made the rooms more difficult to warm—and he had been cold ever since they had arrived. They were using only the two rooms, and had left the rest of the house locked and shuttered. It was a gloomy building, with the smell of damp pervading it. He had only the company of a whining alcoholic, day after cold rainy day. The man was ripe and over-ripe for trouble, for any diversion to break the grinding monotony—but now he was reduced to errand boy and house servant, roles for which he was unsuited by temperament and training, and he scowled darkly as he trudged over the bridge towards the village store, with its row of petrol pumps standing before it like sentries.

The storekeeper saw him coming, and called through into the back of the shop.

"It's himself from down at the Old Manse."

His wife came through, wiping her hands on her apron, a short plump woman with bright eyes and ready tongue.

"City people have no more sense than they need, out in this weather."

"Sure and it's not baked beans nor Jamieson whisky he's after buying."

Speculation about the new occupant of the Old Manse had swiftly become one of the village's main diversions, with regular bulletins broadcast by the girl on the local telephone exchange—two overseas telephone calls, by the postman—no mail deliveries, by the dustman—the disposals into the dustbins were made up mainly of empty Heinz baked beans cans and Jamieson whisky bottles.

"I still think he's from the trouble up north," said the shop-keeper's wife. "He's got the look and the sound of an Ulster man."

"Hush, woman." Her husband cautioned her. "You'll bring bad luck upon us. Get yourself back into the kitchen now."

The man came in out of the rain and swept the tweed cap off his head, beating the water from it against the jamb of the door. He had black straight hair, cut into a ragged fringe above the dark Irish visage and fierce eyes, like those of a falcon when first the leather hood is slipped.

"The top of the morning to you, Mr. Barry," the shopkeeper greeted him heartily. "Like as not it will stop raining, before it clears."

The man grunted, and as he slipped the waterproof cape from his shoulders, swept the cluttered interior of the little general deal-er's store with a quick, all-embracing glance.

He wore a rough tweed jacket over a cable-stitched jersey and brown corduroys tucked into the top of the Wellington boots.

"You finished writing on your book, have you?" Barry had told the milkman that he was writing a book about Ireland. The Wick-low hills were a stronghold of the literary profession; there were a dozen prominent or eccentric writers living within twenty miles, taking advantage of Ireland's tax concessions to writers and artists.

"Not yet," Barry grunted, and went across to the shelves nearest the till. He made a selection of half a dozen items and laid them on the worn counter top.

"When it's good and wrote I'm going to ask the library to keep a copy for me," the shopkeeper promised, as though that was exactly what a writer would want to hear, and began to ring up the purchases on his register.

Barry's upper lip was still unnaturally smoother and paler than the rest of his face. He had shaved away the dark droopy moustache the day before arriving in the village, and at the same time had cut the fringe of hair that hung almost to his eyes.

The shopkeeper picked up one of the purchases and looked inquiringly at Barry, but when the dark Irish face remained impassive and he volunteered no explanation, the shopkeeper dropped his eyes self-consciously and rang up the package with the other purchases and dropped it into a paper carrier.

"That will be three pounds twenty pence," he said, and closed the cash drawer with a clang, waiting while Barry slung the cape over his shoulders and adjusted the tweed cap.

"God be with you then, Mr. Barry."

There was no reply and the shopkeeper watched him set off back across the bridge before he called his wife again.

"He's a surly one, all right, he is."

"He's got him a girlfriend down there." The shopkeeper was bursting with the importance of his discovery. "He's up to a nice little bit of hanky-panky."

"How do you know that?"

"He was after buying woman's things—you know." He hooded a knowing eye.

"No, I don't know," his wife insisted.

"For the curse—you know. Women's things," and his wife glowed with the news, and began to untie her apron.

"You're sure now?" she demanded.

"Would I ever be lying to you?"

"I think I'll go across to Mollie for a cuppa tea," said his wife eagerly; the news would make her the woman of the hour throughout the village.

The man they knew as Barry trudged into the narrow, high-walled lane that led up to the Old Manse. It was only the heavy boots and voluminous cape that gave him a clumsy gait, for he was a lithe, lean man in prime physical condition, and under the brim of his cap the eyes were never still, hunter's eyes probing and darting from side to side.

The wall was twelve feet high, the stonework blotched with silver-grey lichen, and although it was cracked and sagging at places, yet it was still substantial and afforded complete privacy and security to the property beyond.

At the end of the lane there was a pair of rotten and warping double doors, but the lock was a bright new brass Yale and the cracks in the wood and the gaping seams had been covered with fresh white strips of pine so that it was impossible to see into the interior of the garage.

Barry unlocked the brass lock and slipped through, pulling the latch closed behind him.

A dark-blue Austin saloon car was parked facing the doors for immediate departure. It had been stolen in Ulster two weeks before, resprayed and fitted with a roof rack to alter its appearance, and with new licence plates. The engine had been tuned and checked, and Barry had paid nearly twice its market value.

Now he slipped behind the wheel and turned the key in the ignition. The engine fired and caught immediately. He grunted with satisfaction, seconds could mean the difference between success and failure, and in his life failure and death were synonymous. He listened to the engine beat for half a minute, checking the oil pressure and fuel gauges before switching off the engine again and going out through the rear door of the garage into the overgrown kitchen yard.

The old house had the sad unloved air of approaching dereliction. The fruit trees in the tiny orchard were sick with fungus diseases and surrounded by weed banks.

The thatch roof was rotten-green with moss, and the windows were blindman's eyes, unseeing and uncaring.

Barry let himself in through the kitchen door and dropped his cape and cap on the scullery floor and set the carrier on the draining board of the sink. Then he reached into the cutlery drawer and brought out a pistol. It was a British officer's service pistol, had in fact been taken during a raid on a British Army arsenal in Ulster three years previously.

Barry checked the handgun with the expertise of long familiarity and then thrust it into his belt. He had felt naked and vulnerable for the short time that he was without the weapon—but he had reluctantly decided not to risk carrying it in the village.

Now he tapped water into the kettle, and at the sound a voice called through from the dim interior.

"Is that you?"

"None other," Barry answered drily, and the other man came through and stood in the doorway to the kitchen.

He was a thin, stooped man in his fifties with the swollen inflamed face of the very heavy drinker.

"Did you get it?" His voice was husky and rough with whisky, and he had a seedy run-down air, a day's stubble of grey hairs that grew at angles on the blotchy skin.

Barry indicated the package on the sink. "It's all there, doctor."

"Don't call me that, I'm not a doctor any more." The man snapped irritably.

"Oh, but you are a damned fine one. Ask the girls who dropped their bundles—"

"Leave me alone, damn you."

Yes, he had been a damn fine doctor. Long ago, before the whisky. Now however it was the abortions and the gunshot wounds of fugitives, and jobs like this one. He did not like to think about this one. He crossed to the sink and sorted through the packages.

"I asked you for adhesive tape," he said.

"They had none. I brought the bandage."

"I cannot—" the man began, but Barry whirled on him savagely, his face darkening with angry blood.

"I've had a gutful of your whining. You should have brought what you needed, not sent me to get it for you."

"I did not expect the wound—"

"You didn't expect anything but another dram of Jamiesons, man. There is no adhesive tape. Now get on with it and tie the bitch's hand up with the bandage."

The older man backed away swiftly, picked up the packages and shuffled through into the other room.

Barry made the tea and poured it into the thick china mug, put in four spoons of sugar and stirred noisily, staring out of the smeared panes. It was raining again. He thought that the rain and the waiting would drive him mad.

The doctor came back into the kitchen, carrying a bundle of linen soiled with blood and the yellow ooze of sepsis.

"She is sick," he said. "She needs drugs, antibiotics. The finger—"

"Forget it," said Barry.

From the other room there was a long-drawn-out whimper, followed by the incoherent gabble of a young girl deep in the delirium induced by fever and hypnotic drugs.

"If she is not taken to proper care, I won't be responsible."

"You'll be responsible," Barry told him heavily. "I'll see to that."

The doctor dropped the bundle of linen into the sink and let the water run over it.

"Can I have a drink now?" he asked.

Barry made a sadistic display of consulting his watch.

"No. Not yet," he decided.

The doctor poured soap flakes into the sink.

"I don't think I can do the hand," he whispered, shaking his head. "The finger was bad enough—but I can't do the hand."

"You'll do the hand," said Barry. "Do you hear me, you whisky-guzzling old wreck? You'll do the hand, and anything else I tell you to do."

Sir Steven Stride offered a reward of fifty thousand pounds to anyone giving information that led to the recovery of his niece, and the offer was widely reported on television and in the press with reprints of the identikit portrait. It led to a revival of the flagging public interest in the case.

Inspector Richards had been able to reduce his telephone answering staff to one the last few days, but with the renewed spate of informers and speculators, he had to ask for the other policewoman to return to the third floor, and he had two sergeants processing the material that flowed in.

"I feel like Littlewoods," he growled to Peter. "Everybody taking a ticket on the pools, or getting his threepence worth of advertising." He picked up another message slip. "Here is another claim for responsibility—The Democratic People's Party for the Liberation of Hong Kong. Have we ever heard of them before?"

"No, sir." The senior sergeant looked up from his lists. "But that makes one hundred and forty-eight confessions or claims for responsibility so far."

"And 'Enry the Eighth was on again half an hour ago." One of the girls at the switchboard turned and smiled around her mouthpiece. "Hasn't missed a day."

'Enry the Eighth was a sixty-eight-year-old pensioner who lived in a council estate in South London. His hobby was confessing to the latest spectacular crime from rape to bank robbery, and he had called regularly every morning.

"Come and get me," he challenged each time. "But I warn you I won't come peaceful like." When the local constable had made a courtesy call, while on his regular beat, 'Enry the Eighth had his suitcase packed and ready to go. His disappointment was heart-rending when the bobby tactfully explained that they weren't going to arrest him, but when the bobby assured him that they would be keeping him under close surveillance as the Commissioner considered him a very dangerous man, he brightened up considerably and offered the constable a cup of tea.

"The trouble is we dare not dismiss any of it, even the real loonies, it all has to be checked out," Richards sighed, and motioned Peter to go through to the inner office.

"Still nothing?" Richards asked. It was an unnecessary question. They had a tap on his telephone, at the hotel and at Thor Headquarters, to record any contact from the kidnappers.

"No, nothing," Peter lied, but the lie had become easy now—just as he had learned to accept whatever else was necessary for Melissa-Jane's release.

"I don't like it, General. I really don't like the fact that there has been no attempt to contact you. I don't want to be despondent, but every day of silence makes it look more like an act of vengeance—" Richards broke off and covered his embarrassment by lighting a cigarette. "Yesterday the Deputy-Commissioner telephoned me. He wanted my opinion as to how much longer I thought it necessary to maintain this special unit."

"What did you tell him?" Peter asked.

"I told him that if we did not have some firm evidence within ten days, at least some sort of demand from the kidnappers—then I would have to believe that your daughter was no longer alive."

"I see." Peter felt a fatalistic calm. He knew. He was the only one who knew. There were four days to Caliph's deadline, he had worked out his timetable. Tomorrow morning he would request his urgent meeting with Kingston Parker. He expected it would take less than twelve hours to arrange it. He would make it too attractive for Parker to refuse.

Parker would have to come, but against the remote possibility that he did not, Peter had left himself three clear days before the deadline in which to put into action his alternative plan. This would mean going to Kingston Parker. The first plan was the better, the more certain—but if it failed, Peter would accept any risk.

Now he realized that he had been standing in the centre of Richards's office, staring vacantly at the wall above the little inspector's head. He started as he realized that Richards was staring at him with a mingling of pity and concern.

"I am sorry, General. I understand how you feel, but I cannot keep this unit functioning indefinitely. We just do not have enough people—"

"I understand." Peter nodded jerkily, and wiped his face with an open hand. It was a weary, defeated gesture.

"General, I think you should see your doctor. I really do." Richards's voice was surprisingly gentle.

"That won't be necessary—I'm just a little tired."

"A man can take just so much."

"I think that's what these bastards are relying on," Peter agreed. "But I'll be all right."

From the next door office there was the almost constant tinkle of telephone bells, and the murmur of female voices as the two policewomen answered the incoming stream of calls. It had become a steady background effect, so that when the call for which they had prayed and pleaded and waited finally came, neither of the two men was aware of it, and there was no excitement on the switchboard.

The two girls sat side by side on swivel stools in front of the temporary switchboard. The blonde girl was in her middle twenties, she was pretty and pert, with big round breasts buttoned primly under her blue uniform jacket. The blonde hair was twisted into a bun at the back of her neck to free her ears, but the headset made her appear older and businesslike.

The bell pinged and a panel lit in front of her, she plugged in the switch and spoke into the headset.

"Good morning. This is the Police Special Information Unit—" She had a pleasant middle-class accent, but was unable to keep the trace of boredom out of it. She had been on this job for twelve days now. There was the warning tone of a public telephone and then the click of small change fed into the slot.

"Can you hear me?" The accent was foreign.

"Yes, sir."

"Listen carefully. Gilly O'Shaughnessy has her—" No, it was an imitation, the foreign accent slipped a little with the pronunciation of the name.

"Gilly O'Shaughnessy," the police girl repeated.

"That's right. He's holding her at Laragh."

"Spell that, please." Again the accent slipped as the man spelled the name.

"And where is that, sir?"

"County Wicklow, Ireland."

"Thank you, sir. What is your name, please?"

There was the clack of a broken connection and the hum of the dialling tone. The girl shrugged, and scribbled the message on the pad before her, glancing at her wristwatch simultaneously.

"Seven minutes to tea time," she said. "Roll on death, battle with the angels." She tore the sheet off the pad and passed it over her shoulder to the burly, curly-headed sergeant who sat behind her.

"I'll buy you a sticky bun," he promised.

"I'm on a diet," she sighed.

"That's daft, you look a treat—" The sergeant broke off. "Gilly O'Shaughnessy. Why do I know that name?"

The older sergeant looked up sharply.

"Gilly O'Shaughnessy?" he demanded. "Let me see that." And he snatched the sheet, scanning it swiftly, his lips moving as he read the message. Then he looked up again.

"You know the name because you've seen it on the wanted posters, and heard it on telly. Gilly O'Shaughnessy, strewth man, he's the one who bombed the Red Lion at Leicester, and shot the Chief Constable in Belfast."

The curly-headed policeman whistled softly. "This looks like a hot one. A real hot one—" But his colleague was already barging into the inner office without the formality of knocking.

Richards had the connection to the Dublin police within seven minutes.

"Impress upon them that there must be no attempt—" Peter fretted, while they waited, and Richards cut him short.

"All right, General. Leave this to me. I understand what has to be done—" At that moment the Dublin connection was made, and Richards was transferred quickly to a Deputy-Commissioner. He spoke quietly and earnestly for nearly ten minutes before he replaced the receiver.

"They will use the local constabulary, not to waste time in sending a man down from Dublin. I have their promise that no approach will be made if a suspect is located."

Peter nodded his thanks. "Laragh," he said. "I have never heard of it. It cannot have a population of more than a few hundred."

"I've sent for a map," Richards told him, and when it came they studied it together.

"It's on the slopes of the Wicklow hills—ten miles from the coast." And that was about all there was to learn from the large-scale map.

"We'll just have to wait for the Dublin police to call back—"

"No," Peter shook his head. "I want you to call them again, and ask them to contact the surveyor-general. He must have trig maps of the village, aerial photographs, street layouts. Ask them to get them down with a driver to Enniskerry Airfield—"

"Should we do that now? What if this turns out to be another false alarm."

"We'll have wasted a gallon of petrol and the driver's time—" Peter was no longer able to sit still, he jumped out of the chair and began to pace restlessly about the office, it was too small for him suddenly, he felt as though he were on the point of suffocation. "I don't think it is, however. I have the smell of it. The smell of the beast."

Richards looked startled and Peter deprecated the exaggerated phrase with a dismissive gesture. "A manner of speech," he explained, and then stopped as a thought struck him. "The helicopters will have to refuel, they haven't got the range to make it in one hop, and they are so bloody slow!" He paused and reached a decision, then leaned across Richards's desk to pick up the telephone and dialled Colin Noble's private number at Thor.

"Colin." He spoke curtly with the tension that gripped him like a mailed fist. "We've just had a contact. It's still unconfirmed, but it looks the best yet."

"Where?" Colin broke in eagerly.

"Ireland."

"That's to hell and gone."

"Right, what's the flight time for the whirly birds to reach Enniskerry?"

"Stand by." Peter heard him talking to somebody else—probably one of the R.A.F. pilots. He came back within the minute.

"They will have to refuel en route—"

"Yes?" Peter demanded impatiently.

"Four and a half hours," Colin told him.

"It's twenty past ten now—almost three o'clock before they reach Enniskerry. With this weather it will be dark before five." Peter thought furiously; if they sent the Thor team all the way to Ireland on a false trail—and while they were there the correct contact was made in Scotland, or Holland or—

"It's got the smell. It's got to be right," he told himself, and took a deep breath. He could not order Colin Noble to go to Bravo. Peter was no longer commander of Thor.

"Colin," he said. "I think this is it. I have the deep-down gut feel for it. Will you trust me and go to Bravo now? If we wait even another half hour, we'll not get Melissa-Jane out before nightfall—if she is there."

There was a long silence, broken only by Colin Noble's light quick breath.

"Hell, it can only cost me my job," he said easily at last. "Okay, Pete baby, it's Bravo, we'll be airborne in five minutes. We'll pick you up from the helipad in fifteen minutes; be ready."

The cloud was breaking up, but the wind was still bitter and spiteful, and up on the exposed helipad it cut cruelly through Peter's trench coat, blazer and roll-neck jersey. They looked out across the churned surface of the Thames River, eyes watering in the wind, for the first glimpse of the helicopters.

"What if we have a confirmation before you reach Enniskerry?"

"You can reach us on the R.A.F. frequencies, through Biggin Hill," Peter told him.

"I hope I don't have bad news for you." Richards was holding his bowler hat in place with one hand, the skirts of his jacket slapping around his skinny rump and his face blotchy with the cold.

The two ungainly craft came clattering in, low over the roof-tops, hanging on the whirling silver coins of their rotors.

At a hundred feet Peter could plainly recognize the broad shape of Colin Noble in the open doorway of the fuselage, just forward of the brilliant R.A.F. roundels, and the down-draught of the rotors boiled the air about them.

"Good hunting." Richards raised his voice to a shout. "I wish I was coming with you."

Peter ran forward lightly, and jumped before the helicopter gear touched the concrete pad. Colin caught him by the upper arm and helped to swing him aboard without removing the cheroot from his wide mouth.

"Welcome aboard, buddy. Now let's get this circus on the road." And he hitched the big .45 pistol on his hip.

"She's not eating." The doctor came through from the inner room and scraped the plate into the rubbish bin below the sink. "I'm worried about her. Very worried."

Gilly O'Shaughnessy grunted but did not look up from his own plate. He broke a crust off the slice of bread and very carefully wiped up the last of the tomato ketchup. He popped the bread into his mouth and followed it with a gulp of steaming tea, and while he chewed it all together, he leaned back on the kitchen chair and watched the other man.

The doctor was on the verge of cracking up. He would probably not last out the week before his nerve went completely. Gilly O'Shaughnessy had seen better men go to pieces under less strain.

He realized then that his own nerves were wearing away.

It was more than just the rain and the waiting that was working on him. He had been the fox for all of his life, and he had developed the instincts of the hunted animal. He could sense danger, the presence of the pursuers, even when there was no real evidence. It made him restless to stay longer in one place than was necessary, especially when he was on a job. He had been here twelve days, and it was far too long. The more he thought about it the more uneasy he became. Why had they insisted he bring the brat to this isolated, and therefore conspicuous, little dead-end? There was only one road in and out of the village, a single avenue of escape. Why had they insisted that he sit and wait it out in this one place? He would have liked to keep moving. If he

had had the running of it, he would have bought a second-hand
house trailer, and kept rolling from one park to another—his attention wandered for a few moments as he thought how he would
have done it if he had been given the planning of it.

He lit a cigarette and gazed out of the rain-blurred window
panes, hardly aware of the muttered complaints and misgivings of
his companion. What they should have done was crop the brat's
fingers and bottle all of them to send to her father at intervals,
and then they should have held a pillow over her face and buried
her in the vegetable garden or weighted her and dumped her out
beyond the hundred-fathom line of the Irish Sea. That way they
would not have had to bother with a doctor, and the nursing—

Everything else had been done with professional skill, starting
with the contact they had made with him in the *favela* of Rio de
Janeiro, where he was hiding out in a sleazy one-room shack with
the half-caste Indian woman, and down to his last fifty quid.

That had given him a real start. He thought he had covered his
tracks completely but they had him made. They had the passport
and travel papers in the name of Barry, and they did not look like
forgeries. They were good papers, he was sure of it, and he knew a
lot about papers.

Everything else had been as well planned, and swiftly delivered.
The money—a thousand pounds in Rio, another five thousand the
day after they grabbed the brat, and he was confident that the
final ten would be there as it was promised. It was better than an
English gaol, the "Silver City" as the Brits called their concentration camp at the Maze. That was what Caliph had promised if
he didn't take the job.

Caliph, now that was a daft name, Gilly O'Shaughnessy decided for the fiftieth time as he dropped the stub of his cigarette
into the dregs of his teacup and it was extinguished with a sharp
hiss. A real daft name, but somehow it had the ability to put a
chill on the blood, and he shivered not only from the cold.

He stood up and crossed to the kitchen window. It had all been
done with such speed and purpose and planning—everything so
clearly thought out that when there was a lapse it was more trou-
bling.

Gilly O'Shaughnessy had the feeling that Caliph did nothing
without good reason. Then why had they been ordered to back

themselves into this dangerously exposed bottle neck, without the security of multiple escape routes, and to sit here and wait?

He picked up the cyclist cape and tweed cap. "Where are you going?" the doctor demanded anxiously.

"I'm going to take a shufti," Gilly O'Shaughnessy grunted as he pulled the cap down over his eyes.

"You're always prowling around," the doctor protested. "You make me nervous."

The dark Irishman pulled the pistol from under his jacket and checked the load before thrusting it back into his belt. "You just go on playing nursemaid," he said brusquely, "and leave the man's work to me."

The small black Austin crawled slowly up the village street, and the rain hammered on the cab and bonnet in tiny white explosions that blurred the outline, giving the machine a softly focused appearance, and the streaming windscreen effectively hid the occupants. It was only when the Austin parked directly in front of Laragh's only grocery store and both front doors opened that the curiosity of watchers from behind the curtained windows all down the street was satisfied.

The two members of the Irish constabulary wore the service blue winter uniform with darker epaulettes. The soft rain speckled the patent leather peaks of their caps as they hurried into the shop.

"Good morning, Maeve, me old love," the sergeant greeted the plump red-faced lady behind the counter.

"Owen O'Neill, I do declare." She chuckled as she recognized the sergeant—there had been a time, thirty years before, when the two of them had given the priest some fine pickings at the confessional. "And what brings you all the way up from the big city?"

That was a generous description of the quaint seaside resort town of Wicklow, fifteen miles down the road.

"The sight of your blooming smile—"

They chatted like old friends for ten minutes, and her husband came through from the little storeroom when he heard the rattle of teacups.

"So what is new in Laragh, then?" the sergeant asked at last. "Any new faces in the village?"

"No, all the same faces. Nothing changes in Laragh, bless the Lord for that." The shopkeeper wagged his head. "No, indeed— only new face is the one down at the Old Manse, he and his lady friend"—he winked knowingly—"but seeing as how he's a stranger, we aren't after counting him."

The sergeant ponderously delved for his notebook, opened it and extracted a photograph from it, it was the usual side view and full face of police records. He held the name covered with his thumb as he showed it to them.

"No." The woman shook her head positively. "Himself down at the Manse is ten years older than that, and he does not have a moustache."

"This was taken ten years ago," said the sergeant.

"Oh, well, why didn't you say so." She nodded. "Then that's him. That's Mr. Barry for certain sure."

"The Old Manse, you say." The sergeant seemed to inflate visibly with importance, as he put the photograph back into his notebook. "I'm going to have to use your telephone now, dear."

"Where will you be after telephoning?" The shopkeeper asked suspiciously.

"Dublin," the sergeant told him. "It's police business."

"I'll have to charge you for the call," the shopkeeper warned him quickly.

"There," said the wife as they watched the sergeant making his request to the girl on the village switchboard. "I told you he had the look of trouble, now didn't I. The first time I laid eyes on him I knew he was from up in the North, and carrying trouble like the black angel."

Gilly O'Shaughnessy kept close in under the stone wall, keeping out of the slanting rain and out of the line of sight of a casual watcher on the slope beyond the river. He moved carefully and quietly as a tomcat on his midnight business, stopping to examine the earth below the weakened or tumbled places in the wall where a man could have come over, studying the wet drooping weeds for the brush marks where a man might have passed.

At the farthest corner of the garden, he stepped up onto the leaning main stem of an apple tree to see over the wall, wedging himself against the lichen-encrusted stone, so that the silhouette of his head did not show above the wall.

He waited and watched for twenty minutes, with the absolute animal patience of the predator, then he jumped down and went on around the perimeter of the wall, never for a moment relaxing his vigilance, seemingly oblivious to the discomfort of the cold and the insistent rain.

There was nothing, not the least sign of danger, no reason for the nagging disquiet—but still it was there. He reached another vantage point, the iron gate that led into the narrow walled alley, and he leaned against the stone jamb, cupping his hands to protect match and cigarette from the wind, and then shifting slightly so he could see through the crack between wall and gate and cover the walled lane, and the road beyond as far as the bridge.

Once again he assumed the patient watching role, closing his mind against physical discomfort and letting his eyes and his brain work at their full capacity.

Not for the first time he pondered the unusual system of signals and exchanges of material that Caliph had insisted upon.

The payments had been made by bearer deposit certificates, in Swiss francs, sent through the post to his Rio address and then to his collection address in London.

He had made one delivery to Caliph, the bottle and its contents —and two telephone calls. The delivery had been made within two hours of grabbing the girl, while she was still under the effects of the initial shot of the drug. The doctor—Dr. Jamieson—as Gilly O'Shaughnessy liked to think of him, had done the job in the back of the second car. It had been waiting in the car park at Cambridge railway station, a little green Ford delivery van with a completely enclosed rear compartment. They had moved the girl from the maroon Triumph to the Ford in the covering dusk of the autumn evening, and they had parked again in the lot of a roadside cafe on the A.10 while Dr. Jamieson did the job. All the instruments had been ready for him in the van, but he had botched it badly, his hands shaking with nerves and the need for liquor. The brat had bled copiously, and now the hand was infected.

Gilly O'Shaughnessy felt his irritation rising sharply when he thought of the doctor. Everything he touched seemed to turn to disaster.

He had delivered the bottle to a pick-up car that had been exactly where he was told it would be, and it had dipped its headlights in the prearranged signal. Gilly had hardly stopped, but merely drawn up alongside and handed the bottle across, then driven straight into the West, and caught the early morning ferry long before any general alarm was out for the girl.

Then there were the telephone calls. They worried Gilly O'Shaughnessy as much as anything else in this whole bloody business. He had made the first call immediately they reached Laragh. It was an international call, and he had to say one sentence:

"We arrived safely." And then hang up. A week later a call to the same number, and again only one sentence:

"We are enjoying ourselves." And then immediately break the connection.

Gilly remembered how each time the girl on the local exchange had called him back to ask if the contact had been satisfactory—and each time she had sounded puzzled and intrigued.

It was not the way Caliph had worked up until then, it was leaving a trail for the hunters to follow and he would have protested—if there had been somebody to protest to, but there was only the international telephone number, no other way of contacting Caliph. He decided as he stood by the gate that he would not make the next telephone call to that number which was due in four days' time.

Then he remembered that was the day the hand was due—and he would probably receive his orders for delivery of the hand when he made the call—but he didn't like it. Not even for the money—and suddenly his mind went back to an incident long ago.

They had wanted to pass false information to the English, details of an intended operation—which would in fact take place at a different place and a different time. They had fed the detailed but duff information to a young unreliable Provo, one who they knew would not hold out under interrogation, and they had put him in a safe house in the Shankill Road—and that was where the English took him.

Gilly O'Shaughnessy felt a little electric prickle run down his spine like ghost-fire, and that feeling had never let him down before—never. He looked at his cheap Japanese wristwatch, it was almost four o'clock, and evening was lowering on the hills of grey and cold green. When he looked up again, there was movement on the road.

From the top of the hill a vehicle was following the curve of the road, down towards the bridge. It was a small black saloon car, and it went out of sight behind the hedge.

Gilly O'Shaughnessy watched for it to reappear without particular interest, still worrying about those two telephone calls. Trying to find the need for them, why Caliph should want to take that chance.

The small black car turned onto the bridge, and came directly down towards the Manse, but the light was wrong and Gilly could make out only the shape of two heads beyond the rhythmically flogging windscreen wipers.

The car began to slow up, coming down almost to walking speed, and Gilly straightened up instinctively, suddenly completely alert as he peered through the slit. There was the pale blur of faces turned towards him, and the car slowed almost to a halt. The nearest side window was lowered slowly and for the first time he could see clearly into the interior. He saw the peak of the uniform cap, and the silver flash of a cap badge above the straining white face. The ghost-fire flared up Gilly O'Shaughnessy's spine and he felt his breath suddenly scalding his throat.

The small black car disappeared beyond the corner of the stone wall, and he heard it accelerate away swiftly.

Gilly O'Shaughnessy whirled with the cape ballooning around him and he ran back to the house. He felt very cold and sure and calm now that the moment of action had come.

The kitchen was empty and he crossed it in half a dozen strides, and threw open the door to the second room.

The doctor was working over the bed and he looked up angrily. "I've told you to knock."

They had argued this out before. The doctor still retained some bizarre vestige of professional ethics in his treatment of his patient. He might surgically mutilate the child for the money he so desperately needed, but he had protested fiercely when Gilly O'Shaughnessy had lingered at the doorway to ogle the maturing body whenever the doctor stripped it for cleansing, treatment or for the performance of its natural functions.

The dark Irishman had half-heartedly attempted to force him to back down, but when he had encountered surprisingly courageous opposition he had abandoned his voyeuristic pleasures and had returned to the inner room only when called to assist.

Now the child lay face down on the soiled sheets. Her blonde hair was matted and snarled into greasy tresses; the doctor's attempts at cleanliness were as bumbling and ineffectual as his surgery.

The infection and the use of drugs had wasted the flesh off the tender young body, each knuckle of her spine stood out clearly and her naked buttocks seemed pathetically vulnerable, shrunken and white.

Now the doctor pulled the grubby sheet up to her shoulders, and turned to stand protectively over her. It was an absurd gesture, when you looked at the untidy, stained dressing that bound up her left hand—and Gilly O'Shaughnessy snarled at him fiercely.

"We are getting out."

"You can't move her now," protested the doctor. "She's really sick."

"Suit yourself," Gilly agreed grimly. "Then we'll leave her." He reached under the dripping cape, and brought out the pistol. He thumbed back the hammer and stepped up to the bed. The doctor grabbed at his arm, but Gilly pushed him away easily, sending him reeling back against the wall.

"You are right, she'll be a nuisance," he said, and placed the muzzle of the pistol against the base of the child's skull.

"No," shrieked the doctor. "No, don't do that. We'll take her."

"We are leaving as soon as it's dark." Gilly stepped back and uncocked the pistol. "Be ready by then," he warned.

The two helicopters flew almost side by side, with the number two only slightly behind and higher than the leader; below them the Irish Sea was a sheet of beaten lead flecked with feathers of white water.

They had refuelled at Caernarvon and had made good time since leaving the Welsh coast, for the wind drove them on, but still the night was overtaking them and Peter Stride fretted, glancing at his wristwatch every few seconds.

It was only ninety miles of open water to cross, but to Peter it seemed like the entire Atlantic. Colin slumped beside him on the bench that ran the length of the hold, with the cold stump of a cheroot in the corner of his mouth in deference to the "No smoking" light that burned on the bulkhead behind the flight deck. The rest of the Thor team had adopted their usual attitudes of complete relaxation, some of them sprawled on the deck using their equipment as pillows, the others stretched out full length on the benches.

Peter Stride was the only one tensed up, as though his blood fizzed with nervous energy. He stood up once again to peer through the perspex window, checking the amount of daylight and trying to judge the height and position of the sun through the thick cloud cover.

"Take it easy," Colin counselled him as he dropped back into his seat. "You will give yourself an ulcer."

"Colin, we've got to decide What are our priorities on this strike?" He had to shout above the racket of wind and motor.

"There are no priorities. We have only one object—to get Melissa-Jane out, and out safely."

"We aren't going to try for prisoners to interrogate?"

"Peter baby, we are going to hit anything and everything that moves in the target area, and we are going to hit them hard."

Peter nodded with satisfaction. "They will only be goons anyway, you can be certain that their paymaster will not let them connect to him—but what about Kingston Parker, he would want prisoners?"

"Kingston Parker?" Colin removed the stub of cheroot from his mouth. "Never heard of him—around here it's Uncle Colin makes the decisions." And he grinned at Peter, that friendly lopsided grin, and at that moment the flight engineer crossed the cabin and yelled at Colin.

"Irish coast ahead—we'll be landing at Enniskerry in seven minutes, sir."

Air traffic control at Enniskerry had been apprised of the emergency. They stacked the other traffic in holding pattern above circuit altitude and cleared the two R.A.F. helicopters for immediate landing.

They came clattering out of the low grey cloud and rain, and settled on the hangar apron. Immediately a police car, with headlights burning in the gloom, sped out from between the hangars and parked beside the leading machine. Before the rotors had stopped turning, two members of the Irish Constabulary and a representative of the surveyor general's office were scrambling up into the camouflaged fuselage.

"Stride." Peter introduced himself quickly, he was dressed now in Thor assault gear, the one piece fitted black suit and soft boots, the pistol on its webbing belt strapped down to his right thigh.

"General, we've had a confirmation," the police inspector told him while they were still shaking hands. "Local people have identified O'Shaughnessy from a police photograph. He is staying in the area all right."

"Have they found where?" Peter demanded.

"They have, sir. It's an old rambling building on the edge of the village—" He motioned the bespectacled surveyor to come forward with the file he was clutching to his chest. There was no chart-table in the stripped-out hull of the helicopter, and they spread the survey map and photographs on the deck.

Colin Noble ordered across the team from the second helicopter, and twenty men crowded into a huddle about the maps. "There, that's the building." The surveyor placed a circle on the map with a blue pencil.

"Right," grunted Colin. "We've got good fixes—we pick up either the river or the road and follow it to the bridge and the church. The target is between them."

"Haven't we got a blow-up of the building, a plan of the interior?" one of the Thor team asked.

"Sorry, there wasn't time to do a proper search," the surveyor apologized.

"The local police reported again a few minutes ago, and we got a relay on the radio. They say the house is enclosed by a high stone wall and that there are no signs of activity."

"They haven't been near it?" Peter demanded. "They were strictly ordered not to approach the suspects."

"They drove past once on the public road." The inspector looked slightly abashed. "They wanted to make certain that—"

"If it's O'Shaughnessy, he needs only one sniff and he'll be gone." Peter's expression was stony, but his eyes sparked blue with anger. "Why can't these people do what they are told?" He turned quickly to the helicopter pilot in his yellow life jacket and helmet with its built-in microphone and earphones.

"Can you get us in?"

The pilot did not answer immediately but glanced up at the nearest window; a fresh gout of rain splashed against the pane.

"It will be dark in ten minutes, or even earlier, and the ceiling is down to the deck now, we only got down here using the airport V.O.R. beacons." He looked dubious. "There is nobody aboard who will recognize the target, hell—I don't know—I could get you in at first light tomorrow."

"It has to be tonight, now. Right now."

"If you could get the local police to mark the target," the pilot suggested, "with torches or a flare."

"There is no chance of that—we have to go in cold, and the longer we sit here talking the less our chances. Will you give it your best shot?" Peter was almost pleading, the go decision one that cannot be forced on a pilot. Even air traffic control cannot force a pilot-in-command to operate beyond his personal judgement.

"We will have to try and keep ground contact all the way, it's classic conditions for trouble, rising terrain and deteriorating weather—"

"Try it," Peter said, "please."

The pilot hesitated five seconds longer.

"Let's go!" he said abruptly, and there was a concerted rush for the hatchway as the second Thor team made for the other machine, and the police and surveyor made certain they were not included on the passenger list.

Turbulence slogged the helicopter like the punches of a heavyweight prize fighter, and she dipped and staggered to them with a nauseatingly giddy action.

The ground flickered past under them, very close, and yet bleakly insubstantial in the wild night. The headlights of a solitary vehicle on a lonely country road, the cluttered lights of a village, each a distinct yellow rectangle they were so close, these were the only landmarks with any meaning—the rest was black patches of woods, the threads of hedges and stone walls drawn lightly across sombre fields, and every few minutes even that was gone as a fresh squall of grey clouds and rain washed away all vision, and the pilot concentrated all his attention on the dull glow of the flight instruments arranged in their distinctive T layout in front of him.

Each time they emerged from cloud, the light seemed to have

diminished and the menace of earth loomed more threateningly as they were forced lower and lower to keep contact.

Peter was squeezed into the jump seat of the helicopter's flight deck, between the two pilots, and Colin crowded in behind him, all of them peering ahead, all silent and tense as the ungainly machines lumbered low and heavy over the earth, groping for the shoreline.

They hit the coast, the ghostly white line of surf flared with phosphorescence only fifty feet below them, and the pilot swung them to run south with it—and seconds later another brighter field of lights appeared below them.

"Wicklow," said the pilot, and his co-pilot called the new heading, now they had made a fix they could head for Laragh directly.

They swung onto the new heading, following the road inland.

"Four minutes to target," the co-pilot shouted at Peter, stabbing ahead with his finger, and Peter did not try to answer in the clatter and roar of the rotors, but he reached down and checked the Walther in its quick-release holster; it came out cleanly in his fist.

Gilly O'Shaughnessy threw his few personal possessions into the blue canvas airways grip, a change of underclothing and his shaving gear. Then he pulled the iron bedstead away from the wall, ripped back the skirting board and cleared out the hiding-place he had made there by removing a single brick.

There were the new papers and passports. They had even provided papers for the brat—Helen Barry—his daughter. Caliph had thought of everything. With the papers was six hundred pounds sterling in travellers' cheques, and a package of spare ammunition for the pistol. He thrust these into the pocket of his jacket, and took one last look around the bare bleak room. He knew that he had left nothing to lead the hunters, because he never carried anything that could be used to identify him. Yet he was obsessed by the need to destroy all sign of his passing. He had long ago ceased to think of himself by the name of Gilly O'Shaughnessy. He had no name, and only one purpose—that purpose was destruction. The magnificent passion to reduce all life to decay and mortification.

He could recite by heart most of Bakunin's *The Revolutionary Catechism*, especially the definition of the true revolutionary:

The lost man, who has no belongings, no outside interests, no personal ties of any sort—not even a name. Possessed of but one thought, interest and passion—the revolution. A man who has broken with Society, broken with its laws and conventions. He must despise the opinions of others, and be prepared for death and torture at any time. Hard towards himself, he must be hard to others, and in his heart there must be no place for love, friendship, gratitude or even honour.

As he stood now in the empty room, he saw himself in a rare moment of revelation, as the man he had set out to become—the true revolutionary, and his head turned for a moment to indulge in the vanity of regarding his own image in the mirror screwed to the peeling wallpaper above the iron bedstead.

It was the cold face of the lost man, and he felt proud to belong to that élite class, the cutting edge of the sword, that was what he was.

He picked up the canvas grip, and strode through into the kitchen.

"Are you ready?" he called.

"Help me."

He dropped the grip and stepped to the window. The last of the light was fading swiftly, glowing pink and mother of pearl within the drooping, pregnant belly of the sky. It seemed so close he could reach out and touch it. Already the trees of the unkempt orchard were melding as the night encroached.

"I cannot carry her on my own," the doctor whined, and he swung away from the window. It was time to go again. In his life there was always the moving onwards, and always the hunters baying hard upon his scent. It was time to run again, run like the fox.

He went through into the second room. The doctor had the child wrapped in a grey woollen blanket, and he had tried to lift her from the bed, but had failed. She was sprawled awkwardly, half onto the floor.

"Help me," repeated the doctor.

"Get out of the way." Gilly O'Shaughnessy pushed him roughly aside, and stooped over the girl. For a second their faces were within inches of each other.

Her eyes were opened, half conscious, although the pupils were widely dilated by the drug. The lids were pink-rimmed and there were little butter-yellow lumps of mucus in the corners. Her lips were dried to white scales, and cracked through to the raw flesh at three places.

"Please tell my daddy," she whispered. "Please tell him I'm here."

His nostrils flared at the sick sour smell of her body, but he picked her up easily with an arm under her knees and the other under her shoulders, and carried her out across the kitchen, kicking open the door so the lock burst and it slammed back against its hinges.

Quickly he carried her across the yard to the garage, with the doctor staggering along after them carrying a carton of medical supplies and equipment against his chest, cursing miserably at the cold, and sliding and slipping in the treacherous footing.

Gilly O'Shaughnessy waited while the doctor opened the rear door of the car, and then he bundled her in so roughly that the child cried out weakly. He ignored her and went to the double garage doors and dragged them open. It was night now and he could not see as far as the bridge.

"Where are we going?" bleated the doctor.

"I haven't decided yet," Gilly told him brusquely. "There is a safe house up north, or we might go back across the sea to England." He thought of the trailer again, that was a good one—

"But why are we leaving now, so suddenly?"

He did not bother to reply but left the garage and ran back into the kitchen. Always he was obsessed by the need to cover his tracks, to leave no sign for the hunters.

Though he had brought little with him, and was taking that now, yet he knew the old house contained signs, even if it was only his fingerprints. There was also the single remaining appetite for destruction to assuage.

He ripped the wooden doors off the kitchen cupboards and smashed them to splinters under his heel, piled them in the centre of the wood floor. He crumpled the newspapers piled on the table and added them to the pile, threw the table and chairs upon it.

He lit a match and held it to the crumpled newsprint. It flared readily, and he straightened and opened the windows and doors. The flames fed on the cold fresh air and climbed greedily, catching on the splintered doors.

Gilly O'Shaughnessy picked up the canvas grip and stepped out into the night, crouching to the wind and the rain—but halfway to the garage he straightened again abruptly and paused to listen.

There was a sound on the wind, from the direction of the coast. It might have been the engine note of a heavy truck coming up the hills, but there was a peculiar thin whistling sound mingled with the engine beat, and the volume of sound escalated too sharply to be that of a lumbering truck. It was coming on too swiftly, the sound seemed to fill the air, to emanate from the very clouds themselves.

Gilly O'Shaughnessy stood with his face lifted to the fine silver drizzle, searching the belly of the clouds, until a throbbing regular glow began to beat like a pulse in the sky, and it was a moment until he recognized it as the beacon light of a low-flying aircraft, and at the same moment he knew that the shrill whistle was the whirling of rotors bringing the hunters.

He cried aloud in the certainty of betrayal and on-rushing death. "Why? God, why?" he called to the God he had so long ago denied, and began to run.

"It's no good." The pilot twisted his neck to shout at Peter without taking his eyes from the flight instruments which kept the great ungainly machine level and on course. They had lost contact with the other machine.

"We are socked in, blind." The cloud frothed over the canopy like boiling milk over the lip of the pot. "I'm going to have to climb out, and head back for Enniskerry before we run into my number two."

The risk of collision with the other helicopter was now real and imminent.

Th beacon light throbbed above them, reflected off the impenetrable press of soft cloud—but the other pilot would not see it until too late.

"Hold on. Just another minute," Peter shouted back at him, his expression tortured in the glow of the instrument panel. The entire operation was disintegrating about him, would soon end in tragedy or in fiasco, but he must go on.

"It's no good—" the pilot began, and then shouted with fright and hurled the helicopter over onto its side, at the same instant altering pitch and altitude so the machine shuddered and lurched as though she had run into a solid obstruction, and then bounded upwards, gaining a hundred feet in a swoop.

The spire of a church had leapt at them out of the cloud, like a predator from ambush, and now it flickered by only feet from where they crouched in the flight deck, but it had disappeared again instantly as they roared past.

"The church!" Peter yelled. "That's it! Turn back."

The pilot checked the machine, hovering blindly in the chaos of rain and cloud churned to a fury by the down-draught of their own rotor.

"I can't see a damned thing," shouted the pilot.

"We've got one hundred and seventy feet on the radio altimeter," his co-pilot called; that was actual height from the ground and still they could see nothing below them.

"Get us down. For God's sake, get us down," Peter pleaded.

"I can't take the chance. We don't have any idea of what is under us." The pilot's face was sickly orange in the instrument glow, his eyes the shadowed pits of a skull. "I'm climbing out and heading back—"

Peter reached down and the butt of the Walther jumped into his hand, like a living thing. He realized coldly that he was capable of killing the pilot, to force the co-pilot to land—but at the moment there was a hole in the cloud, just enough to make out the dark loom of the earth below them.

"Visual," Peter shouted. "We've visual, get us down!" And the helicopter sank swiftly, breaking out suddenly into the clear.

"The river." Peter saw the glint of water. "And the bridge—"

"There's the churchyard"—Colin roared eagerly—"and that's the target."

The thatched roof was a black oblong, and light spilled from the windows of one side of the building, so they could see the high enclosing wall. The pilot spun the helicopter on its axis like a compass needle, and dived towards the building.

Colin Noble scrambled down into the cabin, shouting to his team. "Delta! We are going to Delta—" And the flight engineer slid the hatch cover open. Immediately a fine swirling mist filled the cabin as the down-draught of the rotors churned the rain filled air.

The Thor team were on their feet, forming up on each side of the open hatch, while Colin towered over the flight engineer as he took lead position—"point" he always called it.

The earth rushed up to meet them, and Colin spat out the cheroot stub and braced himself in the doorway.

"Hit anything that moves," he yelled. "But for Chrissake watch out for the kid. Let's go, gang. Let's go!"

Peter was jammed into the jump seat by the swooping drop of the machine, unable to follow, wasting precious seconds—but he had a clear view ahead through the canopy.

The light in the windows of the building wavered unnaturally, and Peter realized that it was burning. Those were flames, and his concern was heightened by the knowledge, but he did not have a chance to ponder this new development. In the shadows of the walled yard he saw movement, just the blur of it in the glow of the flames, and what was left of the daylight—but it was the shape of a man, running, crouched low, disappearing almost immediately into one of the outbuildings that flanked the narrow stone walled lane.

Peter dragged himself out of the seat against the G force, scrambling awkwardly down into the cabin as the helicopter dropped the last few feet, and then hung, swaying slightly, suspended ten feet above the open yard at the rear of the house—and black-clad figures spilled out of her, dropping lightly onto their feet and racing forward as they touched ground, seeming to disappear again miraculously through the doors and windows of the building. Even in the grinding tension of the moment Peter felt the flare of pride in the way it was done, instant and seemingly effortless penetration, the lead man using the sandbags to break in glass and wooden shutters and the man behind him going in with a clean controlled dive.

Peter was the last man left aboard, and something made him check in the open hatchway before jumping. Perhaps it was that glimpse of movement outside the main building that he had been given; he looked back that way, and suddenly lights leapt in solid white lances down the walled lane—the headlights of a motor vehicle, and at the same moment the vehicle launched itself from the dark derelict outbuilding and rocketed away down the lane.

Peter teetered in the open hatch, for he had been in the very act of jumping, but he caught his balance now, grabbing wildly at the nylon line above the door. The vehicle slowed for the turn into the main road at the bridge—and Peter caught the flight engineer and shook his shoulder violently, pointing after the escaping vehicle. His lips were inches from the man's face.

"Don't let it get away!" he screamed, and the flight engineer was quick and alert, he spoke urgently into his microphone, directly to the pilot in the flight deck above them, and obediently the helicopter swung around and the beat of the engines changed as the rotors altered pitch and roared in forward thrust—the machine lunged forward, skimming the garage roof by mere feet and then hammered out into the night in pursuit of the dwindling glow of headlights.

Peter had to hang out of the hatchway to see ahead, and the wind clamoured around his head and tore at his body, but they were swiftly overhauling the vehicle as it raced down the twisting narrow road towards the coast.

It was two hundred yards ahead, and the tree tops seemed to rush by at the same level as the hatch in which Peter stood. A hundred yards ahead now, the headlights blazed through the drivel of rain, etching fleeting cameos of hedges and starkly lit stone walls from the night.

They were close enough now for Peter to make out that it was a smallish vehicle with an estate car body, not quite large enough to be a station wagon—the driver was throwing it through the curves and twists of the road with reckless skill, but the helicopter crept up behind him.

"Tell him to switch off the beacon light." Peter swung inboard to shout in the flight engineer's ear. He did not want to warn the driver that he was being followed, but as the engineer lifted the microphone to his mouth the headlights snapped out. The driver had become aware, and after the brilliance of the headlights the night seemed black, and the car disappeared into it.

Peter felt the helicopter lurch, as the pilot was taken by surprise, and his own dismay was a lance.

"We have lost them," he thought, and he knew that it was suicide to fly on blindly only a few feet above the tree tops, but the pilot of the helicopter steadied the craft and then suddenly the earth below them was lit by a blaze of stark white light that startled Peter until he realized that the pilot had switched on his landing lights. There were two of them, one on each side of the fuselage; they were aimed down and slightly forward.

The escaping car was caught fairly in their brilliance.

The helicopter dropped lower, edging in between the telegraph poles and trees that lined the narrow road.

Now Peter could see that the car was a deep blue Austin, with a carrying rack bolted to the long roof. It was that carrying rack which decided him. Without it no human being could have hoped for purchase on the smooth rounded roof of the lurching, swaying car.

The doctor in the back seat of the Austin had been the one who spotted the helicopter. The engine noise and the drumming of the wind had covered the whistling whine of the rotors, and Gilly O'Shaughnessy had chuckled with grim triumph and self-congratulation. He had deliberately waited for the helicopter to discharge its load of fighting men before he had switched on his headlights and roared out of the garage into the lane.

He knew it would be many minutes before the assault team realized that the burning house was empty and that it would take as long again to regroup and board the helicopter to continue the hunt—and by that time he would be clear; there was a safe house in Dublin—or there had been, four years previously. Perhaps it was blown now; in that case he would have to get rid of the brat and Dr. Jamieson, a bullet each in the back of the head, and drive the Austin into the Irish Sea.

The wild exhilaration of danger and death was upon him again, the waiting was over at last and he was living again the way he had chosen—the fox running ahead of the hounds, he was alive again, with his right foot thrust flat to the floor boards and the Austin rocketing through the night.

The girl was screaming weakly from the back seat, in pain and panic; the doctor was trying to quiet her, and Gilly laughed aloud. The tyres screeched wildly as he skidded out in the turn, brushing the hedge with the side before he was through.

"They are following," screamed the doctor, as he straightened the car into the next stretch. Gilly glanced back over his shoulder. He could see nothing through the rear windows.

"What?"

"The helicopter—"

Gilly lowered his window and, driving with one hand, thrust his head out. The flashing aircraft beacon was close behind and above, and he ducked back in and looked ahead to make sure that the road ran straight, then he switched off the headlights.

In total darkness he did not diminish speed, and now when he laughed it was a wild and reckless sound.

"You're mad," the doctor shrieked. "You'll kill us all!"

"Right you are, Doctor!" But his night vision was clearing and he caught the Austin before she wandered into the stone wall on the left-hand side, and at the same moment he jerked the pistol from under his cape and laid it on the seat beside him.

"There is not going to be—" he began and then broke off as the blinding light burst over them. The helicopter had switched on its landing lights—the road ahead was brightly lit, and he skidded into the next turn with rubber squealing.

"Stop!" the doctor pleaded, trying to hold the semi-conscious child from being hurled about in the swaying cab. "Let's give up now, before they kill us."

"They've got no fighting men on board," Gilly yelled back at him. "There's nothing they can do."

"Give up," the doctor whined. "Let's get out of this alive." And Gilly O'Shaughnessy threw back his head and roared with laughter.

"I'm keeping three bullets, Doctor, one for each of us—"

"They're right on top of us."

Gilly snatched up the pistol and once again thrust his head and right shoulder out, twisting to look upwards.

The eye-searing lights beamed down upon him, very close above. It was all he could see and he fired at them, the crash of the shots lost in the clattering whistling roar of the rotors and the tearing rush of the wind.

Poised in the hatchway, Peter counted the bright orange spurts of gunfire. There were three of them, but there was no sound of passing shot, no thump of the strike.

"Get lower!" he shouted at the engineer, reinforcing the order with urgent hand signals, and obediently the big machine sank down upon the racing Austin.

Peter gathered himself, judging his moment carefully, and when it came he launched himself clear of the hatchway, and his guts seemed to cram into his throat as he dropped.

He dropped with all four limbs spread and braced to land together, but for a moment he thought he had misjudged it and would fall behind the Austin, into the metalled roadway, to be crushed and shredded by the forward impetus of the low-flying helicopter.

Then the Austin swerved and checked slightly and Peter crashed into its roof with stunning force; he felt the metal buckle and sag under him, and then he was rolling and slipping sideways. His whole left side was numbed by the force of impact, and he clutched wildly with his right hand, his fingernails tearing at the paintwork, but still he slid towards the edge, his legs kicking wildly in black rushing space.

At the last instant before he was hurled into the roadway, his clawed fingers hooked in the framework of the roof rack, and he hung bat-like from his one arm. It had taken only a small part of a second, and immediately the driver of the Austin realized that there was a man on the roof. He slewed the little car from one side of the road to the other, short wrenching turns that brought her over on two outside wheels before slamming back and twisting the other way. The tyres squealed harsh protest, and Peter was flung brutally back and forth, the muscle and tendons of his right arm popping and creaking with the strain of holding on—but feeling was flooding swiftly back into his numbled left side.

He had to move quickly, he could not survive another of those wrenching swerves, and he gathered himself, judged the Austin's momentum, and used it to roll and grab with his free hand; at the same moment the toes of his soft boots found purchase on one of the struts of the roof carrier, and he pressed himself belly down, clinging with both arms and legs to the wildly swinging machine.

The Austin checked and steadied as a steep turn appeared ahead in the arc lights of the helicopter which still hung over them. The driver shot the car into the corner, and ahead of them was a long extended drop as the road twisted down the hills towards the coast.

Peter half lifted himself and was about to slide forward when the metal six inches in front of his nose exploded outwards, leaving a neatly punched hole through the roof, and tiny fragments of flying metal stung his cheek; at the same moment the concussion of the pistol shot beat in upon his eardrums. The driver of the Austin was firing blindly up through the coachwork, and he had misjudged Peter's position above him by inches. Peter threw himself desperately to one side, for an instant almost losing his grip on the struts of the carrier—and another pistol bullet clanged out through the metal roof, that one would have taken him through the belly, and Peter had a fleeting image of the kind of wound that it would have inflicted, the bullet mushroomed and deformed by the roof, and breaking up inside his body.

Desperately Peter threw himself back the opposite way, trying to outguess the gunman below him, and once again the crash of the shot and the metal roof erupted in a little jagged pockmark, flecking the paintwork away so the rim of the bullet hole shone like a polished silver shilling. Again it would have hit him, if he had not moved.

Peter rolled again, tensing his belly muscles in the anticipation of the tearing, paralysing impact, expecting the gunshot—which did not come. Only then he remembered the wasted pistol fire the driver had thrown up at the hovering helicopter. He had emptied his pistol and as the realization dawned on Peter there was another completely compelling sound, very faint in the drumming rush of the wind and the engine roar—but unmistakable. It was the sound of a young girl screaming and it galvanized Peter as nothing else, even the threat of death, could have done.

He came up on toes and fingers, like a cat, and he went forward and to the right, until he was directly above the driver's seat.

The girl screamed again, and he recognized Melissa-Jane's voice. There was no question of it, and he slipped the Walther from its quick-release holster and cocked the hammer with the same movement, one glance ahead and they were rushing down on another turn in the narrow road. The driver would be using both hands to control the swaying and bucking little machine.

"Now!" he told himself, and dropped forward, so that he was peering backwards and upside-down through the windshield directly into the driver's pale face and at a distance of only eighteen inches.

In the thousandth part of a second Peter recognized the wolfish features and the cold, merciless eyes of the killer. He had hunted this man for many years and studied his photograph endlessly when the hunting of Provo terrorists had been his life's work.

Gilly O'Shaughnessy was driving with both hands, the pistol still gripped in one of them and the chamber open for reloading.

He snarled at Peter like an animal through the bars of its cage, and Peter fired with the muzzle of the Walther touching the glass of the windshield.

The glass starred into a glittering sheet, white and opaque, and then it collapsed inwards with the force of the wind, filling the interior of the Austin with flying diamond chips of sparkling glass.

Gilly O'Shaughnessy had thrown up both hands to his face, but bright blood burst from between them, spattering his chest and soaking swiftly into the lank black hair.

Still hanging upside down across the Austin's cab, Peter thrust the Walther in through the shattered windscreen until it almost touched the man's body and he fired twice more into his chest, where the explosive Velex bullets would break up against bone, and would not overpenetrate to harm anybody else in the interior. Melissa-Jane's screams still rang clearly in his ears as he killed Gilly O'Shaughnessy. He did it as coldly as a veterinary surgeon would put down a rabid dog, and with as little pleasure, and the bullets punched Gilly O'Shaughnessy back on the bucket seat, head lolling from side to side, and Peter expected the howl of the engine to cut out now as the dead man's foot slipped from the accelerator.

It did not happen. There was no change in the engine beat, the body had slid forward and jammed the knee under the dashboard, bearing down fully on the pedal, and the little car flew down the slope of the hill, the stone walls on each side blurring past as though down a tunnel in the depths of the earth.

Peter wriggled forward and thrust both arms through the shattered windshield and caught the untended wheel as it began to spin aimlessly. He checked the Austin and swung her back into the road, but she had been driven to her limits, rocking and swaying crazily before she righted herself and flew down the hill.

It was almost impossible to judge the control needed to keep her on the road.

Peter was hanging head down, gripping only with knees and toes, and he had to manipulate the wheel from this inverted position with his upper arms sawing across the teeth of jagged glass still remaining in the frame of the windshield.

The wind whipped and clawed him, and Gilly O'Shaughnessy's body flopped forward bonelessly onto the wheel, jamming it at a critical moment, so that while Peter used one hand to shove him backwards, the side of the Austin touched the stone wall with a screech of rending metal and a shower of orange sparks. Peter wrenched her back into the road, and she began a series of uncontrolled broadsides, swinging wildly from side to side, touching the wall with another jarring shock, then swinging back sideways to bounce over the verge, then back again.

She was going over, Peter knew it, and he would be crushed under the metal roof and smeared along the abrasive surface of the macadam road. He should jump now, and take his chances— but grimly he stayed with the crazed machine, for Melissa-Jane was in her and he could not leave.

She survived one more skid, and ahead Peter had the glimpse of a barred wooden gate in the wall. Deliberately he turned the front wheels into the direction of the next skid, no longer trying to counteract it, but aggravating it—steering directly for the gate, and the Austin smashed into it.

A wooden beam cartwheeled over Peter's head, and a scalding cloud of steam from the shattered radiator stung his face and hands, and then the Austin was into the open field, bouncing and thudding over the rocks that studded it, the drag of soft muddy earth slowing her, and the steep slope of the hillside against her— within fifty feet the front end dropped heavily into a drainage ditch, and the little car shuddered to a halt, canted at an abandoned angle.

Peter slipped over the side and landed on his feet. He jerked open the rear door and a man half fell from the cab. He dropped onto his knees in the mud, blubbering incoherently and Peter drove his right knee into his face. Bone and cartilage crunched sharply and there was the crackle of breaking teeth. His voice was cut off abruptly and, as he dropped, Peter chopped him with the stiffened blade of his right hand, a controlled blow—judged finely to immobilize but not to kill, and before the unconscious body dropped, Peter had gone in over it.

He lifted his daughter out of the Austin, and the frail wasted body felt unsubstantial in his arms, and the heat of fever and infection burned against his chest.

He was possessed by an almost uncontrollable desire to crush her body to him with all the strength of his arms, but instead he carried her as though she was made of some precious and fragile substance, stepping carefully over the uneven rocky surface of the field to where the helicopter was settling cumbersomely.

The Thor doctor was still aboard her; he jumped clear before the helicopter touched and ran towards Peter in the brilliant glare of the landing lights.

Peter found he was crooning softly.

"It's all right now, darling. It's all over now. It's all finished, my baby—I'm here, little one—"

Then Peter made another discovery. It was not sweat running down his cheeks and dripping from his chin, and he wondered unashamedly when last it was he had wept. He could not remember, and it did not seem important, not now, not with his daughter in his arms.

Cynthia came down to London, and Peter relived some of those horrors from their marriage.

"Everybody around you always has to suffer, Peter. Now it's Melissa-Jane's turn."

He could not avoid her, nor her martyred expression, for she was always at Melissa-Jane's bedside. While he bore her recriminations and barbed accusations, he wondered that she had ever been gay and young and attractive. She was two years younger than he, but she already had the shapeless body and greying mind that made her seem twenty years older.

Melissa-Jane responded almost miraculously to the antibiotics, and although she was still weak and skinny and pale, the doctor discharged her on the third day, and Peter and Cynthia had their final degrading haggling and bargaining session which Melissa-Jane settled for them.

"Mommy, I'm still so afraid. Can't I go with Daddy—just for a few days?"

Finally Cynthia agreed with sighs and the pained airs that left them both feeling a little guilty. On the drive down to Abbots Yew, where Steven had invited them for as long as was necessary for Melissa-Jane's convalescence, she sat very quietly beside Peter, her left hand still in the sling and the finger wearing a small neat white turban. She spoke only after they had passed the Heathrow turnoff on the M 4.

"All the time I knew you were going to come. I can't remember much else. It was always dark and giddy-making—things kept changing, I'd look at a face and it would fade away, and then we'd be somewhere else—"

"It was the drug they were giving you," Peter explained.

"Yes, I know that. I remember the prick of the needle." Reflexively she rubbed her upper arm, and shivered briefly. "But even with the drug I always knew you were going to come. I remember lying in the darkness listening for your voice—"

There was the temptation to try to pretend it had never happened, and Melissa-Jane had not spoken about it until now, but Peter knew she must be allowed to talk it out.

"Would you like to tell me about it?" he invited gently, knowing that it was essential to the healing process. He listened quietly as she spilled out drug-haunted memories, disjointed scraps of conversation and impressions. The terror was back in her voice when she spoke of the dark one.

"He looked at me sometimes. I remember him looking at me—" And Peter remembered the cold killer's eyes.

"He is dead now, darling."

"Yes, I know. They told me." She was silent for a moment, and then went on. "He was so different from the one with grey hair. I liked him, the old one. His name was Doctor Jamieson."

"How did you know that?" Peter asked.

"That's what the dark one called him." She smiled. "Doctor Jamieson, I remember he always smelled like cough mixture and I liked him—"

The one who had done the amputation, and would have taken her hand as well, Peter thought grimly.

"I never saw the other one. I knew he was there, but I never saw him."

"The other one?" Peter turned to her sharply. "Which other one, darling?"

"There was another one—and even the dark one was afraid of him. I knew that, they were all afraid of him."

"You never saw him?"

"No, but they were always talking about him, and arguing about what he would do."

"Do you remember his name?" Peter asked, and Melissa-Jane frowned in concentration.

"Did he have a name?" Peter prompted.

"Usually they just talked about *him*, but, yes, I remember now. The dark one called him 'Casper.'"

"Casper?"

"No, not that, not Casper. Oh, I can't remember." Her voice had risen, a shrill note in terror that ripped at Peter's nerves.

"Don't worry about it." He tried to soothe her, but she shook her head with frustration.

"Not Casper, but a name like that. I knew he was the one who really wanted to hurt me—they were just doing what he told them. He was the one I was truly afraid of." Her voice ended with a sob, and she was sitting bolt upright in the seat.

"It's over now, darling." Peter swung into the verge of the road and braked to a halt. He reached for her but she was rigid in his arms and at his touch she began to shake uncontrollably. Peter's alarm flared, and he held her to his chest.

"Caliph!" She whispered. "That's his name. Caliph." And she relaxed against him softly, and sighed. The shaking stopped slowly. Peter went on holding her, trying to control the terrible consuming waves of anger that engulfed him, and it was some little time before he realized suddenly that Melissa-Jane had fallen asleep.

It was as though uttering the name had been a catharsis for her terror, and now she was ready to begin the healing inside.

Peter laid her gently back in the seat and covered her with the angora rug before he drove on, but every few seconds he glanced across to make sure she was at peace.

Twice Peter called Magda Altmann from Abbots Yew, both times to her private number, but she was unobtainable and there was no message for him. That was five days he had not been able to reach her, not since the Delta Strike which had freed Melissa-Jane. She seemed to have disappeared completely, and Peter pondered the implications during the quiet days when he was almost always alone with his daughter.

Then Dr. Kingston Parker arrived at Abbots Yew, and Sir Steven Stride was delighted to have as his guest such a distinguished statesman.

Kingston Parker's giant personality seemed to fill the beautiful old home. When he put himself out, his graciousness was irresistible. Steven was delighted with him, particularly when he discovered that despite Parker's image as a liberal and his well-known concern with human rights, he was also a champion of the capitalist system, and determined that his country should take more seriously its responsibilities as leader of the Western world. They both deplored the loss of the B-1 bomber and the delaying of the neutron bomb programme, and the restructuring of America's intelligence agencies. They spent much of the first afternoon in Steven's redwood-panelled study exploring each other's views, and came out of it fast friends.

When they emerged, Parker completed his conquest of the Stride household by showing he shared with Patricia Stride a scholarly knowledge and love of antique porcelain. His concern and warmth for Melissa-Jane and his relief at her safety were too spontaneous not to be entirely genuine. His conquest of that young lady's affections was complete when he went down with her to the stables to meet Florence Nightingale and prove that he was also a fair judge of horseflesh.

"He's a lovely man. I think he is truly an honourable man," Melissa-Jane told Peter, when he went up to her bedroom to bid her goodnight. "And he's so kind and funny." Then, lest there be any question of disloyalty, "But you are still my most favourite man in all the world."

Her cure and convalescence seemed almost complete, and as Peter went down to rejoin the company he marvelled again at the resilience of young flesh and young minds.

As usual at Abbots Yew there was glittering and stimulating company at dinner, with Kingston Parker at its centre, but afterwards he and Peter exchanged a single glance down the length of Pat Stride's silver- and candle-decorated table, and they left them to the port and cognac and cigars and slipped out unobtrusively into the walled rose garden.

While they paced side by side on the crunching gravel pathway, Kingston Parker stoked his meerschaum and then began to talk quietly. Once his bodyguard coughed in the shadows where he waited just out of range of their subdued voices, but that was the only intrusion and the spring night was still and balmy. Their conversation seemed utterly incongruous in these surroundings, talk of death and violence, the use and abuse of power, and the manipulations of vast fortunes by a single mysterious figure.

"It's been five days since I arrived in England." Kingston Parker shrugged. "One does not rush through the echoing passages of Whitehall. There was much to discuss"—Peter knew that he had met with the Prime Minister on two separate occasions—"and it wasn't just Atlas business, I'm afraid." Parker was one of the President's confidants. They would have taken full advantage of his visit to exchange views with the British Government. "However, we did discuss Atlas in depth and detail. You know very well that Atlas has opponents and critics on both sides of the Atlantic. They tried very hard to squash it, and when they could not they saw to it that its powers and duties were severely curtailed." Parker paused and his pipe gurgled. He flicked out the juices from the mouthpiece onto the gravel path. "The opponents of Atlas are all highly intelligent, concerned and informed men. Their motives and their reasoning in opposing Atlas are laudable. I find myself a little in sympathy despite myself. If you create a strike force such as Atlas, where enormous powers are placed in the hands of a single man or a small élite leadership, you could very well be creating a Frankenstein—a monster more frightening than the one you are setting out to destroy."

"That depends on the man who controls it, Doctor Parker. I believe that they have the right man."

"Thank you, Peter." Parker turned his big shaggy head and smiled. "Won't you please call me Kingston."

Peter nodded agreement, while Parker went on. "Atlas has had some spectacular successes—at Johannesburg and now in Ireland—but that makes it more dangerous. There will be a readier acceptance of the whole concept by the public; if Atlas asks for wider powers, it is more likely they would be granted. And, believe me, if it is to do the job, it needs wider powers, Peter. I find myself torn down the centre—"

"And yet," Peter pointed out, "we cannot take on the most dangerous animal in the world, man the killer—we cannot do it without arming ourselves in every possible way."

Kingston Parker sighed. "And if Atlas achieves those powers, who can say when they will be abused, when will the rule of force supersede the rule of law?"

"The rules have changed. The rule of law is so often powerless in the face of those who have no respect for the law."

"There is another aspect, Peter. One that I have thought about half my life. What about the rule of unjust law? The laws of oppression and greed. A law that enslaves or deprives a man because of the colour of his face or the God he worships? If a duly constituted parliament makes racial laws—or if the General Assembly of the United Nations declares that Zionism is a form of Imperialism and must be outlawed—what if a handful of men gain control of the world's resources and legally manipulate them in a manner dictated by personal greed to the detriment of all humankind, such as the Committee of OPEC, the King of Saudi Arabia"—Kingston Parker made a helpless gesture, spreading those long sensitive fingers. "Must we respect those laws? The rule of law, even unjust law, is it sacrosanct?"

"Balance," said Peter. "There has to be a balance between law and force."

"Yes, but what is the balance, Peter?" He abruptly closed his hands into fists. "I have asked for greater powers for Atlas, wider scope for its use, and I think these will be granted. When they are, we will have need of good men, Peter." Kingston Parker reached out and took Peter's shoulder in a surprisingly powerful grip. "Just men, who can recognize when the rule of law has either failed or is unjust, and who have the courage and the vision to act to restore the balance that you spoke of a moment ago."

His hand was still on Peter's shoulder and he left it there. It was a natural gesture, without affectation.

"I believe you are one of those men." He let the hand drop, and his manner changed. "Tomorrow I have arranged that we meet with Colonel Noble. He has been busy breaking down and examining the entire Irish operation, and I hope he will have come up with something for us to get our teeth into. Then there is much else to discuss. Two o'clock at Thor Command, will it suit you, Peter?"

"Of course."

"Now let's go in and join the company."

"Wait." Peter stopped him. "I have something I must tell you, Kingston. It's been tearing at my guts, and after you have heard it you may alter your opinion of me—my suitability for my role at Atlas."

"Yes?" Parker turned back and waited quietly.

"You know that the people who kidnapped my daughter made no demands for her return, made no attempt to contact me or the police to negotiate."

"Yes," Parker answered. "Of course. It was one of the puzzling things about the whole business."

"It was untrue. There was a contact and a demand."

"I don't understand." Parker frowned and thrust his face closer to Peter's, as though trying to study his expression in the poor light from the windows.

"The kidnappers contacted me. A letter which I destroyed—"

"Why?" Parker shot at him.

"Wait. I'll explain," Peter replied. "There was a single condition for my daughter's release, and a deadline of two weeks. If I did not meet the condition by that time, they would have sent me parts of my daughter's body—her hands, her feet, and finally her head."

"Diabolical," Parker whispered. "Inhuman. What was the condition?"

"A life for a life," said Peter. "I was to kill you in exchange for Melissa-Jane."

"Me!" Parker started, throwing back his head with shock. "They wanted me?"

Peter did not reply, and they stood staring at each other, until Parker raised his hand and combed at his hair, a distracted gesture.

"That changes it all. I will have to think it out carefully—but it makes a whole new scenario." He shook his head. "Me. They were going for the head of Atlas. Why? Because I was the champion of Atlas, and they opposed its formation? No! That's not it. There seems only one logical explanation. I told you last time I saw you that I suspected the existence of a central figure—the puppet-master who was taking control of all known militant organizations and welding them into a single cohesive and formidable entity. Well, Peter, I have been hunting this figure. I have learned much to confirm my suspicions since last we met. I believe this person, or assembly of persons, does in fact exist—part of the new powers I have asked for Atlas were to be used to hunt and destroy this organization before it does grave damage—before it succeeds in so terrifying the nations of the world that it becomes itself a world power." Parker stopped as though to gather his thoughts, and then went on in quieter more measured tones. "I think now that this is absolute proof that it does exist, and that it is aware of my suspicions and intentions to destroy it. When I set you up as

Atlas agent at large, I believed you would make contact with the enemy—but, God knows, I did not expect it to come like this."

He paused again, considering it. "Incredible!" He marvelled. "The one person whom I would never have suspected, you, Peter. You could have reached me at any time, one of the few people who could. And the leverage! Your daughter—the protracted mutilations—I may have just misjudged the cunning and ruthlessness of the enemy."

"Have you ever heard the name Caliph?" Peter asked.

"Where did you hear that?" Parker demanded harshly.

"The demand letter was signed Caliph, and Melissa-Jane heard her captors discussing it."

"Caliph." Parker nodded. "Yes, I have heard the name, Peter. Since I last spoke to you. I have heard the name. Indeed I have." He was silent again, sucking distractedly on his pipe, then he looked up. "I will tell you how and when tomorrow when we meet at Thor, but now you have given me much to keep me awake tonight."

He took Peter's arm and led him back towards the house. Warm yellow light and laughter spilled out from the downstairs windows, welcoming and gay, but both of them were withdrawn and silent as they trudged up the smoothly raked path.

At the garden door Kingston Parker paused, holding Peter back from entering.

"Peter, would you have done it?" he asked gruffly.

Peter answered him levelly without attempting to avoid his eyes. "Yes, Kingston, I would have done it. "

"How?"

"Explosives."

"Better than poison," Parker grunted. "Not as good as the gun." And then angrily, "We have to stop him, Peter. It is a duty that supersedes every other consideration."

"What I have just told you does not alter our relationship?" Peter asked. "The fact that I would have been your assassin—does not change it?"

"Strangely enough, it merely confirms what I have come to believe of you, Peter. You are a man with the hard ruthless streak we need, if we are to survive." He smiled bleakly. "I might wake up sweating in the night—but it doesn't alter what we have to do— you and I."

Colin Noble with his cheroot, and opposite him Kingston Parker with the amber meerschaum, seemed to be in competition as to who could soonest render the air in the room incapable of supporting human life. It was already thick and blue, and the temporary headquarters of Thor Command lacked air-conditioning—but within minutes Peter had become so immersed in what he was hearing that the discomfort was forgotten.

Colin Noble was going over the details of the Irish operation, and all that had been gleaned from it.

"The house, the Old Manse, was burned to the ground, of course, the Irish constabulary had twenty men sifting through the ashes—" He spread his hands. "A big nix. Nothing at all."

"Next the contents of the Austin and its—provenance—how do you like that word, Peter baby? Provenance, that's a classy word."

Parker smiled indulgently. "Please go on, Colin."

"The Austin was stolen in Dublin, and resprayed and fitted with the roof carrier. It contained nothing, no papers, nothing in the glove compartment or boot, it had been stripped and cleaned out by an expert—"

"The men," Parker prompted him.

"Yes, sir. The men. The dead one first. Name of Gerald O'Shaughnessy, also known as 'Gilly,' born Belfast 1946." As he spoke Colin picked up the file that lay on the table in front of him. It was five inches thick. "Do we want to read all of it? It's a hell of a story. The guy had a track record—"

"Only as far as it concerns Atlas," Parker told him.

"There is no evidence as to when or how he became involved with this business." Colin sketched the facts swiftly and succinctly. "So we end with the contents of his pockets. Six hundred pounds sterling, thirty-eight rounds of .38 ammunition, and papers in the name of Edward and Helen Barry—forged, but beautifully forged." Colin closed the file with a slap. "Nothing," he repeated. "Nothing we can use. Now the other man. Morrison —Claude Bertram Morrison—celebrated abortionist and dedicated alcoholic. Struck off the medical rolls in 1969." Again he recounted the sordid history swiftly and accurately. "His price for the digital surgery was three thousand pounds—half in advance. Hell, that's cheaper than Blue Cross." Colin grinned, but his eyes were black and bright with anger. "I am pleased to report that he can expect a sentence of approximately fifteen years. They are going to throw the book at him. There is only one item of any possible interest which he could give us. Gilly O'Shaughnessy was the leader from whom he took his orders. O'Shaughnessy, in turn, took his orders from somebody called—" He paused dramatically. "Yes, that's right. The name we have all heard before. Caliph."

"Just one point here," Kingston Parker interrupted. "Caliph likes to use his name. He signs it on his correspondence. Even his lowliest thugs are given the name to use. Why?"

"I think I can answer that." Peter stirred and raised his head. "He wants us to know that he exists. We must have a focal point for our fear and hatred. When he was merely a nameless, faceless entity he was not nearly as menacing as he is now."

"I think you are right." Parker nodded his head gravely. "By using the name he is building up a store of credibility which he will draw upon later. In the future, when Caliph says he will kill or mutilate we know he is in deadly earnest, there will be no compromise. He will do exactly as he promises. The man, or men, are clever psychologists."

"There is just one aspect of the Irish operation we have not yet considered," Peter broke in, frowning with concentration. "That is—who was it that tipped us off, and what was the reason for that telephone call?"

They were all silent, until Parker turned to Colin.

"What do you think of that one?"

"I have discussed it with the police, of course. It was one of the first things that puzzled us. The police believe that Gilly O'Shaughnessy picked his hideout in Ireland because he was familiar with the terrain, and had friends there. It was his old stamping ground when he was with the Provos. He could move and disappear, get things fixed." Colin paused and saw the sceptical expression on Peter's face. "Well, look at it this way, Pete. He had a woman negotiate the lease on the Old Manse—Kate Barry, she called herself and signed it on the lease—so that was one ally, there must have been others, because he was able to buy a stolen and reworked automobile—he would have had difficulty doing that in Edinburgh or London without the word getting about."

Peter nodded reluctantly. "All right, having the Irish connection helped him."

"But there was the other side of the coin. O'Shaughnessy had enemies, even in the Provos. He was a ruthless bastard with a bloody record. We can only believe that one of those enemies saw the chance to make a score—the one who sold him the stolen auto, perhaps. We have had the recording of the tip-off call examined by language experts and had a run against the voice prints on the computer. Nothing definite. The voice was disguised, probably through a handkerchief and nose plugs, but the general feeling is that it was an Irishman who made the call. The boffins from the telephone department were able to test the loading of the line and guess that it was a call from a foreign country—very likely Ireland, although they cannot be certain of that."

Peter Stride raised one eyebrow slightly, and Colin chuckled weakly and waved the cheroot at him in a wide gesture of invitation.

"Okay. That's my best shot," he said. "Let's hear you do better. If you don't like my theories, you must have one of your own."

"You are asking me to believe it was all a coincidence; that O'Shaughnessy just happened to run into an old enemy who just happened to tip us off twenty-four hours before the deadline for Melissa-Jane's hand to be amputated. Then it just so happened that we reached Laragh at exactly the same moment as O'Shaughnessy was pulling out and making a run for it. Is that what you want me to believe?"

"Something like that," Colin admitted.

"Sorry, Colin. I just don't like coincidence."

"Shoot!" Colin invited. "Let's hear how it really happened."

"I don't know," Peter grinned placatingly. "It is just that I have this feeling that Caliph doesn't deal in coincidence either. I have this other feeling that somehow Gilly O'Shaughnessy had the death mark on his forehead from the beginning. I have this feeling it was all part of the plan."

"It must be great fun to have these feelings." Colin was prickling a little. "But they sure as hell aren't much help to me."

"Take it easy." Peter held up one hand in surrender. "Let's accept tentatively that it happened your way, then—"

"But?" Colin asked.

"No buts—not until we get some more hard evidence—"

"Okay, buster." There was no smile on Colin's face now, the wide mouth clamped in a grim line. "You want hard evidence, try this one for size—"

"Hold it, Colin," Parker shot in quickly, authoritatively. "Wait for a moment before we come to that." And Colin Noble deflated with a visible effort, the cords in his throat smoothing out and the line of mouth relaxed into the old familiar grin as he deferred to Kingston Parker.

"Let's backtrack here a moment," Parker suggested. "Peter came up with the name Caliph. In the meantime we had picked up the same name—but from an entirely different source. I promised Peter I would tell him about our source—because I think it gives us a new insight into this entire business." He paused and tinkered with his pipe, using one of those small tools with folding blades and hooks and spikes with which pipe smokers arm themselves. He scraped the bowl and knocked a nub of half-burned tobacco into the ashtray, before peering into the pipe the way a rifleman checks the bore of his weapon. Peter realized that Parker used his pipe as a prop for his performances, the way a magician distracts his audience with flourishes and mumbo-jumbo. He was not a man to underestimate, Peter thought again for the hundredth time. Kingston Parker looked up at him and smiled, a conspiratorial smile as if to acknowledge that Peter had seen through his little act.

"Our news of Caliph comes from an unlikely direction—or rather, considering the name, a more likely direction. East. Riyadh to be precise. Capital city of Saudi Arabia, seat of King Khalid's oil Empire. Our battered and beleaguered Central Intelligence Agency has received an appeal from the King following the murder of one of his grandsons. You recall the case, I'm sure—" Peter had a strange feeling of *déjà-vu* as he listened to Kingston Parker confirming exactly the circumstances that he and Magda Altmann had discussed and postulated together, was it only three weeks before? "You see the King and his family are in a very vulnerable position really. Did you know that there are at least seven hundred Saudi princes who are multi-millionaires, and who are close to the King's affections and power structure? It would be impossible to guard that many potential victims adequately. It's really damned good thinking—you don't have to seize a hostage with all the attendant risks. There is virtually an unlimited supply of them walking around, ripe for plucking, and an inexhaustible supply of assassins to be either pressured or paid to do the job, just as long as you have the information and leverage, or just enough money. Caliph seems to have all that."

"What demand has been made upon Khalid?" Peter asked.

"We know for certain that he has received a demand, and that he has appealed to the CIA for assistance to protect and guard his family. The demand came from an agency or person calling himself Caliph. We do not know what the demand is—but it may be significant that Khalid has agreed that he will not support a crude oil price increase at the next pricing session of OPEC, but on the contrary he will push for a five per cent decrease in the price of crude."

"Caliph's thinking has paid off again," Peter murmured.

"It looks like it, doesn't it." Parker nodded, and then chuckled bitterly. "And once again you get the feeling, as with his demands to the South African Government, that his final objective is desirable—even if the way he goes about procuring it is slightly unconventional, to say the least."

"To say the very least," Peter agreed quietly, remembering the feel of Melissa-Jane's fever-racked body against his chest.

"So there is no doubt now that what we feared, is fact. Caliph exists," said Parker.

"Not only exists, but flourishes," Peter agreed.

"Alive and well with a nice house in the suburbs." Colin lit the stub of his cheroot before going on. "Hell! He succeeded at Johannesburg. He is succeeding at Riyadh—where does he go from there—why not the Federation of Employers in West Germany? The Trade Union leaders in Great Britain?—Any group powerful enough to affect the fate of nations, and small enough to be terrorized as individuals."

"It's a way to sway and direct the destiny of the entire world. You just cannot guard all the world's decision-makers from personal attack," Peter agreed. "And it's no argument to point out that because his first two targets have been South Africa and the oil monopoly, then the long term results will be to the benefit of mankind. His ultimate target will almost certainly be the democratic process itself. I don't think there can be any doubt that Caliph sees himself as a god. He sees himself as the paternal Tyrant. His aim is to cure the ills of the world by radical surgery, and to maintain its health by unrestrained force and fear."

Peter could remain seated no longer. He pushed back his chair and crossed to the windows, standing there in the soldier's stance, balanced on the balls of his feet with both hands clasped lightly behind his back. There was an uninspiring view of the high barbed-wire fence, part of the airfield and the corrugated sheet wall of the nearest hangar. A Thor sentry paced before the gates with a white M.P. helmet on his head and side arm strapped to his waist. Peter watched him without really seeing him, and behind Peter the two men at the table exchanged a significant glance. Colin Noble asked a silent question and Parker answered with a curt nod of affirmative.

"All right," Colin said. "A little while back you asked for hard facts. I promised to give you a few."

Peter turned back from the window and waited.

"Item One. During the time that Gilly O'Shaughnessy held Melissa-Jane in Laragh, two telephone calls were made from the Old Manse. They were both international calls. They both went through the local telephone exchange. The first call was made at seven P.M. local time on the first of this month. That would have been the first day that they could have reached the hideout. We have to guess it was an 'All Well' report to the top management. The second call was exactly seven days later again at seven o'clock local time precisely. To the same number. We have to guess that it was another report, 'All is still well.' Both calls were less than one minute in duration. Just time enough to pass a pre-arranged code message—" Colin broke off and looked again at Kingston Parker.

"Go on," Parker instructed.

"The calls were to a French number. Rambouillet 47-87-47."

Peter felt it hit him in the stomach, a physical blow, and he flinched his head. For a moment closing both his eyes tightly. He had called that number so often, the numerals were graven on his memory.

"No." He shook his head, and opened his eyes. "I'm not going to believe it."

"It's true, Peter," Parker said gently.

Peter walked back to his seat. His legs felt rubbery and shaky under him. He sat down heavily.

The room was completely silent. Neither of the other two looked directly at Peter Stride.

Kingston Parker made a gesture to Colin and obediently he slid the red box file, tied with red tapes, across the cheap vinyl-topped table.

Parker untied the tapes and opened the file. He shuffled the papers, scanning them swiftly. Clearly he was adept at speed reading and was able to assimilate each typed double-spaced page at a glance—but now he was merely waiting for Peter to recover from the shock. He knew the contents of the red file almost by heart.

Peter Stride slumped in the steel-framed chair with its uncushioned wooden seat, staring sightlessly at the bulletin board on the opposite wall on which were posted the Thor rosters.

He found it hard to ride the waves of dismay that flooded over him. He felt chilled and numbed, the depth of this betrayal devastated him, and when he closed his eyes again he had a vivid image of the slim, tender body with the childlike breasts peeping through a silken curtain of dark hair.

He straightened in his seat, and Kingston Parker recognized the moment and looked up at him, half-closing the file and turning it towards him.

The cover bore the highest security gradings available to Atlas Command—and below them was typed:

ALTMANN   MAGDA   IRENE.
Born KUTCHINSKY.

Peter realized that he had never known her second name was Irene. Magda Irene. Hell, they were really ugly names—made special only by the woman who bore them.

Parker turned the file back to himself and began to speak quietly.

"When last you and I met, I told you of the special interest we had in this lady. That interest has continued, unabated, since then, or rather it has gathered strength with every fresh item of information that has come to us." He opened the file again and glanced at it as if to refresh his memory. "Colin has been very successful in enlisting the full co-operation of the intelligence agencies of both our countries, who in turn have been able to secure that of the French and—believe it or not—the Russians. Between the four countries we have been able to at last piece together the woman's history—" He broke off. "Remarkable woman," and shook his head in admiration. "Quite incredible really. I can understand how she is able to weave spells around any man she chooses. I can understand, Peter, your evident distress. I am going to be blunt now—we have no time nor space in which to maneuvre tactfully around your personal feelings. We know that she has taken you as a lover. You notice that I phrase that carefully. Baroness Altmann takes lovers, not the other way around. She takes lovers deliberately and with careful forethought. I have no doubt that once she has made the decision, she accomplishes the rest of it with superb finesse."

Peter remembered her coming to him and the exact words she had used. "I am not very good at this, Peter, and I want so badly to be good for you."

The words had been chosen with the finesse that Kingston Parker had just spoken of. They were exactly turned to make herself irresistible to Peter—and afterwards she had given the gentle lie to them with the skill and devilish cunning of her hands and mouth and body.

"You see, Peter. She had special and expert training in all the arts of love. There are probably few women in the Western world who know as much about reading a man, and then pleasing him. What she knows she did not learn in Paris or London or New York—" Kingston Parker paused and frowned at Peter. "This is all theory and hearsay, Peter. You are in a better position to say just how much of it is false?"

The ultimate skill in pleasing a man is to fuel his own belief in himself, Peter thought, as he returned Parker's inquiring gaze with expressionless eyes. He remembered how with Magda Altmann he had felt like a giant, capable of anything. She had made him feel like that with a word, a smile, a gift, a touch—that was the ultimate skill.

He did not answer Parker's question. "Go on please, Kingston," he invited. Externally, he had himself completely under control now. His right hand lay on the table top, with the fingers half open, relaxed.

"I told you that even as a child she showed special talents. In languages, mathematics—her father was an amateur mathematician of some importance—chess and other games of skill. She attracted attention. Especially she attracted attention because her father was a member of the Communist Party"—Parker broke off as Peter lifted his head in sharp inquiry. "I'm sorry, Peter. We did not know that when last we met. We have learned it since from the French, they have access to the party records in Paris, it seems, and it was confirmed by the Russians themselves. Apparently the child used to accompany her father to meetings of the party, and soon showed a precocious political awareness and understanding. Her father's friends were mostly party members, and after his death—there still remains a mystery around his death. Neither the French nor the Russians are forthcoming on the subject. Anyway, after his death, Magda Kutchinsky was cared for by these friends. It seemed she was passed on from family to family"—Kingston Parker slid a postcard-sized photograph from a marbleized envelope and passed it across the table to Peter—"from this period."

It showed a rather skinny little girl in short skirts and dark stockings, wearing the yoked collar and straw bonnet of the French schoolgirl. Her hair was in two short braids, tied with ribbons, and she held a small fluffy white dog in her arms. The background was a Parisian summer park scene, with a group of men playing *boule* and chestnut trees in full leaf.

The child's face was delicately featured with huge beautiful eyes, somehow wise and compassionate beyond her age, and yet still imbued with the fresh innocence of childhood.

"You can see she already had all the markings of spectacular beauty." Kingston Parker grunted, and reached across to take back the photograph. For a moment Peter's fingers tightened instinctively, he would have liked to have kept it, but he relaxed and let it go. Parker glanced at it again and then slipped it back into the envelope.

"Yes. She attracted much interest, and very soon an uncle from the old country wrote to her. There were photographs of her father and the mother she had never known, anecdotes of her infancy and her father's youth. The child was enchanted. She had never known she had an uncle. Her father had never spoken of his relatives, but now at last the little orphan found she had family. It took only a few more letters, exchanges of delight and affection, and then it was all arranged. The uncle came to fetch her in person—and Magda Kutchinsky went back to Poland." Parker spread his hands. "It was easy as that."

"The missing years," Peter said, and his voice sounded strange in his own ears. He cleared his throat and shifted uncomfortably under Parker's piercing but understanding gaze.

"No longer missing, Peter. We have been fed a little glimmering of what happened during those years—and we have been able to fill in the rest of it from what we knew already."

"The Russians?" Peter asked, and when Parker nodded, Peter went on with a bitter tang to his voice. "They seem to be very forthcoming, don't they? I have never heard of them passing information—at least not valuable information—so readily."

"They have their reasons in this case," Parker demurred. "Very good reasons as it turns out—but one will come to those in due course."

"Very well."

"The child returned with her uncle to Poland, Warsaw. And there was an extravagant family reunion. We are not certain if this was her real family, or whether the child was provided with a foster family for the occasion. In any event, the uncle soon announced that if Magda would submit to examination there was an excellent chance that she would be provided with a scholarship to one of the élite colleges of the U.S.S.R. We can imagine that she passed her examination with great distinction and her new masters must have congratulated themselves on their discovery.

"The college is on the shores of the Black Sea near Odessa. It does not have a name, nor an old school tie. The students are very specially selected, the screening is rigorous and only the brightest and most talented are enrolled. They are soon taught that they are an élite group, and are streamed in the special direction that their various talents dictate. In Magda's case it was languages and politics, finance and mathematics. She excelled and at the age of seventeen graduated to a higher, more specialized branch of the Odessa college. There she was trained in special memory techniques, the already bright mind was honed down to a razor edge. I understand that one of the less difficult exercises was to be given access to a list of one hundred diverse items for sixty seconds. The list had to be repeated from memory, in the correct order, twenty-four hours later." Parker shook his head again, expressing his admiration.

"At the same time she was also trained to fit naturally into upper-class international Western society. Dress, food, drink, cosmetics, manners, popular music and literature, cinema, theatre, democratic politics, business procedures, the operation of stocks and commodities markets, the more mundane secretarial skills, modern dancing, the art of love-making and pleasuring men—that and much else, all of it taught by experts—flying, skiing, weapons, the rudiments of electronics and mechanical engineering and every other skill that a top-class agent might have to call upon.

"She was the star of her course and emerged from it much as the woman you know. Poised, skilled, beautiful, motivated—and deadly.

"At the age of nineteen she knew more, was capable of more, than most other human beings, male or female, twice her age.' The perfect agent, except for a small flaw in her make-up that only showed up later. She was too intelligent and too personally ambitious." Kingston Parker smiled for the first time in twenty minutes. "Which of course is a pseudonym for Greed. Her masters did not recognize it in her, and perhaps at that age it was only latent greed. She had not yet been fully exposed to the attractions of wealth—or of unlimited power."

Kingston Parker broke off, leaned across the table towards Peter. He seemed to change direction then, smiling an inward knowledgeable smile, as though pondering a hidden truth.

"Greed for wealth alone belongs essentially to the lower levels of human intelligence. It is only the developed and advanced mind that can truly appreciate the need for power"—he saw the protest in Peter's expression—"no, no, I don't mean merely the power to control one's own limited environment, merely the power of life and death over a few thousand lives—not that, but true power. Power to change the destiny of nations, power such as Caesar or Napoleon wielded, such as the President of the United States wields—that is the ultimate greed, Peter. A magnificent and noble greed."

He was silent a moment, as though glimpsing some vision of splendour. Then he went on,

"I digress. Forgive me," and turned to Colin Noble. "Do we have some coffee, Colin? I think we could all do with a cup now."

Colin went to the machine that blooped and gurgled and winked its red eye in the corner, and while he filled the cups, the charged atmosphere in the room eased a little, and Peter tried to arrange his thoughts in some logical sequence. He looked for the flaws and weak places in the story but could find none—instead he remembered only the feel of her mouth, the touch of her hands on his body. Oh God, it was a stab of physical pain, a deep ache in the chest and groin, as he remembered how she had coursed him like a running stag, driving and goading him on to unvisited depths of his being. Could such skills be taught, he wondered, and if so, by whom? He had a horrifying thought of a special room set on the heights above the Black Sea, with that slim, vulnerable, tender body practising its skills, learning love as though it were cookery or small arms practice—and then he shut his mind firmly against it, and Kingston Parker was speaking again, balancing his coffee cup primly with his pinky finger raised, like an old maid at a tea party.

"So she arrived back in Paris and it fell at her feet. It was a triumphant progress." Kingston Parker prodded in the file with his free hand, spilling out photographs of Magda—Magda dancing in the ballroom of the Élysée Palace, Magda leaving a Rolls-Royce limousine outside Maxim's in the rue Royale, Magda skiing, riding, beautiful, smiling, poised—and always there were men. Rich, well-fed, sleek men.

"I told you once there were eight sexual liaisons." Kingston Parker used that irritating expression again. "We have had reason to revise that figure. The French take a very close interest in that sort of thing, they have added to the list." He flicked over the photographs. "Pierre Hammond, Deputy Minister of Defence—" And another. "Mark Vincent, head of mission at the American Consulate—"

"Yes," Peter cut in short, but still there was a sickly fascination in seeing the faces of these men. He had imagined them accurately, he realized, without particular relish.

"Her masters were delighted—as you can imagine. With a male agent it is sometimes necessary to wait a decade or more for results while he moles his way into the system. With a young and beautiful woman she has her greatest value when those assets are freshest. Magda Kutchinsky gave them magnificent value. We do not know the exact extent of her contributions—our Russian friends have not bared everything to us, I'm afraid, but I estimate that it was about this time they began to realize her true potential. She had the magical touch, but her beauty and youth could not last forever—" Kingston Parker made a deprecating gesture with the slim pianist's hands. "We do not know if Aaron Altmann was a deliberate choice by her masters. But it seems likely. Think of it—one of the richest and most powerful men in Western Europe, one who controlled most of the steel and heavy engineering producers, the single biggest armaments complex, electronics—all associated and sensitive secondary industries. He was a widower, childless, so under French law his wife could inherit his entire estate. He was known to be fighting a slowly losing battle with cancer, so his life term was limited—and he was also a Zionist and one of the most trusted and influential members of Mossad. It was beautiful. Truly beautiful," said Kingston Parker. "Imagine being able to undermine a man of that stature, perhaps being able to double him! Though that seemed an extravagant dream—not even the most beautiful siren of history could expect to turn a man like Aaron Altmann—he is a separate study on his own, another incredible human being with the strength and courage of a lion—until the cancer wore him out. Again I digress, forgive me. Somebody, either the Director of the NKVD in Moscow or Magda Kutchinsky's control at the Russian Embassy in Paris—who was, incidentally, the Chief NKVD Commissar for Western Europe, such was her value—or Magda Kutchinsky herself, picked Aaron Altmann. Within two years she was indispensable to him. She was cunning enough not to use her sexual talents upon him immediately. Altmann could have any woman who took his fancy, and he usually did. His sexual appetites were legendary, and they probably were the cause of his remaining childless. A youthful indiscretion resulted in a venereal disease with complications. It was later completely cured, but the damage was irreversible, he never produced an heir."

He was a man who would have toyed with her and cast her aside as soon as he tired of her, if she had been callow enough to make herself immediately available to him. First, she won his respect and admiration. Perhaps she was the first woman he had ever met whose brain and strength and determination matched his own.

Kingston Parker selected another photograph and passed it across the table. Fascinated, Peter stared at the black-and-white image of a heavily built man with a bull neck, and a solid thrusting jaw. Like so many men of vast sexual appetite, he was bald except for a Friar Tuck frill around the cannon-ball dome of his skull. But there were humorous lines chiselled about his mouth,

and his eyes, though fierce, looked as though they too could readily crinkle with laughter lines. Portrait of Power, Peter thought.

"When at last she gave him access to her body, it must have
been like some great electrical storm." Kingston Parker seemed to
be deliberately dwelling on her past love affairs, and Peter would
have protested had not the information he was receiving been so
vital. "This man and woman must have been able to match each
other once again. Two very superior persons, two in a hundred million probably—it is interesting to speculate what might have happened if they had been able to produce a child." Kingston Parker
chuckled. "It would probably have been a mongolian idiot—life is
like that."

Peter moved irritably, hating this turn in the conversation, and
Parker went on smoothly.

"So they married, and the NKVD had a mole in the centre of
Western industry. Narmco, Altmann's armaments complex, was
manufacturing top-secret American, British and French missile
hardware for NATO. The new Baroness was soon on the Board,
became in fact Deputy Chairman of Narmco. We can be sure that
armaments blueprints were passed, not by the sheet but by the
truckload. Every night, the leaders and decision-makers of the
Western world sat at the new Baroness's table and swilled her
champagne. Every conversation, every nuance and indiscretion
was recorded by that specially trained memory, and slowly, inevitably, the Baron's strength was whittled away. He began to rely
more and more upon her. We do not know exactly when she began
to assist him with his Mossad activities—but when it happened
the Russians had succeeded in their design. In effect they had succeeded in turning Baron Aaron Altmann, they had his right hand
and his heart—for by this time the dying Baron was completely
besotted by the enchantress. They could expect to inherit the
greater part of Western European heavy industry. It was all very
easy—until the latent defect in the Baroness' character began to
surface. We can only imagine the alarm of her Russian masters
when they detected the first signs that the Baroness was working
for herself alone. She was brighter by far than any of the men who
had up until that time controlled her, and she had been given a
taste of real power. The taste seemed very much to her liking. We
can only imagine the gargantuan battle of wills between the puppet masters and the beautiful puppet that had suddenly developed

a mind and ambitions of her very own. Quite simply her ambition now was to be the most wealthy and powerful woman since Catherine of Russia, and the makings were almost within her pretty hands, except—"

Kingston Parker stopped; like a born storyteller, he knew instinctively how to build up the tension in his audience. He rattled his coffee cup.

"This talking is thirsty business." Colin and Peter had to rouse themselves with a physical effort. They had been mesmerized by the story and the personality of the storyteller. When Parker had his cup refilled, he sipped at it, then went on speaking.

"There was one last lever her Russian masters had over her. They threatened to expose her. It was quite a neat stroke, really. A man like Aaron Altmann would have acted like an enraged bull if he had known how he had been deceived. His reaction was predictable. He would have divorced Magda immediately. Divorce is difficult in France—but not for a man like the Baron. Without his protection Magda was nothing, less than nothing, for her value to the Russians would have come to an end. Without the Altmann Empire her dreams of power would disappear like a puff of smoke. It was a good try—it would have worked against an ordinary person, but of course they were not dealing with an ordinary person—"

Parker paused again.

"I have been doing a lot of talking," he smiled at Peter. "I'm going to let you have a chance now, Peter. You know her a little, you have learned a lot more about her in the last hour. Can you guess what she did?"

Peter began to shake his head—and then it crashed in upon him with sickening force, and he stared at Parker, the pupils of his eyes dilating with the strength of his revulsion.

"I think you have guessed." Parker nodded. "Yes, we can imagine that by this stage she was becoming a little impatient herself. The Baron was taking a rather long time to die."

"Christ, it's horrible." Peter grunted, as though in pain.

"From one point of view, I agree." Parker nodded. "But if you look at it like a chess player, and remember she is a player of Grand Master standard, it was a brilliant stroke. She arranged that the Baron be kidnapped. There are witnesses to the fact that she insisted on the Baron accompanying her that day. He was feeling very badly, and he did not want to go sailing, but she insisted that the sun and fresh air would be good for him. He never took his bodyguard when he went sailing. Thre were just the two of them. A very fast cruiser was waiting offshore"—he spread his hands—"you know the details?"

"No," Peter denied it.

"The cruiser rammed the yacht. Picked the Baron out of the water, but left the Baroness. An hour later there was a radio message to the coastguard, they went out and found her still clinging to the wreckage. The kidnappers were very concerned that she survive."

"They may have wanted a loving wife to bargain with," Peter suggested swiftly.

"That is possible, of course, and she certainly played the role of the bereaved wife to perfection. When the ransom demand came it was she who forced the Board of Altmann Industries to ante up the twenty-five million dollars. She personally took the cash to the rendezvous—alone." Parker paused significantly.

"She didn't need the money."

"Oh, but she did," Parker contradicted. "The Baron was not in his dotage, you know. His hands were still very firmly on the reins —and the purse strings. Magda had as much as any ordinary wife could wish for, furs, jewellery, servants, clothes, cars, boats— pocket money, around two hundred thousand dollars a year, paid to her as a salary from Altmann Industries. Any ordinary wife would have been well content—but she was not an ordinary wife. We must believe she had already planned how to carry forward her dreams of unlimited power—and it needed money, not thousands but millions. Twenty-five million would be a reasonable stopgap, until she could get her pretty little fingers on the big apple. She drove the cash, in thousand-Swiss-franc bills, I understand; she drove alone to some abandoned airfield and had a plane come pick it up and fly it out to Switzerland. Damned neat."

"But"—Peter searched for some means of denial—"the Baron was mutilated. She couldn't—"

"Death is death, mutilation may have served some obscure purpose. God knows, we are dealing with an Eastern mind, devious, sanguinary—perhaps the mutilation was merely to make any suspicion of the wife completely far-fetched—just as you immediately used it to protect her."

He was right, of course. The mind that could plan and execute the rest of such a heinous scheme would not balk at the smaller niceties of execution. He had no more protest to make.

"So let us review what she had achieved by this stage. She was rid of the Baron, and the restrictions he placed upon her. An example of these restrictions, for we will find it significant later: She was very strongly in favour of Narmco banning the sale of all weapons and armaments to the South African Government. The Baron, ever the businessman, looked upon that country as a lucrative market. There was also the South African sympathy for Zionism. He overruled her, and Narmco continued to supply aircraft, missiles and light armament to that country right up until the official UN resolution to enforce a total arms embargo, with France ratifying it. Remember the Baroness's anti-South African attitude. We come to it again later.

"She was rid of the Baron. She was rid of her Russian control, well able to maintain a small army to protect herself. Even her former Russian masters would hesitate to take revenge on her. She was a French Grande Dame now. She had gained significant working capital—25 million for which she was not accountable to another living human being. She had gained an invincible power base at Altmann Industries. Although she was still under certain checks and safeguards from the Board of Directors, yet she had access to all its information-gathering services, to its vast resources. As the head of such a colossus she had the respect of and sympathy of the French Government, and as a fringe benefit—limited but significant access to their intelligence systems. Then there was the Mossad connection, was she not the heir to Aaron Altmann's position—"

Peter suddenly remembered Magda speaking of her "sources"—and never identifying them. Was she really able to use the French and Israeli intelligence as her own private agencies? It seemed impossible. But he was learning swiftly that when dealing with Magda Altmann, anything was possible.

"There was a period then of consolidation, a time when she gathered up the reins that Aaron had dropped. There were changes amongst the top management throughout Altmann Industries as she replaced those who might oppose her with her own minions. A time of planning and organizing, and then the first attempt to govern and prescribe the destiny of nations. She chose the nation which most offended her personal view of the new world she was going to build. We will never know what made her choose the name of Caliph—"

"You have to be wrong." Peter squeezed his eyelids closed with thumb and forefinger. "You just don't know her."

"I don't think anybody knows her, Peter," Kingston Parker murmured, and fiddled with his pipe. "I'm sorry, we are going pretty fast here. Do you want to back up and ask any questions?"

"No, it's all right." Peter opened his eyes again. "Go on, will you, Kingston?"

"One of the most important lessons that Baroness Altmann had learned was the ease with which force and violence can be used, and their tremendous effect and profitability. Bearing this lesson in mind, the Baroness chose her first act as the new ruler of mankind, and the choice was dictated by her early political convictions, those convictions formed at her father's knee and at the Communist Party meetings that she had attended as a precocious child in Paris. There is a further suggestion that the choice was reinforced by the Altmann banking corporation's interests in South African gold sales, for by this time the Baroness had tempered her socialist and communist leanings with a good healthy dollop of capitalistic self-interest. We can only guess, but if the scheme to bring out forty tons of gold—and a black-based government-in-exile—had succeeded, it would not have taken very long for Caliph to gain control of both government and gold." Parker shrugged. "We just cannot say how ambitious, even grandiose, those plans were. But we can say that Caliph, or the Baroness, recruited her team for the execution of the plan with the skill she brought to anything she handled." He broke off, and smiled. "I think all three of us remember the taking of Flight 070 vividly enough not to have to go once more over the details. Let me just remind you that it would have succeeded, in fact it had actually succeeded, when Peter here made his unscheduled move that brought it all down. But it succeeded. That was the important thing. Caliph could afford to congratulate herself. Her information was impeccable. She had chosen the right people for the job. She even knew the name of the officer who would command the anti-terrorist force which would be sent to intervene, and her psychology had been excellent. The execution of the four hostages had so shocked and numbed the opposition that they were powerless—the cup had been dashed from her lips by one man alone. Inevitably her interest in that man was aroused. Possibly with feminine intuition she was able to recognize in him the qualities which could be turned to her own purpose. She had that indomitable streak in her make-up that is able to recognize even in the dust of disaster that material for future victory." Parker shifted his bulk, and made a small deprecatory gesture. "I hope it will not seem immodest if I bring myself into the story at this stage. I had been given the hint that something like Caliph existed. In fact, this may not have been her first act after the killing of Aaron Altmann. Two other succcessful kidnappings have her style—one of them the OPEC ministers in Vienna—but we cannot be sure. I had been warned and I was waiting for Caliph to surface. Dearly I would have loved a chance to interrogate one of the hijackers—"

"They would have had nothing to tell you," Peter interjected brusquely. "They were merely pawns, like the doctor we captured in Ireland."

Parker sighed. "Perhaps you are right, Peter. But at the time I believed that our only lead to Caliph had been severed. Later when the thing had been done and I had recovered from the shock of it, it suddenly occurred to me that the lead was still there —stronger than ever. You were that lead, Peter. That was why I recommended that your resignation be accepted. If you had not resigned, I would have forced you out anyway, but you played along superbly by resigning." He smiled again. "I have never thanked you for that."

"Don't mention it," said Peter, grimly. "I like to be of service."

"And you were. Almost immediately you were on the loose, the Baroness began making her approach. First she collected every known fact about you. Somehow she even got a computer run on you. That's a fact. An unauthorized run was made on the Central Intelligence computer four days after your resignation. She must have liked what she got, for there was the Narmco offer—through conventional channels. Your refusal must have truly excited her interest, for she used her connections to have herself invited down to Sir Steven's country house." Parker chuckled. "My poor Peter, you found yourself without warning in the clutches of one of history's most accomplished enchantresses. I know enough about the lady to guess that her approach to you was very carefully calculated from the complete information that she had on you. She knew exactly what type of woman attracted you. Fortunately, she fitted the general physical description—"

"What is that?" Peter demanded. He was unaware that he had a specific type of physical preference.

"Tall, slim and brunette," Parker told him promptly. "Think about it," he invited. "All your women have been that."

He was right, of course, Peter realized. Hell, even at thirty-nine years of age it was still possible to learn something about yourself.

"You're a cold-blooded bastard, Kingston. Did anybody ever tell you that?"

"Frequently." Kingston smiled. "But it's not true, and compared to Baroness Altmann I am Father Christmas." And he became serious again. "She wanted to find out what we at Atlas knew about her activities. She knew by this stage that we had our suspicions, and through you she had an inside ear. Of course, your value would deteriorate swiftly the longer you were out of Thor— but you could still be useful in a dozen other ways. As a bonus, you could be expected to do a good job at Narmco. All her expectations were fulfilled, and exceeded. You even thwarted an assassination attempt on her life—"

Peter lifted an eyebrow in inquiry.

"—on the road to Rambouillet that night. Here we are only guessing, but it's a pretty well-informed guess. The Russians had by this time despaired of returning her to the fold. They had also suspicions as to her role as Caliph. They decided on a radical cure for their one-time star agent. They either financed and organized the assassination attempt themselves, or they tipped off Mossad that she had murdered Aaron Altmann. I would be inclined to believe that they hired the killers themselves—because the Mossad usually do their own dirty work. Anyway, with NKVD or Mossad as paymasters, an ambush was set up on the Rambouillet road and you drove into it. I know you don't like coincidence, Peter, but I believe it was merely coincidence that you were driving the Baroness' Maserati that night."

"All right," Peter murmured. "If I swallow the rest of the hog, that little crumb goes down easily enough."

"That attempt severely alarmed the Baroness. She was not certain who had been the author. I think she believed it was Atlas Command, or at the very least that we had something to do with it. Almost immediately after that you were able to confirm our interest in her, and our knowledge that Caliph existed. I invited you to America, Colin brought you to meet me, and when you returned you either told her about it, or in some way confirmed her suspicions of Atlas Command and Kingston Parker. I am guessing again—but how close am I, Peter? Be honest."

Peter stared at him, trying to keep his face expressionless while his mind raced. That was exactly how it had happened.

"We were all hunting Caliph. You saw no disloyalty in discussing it with her." Parker prompted him gently, and Peter nodded once curtly.

"You believed that we had common goals," Parker went on with deep understanding and compassion. "You thought we were all hunting Caliph. That is right."

"She knew I had been to America to see you before I told her. I don't know how—but she knew," Peter said stiffly. He felt like a traitor.

"I understand," Parker said simply. He reached across the table and once again placed his hand on Peter's shoulder. He squeezed it while he looked into Peter's eyes, a gesture of affirmation and trust. Then he laid both hands on top of the table.

"She knew who was the hunter then, and she knew enough about me to know I was dangerous. You were probably the only man in the world who could reach me and do the job—but you had to be motivated. She picked the one and only lever that would move you. She picked it unerringly—just as she had done everything else. It would have worked—in one stroke she would have gotten rid of the hunter, and she would have acquired a top-class assassin. When you had done the job, you would have belonged to Caliph for all time. She would have used you to kill again and again, and each time you killed you would be more deeply enmeshed in her net. You really were a very valuable prize, Peter. Valuable enough for her to find it worthwhile to use her sexual wiles upon you."

He saw the lumps of clenched muscle at the corner of Peter's jaw, and the fire in his eyes.

"You are also a very attractive man, and who knows but she felt the need to combine business and pleasure? She is a lady with strongly developed sexual appetites."

Peter felt a violent urge to punch him in the face. He needed some outlet for his rage. He felt belittled, soiled and used.

"She was clever enough to realize that the sex was not enough of a hold to force you to commit murder. So she took your daughter, and immediately had her mutilated—just as at Johannesburg she had executed hostages without hesitation. The world must learn to fear Caliph."

There was no smile on Parker's face now.

"I truly believe that if you had not been able to deliver my head by the deadline, she would not have hesitated to carry out the next mutilation, and the one after that."

Again Peter was assailed by a wave of nausea as he remembered that shrivelled white lump of flesh with the scarlet fingernail floating horribly in its tiny bottle.

"We were saved from that by the most incredible piece of luck. The Provo informer," said Parker. "And again the understandable eagerness of the Russians to co-operate with us. It is a wonderful opportunity for them to hand us their problem. They have let us have an almost full account of the lady and her history."

"But what are we going to do about it?" Colin Noble asked. "Our hands are tied. Do we just have to wait for the next atrocity —do we have to hope we will get another lucky break when Caliph kills the next Arab prince?"

"That will happen—unless they push through the OPEC decision," Parker predicted levelly. "The lady has converted very easily to the capitalist system now that she owns half of Europe's industry. A reduction in the oil price would benefit her probably more than any other individual on earth—and at the same time it will also benefit the great bulk of humanity. How nicely that squares all her political and personal interests."

"But if she gets away with it?" Colin insisted. "What will be her next act of God?"

"Nobody can predict that," Parker murmured, and they both turned their heads to look at Peter Stride.

He seemed to have aged twenty years. The lines at the corners of his mouth were cut in deeply like the erosion of weathered granite. Only his eyes were blue and alive and fierce as those of a bird of prey.

"I want you to believe what I am going to say now, Peter. I have not told you all this to put pressure on you," Parker assured him quietly. "I have told you only what I believe is necessary for you to know—to protect yourself if you should elect to return into the lion's den. I am not ordering you to do so. The risks involved cannot be overestimated. With a lesser man I would term it suicidal. However, now that you are forewarned, I believe you are the one man who could take Caliph on her own ground. Please do not misunderstand what I mean by that. I am not for a moment suggesting assassination. In fact, I expressly forbid you to even think in that direction. I would not allow it, and if you acted independently, I would do my utmost to see that you were brought to justice. No, all I ask is that you keep close to Caliph and try to outguess her. Try to expose her so we can lawfully act to take her out of action. I want you to put out of your mind the emotional issues—those hostages at Johannesburg, your own daughter—try to forget them, Peter. Remember we are neither judge nor executioner—" Parker went on speaking quietly and insistently, and Peter watched his lips with narrowed eyes, hardly listening to the words, trying to think clearly and see his course ahead—but his thoughts were a children's carousel, going around and around with fuss and fury but returning with every revolution to the one central conclusion.

There was only one way to stop Caliph. The thought of attempting to bring someone like Baroness Magda Altmann to justice—in a French Court—was laughable. Peter tried to force himself to believe that vengeance had no part in his decisions, but he had lived too long with himself to be able to pull off such a deceit. Yes, vengeance was part of it—and he trembled with the rage of remembrance, but it was not all of it. He had executed the German girl, Ingrid, and Gilly O'Shaughnessy—and had not regretted the decision to do so. If it was necessary for them to die—then surely Caliph deserved to die a thousand times more.

And there is only one person who can do it, he realized.

Her voice was quick and light and warm, with just that fascinating trace of accent; he remembered it so well, but had forgotten the effect it could have upon him. His heart pounded as though he had run a long way.

"Oh Peter. It's so good to hear your voice. I have been so worried. Did you get my cable?"

"No, which cable?"

"When I heard that you had freed Melissa-Jane. I sent you a cable from Rome."

"I didn't get it—but it doesn't matter."

"I sent it to you via Narmco—in Brussels."

"It's probably waiting for me there. I haven't been in touch."

"How is she, Peter?"

"She is fine now—" He found it strangely difficult to use her name, or any form of endearment. He hoped that the strain would not sound in his voice. "But we went through a hell of a time."

"I know. I understand. I felt so helpless. I tried so hard, that's why I was out of contact, Peter *chéri*, but day after day there was no news."

"It's all over now," Peter said gruffly.

"I don't think so," she said swiftly. "Where are you calling from?"

"London."

"When will you come back?"

"I telephoned Brussels an hour ago. Narmco wants me back urgently. I am taking a flight this afternoon."

"Peter, I have to see you. I've been too long without you—but, oh *mon Dieu*, I have to be in Vienna tonight. Wait, let me see, if I sent the Lear to fetch you now we could meet, even for an hour. You could take the late flight from Orly to Brussels and I could go on to Vienna with the Lear—please, Peter. I missed you so. We could have an hour together."

One of the airport sub-managers met Peter as he disembarked from the Lear and led him to one of the VIP lounges above the main concourse.

Magda Altmann came swiftly to meet him as he stepped into the lounge—and he had forgotten how her presence could fill a room with light.

She wore a tailored jacket over a matching skirt, severe gunmetal grey and tremendously effective. She moved like a dancer on long graceful legs which seemed to articulate from the narrow waist—and Peter felt awkward and heavy-footed, for the awareness that he was in the presence of evil sat heavily upon him, weighting him down.

"Oh Peter. What have they done to you?" she asked with quick concern flaring in those huge compassionate eyes. She reached up to touch his cheek.

The strain and horror of the last days had drawn him out to the edge of physical endurance. His skin had a greyish, sickly tone against which the new beard darkening his jaws contrasted strongly. There were more fine silver threads at his temples, gull's wings against the thicker darker waves of his hair, and his eyes were haunted. They had sunk deeply into their sockets.

"Oh darling, darling," she whispered, low enough so that the others in the room could not hear her, and she reached up with her mouth for his.

Peter had carefully schooled himself for this meeting. He knew how important it was that he should not in any way betray the knowledge he had. Magda must never guess that he had found her out. That would be deadly dangerous. He must act completely naturally. It was absolutely vital, but there was just that instant's remembrance of his daughter's pale wasted fever-racked features, and then he stooped and took Magda's mouth.

He forced his mouth to soften, as hers was soft and warm and moist, tasting of ripe woman and crushed petals. He made his body welcoming as hers was melting and trusting against his—and he thought he had succeeded completely until she broke gently from his embrace and leaned back, keeping those slim strong hips still pressed against his. She studied his face again, a swift probing, questioning gaze, and he saw it change deep in her eyes. The flame going out of them leaving only a cold merciless green light, like the beautiful spark in the depths of a great emerald.

She had seen something, no, there had been nothing to see. She had sensed something in him, the new awareness. Of course, she would have been searching for it. She needed only the barest confirmation—the quirk of expression on his mouth, the new wariness in his eyes, the slight stiffness and reserve in his body—all of which he thought he had been able to control perfectly.

"Oh, I am glad you are wearing blue now." She touched the lapel of his casual cashmere jacket. "It does suit you so well, my dear."

He had ordered the jacket with her in mind, that was true—but now there was something brittle in her manner. It was as though she had withdrawn her true self, bringing down an invisible barrier between them.

"Come." She turned away, leading him to the deep leather couch below the picture windows. Some airport official had been able to find flowers, yellow tulips, the first blooms of spring, and there was a bar and coffee machine.

She sat beside him on the couch, but not touching him, and with a nod dismissed her secretary. He moved across the room to join the two bodyguards, her grey wolves, and the three of them remained out of earshot, murmuring quietly amongst themselves.

"Tell me, please, Peter." She was still watching him, but the cold green light in her eyes had been extinguished—she was friendly and concerned, listening with complete attention as he went step by step over every detail of Melissa-Jane's kidnapping.

It was an old rule of his to tell the complete truth when it would serve—and it served now, for Magda would know every detail. He told her of Caliph's demand for Kingston Parker's life, and his own response.

"I would have done it," he told her frankly, and she hugged her own arms and shuddered once briefly.

"God, such evil can corrupt even the strongest and the best—" and now there was understanding softening her lips.

Peter went on to tell her of the lucky tip-off and the recovery of Melissa-Jane. He went into details of the manner in which she had been abused, of her terror and the psychological damage she had suffered—and he watched Magda's eyes carefully. He saw something, emphasized by the tiny frown that framed them. He knew that he could not expect feelings of guilt. Caliph would be far beyond such mundane emotion—but there was something there, not just stagy compassion.

"I had to stay with her. I think she needed those few days with me," he explained.

"Yes. I am glad you did that, Peter." She nodded, and glanced at her wristwatch. "Oh, we have so little time left," she lamented. "Let's have a glass of champagne. We have a little to celebrate. At least Melissa-Jane is alive, and she is young and resilient enough to recover completely."

Peter eased the cork and when it popped he poured creaming pale yellow Dom Perignon into the flutes, and smiled at her over the glass as they saluted each other.

"It's so good to see you, Peter." She was truly a superb actress, she said it with such innocent spontaneity that he felt a surge of admiration for her despite himself. He crushed it down and thought that he could kill her now and here. He did not really need a weapon. He could use his hands if he had to, but the Cobra parabellum was in the soft chamois leather holster under his left armpit. He could kill her, and the two bodyguards across the room would gun him down instantly. He might take one of them, but the other one would get him. They were top men. He had picked them himself. They would get him.

"I'm sorry we will not be together for very long," he countered, still smiling at her.

"Oh, *chéri*. I know, so am I." She touched his forearm, the first touch since the greeting embrace. "I wish it were different. There are so many things that we have to do, you and I, and we must forgive each other for them."

Perhaps the words were meant to have a special significance; there was a momentary flash of the warm green fire in her eyes, and something else—perhaps a deep and unfathomable regret. Then she sipped the wine, and lowered the long curled lashes across her eyes, shielding them from his scrutiny.

"I hope we will never have anything terrible to forgive—"

For the first time he faced the act of killing her. Before it had been something clinical and academic, and he had avoided considering the deed itself. But now he imagined the impact of an explosive Velex bullet into that smooth sweet flesh. His guts lurched, and for the first time he doubted if he were capable of it.

"Oh Peter, I hope so. More than anything in life, I hope that." She lifted her lashes for a moment, and her eyes seemed to cling to his for an instant, pleading for something—forgiveness, perhaps. If he did not use the gun, then how would he do it, he wondered. Could he stand the feeling of cartilage and bone snapping and crackling under his fingers, could he hold the blade of knife into her flat hard belly and feel her fight it like a marlin fights the gleaming curved hook of the gaff?

The telephone on the bar buzzed, and the secretary picked it up on the second ring. He murmured into it.

"*Oui, oui. D'accord.*" And hung up. "Ma Baronne, the aircraft is refuelled and ready to depart."

"We will leave immediately," she told him, and then to Peter, "I am sorry."

"When will I see you?" he asked.

She shrugged, and a little shadow passed over her eyes. "It is difficult. I am not sure—I will telephone you. But now I must go, Peter. *Adieu*, my darling."

When she had gone, Peter stood at the windows overlooking the airfield. It was a glorious spring afternoon, the early marguerites were blooming wild along the grassy verges of the main runways, like scattered gold sovereigns, and a flock of black birds hopped amongst them, probing and picking for insects, completely undisturbed by the jet shriek of a departing Swissair flight.

Peter ran his mind swiftly over the meeting. Carefully identifying and isolating the exact moment when she had changed. When she had ceased to be Magda Altmann and become Caliph.

There was no doubt left now. Had there ever been, he wondered, or had it merely been his wish to find doubt?

Now he must harden himself to the act. It would be difficult, much more difficult than he had believed possible. Not once had they been alone, he realized then—always the two grey wolves had hovered around them. It was just another sign of her new wariness. He wondered if they would ever be alone together again —now that she was alerted.

Then abruptly he realized that she had not said, "*Au revoir*, my darling" but instead she had said, "*Adieu*, my darling."

Was there a warning in that? A subtle hint of death—for if Caliph suspected him, he knew what her immediate reaction must be. Was she threatening, or had she merely discarded him, as Kingston Parker had warned that she would?

He could not understand the desolate feeling that swamped him at the thought that he might never see her again—except through the gunsight.

He stood staring out of the window, wondering how his career and his life had begun to disintegrate about him since first he had heard the name Caliph.

A polite voice at his shoulder startled him and he turned to the airport sub-manager. "They are calling the KLM flight to Brussels now, General Stride."

Peter roused himself with a sigh and picked up his overcoat and the crocodile skin Hermes briefcase that had been a gift from the woman he must kill.

There was such a volume of correspondence and urgent business piling the long desk in his new office that Peter had excuse to put aside the detailed planning of the pre-emptive strike against Caliph.

To his mild surprise he found himself enjoying the jostle and haggle, the driving pace and the challenge of the market-place. He enjoyed pitting wits and judgement against other sharp and pointed minds, he enjoyed the human interaction—and for the first time understood the fascination which this type of life had exerted over his brother, Steven.

Three days after arriving back at his desk, the Iranian Air Force made their first order of the Narmco Kestrel missiles. One hundred and twenty units, over a hundred and fifty million dollars' worth. It was a good feeling, and could grow stronger, could finally become addictive, he realized.

He had always looked upon money as rather a nuisance, those degrading and boring sessions with bank managers and clerks of the income tax department, but now he realized that this was a different kind of money. He had glimpsed the world in which Caliph existed, and realized how once a human being became accustomed to manipulating this kind of money, then dreams of god-like power became believable, capable of being transmuted into reality.

He could understand, but could never forgive, and so at last, seven days after his return to Brussels, he forced himself to face up to what he must do.

Magda Altmann had withdrawn. She had made no further contact since that brief and unsatisfactory hour at Orly Airport.

He must go to her, he realized. He had lost his special inside position which would have made the task easier.

He could still get close enough to kill her, of that he was certain. Just as he had the opportunity to do so at Orly. However, if he did it that way it would be suicidal. If he survived the swift retribution of her guards, there would be the slower but inexorable processes of the law. He knew without bothering to consider it too deeply that he would be unable to use the defence of the Caliph story. No court would believe it. Without the support of Atlas or the Intelligence systems of America and Britain, it would sound like the rantings of a maniac. That support would not be forthcoming—of that he was certain. If he killed Caliph they would be delighted, but they would let him go to the guillotine without raising a voice in his defence. He could imagine the moral indignation of the civilized world if they believed that an unorthodox organization such as Atlas was employing assassins to murder the prominent citizens of a foreign and friendly nation.

No. He was on his own, completely. Parker had made that quite clear. And Peter realized that he did not want to die. He was not prepared to sacrifice his life to stop Caliph—not unless there was no other way. There had to be another way, of course.

As he planned it he thought of the victim only as Caliph—never as Magda Altmann. That way he was able to bring a cold detachment to the problem. The where, the when and the how of it.

He had complicated the task by replanning her personal security, and his major concern when he did so had been to make her movements as unpredictable as possible. Her social calendar was as closely guarded as a secret of state, there were never any forward press reports of attendance at public or state events. If she were invited to dine at the Élysée Palace, the fact was reported the day after, not the day before. But there were some annual events that she would never miss. Together they had discussed these weaknesses in her security.

"Oh Peter—you cannot make a convict of me." She had laughed in protest when he mentioned them. "I have so few real pleasures—you would not take them from me, would you?"

The first seasonal showing of Yves St. Laurent's collections, that she would never miss—or the Grande Semaine of the spring racing season which culminates with the running of the Grand Prix de Paris at Longchamp. This year she had high hopes of victory with her lovely and courageous bay mare, Ice Leopard. She would be there. It was certain.

Peter began to draw up the list of possible killing grounds, and then crossed off all but the most likely. The estate at La Pierre Bénite, for instance. It had the advantage of being familiar ground for Peter. With a soldier's eye he had noticed fields of fire across the wide terraced lawns that dropped down to the lake; there were stances for a sniper in the forests along the far edge of the lake, and in the little wooded knoll to the north of the house which commanded the yard and stables. However, the estate was well guarded and even there the victim's movements were unpredictable. It would be possible to lie in ambush for the week when she was in Rome or New York. Then again the escape route was highly risky, through a sparsely populated area with only two access roads—both easily blocked by swift police action. No, La Pierre Bénite was crossed from the list.

In the end Peter was left with the two venues that had first sprung to mind—the members' enclosure at Longchamp or Yves St. Laurent's premises, at 46 Avenue Victor Hugo.

Both had the advantages of being public and crowded, circumstances favouring pickpockets and assassins, Peter thought wryly. Both had multiple escape routes, and crowds into which the fugitive could blend. There were good stances for a sniper in the grandstands and buildings overlooking the members' enclosure and the saddling paddock at Longchamp or in the multi-storied buildings opposite No. 46 in Avenue Victor Hugo.

It would probably be necessary to rent an office suite in one of the buildings—with the attendant risks, even if he used a false name, which put the probability slightly in favour of the racecourse. However, Peter delayed the final decision until he had a chance to inspect each site critically.

There was one last advantage in doing it this way. It would be a stand-off kill. He would be spared the harrowing moments of a kill at close range, with handgun or knife or garrotte.

There would be the detached view of Caliph through the lens of a telescopic sight. The flattened perspectives and the altered colour balances always made for a feeling of unreality. The intervening distance obviated the need for confrontation. He would never have to watch the green light go out in those magnificent eyes, nor hear the last exhalation of breath through the soft and perfectly sculptured lips that had given him so much joy—quickly he thrust those thoughts aside. They weakened his resolve, even though the rage and the lust for vengeance had not abated.

If he could get one of the Thor .222 sniper rifles it would be the perfect tool for this task. With the extra long, accurized barrels designed for use with match grade ammunition and the new laser sights, the weapon could throw a three-inch group at seven hundred yards.

The sniper had only to depress the button on the top of the stock with the forefinger of his left hand. This activated the laser and the beam swept precisely down the projected flight of the bullet. It would show as a bright white coin the size of a silver dime. The sniper looked for the spot of light through the telescopic lens of the sight, and the moment it was exactly on the target he pressed the trigger. Even an unskilled marksman could hardly miss with this sight, in Peter's hands it would be infallible—and Colin Noble would give him one. Not only would Colin give him one, hell, he would probably have it delivered with the compliments of the American Marine Corps by the senior military attaché of the U.S. Embassy in Paris.

Yet Peter found himself drawing out the moment of action, going over his plans so often and with such a critical eye that he knew he was procrastinating.

The sixteenth day after his return to Brussels was a Friday. Peter spent the morning on the NATO range north of the city at a demonstration of the new electronic shield that Narmco had developed to foil the radar guidance on short-range anti-tank missiles. Then he helicoptered back with the three Iranian officers who had attended the demonstration and they lunched at Épaule de Mouton, a magnificent and leisurely meal. Peter still felt guilty spending three hours at the lunch table, so he worked until eight o'clock that evening, on the missile contracts.

It was long after dark when he left through the rear entrance, taking all his usual precautions against the chance that Caliph had an assassin waiting for him in the shadowed streets. He never left at the same time nor followed the same route, and this evening he bought the evening papers from a *marchand du tabac* in the Grand'Place and stopped to read them at one of the outdoor cafés overlooking the square.

He began with the English papers, and the headlines filled the page from one side to the other; black and bold, they declared:

DROP IN PRICE OF CRUDE OIL

Peter sipped the whisky thoughtfully as he read the article through, turning to page six for the continuation.

Then he crumpled the newsprint in his lap, and stared at the passing jostle of spring tourists and early evening revellers.

Caliph had achieved her first international triumph. From now on there would be no bounds to her ruthless rampage of power and violence.

Peter knew he could delay no longer. He made the go decision then, and it was irrevocable. He would arrange to visit London on

Monday morning, there was excuse enough for that. He would ask Colin to meet him at the airport, and it would be necessary to tell him of his plan. He knew he could expect full support. Then he could move on to Paris for the final reconnaissance and choice of killing ground. There was still two weeks until the showing of the spring collections—two weeks to plan it so carefully that there would be no chance of failure.

He felt suddenly exhausted, as though the effort of decision had required the last of his reserves. So exhausted that the short walk back to the hotel seemed daunting. He ordered another whisky and drank it slowly before he could make the effort.

Narmco maintained two permanent suites at the Hilton for their senior executives and other important visitors. Peter had not yet made the effort of finding private accommodation in the city, and he was living out of the smaller of the two suites. It was merely a place to wash and sleep and leave his clothes, for he could not shake off the feeling of impermanence, of swiftly changing circumstances, by which he found himself surrounded.

My books are in storage again, he thought with a little chill of loneliness. His collection of rare and beautiful books had been in storage for the greater part of his life, as he roamed wherever his duty took him, living out of barracks and hotel rooms. His books were his only possessions, and as he thought about them now he was filled with an unaccustomed longing to have a base, a place that was his own—and immediately he thrust it aside, smiling cynically at himself as he strode through the streets of another foreign city, alone again.

It must be old age catching up with me, he decided. There had never been time for loneliness before—but now, but now? Unaccountably he remembered Magda Altmann coming into his arms and saying quietly,

"Oh Peter, I have been alone for so long."

The memory stopped him dead, and he stood in the light of one of the street lamps, a tall figure in a belted trench coat with a gaunt and haunted face.

A blonde girl with lewdly painted lips sauntered towards him down the sidewalk, pausing to murmur a proposition, and it brought Peter back to the present.

"*Merci.*" He shook his head in curt refusal and walked on.

As he passed the bookstall in the lobby of the Hilton, a rack of magazines caught his attention and he stopped at the shelf of women's magazines. There would be announcements of the Paris haute couture showings soon, and he thumbed the pages of *Vogue* looking for mention of Yves St. Laurent's show—instead he was shocked by the image of a woman's face that leapt out of the page at him.

The elegant cheekbone structure framing the huge slanted Slavic eyes. The shimmering fall of dark hair, the feline grace of movement frozen by the camera flash.

In the photograph she was in a group of four people. The other woman was the estranged wife of a pop singer, the sulky expression, slightly skew eyes and bee-stung lips a landmark on the Parisian social scene. Her partner was a freckled, boyish-faced American actor in a velvet suit with gold chains around his throat, more famous for his sexual exploits than his film roles. They were not the type of persons with whom Magda Altmann habitually associated, but the man beside her, on whose arm she leaned lightly, was much more her style. He was fortyish, dark and handsome in a fleshy heavily built way, with dense wavy hair, and he exuded the special aura of power and confidence that befitted the head of the biggest German automobile manufacturing complex.

The caption below the photograph had them attending the opening of an exclusive new Parisian discothèque—again this was not Magda Altmann's habitual territory, but she was smiling brilliantly at the tall handsome German, so obviously enjoying herself that Peter felt a stinging shaft of emotion thrust up under his ribs. Hatred or jealousy—he was not certain—and he slapped the magazine closed and returned it to its rack.

In the impersonal antiseptically furnished suite he stripped and showered, and then standing naked in the small lounge of the suite he poured himself a whisky. It was his third that evening.

Since the kidnapping he had been drinking more than ever before in his life, he realized. It could exert an insidious hold when a man was lonely and in grave doubt. He would have to begin watching it. He took a sip of the smoky amber liquid and turned to look at himself in the mirror across the room.

Since he had been back in Brussels, he had worked out each day in the gymnasium at the NATO officers' club where he still had membership, and his body was lean and hard with a belly like a greyhound's. Only the face was ravaged by strain and worry—and, it seemed, by some deep unutterable regret.

He turned back towards the bedroom of the suite, and the telephone rang.

"Stride," he said into the mouthpiece, standing still naked with the glass in his right hand.

"Please hold on, General Stride. We have an international call for you."

The delay seemed interminable with heavy buzzing and clicking on the line, and the distant voices of other operators speaking bad French or even worse English.

Then suddenly her voice, but faint and so far away that it sounded like a whisper in a vast and empty hall.

"Peter, are you there?"

"Magda?" He felt the shock of it, and his voice echoed back at him from the receiver; there was the click before she spoke again, that switch of carrier wave that told him they were on a radio telephone link.

"I have to see you, Peter. I cannot go on like this. Will you come to me, please, Peter?"

"Where are you?"

"Les Neuf Poissons." Her voice was so faint, so distorted, that he asked her to repeat it.

"Les Neuf Poissons—The Nine Fishes," she repeated. "Will you come, Peter?"

"Are you crying?" he demanded, and the silence echoed and clicked and hummed so he thought they had lost contact, and he felt a flare of alarm so his voice was harsh as he asked again. "Are you crying?"

"Yes." It was only a breath, he might have imagined it.

"Why?"

"Because I am sad and frightened, Peter. Because I am alone, Peter. Will you come, please, will you come?"

"Yes," he said. "How do I get there?"

"Ring Gaston at La Pierre Bénite. He will arrange it. But come quickly, Peter. As quickly as you can."

"Yes. As soon as I can—but where is it?"

He waited for her reply, but now the distances of the ether echoed with the sound of utter finality.

"Magda? Magda?" He found himself shouting desperately, but

the silence taunted him and reluctantly he pressed a finger down on the cradle of the telephone.

"Les Neuf Poissons," he repeated softly, and lifted the finger. "Operator," he said, "please get me a call to France Rambouillet 47-87-47." And while he waited he was thinking swiftly.

This was what he had been subconsciously waiting for, he realized. There was a feeling of inevitability to it, the wheel could only turn—it could not roll sideways. This was what had to happen.

Caliph had no alternative. This was the summons to execution. He was only surprised that it had not come sooner. He could see why Caliph would have avoided the attempt in the cities of Europe or England. One such attempt well planned and executed with great force had failed that night on the road to Rambouillet. It would have been a warning to Caliph not to underestimate the victim's ability to retaliate—for the rest, the problems would have been almost the same as those that Peter had faced when planning the strike against Caliph herself.

The when and the where and the how—and Caliph had the edge here. She could summon him to the selected place—but how incredibly skilfully it had been done. As he waited for the call to Rambouillet, Peter marvelled at the woman afresh. There seemed no bottom to her well of talent and accomplishments—despite himself, knowing full well that he was listening to a carefully rehearsed act, despite the fact that he knew her to be a ruthless and merciless killer, yet his heart had twisted at the tones of despair in her voice, the muffled weeping perfectly done, so he had only just been able to identify it.

"This is the residence of Baroness Altmann."

"Gaston?"

"Speaking, sir."

"General Stride."

"Good evening, General. I was expecting your call. I spoke to the Baroness earlier. She asked me to arrange your passage to Les Neuf Poissons. I have done so."

"Where is it, Gaston?"

"Les Neuf Poissons—it's the Baroness' holiday island in the Îles sous le Vent—it is necessary to take the UTA flight to Papeete-Faaa on Tahiti where the Baroness' pilot will meet you. It's another hundred miles to Les Neuf Poissons, and unfortunately the airstrip is too short to accommodate the Lear jet—one has to use a smaller aircraft."

"When did the Baroness go to Les Neuf Poissons?"

"She left seven days ago, General," Gaston answered, and immediately went on in the smooth, efficient secretarial voice to give Peter the details of the UTA flight. "The ticket will be held at the UTA check-in counter for you, General, and I have reserved a non-smoking seat at the window."

"You think of everything. Thank you, Gaston."

Peter replaced the receiver, and found that his earlier exhaustion had left him—he felt vital and charged with new energy. The elation of a trained soldier facing the prospect of violent action, he wondered, or was it merely the prospect of an end to the indecision and the fear of unknown things? Soon, for good or for evil, it would be settled and he welcomed that.

He went through into the bathroom and pitched the whisky that remained in his glass into the handbasin.

The UTA DC-10 made its final approach to Papeete-Faaa from the east, slanting down the sky with the jagged peaks of Moorea under the port wing. Peter remembered the spectacularly riven mountains of Tahiti's tiny satellite island as the backdrop of the musical movie *South Pacific* that had been filmed on location here. The volcanic rock was black and unweathered so that its crests were as sharp as sharks' fangs.

They arrowed down across the narrow channel between the two islands, and the runway seemed to reach out an arm into the sea to welcome the big silver machine.

The air was heavy and warm and redolent with the perfume of frangipani blossoms, and there were luscious brown girls swinging and swaying gracefully in a dance of welcome. The islands reached out with almost overpowering sweetness and friendliness —but as Peter picked his single light bag out of the hold luggage and started for the exit doors, something unusual happened. One of the Polynesian customs officers at the gate exchanged a quick word with his companion and then politely stepped into Peter's path.

"Good afternoon, sir." The smile was big and friendly, but it did not stretch as far as the eyes. "Would you be kind enough to step this way." The two customs men escorted Peter into the tiny screened office.

"Please open your bags, sir." Swiftly but thoroughly they went through his valise and crocodile-skin briefcase; one of them even used a measuring stick to check both cases for a hidden compartment.

"I must congratulate you on your efficiency," said Peter, smiling also, but his voice tight and low.

"A random check, sir." The senior officer answered his smile. "You were just unlucky to be the ten thousandth visitor. Now, sir, I hope you won't object to a body search?"

"A body search?" Peter snapped, and would have protested further, but instead he shrugged and raised both arms. "Go ahead."

He could imagine that Magda Altmann was as much the Grande Dame here as she was in mother France. She owned an entire island group, and it would need only a nod to have an incoming visitor thoroughly searched for weapons of any sort.

He could image also that Caliph would be very concerned that the intended victim should be suitably prepared for execution, lest he should inadvertently become the executioner.

The one customs officer checked his arms and flanks from armpit to waist, while the other knelt behind him and checked inside and outside of his legs from crotch to ankle.

Peter had left the Cobra in the safe deposit box in the Hilton in Brussels. He had anticipated something like this, it was the way Caliph would work.

"Satisfied?" he asked.

"Thank you for your co-operation, sir. Have a lovely stay on our island."

Magda's personal pilot was waiting for Peter in the main concourse, and hurried forward to shake his hand.

"I was worried that you were not on the flight."

"A small delay in customs," Peter explained.

"We should leave immediately, if we are to avoid a night landing on Les Neuf Poissons—the strip is a little difficult."

Magda's Gates Lear was parked on the hard-stand near the service area, and beside it the Norman Britten Trislander looked small and ungainly, a stork-like ugly aircraft capable of the most amazing performance in short take-off and landing situations.

The body of the machine was already loaded with crates and

cartons of supplies, everything from toilet rolls to Veuve Cliquot champagne, all tied down under a wide-meshed nylon net.

Peter took the right-hand seat, and the pilot started up and cleared with control, then to Peter,

"One hour's flying. We will just make it."

The setting sun was behind them as they came in from the west and Les Neuf Poissons lay like a precious necklace of emeralds upon the blue velvet cushion of the ocean.

There were nine islands in the characteristic circular pattern of volcanic formation, and they enclosed a lagoon of water so limpid that every whorl and twist of the coral outcrops showed through as clearly as if they were in air.

"The islands had a Polynesian name when the Baron purchased them back in 1945," the pilot explained in the clearly articulated, rather pedantic French of the Midi. "They were given by one of the old kings as a gift to a missionary he favoured, and the Baron purchased them from his widow. The Baron could not pronounce the Polynesian name so he changed it." The pilot chuckled. "The Baron was a man who faced the world on his own terms."

Seven of the islands were merely strips of sand and fringes of palms, but the two to the east were larger with hills of volcanic basalt glittering like the skin of a great reptile in the rays of the lowering sun.

As they turned onto their downwind leg, Peter had a view through the window at his elbow of a central building with its roof of palm thatch elegantly curved like the prow of a ship in the tradition of the islands, and around it half-hidden in luscious green gardens were other smaller bungalows. Then they were over the lagoon and there were a clutter of small vessels around the long jetty which reached out into the protected waters—hobie-cats with bare masts, a big powered schooner which was probably used to ship the heavy stores such as dieseline down from Papeete, power boats for skiing and diving and fishing. One of them was out in the middle of the lagoon, tearing a snowy ostrich feather of wake from the surface as it ran at speed, a tiny figure towed on skis behind it lifted an arm and waved a greeting. Peter thought it might be her, but at that moment the Trislander banked steeply onto its base leg and he was left with only a view of cumulus cloud bloodied by the setting sun.

The runway was short and narrow, hacked from the palm plantation on the strip of level land between beach and hills. It was surfaced with crushed coral. They made their final approach over a tall palisade of palm trees. Peter saw that the pilot had not exaggerated by calling it a little difficult. There was a spiteful crosswind rolling in and breaking over the hills, and it rocked the Trislander's wings sickeningly. The pilot crabbed her in, heading half into the wind, and as he skimmed in over the palm tops, closed the throttles, kicked her straight with the rudders, lowered a wing into the wind to hold her from drifting and dropped her neatly fifty feet over the threshold, perfectly aligned with the short runway so she kissed and sat down solidly; instantly the pilot whipped the wheel to full lock into the crosswind to prevent a ground loop and brought her up short.

"*Parfait!*" Peter grunted with involuntary admiration, and the man looked slightly startled as though the feat deserved no special mention. Baroness Altmann employed only the very best.

There was an electric golf cart driven by a young Polynesian girl waiting at the end of the strip amongst the palm trees. She wore only a pareo wrapped around her body below the armpits, a single length of crimson-and-gold patterned cloth that fell to mid-thigh. Her feet were bare, but around her pretty head she wore a crown of fresh flowers—the maeva of the islands.

She drove the golf cart at a furious pace along narrow winding tracks through the gardens that were a rare collection of exotic plants, skilfully laid out, so that there was an exquisite surprise around each turn of the path.

His bungalow was above the beach with white sand below the verandah and the ocean stretching to the horizon, secluded as though it were the only building on the island. Like a child the island girl took his hand, a gesture of perfect innocence, and led him through the bungalow, showing him the controls for the air-conditioning, lighting and the video screen, explaining it all in lisping French patois, and giggling at his expression of pleasure.

There was a fully stocked bar and kitchenette, the small library contained all the current best-sellers, and the newspapers and magazines were only a few days old. The offerings on the video screen included half a dozen recent successful features and Oscar winners.

"Hell, Robinson Crusoe should have landed here," Peter chuckled, and the girl giggled and wriggled like a friendly little puppy in sympathy.

She came to fetch him again two hours later, after he had showered and shaved and rested and changed into a light cotton tropical suit with open shirt and sandals.

Again she held his hand and Peter sensed that if a man had taken the gesture as licence, the girl would have been hurt and confused. By the hand she led him along a path that was demarcated by cunningly concealed glow lights, and the night was filled with the murmur of the ocean and the gentle rustle and clatter of palm fronds moving in the wind.

Then they came to the long ship-roofed building he had seen from the air. There was soft music and laughter, but when he stepped into the light the laughter stopped and half a dozen figures turned to him expectantly.

Peter was not sure what he had expected, but it was not this gay, social gathering, tanned men and women in expensive and elegant casual wear, holding tall frosted glasses filled with ice and fruit.

"Peter!" Magda Altmann broke from the group, and came to him with that gliding hip-swinging walk.

She wore a soft, shimmering, wheaten gold dress, held high at the throat with a thin gold chain, but completely nude across the shoulders and down her back to within an inch of the cleft of her buttocks. It was breath-taking for her body was smooth as a rose petal and tanned to the colour of new honey. The dark hair was twisted into a rope as thick as her wrist and piled up onto the top of her head, and she had touched her eyes with shadows so they were slanting and green and mysterious.

"Peter," she repeated, and kissed him lightly upon the lips, a brush like a moth's wing, and her perfume touched him as softly, the fragrance of Quadrille flowering with the warmth and magic of her body.

He felt his senses tilt. With all he knew of her, yet he was still not hardened to her physical presence.

She was as cool and groomed and poised as she had ever been, there was no trace at all of the confusion and fearsome loneliness that he had heard in those muffled choked-down sobs from half-way across the world—not until she stepped back to tilt her head on one side, surveying him swiftly, smiling lightly.

"Oh, *chéri,* you are looking so much better. I was so worried about you when last I saw you."

Only then he thought he was able to detect the shadows deep in her eyes, and the tightness at the corners of her mouth.

"And you are more beautiful than I remembered."

It was true, so he could say it without reserve, and she laughed, a single soft purr of pleasure.

"You never said that before," she reminded him, but still her manner was brittle. Her show of affection and friendliness might have convinced him at another time, but not now. "And I am grateful."

Now she took his arm, her fingers in the crook of his elbow, and she led him to the waiting group of guests as though she did not trust herself to be alone with him another moment lest she reveal some forbidden part of herself.

There were three men and their wives: an American Democratic senator of considerable political influence, a man with a magnificent head of silver hair, eyes like dead oysters, and a beautiful wife at least thirty years his junior who looked at Peter the way a lion looks at a gazelle and held his hand seconds longer than was necessary.

There was an Australian, heavy in the shoulder and big in the gut. His skin was tanned leathery and his eyes were framed in a network of wrinkles. They seemed to be staring through dust and sun glare at distant horizons. He owned a quarter of the world's known uranium reserves, and cattle stations whose area was twice the size of the British Isles. His wife was as tanned and her handshake was as firm as his.

The third man was a Spaniard whose family name was synonymous with sherry, an urbane and courtly Don, but with that fierce Moorish rake to his thin features. Peter had read somewhere that the sherry and cognac ageing in this man's cellars was valued at over five hundred million dollars, and that formed only a small part of his family's investments. His wife was a darkly brooding Spanish beauty with an extraordinary streak of chalk white through the peak of her otherwise black hair.

As soon as the group had assimilated Peter, the talk turned back easily to the day's sport. The Australian had boated a huge black marlin that morning, a fish over one thousand pounds in weight and fifteen feet from the point of its bill to the tip of the deep sickle tail, and the company was elated.

Peter took little part in the conversation, but watched Magda Altmann covertly. Yet she was fully aware of his scrutiny, he could see it in the way she held her head, and the tension in her whole long slim body, but she laughed easily with the others and glanced at Peter only once or twice, each time with a smile, but the shadows were in the green depths of her eyes.

Finally she clapped her hands. "Come, everybody, we are going to open the feast." She linked arms with the Senator and the Australian and led them down onto the beach. Peter was left to cope with the Senator's wife, and she pushed her bosom against his upper arm and ran her tongue lightly over her lips as she clung to him.

Two of the Polynesian servants were waiting beside a long mound of white beach sand, and at Magda's signal they attacked it with shovels, swiftly exposing a thick layer of seaweed and banana leaves from which poured columns of thick and fragrant steam. Below that was a rack of banyan wood and palm fronds which suspended the feast over another layer of seaweed and live coals.

There were exclamations of delight as the aromas of chicken and fish and pork mingled with those of bread-fruit and plantains and spices.

"Ah, a success," Magda declared gaily. "If any air is allowed to enter the bake we lose it all. It burns, poof! And we are left with only charcoal."

While they feasted and drank the talk and laughter became louder and less restrained, but Peter made the single drink last the evening and waited quietly—not joining the conversation and ignoring the blandishments of the Senator's wife.

He was waiting for some indication of when and from what direction it would come. Not here, he knew, not in this company. When it came it would be as swift and efficient as everything else that Caliph did. And suddenly he wondered at his own conceit, that had allowed him to walk, entirely unarmed and unsupported, into the arena selected and prepared by his enemy. He knew his best defence was to strike first, perhaps this very night if the opportunity offered. The sooner the safer, he realized, and Magda smiled at him across the table set under the palm trees and laden with enough food to feed fifty. When he smiled back at her, she beckoned with a slight inclination of her head, and then while the men argued and bantered loudly, she murmured an apology to the women and slipped unobtrusively into the shadows.

Peter gave her a count of fifty before he followed her. She was waiting along the beach. He saw the flash of her bare smooth back in the moonlight and he went forward to where she stood staring out across the wind-ruffled waters of the lagoon.

He came up behind her, and she did not turn her head but her voice was a whisper.

"I am so glad you came, Peter."

"I am so glad you asked me to."

He touched the back of her neck, just behind her ear. The ear had an almost elfin point to it that he had not noticed before and the upswept hair at her nape was silken under his fingertips. He could just locate the axis, that delicate bone at the base of the skull which the hangman aims to crush with the drop. He could do it with the pressure of thumb and it would be as quick as the knot.

"I am so sorry about the others," she said. "But I am getting rid of them—with almost indecent haste, I'm afraid." She reached up over her shoulder and took his hand from her neck, and he did not resist. Gently she spread the hand, and then pressed the open palm to her cheek. "They will leave early tomorrow. Pierre is flying them back to Papeete, and then we will have Les Neuf Poissons to ourselves—just you and I"—and then that husky little chuckle—"and thirty odd servants."

He could understand exactly why it would be that way. The only witnesses would be the faithful retainers of the Grande Dame of the islands.

"Now we must go back. Unfortunately my guests are very important, and I cannot ignore them longer—but tomorrow will come. Too slowly for me, Peter—but it will come."

She turned in the circle of his arms and kissed him with a sudden startling ferocity, so his lips were crushed against his teeth, and then she broke from him and whispered close to his ear, "Whatever way it goes, Peter, we have had something of value, you and I. Perhaps the most precious thing I have had in my life. They can never take that from me."

And then she was out of his arms with that uncanny speed and grace of movement and gliding back along the path towards the lights. He followed her slowly, confused and uncertain as to what she had meant by those last words, concluding finally that the purpose had been exactly that—to confuse and unbalance him, and at that moment he sensed rather than heard movement behind him, and instantly whirled and ducked.

The man was ten paces behind him, had come like a leopard, silently from the cover of a fall of lianas and flowering creepers beside the path; only some animal instinct had warned Peter—and his body flowed into the fighting stance, balanced, strung like a nocked arrow, at once ready both to attack and meet attack.

"Good evening, General Stride." Peter only just managed to arrest himself, and he straightened slowly but with each hand still extended stiffly at his side like the blade of a meat cleaver, and as lethal.

"Carl!" he said. So the grey wolves had been close, within feet of them, guarding their mistress even in that intimate moment.

"I hope I did not alarm you," said the bodyguard—and though Peter could not see the man's expression, there was a faint mockery in his voice. If there was confirmation needed, complete and final, this was it. Only Caliph would have need of a guard on a romantic assignment. Peter knew then beyond any doubt that either he or Magda Altmann would be dead by sunset the following evening.

Before going into the bungalow he made a stealthy prowling circuit of the bushes and shrubs that surrounded it. He found nothing suspicious but in the interior the bed had been prepared and his shaving gear cleaned and neatly rearranged. His soiled clothing had been taken for cleaning and the other clothing had been pressed and rearranged more neatly than his own unpacking. He could not therefore be certain that his other possessions had not been searched, but it was safe to presume they had. Caliph would not neglect such an elementary precaution.

The locks on doors and windows were inadequate, had probably not been used in years, for there had been no serpents in this paradise, not until recently. So he placed chairs and other obstacles in such a way that an intruder should stumble over them in the dark, and then he rumpled the bed and arranged the pillows to look like a sleeping figure, but took a single blanket to the long couch in the private lounge. He did not really expect an attempt before the other guests left the island, but if it came he would confuse Caliph's scenario as much as possible.

He slept fitfully, jerking awake when a falling palm frond rattled across the roof, or the moon threw picture shadows on the wall across the room. Just before dawn he fell into a deeper sleep and his dreams were distorted and nonsensical, only the sharp clear image of Melissa-Jane's terror-stricken face and her silent screams of horror remained with him when he woke. The memory roused in him the cold lust for vengeance which had abated a little in the weeks since her rescue, and he felt reaffirmed, possessed of a steely purpose once more, determined to resist the softening, fatal allure of Caliph.

He rose in the slippery pearl light of not yet dawn, and went down to the beach. He swam out a mile beyond the reef, and had a long pull back against a rogue current, but he came ashore feeling good and hard and alert as he had not been in weeks.

All right, he thought grimly. Let it come. I'm as ready as I'll ever be.

There was a farewell breakfast for the departing guests, on the sugary sands of the beach that had been swept smooth by the night tide—pink Laurent Perrier champagne and hot-house strawberries flown in from Auckland, New Zealand.

Magda Altmann wore brief green shorts that showed off her long shapely legs to perfection, and a matching "boob tube" across her small neat breasts—but her belly and shoulders and back were bare. It was the body of a finely trained athlete, but drawn by a great artist.

She seemed unnaturally elated to Peter, her gaiety was slightly forced and the low purring laughter just a little too ready—and with a saw edge to it. It was almost as though she had made some hard decision, and was steeling herself to carry it through. Peter thought of them as true opponents who had trained carefully for the coming configuration—like prize fighters at the weigh-in.

After the breakfast they rode up in a cavalcade of electric carts to the airfield. The Senator, revved up with pink champagne and sweating lightly in the rising heat, gave Magda an over-affectionate farewell, but she skilfully avoided his hands and shunted him expertly into the Trislander after the other passengers.

Pierre, Magda's pilot, stood on the brakes at the end of the runway while he ran all three engines up to full power. Then he let her go, and the moment she had speed he rotated her into a nose-high obstacle-clearance attitude. The ungainly machine jumped into the sky and went over the palms at the end of the short strip with five hundred feet to spare—and Magda turned to Peter ecstatically.

"I hardly slept last night," she admitted, as she kissed him.

"Neither did I," Peter told her—and then he added silently "for the same reasons, I'm sure."

"I've planned a special day for us," she went on. "And I don't want to waste another minute of it."

The head boatman had Magda's big forty-five-foot Chris-Craft Fisherman singled up at the end of the jetty. It was a beautiful boat, with long low attacking lines that made it seem to be flying even when on its mooring lines, and loving care had very obviously been lavished upon it. The paintwork was unmarked and the stainless steel fittings were polished to a mirror finish. The boatman beamed happily when Magda commended him with a smile and a word.

"Tanks are full, Baronne. The scuba bottles are charged and the light rods are rigged. The water skis are in the main racks, and the chef came down himself to check the ice box."

However, his wide white smile faded when he learned that Magda was taking the boat out alone.

"Don't you trust me?" she laughed.

"Oh, of course, Baronne," but he could not hide his chagrin at having to give over his charge—even to such a distinguished captain.

He handled the lines himself, casting her off, and calling anxious last-minute advice to Magda as the gap between jetty and vessel opened.

"*Ne t'inquiet pas!*" she laughed at him, but he made a dejected figure standing on the end of the jetty as Magda slowly opened up both diesels and the Chris-Craft came up on the plane and seemed almost to break free of the surface. Her wake was scored deep and clean and straight through the gin-clear water of the lagoon, a tribute to the design of her hull, and then it curved out gracefully behind them as Magda made the turn between the channel markers and lined her up for the passage through the reef, and out into the open Pacific.

"Where are we going?"

"There is an old Japanese aircraft carrier lying in a hundred feet of water beyond the reef. Yankee aircraft sank her back in 'forty-four. It is a beautiful site for scuba diving. We will go there first."

How? Peter wondered. Perhaps one of the scuba bottles had been partially filled with carbon monoxide gas. It was simply done, with a hose from the exhaust of the diesel generator, simply pass the exhaust gases through a charcoal filter to remove the taste and smell of unconsumed hydro-carbons and the remaining carbon monoxide gas would be undetectable. Fill the bottle to 30 atmospheres of pressure then top it up with clean air to its operating pressure of 110 atmospheres. It would be swift, but not too swift to alarm the victim, a gentle long sleep. When the victim lost his mouthpiece, the bottles would purge themselves of any trace of the gas. That would be a good way to do it.

"After that we can go ashore on Île des Oiseaux. Since Aaron stopped the islanders stealing the eggs to eat, we've got one of the biggest nesting colonies of terns and noddies and frigate birds in the Southern Pacific."

Perhaps a spear-gun. That would be direct and effective. At short range, say two feet, even below the surface, the spear arrow would go right through a human torso—in between the shoulder blades and out through the breast bone.

"Afterwards we can water ski."

With an unsuspecting skier in the water, awaiting the pick-up, what could be more effective than opening up both those tremendously powerful diesels to the gates and running the victim down? If the hull did not crush him, the twin screws turning at 500 revolutions per minute would cut him up as neatly as a loaf of pre-sliced bread.

Peter found himself intrigued with the guessing-game. He found himself regretting the fact that he would never know what she intended, and he looked back from where they stood side by side on the tall flying bridge of the Chris-Craft. The main island was lowering itself into the water, already they were out of sight of anybody who did not have a pair of powerful binoculars.

Beside him Magda pulled the retaining ribbon out of her hair, and shook loose a black rippling banner that streamed in the wind behind her.

"Let's do this for ever," she shouted above the wind and the boom of the engines.

"Sold to the lady with the sexy backside," Peter shouted back, and he had to remind himself that she was one of the most carefully trained killers he would ever meet. He must not allow himself to be lulled by the laughter and the beauty—and he must not allow her to make the first stroke. His chances of surviving that were remote.

He glanced back again at the land. Any minute now, he thought, and moved as though to glance over the side, getting slightly into her rear, but still in the periphery of her vision; she shifted slightly towards him still smiling.

"At this state of the tide there are always amberjack in the channel. I promised the chef I would bring him a couple of them kicking fresh," she explained. "Won't you go down and get two of the light rods ready, *chéri?* The feather lures are in the forward starboard seat locker."

"Okay," he nodded.

"I'll throttle back to trolling speed when I make the turn into the channel—put the lines in then."

"*D'accord.*" And then on an impulse. "But kiss me first."

She held up her face to him, and he wondered why he had said that. It was not to take farewell of her. He was sure of that. It was to lull her just that fraction, and yet as their lips met he felt the deep ache of regret that he had controlled for so long and as her mouth spread slowly and moistly open under his, he felt as though his heart might break then. For a moment he felt that he might die himself before he could do it, dark waves of despair poured over him.

He slid his hand over her shoulder to the nape of her neck and her body flattened against his, he caressed her lightly, feeling for the place, and then settling thumb and forefinger—a second, another second passed, and then she pulled back softly.

"Hey, now!" she whispered huskily. "You stop that before I pile us on the reef."

He had not been able to do it with his bare hands. He just could not do it like that—but he had to do it quickly, very quickly. Every minute delayed now led him deeper and deeper into deadly danger.

"Go!" she ordered, and struck him a playful blow on the chest.

"We've got time for that later—all the time in the world. Let's savour it, every moment of it."

He had not been able to do it, and he turned away. It was only as he went down the steel ladder into the cockpit of the Chris-Craft that it suddenly occurred to him that during the lingering seconds of that kiss the fingers of her right hand had cupped lovingly under his chin. She could have crushed his larynx, paralysing him with a thumb driven up into the soft vulnerable arch of his throat at the first offensive pressure of his thumb and forefinger.

As his feet hit the deck of the cockpit another thought came to him. Her other hand had lain against his body, stroking him softly under the ribs. That hand could have struck upwards and inwards to tear through his diaphragm—his instincts must have warned him. She had been poised for the stroke, more so than he was; she had been inside the circle of his arms, inside his defences, waiting for him—and he shivered briefly in the hot morning sun at the realization of how close he had been to death.

The realization turned instantly to something else, that slid down his spine cold as water down a melting icicle. It was fear, not the crippling fear of the craven, but fear that edged him and hardened him. Next time he would not hesitate—he could not hesitate.

He was instinctively carrying out her instructions as his mind raced to catch up with the problem. He lifted the lid of the seat locker. In the custom-fitted interior were arranged trays of fishing gear, swivels of brass and stainless steel in fifty different sizes; sinkers shaped for every type of water and bottom; lures of plastic and feathers, of enamel and bright metal; hooks for gigantic bill fish or for fry—and in a separate compartment in the side tray a bait knife.

The knife was a fifty-dollar Ninja with a lexan composition handle, chequered and moulded for grip. The blade was seven inches of hollow ground steel, three inches broad at the hilt and tapering to a stiletto point. It was a brutal weapon, you could probably chop through an oak log with it, as the makers advertised. Certainly it would enter human flesh and go through bone as though it were Cheddar cheese.

It balanced beautifully in Peter's fist as he made one testing slash and return cut with it. The blade hissed in the air, and when he tested the edge too hurriedly it stung like a razor and left a thin line of bright blood across the ball of his thumb.

He kicked off his canvas sneakers, so the rubber soles did not squeak on the deck. He was dressed now in only a thin cotton singlet and boxer-type swimming trunks, stripped down for action.

He went up the first three rungs of the ladder on bare silent feet, and lifted his eyes above the level of the flying bridge.

Magda Altmann stood at the controls of the Chris-Craft, conning the big vessel into the mouth of the channel, staring ahead in complete concentration.

Her hair still flew in the wind, snaking and tangling into thick shimmering tresses. Her naked back was turned to him, the deeply defined depression running down her spine and the crest of smooth hard muscle rising on each side of it.

One leg of her shorts had rucked up slightly exposing a half moon of round white buttock, and her legs were long and supple as a dancer's as she balanced on the balls of her narrow feet, raising herself to see ahead over the bows.

Peter had been gone from the bridge for less than a minute, and she was completely unaware, completely unsuspecting.

Peter did not make the same mistake again, he went up the ladder in a single swift bound, and the bellow of the diesels covered any sound he might have made.

With the knife you never take the chance of the point turning against bone, if you have a choice of target.

Peter picked the small of the back, at the level of the kidneys where there was no bone to protect the body cavity.

It is essential to put the blade in with all possible power; this decreases the chance of bone-deflection and it peaks the paralysing effect of impact-shock.

Peter put the full weight of his rush behind the thrust.

The paralysis is total if the blade is twisted a half turn at the same instant that the blade socks in hilt-deep.

The muscles in Peter's right forearm were bunched in anticipation of the moment in which he would twist the blade viciously in her flesh, quadrupling the size and the trauma of the wound.

The polished stainless steel fascia of the Chris-Craft's control panel reflected a distorted image, like those funny mirrors of the fairground. Only at the moment that Peter had committed himself completely, at the moment when he had thrown all his weight into the killing stroke, did he realize with a sickening flash that she was watching him in the polished steel control panel, she had been watching him from the moment he reappeared at the head of the ladder.

The curved surface of the steel distorted her face, so that it appeared to consist only of two enormous eyes, it distracted him in that thousandth part of a second before the point of the blade entered flesh. He did not see her move.

Blinding, numbing agony shot down his right flank and arm, from a point in the hollow where his collar bone joined the upper arm, while at the same instant something hit him on the inside of his forearm just below the elbow. The knife stroke was flung outwards, passing an inch from her hip, and the point of the blade crashed into the control panel in front of her, scoring the metal with a deep bright scratch, but Peter's numbed fingers could not keep hold on the hilt. The weapon spun from his grip, ringing like a crystal wine glass as it struck the steel handrail and rebounded over the side of the bridge into the cockpit behind him. He realized that she had struck backwards at him, not turning to face him but using only the reflection in the control panel to judge her blow with precision into the pressure point of his shoulder.

Now pain had crippled him and the natural reaction was to clutch at the source of it. Instead with some reflexive instinct of survival he flung up his left hand to protect the side of his neck and the next blow, also thrown backwards, felt as though it had come from a full-blooded swing of a baseball bat. He hardly saw it, it came so fast and hard there was just the flicker of movement across his vision, like the blur of a humming-bird's wing, and then the appalling force of it crushing into the muscle of his forearm.

Had it taken him in the neck where it was aimed, it would have killed him instantly; instead it paralysed his other arm, and she was turning into him now effortlessly, matching his bull strength with a combination of speed and control.

He knew he must try and keep her close, smother her with his weight and size and strength and he hooked at her with the clawed crippled fingers of his knife hand; they caught for a moment and then she jerked free. He had ripped away the flimsy strip of elasticized cloth that covered her breasts, and she spun lightly under and out of the sweep of his other arm as he tried desperately to club her down with his forearm.

He saw that her face was bone-white with the adrenalin over-dose coursing her blood. Her lips were drawn back into a fixed snarl of concentration and fury and her teeth seemed as sharp as those of a female leopard in a trap.

It was like fighting a leopard, she attacked with an unrelenting savagery and total lack of fear, no longer human, dedicated only to his total destruction.

The long hair swirled about him, at one moment flicking like a whiplash into his eyes to blind and unbalance him, and she weaved and dodged and struck like a mongoose at the cobra, every movement flowing into the next, her taunting red-tipped breasts dancing and jerking with each blow she hurled at him.

With a jar of disbelief, Peter realized that she was beating him down. So far he had managed barely to survive each blow that he caught on arm and shoulder; each time her bare feet crashed into his thigh or lower belly, each time her knees drove for his groin and jarred against the bone of his pelvis, he felt a little more of his strength dissipate, felt his reactions becoming more rubbery, just that instant slower. He had countered her attack with luck and instinct, but any instant she must land solidly and drop him, for she was never still, cutting him with hands and feet, keeping him off balance—and he had not hurt her yet, had not touched her with any of his counterstrokes. Still there was no feeling in his hands and fingers. He needed respite, he needed a weapon, and he thought desperately of the knife that had fallen into the cockpit behind him.

He gave ground to her next attack, and the bridge rail caught him in the small of the back; at the same moment another of her strokes—aimed at the soft of his throat—deflected off his arm and crunched into his nose. Instantly his eyes flooded with tears, and he felt the warm salt flood of blood over his upper lip and down the back of his throat; he doubled over swiftly, then in the same movement he threw himself backwards, like a diver making a one-and-a-half from the three-metre board. The rail behind him helped his turn in the air, and he had judged it finely. He landed like a cat on both feet on the deck of the cockpit ten feet below the bridge, flexing at the knees to absorb the shock, and flicking the tears from his eyes, wringing his arms to return blood and feeling.

As he spun into a crouch he saw the knife. It had slid down the cockpit into the stern scuppers. He went for it.

The dive had taken her by surprise, just as she was poised for the final killing stroke to the back of his exposed neck, but she swirled to the head of the ladder and gathered herself while below her, Peter launched himself across the cockpit for the big ugly Ninja knife.

She went for him feet first, dropping from ten feet, and the bare soles of her feet hit him together, the impetus of her falling body enhanced by the stabbing kick that she released at the moment that she hit him.

She caught him high in the back, hurling him forward so that the top of his head cracked into the bulkhead and darkness rustled through his head. He felt his senses going, and it required all of his resolve to roll over and pull his knees swiftly to his chest, to guard himself against the next killing stroke. He caught it on his shins, and once again launched himself after the knife. His fingers felt swollen and clumsy on the rough chequered surface of the hilt, and at the moment they touched he unwound his doubled-up body like a steel coil spring, lashing out with both feet together. It was a blind stroke, delivered in complete desperation.

It was the first solid blow he had landed, it caught her at the moment when she had already launched herself into her next onslaught; both his feet slammed into her belly just below the ribs, and had the flesh there been soft or yielding it would have ended it; but she was just able to absorb the force of it with flat hard muscle—though it hurled her backwards across the cockpit with the breath hissing from her lungs and the long slim body doubling over in an agonized convulsion.

Peter realized that this was the only chance that he had had, and the only one he would ever have—yet his body was racked with such pain that he could hardly drag himself up onto his elbow, and his vision swam and blurred with tears and blood and sweat.

He did not know how he had managed it, some supreme exertion of will, but he was on his feet with the knife in his hand, instinctively extending the blade down the back of his right thigh to keep it protected until the moment it had to be used, crouching as he went in, left arm raised as a shield—and knowing that now he had to end it swiftly, he could not go on longer. This was his last effort.

Then she had a weapon also. Moving so swiftly that it had happened before she was half-way across the cockpit, she had knocked the retaining clip off the boat hook that stood in the rack beside the cabin entrance.

It was eight feet of heavy varnished ash, with an ornate but vicious brass head, and she cut at him with it, a low swinging warning blow to hold him off while she forced air back into her empty lungs.

She was recovering swiftly, much more swiftly than Peter himself. He could see the cold killing light rekindle in her eyes. He knew he could not go on much longer, he must risk it all in one last total effort.

He threw the knife, aiming at her head. The Ninja was not designed as a throwing weapon, it rolled out of line of flight, hilt foremost—but still it forced her to lift the staff of the boat hook and deflect it. It was the distraction he had wanted.

Peter used the momentum of his throw to go in under the swinging staff, and he hit her with his shoulder while her arms were raised.

Both of them reeled backwards into the cabin bulkhead, and Peter groped desperately for a grip. He found it is the thick lustrous tresses of her hair, and he wove his fingers into it.

She fought like a dying animal with strength and fury and courage that he could never have believed possible, but now at last he could pit his superior weight and strength directly against hers.

He smothered her against his chest, trapping one arm between their bodies, while he was able to pull her head backwards at an impossible angle, exposing the long smooth curve of her throat.

And then he scissored his thighs across hers, so that those lethal feet and legs were unable to reach him, and they crashed over onto the deck.

She managed with an incredible effort to swing her weight so that she landed on top of him, her breasts sliding against his chest, lubricated by sweat and the blood that had dribbled down from his nose, but Peter heaved all his remaining strength into his shoulders and rolled back on top of her.

They were locked breast to chest and groin to groin in some bizarre parody of the act of love, only the stock of the boat hook between them.

Peter twisted down hard on the rope of hair in his left hand, pinning her head to the deck so that her eyes were only six inches from his and blood from his nose and mouth dripped onto her upturned face.

Neither of them had spoken a word, the only sound the hiss and suck of laboured breathing, the explosive grunt of a blow delivered or the involuntary gasp of pain as it landed.

They glared into each other's eyes, and at that moment neither of them was a human being, they were two animals fighting to the death, and Peter shifted quickly so the stock of the boat hook fell across her unprotected throat. She had not been ready for that and she ducked her chin too late.

Peter knew he could not dare to release his grip on her hair, nor the arm around her body, nor the scissors that enfolded her legs. He could feel the steely tension of her whole body that required all his own strength to hold. If he relaxed his grip in the slightest, she would twist away, and he would not have the strength to go on after that.

With the elbow of the hand that held her hair, he began to bear down on the ash staff of the boat hook, slowly it crushed down into her throat.

She knew it was over then, but still she fought on. As she weakened Peter was able to transfer more and more of his weight onto the stock of the boat hook. Slowly blood suffused her face, turning it dark mottled plum, her lips quivered with each painful rasping breath and a little frothy saliva broke from the corners of her mouth and ran back down her cheek.

Watching her die was the most horrible thing Peter had ever had to do. He shifted cautiously, going for the few extra ounces of weight which would force the heavy wooden stock down that last eighth of an inch and crush in her throat, and she recognized the moment in his eyes.

She spoke for the first time. It was a croak slurred through swollen and gaping lips.

"They warned me." He thought he had misheard her, and he checked the final thrust downwards which would pinch out the last spark of life. "I couldn't believe it." The faintest whisper, only just intelligible. "Not you."

Then the last resistance went out of her, her body relaxed, the complete acceptance of death at last. The fierce green light went out in her eyes, replaced at the very end with a sadness so heavy that it seemed to acknowledge the ultimate betrayal of all goodness and trust.

Peter could not force himself to make the final thrust downwards that would end it. He rolled off her and flung the heavy wooden stock across the cockpit. It crashed into the bulkhead and he sobbed as he crawled painfully across the deck, turning his back to her completely, knowing that she was still alive and therefore still as dangerous as she had ever been—yet no longer caring. He had gone as far as he could go. It didn't matter any more if she killed him, something in him even welcomed the prospect of release.

He reached the rail and tried to drag himself onto his feet, expecting at any moment the killing blow into the nape of his neck as she attacked him again.

It did not come, and he managed to get onto his knees, but his whole body was trembling violently so that his teeth chattered in his jaws and every strained and bruised tendon and muscle screamed for surcease. Let her kill me, he thought, it doesn't matter. Nothing matters now.

Half supporting himself on the rail, he turned slowly and his vision swam and flickered with patches of darkness and little shooting stars of crimson and white flame.

Through the swirl of senses at the end of their usefulness, he saw that she was kneeling in the centre of the cockpit, facing him.

Her naked torso was splattered and smeared with his blood and the smooth tanned skin oiled with slippery sweat of near death. Her face was still swollen and inflamed, wreathed in a great tangle of matted and disordered hair. There was a flaming livid weal across her throat where the stock had crushed her, and as she fought for breath her small pert breasts lifted and dropped to the painful pumping of her chest.

They stared at each other, far beyond speech, driven to the very frontiers of their existence.

She shook her head, as though trying desperately to deny the horror of it all, and at last she tried to speak, no sound came and she licked her lips and lifted one slim hand to her throat as though to ease the pain of it.

She tried again, and this time she managed one word. "Why?"

He could not reply for fully half a minute, his own throat seemed to have closed, grown together like an old wound. He knew that he had failed in his duty and yet he could not yet hate himself for it. He formed the words in his own mind, as though he were trying to speak a foreign language, and when he spoke his voice was a stranger's broken and coarsened by the knowledge of failure.

"I couldn't do it," he said.

She shook her head again, and tried to frame the next question. But she could not articulate it, only one word came out, the same word again.

"Why—?"

And he had no answer for her.

She stared at him, then slowly her eyes filled with tears, they ran down her cheeks and hung from her chin like early morning dew on the leaf of the vine.

Slowly she pitched forward onto the deck, and for many seconds he did not have the strength to go to her, and then he lurched across the deck and dropped to his knees beside her; he lifted her upper body in his arms suddenly terrified that he had succeeded after all, that she was dead.

His relief soared above the pain of his battered body as he felt her breathing still sawing through her damaged throat, and as her head lolled against his shoulder he realized that fat oily tears still welled out from between her closed eyelids.

He began to rock her like a child in his arms, a completely useless gesture, and only then did her words begin to make any sense to him.

"They warned me," she had whispered.

"I couldn't believe it," she had said.

"Not you."

He knew then that had she not spoken he would have gone through with it. He would have killed her and weighted her body and dropped it beyond the 1,000-fathom line—but the words, although they did not yet make sense, had reached deep into some recess of his mind.

She stirred against his chest. She said something, it sounded like his name. It roused him to reality. The big Chris-Craft was still roaring blindly through the channels and reefs of the outer passage.

He laid her back gently on the deck, and scrambled up the ladder to the flying bridge. The whole of that horrific conflict had taken less than a minute, from his knife-stroke to her collapse under him.

The steering of the Chris-Craft was locked into the automatic pilot and the vessel had run straight out through the channel into the open sea. It reinforced his knowledge that she had been ready for his attack. She had been acting that total concentration in steering the vessel, luring him into the attack while the Chris-Craft was on automatic pilot and she was ready to throw that backward blow at him.

It did not make sense, not yet. All that he knew was that he had made some terrible miscalculation. He threw out the switch of the automatic steering, and shut down both throttles to the idle position before disengaging the main drive. The diesels burbled softly, and she rounded up gently into the wind and wallowed beam-on to the short steep blue seas of the open ocean.

Peter took one glance back over the stern. The islands were just a low smudge on the horizon, and then he was stumbling back to the ladder.

Magda had dragged herself into a half sitting position, but she recoiled swiftly as he came to her and for the first time he saw fear pass like cloud shadow across her eyes.

"It's all right," he told her, his own voice still ragged. Her fear offended him deeply. He did not want her ever to be afraid of him again.

He took her up in his arms, and her body was stiff with uncertainty, like that of a cat picked up against its will, but too sick to resist.

"It's all right," he repeated awkwardly, and carried her down into the saloon of the Chris-Craft. His own body felt battered as though his very bones were bruised and cracked, but he handled her so tenderly that slowly the resistance went out of her and she melted against him.

He lowered her onto the leather padded bench, but when he tried to straighten up she slid one arm around his neck and restrained him, clinging to him.

"I left the knife there," she whispered huskily. "It was a test."

"Let me get the medicine chest." He tried to pull away.

"No." She shook her head and winced at the pain in her throat. "Don't go away, Peter. Stay with me. I am so afraid. I was going to kill you if you took the knife. I nearly did. Oh Peter, what is happening to us, are we both going mad?"

She held him desperately and he sank to his knees on the deck and bowed over her.

"Yes," he answered her, holding her to his chest. "Yes, we must be going mad. I don't understand myself or any of it any more."

"Why did you have to take the knife, Peter? Please—you must tell me. Don't lie, tell me the truth, I have to know why."

"Because of Melissa-Jane—because of what you had done to her—"

He felt her jerk in his arms as though he had struck her again. She tried to speak but now her voice was only a croak of despair, and Peter went on to explain it to her.

"When I discovered that you were Caliph, I had to kill you."

She seemed to be gathering herself for some major effort, but then when she spoke it was still in that scratchy broken whisper.

"Why did you stop yourself, Peter?"

"Because"—he knew the reason then—"suddenly I knew that I loved you. Nothing else counted."

She gasped and was silent again for nearly a minute.

"Do you still think that I am Caliph?" she asked at last.

"I don't know. I don't know anything any more—except that I love you. That's all that matters."

"What happened to us, Peter?" She lamented softly. "Oh God, what has happened to us?"

"Are you Caliph, Magda?"

"But Peter, you tried to kill me. That was the test with the knife. You are Caliph."

Under Magda's direction Peter took the Chris-Craft in through a narrow passage in the coral reef that surrounded Île des Oiseaux, while the seabirds wheeled about them in a raucous cloud, filling the air with their wingbeats.

He anchored in five fathoms in the protected lee, and then called the main island on the VHF radio, speaking to the head boatman.

"The Baronne has decided to sleep on board overnight," he explained. "Don't worry about us."

When he went down to the saloon again Magda had recovered sufficiently to be sitting up. She had pulled on one of the terry-cloth track suits from the clothes locker, and she had wound a clean towel around her throat to protect it and to hide the fierce fresh bruise that was already staining her skin like the squeezed juice of an overripe plum.

Peter found the medicine box in a locker above the toilet bowl of the head, and she protested when he brought two Temprapain capsules for the pain, and four tablets of Brufin for the swelling and bruising of her throat and body.

"Take them," he commanded and held the glass while she did so.

Then he carefully unwrapped the towel from her throat and lightly rubbed a creamy salve into the bruise with his fingertips.

"That feels better already," she whispered, but now she had lost her voice almost entirely.

"Let's have a look at your stomach." He pushed her down gently on her back on the long padded bench and unzipped the top of the towelling suit to the waist. The bruise where he had kicked her had spread from just below her small pale breasts to the tiny sculpted navel in the flat hard plane of her belly, again he massaged the soothing cream into her skin and she sighed and murmured with the comfort of it. When he finished she was able to hobble, still painfully doubled over, to the head. She locked herself in for fifteen minutes while Peter tended his own injuries, and when she emerged again she had bathed her face and combed out her hair.

He poured two crystal old-fashioned glasses half full of Jack Daniel's bourbon and he handed one to her as she sank onto the padded bench beside him. "Drink it. For your throat," he ordered, and she drank and gasped at the sting of the liquor and set the glass aside.

"And you, Peter?" She husked with sudden concern. "Are you all right?"

"Just one thing," he said. "I'd hate you to get really mad at me." Then he smiled, and she started to chuckle but choked on the pain and ended up clinging to him.

"When can we talk?" he asked her gently. "We have to talk this out."

"Yes, I know, but not yet, Peter. Just hold me for a while." And he was surprised at the comfort that it afforded him. The warm woman shape pressed to him seemed to ease the pain of body and of mind, and he stroked her hair as she nuzzled softly against his throat.

"You said you loved me?" she murmured at last, making it a question. Seeking reassurance, as lovers always must.

"Yes. I love you. I think I knew it all along, but when I learned that you were Caliph, I had to bury it deep. It was only there at the end I had to admit it to myself."

"I'm glad," she said simply. "Because you see I love you also. I thought I would never be able to love. I had despaired of it, Peter. Until you. And then they told me you would kill me. That you were Caliph. I thought then I would die—having found you and then lost you. It was too cruel, Peter. I had to give you the chance to prove it wasn't true!"

"Don't talk," he commanded. "Just lie there and listen. There is nothing wrong with my voice, so I will tell it first. The way it was with me, and how I knew you were Caliph."

And he told it to her, holding her to him and speaking softly, steadily. The only other sounds in the cabin were the slap of the wavelets against the hull and the subdued hum of the air-conditioning unit.

"You know everything up to the day Melissa-Jane was taken, all of it. I told you all of it, without reservation and without lying, not once—" he started, and then he went on to tell her in detail of the hunt for Melissa-Jane.

"I think something must have snapped in my mind during those days. I was ready to believe anything, to try anything to get her back. I would wake up in the night and go to the toilet and vomit with the thought of her hand in a glass jar."

He told her how he had planned to kill Kingston Parker to meet Caliph's demands, exactly how he intended doing it, the detailed how and where, and she shuddered against him.

"The power to corrupt even the best," she whispered.

"Don't talk," he admonished her, and went on to tell her of the tip-off that had led them at last to the Old Manse in Laragh.

"When I saw my daughter like that, I lost what little was left of my reason. When I held her and felt the fever and heard her scream with lingering terror, I would have killed—" He broke off and they were silent until she protested with a small gasp and he realized that his hand had closed on her upper arm and his fingers were biting into her flesh with the force of his memories.

"I'm sorry." He relaxed his grip, and lifted the hand to touch her cheek. "Then they told me about you."

"Who?" she whispered.

"The Atlas Command."

"Parker?"

"Yes, and Colin Noble."

"What did they tell you?"

"They told me how your father brought you to Paris when you were a child. They told me that even then you were bright and pretty and special—" He began to recite it for her. "When your father was killed"—she moved restlessly against his chest as he said it—"you went to live with foster parents, all of them members of the party, and in the end you were so special that they sent somebody to take you back to Poland. Somebody who posed as your uncle—"

"I believed he was"—she nodded—"for ten years I believed it. He used to write to me—" She stopped herself with an effort, was silent a moment and then, "He was all I ever had after Papa."

"You were selected to go to Odessa," Peter went on, and felt her go very still in his arms, so he repeated it with the harshness unconcealed in his tone, "to the special school in Odessa."

"You know about Odessa?" she whispered. "Or you think you know—but nobody who has never been there could ever really know."

"I know they taught you to—" he paused, imagining again a beautiful young girl in a special room overlooking the Black Sea, learning to use her body to trap and beguile a man, any man. "They taught you many things." He could not make the accusation.

"Yes," she murmured, "many, many things."

"Like how to kill a man with your hands."

"I think that subconsciously I could not bring myself to kill you, Peter. God knows you should not have survived. I loved you, even though I hated you for betraying me. I could not really do it—"

She sighed again, a broken gusty sound.

"And when I thought that you were going to kill me—it was almost a relief. I was ready to accept that, against living on without the love that I thought I had found."

"You talk too much." He stopped her. "You'll damage your throat further." He touched her lips with his fingers, to silence her, and then went on. "And at Odessa you became one of the chosen, one of the élite."

"It was like entering the church, a beautiful mystic thing," she whispered. "I cannot explain it. I would have done everything or anything for the State, for what I knew was right for 'Mother Russia.'"

"All of this is true?" He marvelled that she made no effort to deny it.

"All of it," she nodded painfully. "I will never lie to you again, Peter. I swear it."

"Then they sent you back to France—to Paris?" he asked, and she nodded.

"You did your job, even better than they had expected you to do it. You were the best, the very best. No man could resist you."

She did not answer, but she did not lower her eyes from his. It was not a defiance but merely a total acceptance of what he was saying.

"There were men. Rich and powerful men—" His voice was bitter now. He could not help himself. "Many, many men. Nobody knows how many, and from each of them you gathered harvest."

"Poor Peter," she whispered. "Have you tortured yourself with that?"

"It helped me to hate you," he said simply.

"Yes, I understand that. There is nothing that I can give you for your comfort—except this. I never loved a man until I met you."

She was keeping her word. There were no more lies nor deceptions now. He was certain of it.

"Then they decided that you could be used to take over control of Aaron Altmann and his Empire—"

"No," she whispered, shaking her head. "I decided on Aaron. He had been the only one man who I had not been able to—" Her voice pinched out and she took a sip of the bourbon and let it trickle slowly down her throat before she went on. "He fascinated me. I had never met a man like that before. So strong, such raw power."

"All right," Peter agreed. "You might even have grown tired of the other role by then—"

"It's hard work being a courtesan." She smiled for the first time since he had begun speaking, but it was a sad self-mocking smile.

"You went about it exactly the right way. First you made yourself indispensable to him. Already he was a sick man, beginning to need a crutch, somebody he could trust entirely. You gave him that—"

She said nothing, but memories passed across her eyes, changing the green shadows like sunlight through a deep still pool.

"And when he trusted you there was nothing you could not supply to your masters. Your value had increased a hundredfold."

He went on talking quietly while outside the day died in a fury of crimsons and royal purples, slowly altering the light in the cabin and dimming it down so that her face was all that existed in the soft gloom. A pale intense expression, listening quietly to the accusations, to the recitation of betrayals and deceits. Only occasionally she made a little gesture of denial, a shake of her head or the pressure of fingers on his arms. Sometimes she closed her eyes briefly as though she could not accept some particularly cruel memory, and once or twice an exclamation was wrung from her in that strained and tortured whisper.

"Oh God, Peter! It's true!"

He told her how she had gradually developed the taste for the power she was able to wield as Aaron Altmann's wife, and how that flourished as Aaron's strength declined. How she at last even opposed the Baron on some issues.

"Like that of supplying arms to the South African Government," Peter said, and she nodded and made one of her rare comments.

"Yes. We argued. That was one of the few times we argued." And she smiled softly, as though at a private memory that she could not share even with him.

He told her how the taste of power and the trappings of power gradually eroded her commitment to her earlier political ideals, how her masters slowly realized they were losing their hold over her and of the pressures they attempted to apply to force her back into the fold. "But you were too powerful now to respond to the usual pressures. You had even succeeded in penetrating Aaron's Mossad connections, and had that protection."

"This is incredible!" she whispered. "It's so close, so very close that it is the truth." He waited for her to elaborate, but instead she motioned him to continue.

"When they threatened to expose you to the Baron as a communist agent, you had no choice but to get rid of him—and you did it in such a way that you not only got rid of the threat to your existence, but you also achieved control of Altmann Industries, and to put the cherry on top of the pie you got yourself twenty-five million in operating capital. You arranged the abduction and killing of Aaron Altmann, you paid yourself the twenty-five million and personally supervised its transfer, probably to a numbered account in Switzerland."

"Oh God, Peter!" she whispered, and in the darkening cabin her eyes were fathomless and huge as the empty cavities of a skull.

"Is it true?" Peter asked for confirmation for the first time.

"It's too horrible. Go on, please."

"It worked so well that it opened up a new world of possibilities for you. Just about this time you truly became Caliph. The taking of Flight 070 was possibly not the first stroke after the kidnapping of Aaron Altmann—there may have been others. Vienna and the OPEC ministers, the Red Brigade activities in Rome—but 070 was the first time you used the name Caliph. It worked, except for the dereliction of duty by a subordinate officer." He indicated himself. "That was all that stopped it—and that was how I attracted your attention originally."

Now it was almost totally dark in the cabin and Magda reached across and switched on the reading light beside them, adjusting the rheostat down to a soft golden glow. In its light she studied his face seriously as he went on.

"By this time you were aware through your special sources, probably the Mossad connection and almost certainly through the French SID, that somebody was onto Caliph. That somebody turned out to be Kingston Parker and his Atlas organization, and I was the ideal person firstly to confirm that Parker was the hunter—and secondly, to assassinate him. I had the special training and talents for the job, I could get close to him without arousing his suspicions, and I needed only to be sufficiently motivated."

"No," she whispered, unable to take her eyes from his face.

"It holds together," he said. "All of it." And she had no reply.

"When I received Melissa-Jane's finger, I was ready for anything—"

"I think I am going to be sick."

"I'm sorry." He gave her the glass and she drank the finger of liquor it contained, gagging a little on it. Then she sat for a few moments with her eyes closed and her hand on her bruised throat.

"All right?" he asked at last.

"Yes. All right now. Go on."

"It worked perfectly—except for the tip-off to the hide-out in Ireland. But nobody could have foreseen that, not even Caliph."

"But there was no proof!" she protested. "It was all conjecture. No proof that I was Caliph."

"There was," he told her quietly. "O'Shaughnessy, the head of the gang that kidnapped Melissa-Jane, made two telephone calls. They were traced to Rambouillet 47-87-47."

She stared at him wordlessly.

"He was reporting to his master—to Caliph, you see." And he waited for her reply. There was none, so after a minute of silence he went on to tell her the arrangements he had made for her execution—the sites he had chosen at Longchamp race course and in the Avenue Victor Hugo, and she shuddered as though she had felt the brush of the black angels' wings across her skin.

"I would have been there," she admitted. "You chose the two best sites. Yves has arranged a private showing for me on the sixth of next month. I would have gone to it."

"Then you saved me the trouble. You invited me here. I knew that it was an invitation to die, that you knew I had become aware, that I had learned you were Caliph. I saw it in your eyes during that meeting at Orly Airport. I saw it proven by the way you were suddenly avoiding me, the way you were giving me no opportunity to do the job I had to do."

"Go on."

"You had me searched when I landed at Papeete-Faaa."

She nodded.

"You had the grey wolves search my room again last night, and you set it up for today. I knew I had to strike first, and I did."

"Yes," she murmured. "You did." And rubbed her throat again.

He went to recharge the glasses from the concealed liquor cabinet behind the bulkhead, and came back to sit beside her.

She shifted slightly, moving inside the circle of his arm, and he held her in silence. The telling of it had exhausted him, and his body ached relentlessly, but he was glad it was said, somehow it was like lancing a malignant abscess—the release of poisons was a relief, and now the healing process could begin.

He could feel his own exhaustion echoed in the slim body that drooped against him, but he sensed that hers was deeper, she had taken too much already—and when he lifted her in his arms again she made no protest, and he carried her like a sleeping child through to the master cabin and laid her on the bunk.

He found pillows and a blanket in the locker below. He slid into the bunk with her, under the single blanket, and she fitted neatly into the curve of his body, pressing gently against him, her back against his chest, her hard round buttocks against the front of his thighs, and her head pillowed into the crook of his arm, while with his other arm he cuddled her close and his hand naturally cupped one of her breasts. They fell asleep like that, pressing closely, and when he rolled over she moved without waking, reversing their positions, moulding herself to his back and pressing her face into the nape of his neck, clasping him with one arm and with a leg thrown over his lower body as though to enfold him completely.

Once he woke and she was gone, and the strength of his alarm surprised him, a hundred new doubts and fears assailed him from the night, then he heard the liquid purr in the bowl of the head and he relaxed. When she returned to the bunk, she had stripped off the terry-cloth track suit and her naked body felt somehow very vulnerable and precious in his arms.

They woke together with sunlight pouring into the cabin through one porthole like stage lighting.

"My God—it must be noon." She sat up, and tossed back the long mane of dark hair over her tanned bare shoulders, but when Peter tried to rise, he froze and groaned aloud.

"Qu'a tu, chéri?"

"I must have got caught in a concrete mixer," he moaned. His bruises had stiffened during the night, torn muscle and strained sinews protested his slightest movement.

"There is only one cure for both of us," she told him. "It's in three parts."

And she helped him off the bunk as though he was an old man. He exaggerated the extent of his injuries a little to make her chuckle. The chuckle was a little hoarse, but her voice was stronger and clearer and she favoured her own bruises only a little as she led him up onto the deck. Her powers of recuperation were those of a young and superbly fit thoroughbred animal.

They swam from the diving platform over the Chris-Craft's stern.

"It's working," Peter admitted as the support of warm salt-water soothed his battered body. They swam side by side, both naked, slowly at first and then faster, changing the sedate breast-stroke for a hard overarm crawl, back as far as the reef, treading water there and gasping at the exertion.

"Better?" she panted with her hair floating around her like the tendrils of some beautiful water plant.

"Much better."

"Race you back."

They reached the Chris-Craft together and clambered up into the cockpit, cascading water and laughing and panting, but when he reached for her, she allowed only a fleeting caress before pulling away.

"First Phase Two of the cure."

She worked in the galley with only a floral apron around her waist which covered the bruises of her belly.

"I never thought an apron could be provocative before."

"You are supposed to be doing the coffee," she admonished him and gave him a lewd little bump and grind with her bare backside.

Her omelettes were thick and golden and fluffy, and they ate them in the early sunlight on the upper deck. The trade wind was sheep-dogging a flock of fluffy silver cloud across the heavens, and in the gaps the sky was a peculiar brilliant blue.

They ate with huge appetites, for the bright new morning seemed to have changed the mood of doom that had overpowered them the previous night. Neither of them wanted to break this mood, and they chattered inconsequential nonsense, and exclaimed at the beauty of the day and threw bread crusts to the seagulls, like two children on a picnic.

At last she came to sit in his lap, and made a show of taking his pulse.

"The patient is much improved," she announced; "is now probably strong enough for Phase Three of the cure."

"Which is?" he asked.

"Peter *chéri*, even if you *are* English, you are not that dense." And she wriggled her bottom in his lap.

They made love in the warm sunlight, on one of the foam mattresses, with the trade wind teasing their bodies like unseen fingers.

It began in banter and with low gurgles of laughter, little gasps of rediscovery, and murmurs of welcome and encouragement—then suddenly it changed, it became charged with almost unbearable intensity, a storm of emotion that sought to sweep away all the ugliness and doubt. They were caught up in the raging torrent that carried them helplessly beyond mere physical response into an unknown dimension from which there seemed no way back, a total affirmation of their bodies and their minds that made all else seem inconsequential.

"I love you," she cried at the very end, as though to deny all else that she had been forced to do. "I have loved only you." It was a cry torn from the very depths of her soul.

It took a long time for them to return from the far place to which they had been driven, to become two separate people again, but when they did somehow they both sensed that they would never again be completely separated; there had been a deeper more significant union than just that of their two bodies, and the knowledge sobered them and yet, at the same time, gave them both new strength and a deep elation that neither had to voice—it was there, and they both simply knew it.

They slid the big inflatable Avon S-650 dinghy over the stern, and went ashore, pulling the rubber craft above the high-water level and mooring it to one of the slanting palm boles.

Then they wandered inland, picking their way hand in hand between the seabird nests that had been crudely scraped in the earth. Half a dozen different species of birds were breeding together in one sprawling colony that covered most of the twenty-acre island. Their eggs varied from cool pale blue as big as that of a goose's, to others the size of a pullet's and speckled and spotted in lovely free-form designs. The chicks were either grotesquely ugly with bare parboiled bodies or were cute as Walt Disney animations. The entire island was pervaded by an endless susurration of thousands of wings and the uproar of squawking, screeching, feuding and mating birds.

Magda knew the zoological names of each species, its range and its habits, and its chances of survival or extinction in the changing ecosystems of the oceans.

Peter listened to her tolerantly, sensing that behind this chatter and studied gaiety she was steeling herself to answer the accusations that he had levelled at her.

At the far end of the island was a single massive takamaka tree, with dense green foliage spreading widely over the fluffy white sand. By now the sun was fiercely bright and the heat and humidity smothered them like a woolen blanket dipped in hot water.

They sought the shade of the takamaka gratefully, and sat close together on the sand staring out across the unruffled waters of the lagoon to the silhouette of the main island, five miles away. At this range and angle there was no sign of the buildings nor of the jetty, and Peter had an illusion of the primeval paradise with the two of them the first man and woman on a fresh and innocent earth.

Magda's next words dispelled that illusion entirely.

"Who ordered you to kill me, Peter? How was the command given? I must know that before I tell you about myself."

"Nobody," he answered.

"Nobody? There was no message like the one you received ordering you to kill Parker?"

"No."

"Parker himself or Colin Noble? They did not order you to do it—or suggest it?"

"Parker expressly ordered me not to do it. You were not to be touched—until you could be taken in jeopardy."

"It was your own decision?" she insisted.

"It was my duty."

"To avenge your daughter?"

He hesitated, would have qualified it, then nodded with total self-honesty. "Yes, that was the most part of it. Melissa-Jane, but I saw it also as my duty to destroy anything evil enough to envisage the taking of 070, the abduction of Aaron Altmann and the mutilation of my daughter."

"Caliph knows about us. Understands us better than we understand ourselves. I am not a coward, Peter, but now I am truly afraid."

"Fear is the tool of his trade," Peter agreed, and she moved slightly, inviting physical contact. He placed one arm about her bare brown shoulders and she leaned lightly against him.

"All that you told me last night was the truth, only the inferences and conclusions were false. Papa's death, the lonely years with strangers as foster-parents—of that period my clearest memories are of lying awake at night and trying to muffle the sound of my weeping with a false blanket. The return to Poland, yes, that was right, and the Odessa school—all of that. I will tell you about Odessa one day, if you truly want to hear it—?"

"I don't think I do," he said.

"Perhaps you are wise; do you want to hear about the return to Paris?"

"Only what is necessary."

"All right, Peter. There were men. That was what I had been selected and trained for. Yes, there were men—" She broke off, and reached up to take his face between her hands, turning it so she could look into his eyes. "Docs that make a difference between us, Peter?"

"I love you," he replied firmly.

She stared into his eyes for a long time looking for evidence of deceit, and then when she found none, "Yes. It is so. You really mean that."

She sighed with relief and laid her head against his shoulder, speaking quietly with just that intriguing touch of accent and the occasional unusual turn of phrase.

"I did not like the men, either, Peter. I think that was why I chose Aaron Altmann. One man, yes I could still respect myself—" She shrugged lightly. "I chose Aaron, and Moscow agreed. It was, as you said, delicate work. First I had to win his respect. He had never respected a woman before. I proved to him I was as good as any man, at any task he wished to set me. After I had his respect, all else followed." She paused and chuckled softly. "Life plays naughty tricks. I found firstly that I liked him, then I grew to respect him also. He was a great ugly bull of a man, but the power . . . a huge raw power, like some cosmic force, became the centre of my existence." She lifted her head to touch Peter's cheek with her lips in reassurance. "No. Peter, I never came to love him. I never loved before you. But I stood in vast awe of him, like a member of a primitive tribe worships the lightning and the thunder. It was like that. He dominated my existence—more than a father, more than a teacher, as much as a god—but less, very much less than a lover. He was crude and strong. He did not make love, he could only rut and tup like the bull he was."

She broke off and looked seriously at him. "Do you understand that, Peter? Perhaps I explained it badly?"

"No," he assured her. "You explained it very well."

"Physically he did not move me, his smell and the hairiness. He had hair on his shoulders and like a pelt down his back. His belly was bulging and hard as iron"—she shivered briefly—"but I had been trained to be able to ignore that. To switch off something in the front of my brain. Yet in all other ways he fascinated me. He goaded me to think forbidden thoughts, to open vaults of my mind that my training had securely locked. All right, he taught me about power and its trappings. You accused me of that, Peter, and I admit it. The flavour of power and money was to my taste. I like it. I like it very much indeed. Aaron introduced me to that. He showed me how to appreciate fine and beautiful things, for he was only physically a bull and he had a wonderful appreciation of the refinements of life—he made me come completely alive. Then he laughed at me. God, I can still hear the bellow of his laughter, and see that great hairy belly shaking with it."

She paused to remember it, almost reverently, and then she chuckled her own husky little laugh.

"'My fine little communist lady,'" he mocked me. "Yes, Peter, it was I who was deceived, he had known from the beginning who I was. He also knew about the school at Odessa. He had accepted me as a challenge, certainly he loved me—or his version of love, but he took me knowingly and corrupted my pure ideological convictions. Only then did I learn that all the information which I had been able to pass to Moscow had been carefully screened by Aaron. He doubled me, as I had been sent to double him. He was Mossad, but of course you know that. He was a Zionist, you know that also. And he made me realize that I was a Jewess, and what it meant to be that. He showed me every fatal flaw in the doctrine of Universal Communism, he convinced me of democracy and the Western Capitalist system, and then he recruited me to Mossad—"

She stopped again, and shook her head vehemently.

"To believe that I could have wished to destroy such a one. That I could have ordered his abduction and mutilation. Towards the end, when he was getting weak, when the pain was very bad, that was the closest I ever came to loving him, the way a mother loves a child. He became pathetically dependent upon me, he used to say the only thing that could lull the pain was my touch. I used to sit for hours rubbing that hairy belly—feeling that awful thing growing bigger inside him each day, like a cauliflower or a grotesque foetus. He would not let them cut it. He hated them— 'butchers' he called them. 'Butchers with their knives and rubber tubes—' "

She broke off and Peter realized that her eyes were filled with tears. He hugged her a little more firmly and waited for her to recover.

"It must have been about this time that Caliph made contact with Aaron. Thinking back I can remember the time when he became suddenly terribly agitated. It made little sense to me then, but he held long diatribes about right-wing tyranny being indistinguishable from tyranny of the left. He never mentioned the name Caliph—I do not think Caliph had yet used that name—and I do believe that Aaron would eventually have told me of the contact in detail, if he had lived. It was the way he was, even with me, he could be as wary and subtle as he could be overpowering. He would have told me of Caliph—but Caliph saw to it that he did not."

She pulled away from Peter's arm so she could again see his face.

"You must understand, *chéri*, that much of this I have learned only recently—in the last few weeks. Much of it I can only piece together like a jig puzzle—pardon, a jig-saw puzzle." She corrected herself swiftly. "But this is what must have happened. Caliph contacted Aaron with a proposition. It was a very simple proposition. He was invited to become a partner of Caliph. Aaron was to make a substantial financial contribution to Caliph's war-chest, and to place his privileged knowledge and lines of influence at Caliph's disposal. In return, he would have a hand in engineering Caliph's brave new world. It was a miscalculation on Caliph's part, perhaps the only mistake he has made up to now. He had misjudged Aaron Altmann. Aaron turned him down flat. But much more dangerously Caliph had made the mistake of revealing his identity to Aaron. I expect that he had to do that in an effort to convince Aaron. You see, Aaron was not a man who would indulge in a game of code-names and hidden identities. That much Caliph had divined correctly. So he had to confront Aaron face to face, and when he discovered that Aaron would not join in a campaign of murder and extortion—no matter how laudable the ultimate ends—Caliph had no choice. He took Aaron, killed him after torturing him hideously for information that could have been useful, mainly information about his Mossad connection, I imagine. Then he persuaded me to pay the ransom. He won two major tricks with a single card. He silenced Aaron, and he gained the twenty-five million for his war-chest."

"How did you learn this? If only you had explained to me before—" Peter heard the bitterness in his own voice.

"I did not know it when we first met, *chéri*, please believe me. I will tell you how I learned it, but please be patient with me. Let me tell it as it happened."

"I am sorry," he said simply.

"The first time I heard the name 'Caliph' was the day I delivered the ransom. I told you about that, didn't I?"

"Yes."

"So we come now to your part. I heard of you for the first time with the Johannesburg hijacking of Flight 070. I thought that you might be the one to help me hunt down Caliph. I found out about you, Peter. I was even able to have a computer print-out on you." She paused, and there was that mischievous flash in her eye again. "I will admit to being very impressed with the formidable list of your ladies."

Peter held up both hands in a gesture of surrender.

"Never again," he pleaded. "Not another word—agreed?"

"Agreed." She laughed, and then, "I'm hungry, and my throat is sore again with all this talking."

They crossed the island again, with their bare feet baking on the sun-heated sand, and went back on board the Chris-Craft.

The chef had stocked the refrigerator with a cornucopia of food, and Peter opened a bottle of Veuve Cliquot champagne.

"You've got expensive tastes," he observed. "I don't know if I can afford to keep you—on my salary."

"I'm sure we could arrange a raise from your boss," she assured him with the twinkle in her eyes. In tacit agreement they did not mention Caliph again until they had eaten.

"There is one other thing you must understand, Peter. I am of Mossad, but I do not control them. They control me. It was the same with Aaron. Both of us were and are very valuable agents, possibly amongst the most valuable of all their networks, but I do not make decisions, nor am I able to have access to all their secrets.

"Mossad's single-minded goal is the safety and security of the state of Israel. It has no other reason for existence. I was certain that Aaron had made a full report to Mossad of Caliph's identity, that he had detailed the proposition that Caliph had proposed— and I suspect that Mossad had ordered Aaron to co-operate with Caliph."

"Why?" Peter demanded sharply.

"I do not know for certain—but I can think of two reasons. Caliph must have been such a powerful and influential man that his support would have been valuable. Then again I suspect that Caliph had pro-Israeli leanings, or professed to have those leanings. Mossad finds allies where it can, and does not question their morals. I think they ordered Aaron to co-operate with Caliph— but—"

"But?" Peter prompted her.

"But you do not order a man like Aaron to go against his deepest convictions, and under that forbidding exterior Aaron Altmann was a man of great humanity. I think that the reason for his agitation was the conflict of duty and belief that he was forced to endure. His instinct warned him to destroy Caliph, and his duty—"

She shrugged, and picked up her fluted champagne glass, twisting it between those long slim fingers and studying the pinpricks of bubbles as they rose slowly through the pale golden wine. When she spoke again she had changed direction disconcertingly.

"A thousand times I had tried to discover what was so different between you and me than with the other men I have known. Why none of them could move me—and yet with you it was almost instantaneous." She looked up at him again as though she was still seeking the reason. "Of course, I knew so much about you. You had the qualities I admire in another human being, so I was disposed favourably—but there are other qualities you cannot detail on a computer print-out or capture in a photograph. There was something about you that made me"—she made a helpless gesture as she searched for the word—"you made me tingle."

"That's a good word," Peter smiled.

"And I had never tingled before. So I had to be very sure. It was a new experience to want a man merely because he is gentle and strong and"—she chuckled—"just plain sexy. You are sexy, you know that, Peter, but also you are something else—" She broke off. "No, I am not going to flatter you any more. I do not want you to get swollen ankles," mixing the French idiom quaintly with the English, and this time not correcting herself. She went straight on. "Caliph must have realized that I had recruited a dangerous ally. He made the attempt to kill you that night on the Rambouillet road—"

"They were after you," Peter cut in.

"Who, Peter? Who was after me?"

"The Russians. By that time they knew you were a double agent."

"Yes, they knew—" She cocked her head and narrowed her eyes. "I had thought about it, of course, and there had been two previous attempts on me, but I do not think the attempt on the Rambouillet road was Russian."

"All right, Caliph then, but after you—not me," Peter suggested.

"Perhaps, but again I do not think so. My instinct tells me they had the right target. They were after you."

"Yes, I would have to agree," Peter said. "I think I was followed when I left Paris that evening—" and he told her about the Citroën. "I think they knew that I was alone in the Maserati."

"Then we accept it was Caliph," she stated flatly.

"Or Mossad," Peter murmured, and her eyes slowly widened, turning a darker thoughtful green as Peter went on.

"What if Mossad did not want an Atlas man getting close to their star agent—they didn't want you to have an ally in your hunt for Caliph? What if they just didn't want me cluttering up the carefully rehearsed scenario?"

"Peter, it's very deep water—"

"—and there are packs of sharks."

"Let's leave that night on the Rambouillet road for the moment," she suggested. "It merely complicates the story I am trying to tell you."

"All right," Peter agreed. "We can come back to it, if we have to."

"The next significant move was the abduction of Melissa-Jane," she said, and Peter's expression changed, becoming flat and stony.

"The choice of the victim was genius-inspired," she said. "But it required no special knowledge of you or your domestic arrangements. There was no secret that you had an only child, and it needed but a casual appraisal of your character to understand how powerful a lever she could be." Magda dipped the tip of her finger into the champagne and then sucked it thoughtfully, pursing her lips and frowning slightly.

"You must understand that by this time I had faced the fact that I was in love with you. The gift was supposed to affirm that—" She flushed slightly under her honey tan, and it was appealing and childlike. He had never seen her blush before and it twisted something in his chest.

"The book," he remembered. "The Cornwallis Harris first edition."

"My first love gift ever. I bought it when I finally admitted it to myself—but I was determined that I would not admit it to you. I am old-fashioned enough to believe the man must speak first."

"I did."

"God, I'll never forget it," she said fervently, and they both thought of the savage confrontation the previous day which had ended incongruously in a declaration of love.

"I try to be unconventional," he said, and she shook her head, smiling.

"You succeed, *mon amour*, oh, how you succeed." Then she sobered again. "I was in love with you. Your distress was mine. The child was a lovely girl, she had captivated me when we met—and on top of all that I felt deadly responsible for her plight. I had inveigled you into joining my hunt for Caliph, and because of that you had lost your daughter."

He bowed his head slightly, remembering how he had believed that she had engineered it. She recognized the gesture.

"Yes, Peter. For me it was the cruellest stroke. That you should believe it of me. There was nothing that I would not have done to give her back to you—and yet there seemed nothing that I could do. My contacts with French intelligence had nothing for me. They had no inkling of how or where the child was being held—and my control at Mossad was unaccountably evasive. Somehow I had the feeling that Mossad had the key to the kidnapping. If they were not directly involved, they knew more than anybody else. I have already explained that I believed Aaron had given them the identity of Caliph. If that was so, then they must know something that could have helped you to recover your child—but from Paris I was powerless to gather that information. I had to go in person to Israel and confront my control there. It was the one chance that I could get them to co-operate. They might believe my value as an agent was worth enough to give me a lead to Melissa-Jane."

"You threatened Mossad with resignation?" Peter asked wonderingly. "You would have done that for me?"

"Oh Peter, don't you understand, I loved you—and I had never been in love before. I would have done anything for you."

"You make me feel humble," he said.

She did not reply, but let the statement stand as though she were savouring it, then she sighed contentedly and went on. "I left everything in Paris. I have an established routine for disappearing when it is necessary. Pierre took me to Rome in the Lear; from there I telephoned you, but I could not tell you what I was going to do. Then I switched identity and took a commercial flight to Tel Aviv. My task in Israel was difficult, much more difficult than I had bargained for. It was five days before my control would see me. He is an old friend. No! Perhaps not a friend, but we have known each other a long time. He is the deputy-director of Mossad. That is how highly they value my services, to give me such an important controller, but still it took five days before he would see me, and he was cold. There was no help they could give me, he said. They knew nothing." She chuckled. "You have never seen me when I want something really badly, Peter. Ha! What a battle. There is much I knew that would embarrass Mossad with her powerful allies of the West—with France and Great Britain and the U.S.A. I threatened to hold a press conference in New York. He became less cold, he told me that the security of the State took precedence over all personal feelings, and I said something very rude about the security of the State, and reminded him of some outstanding business which I would happily leave outstanding. He became warmer—but all this was taking time, days, many days, too many days. I was going crazy. I remembered how they had found Aaron's body, and I could not sleep at night for worrying about that lovely child. And you, oh Peter, you will never know how I prayed to a God that I was not too sure of. You will never know how I wanted to be with you to comfort you. I wanted so desperately just to hear your voice—but I could not break my cover from Tel Aviv. I could not even telephone you, nor send you a letter—" She broke off. "I hoped you would not believe bad things of me. You would not believe that I did not care. That I was not prepared to help you. I could only hope that I would be able to bring you some information of value to prove it was not true—but I never dreamed that one day you would believe that it was I who had taken your daughter and tortured her."

"I am sorry," he said quietly.

"No, do not say you are sorry. We were both Caliph's playthings. There is no blame on you." She laid her hand upon his arm and smiled at him. "It was not you alone who believed bad things. For at last I had prevailed on my Mossad control to give me some little scraps of information. At first he denied completely that they had ever heard of Caliph, but I risked lying to him. I told him that Aaron had told me he had reported the Caliph contact. He gave ground. Yes, he admitted. They knew of Caliph, but they did not know who he was. I hammered on, demanding to see my controller each day, driving him as mad as I was—until he threatened to have me deported even. But each time we met I wheedled and bullied a little more from him.

"At last he admitted, 'All right, we know Caliph, but he is very dangerous, very powerful—and he will become more powerful— God willing, he will become one of the most powerful men in the world, and he is a friend of Israel. Or rather we believe he is a friend of Israel.'

"I bullied some more and he told me, 'We have put an agent close to Caliph, very close to him, and we cannot jeopardize this agent. He is a valuable agent, very valuable but very vulnerable to Caliph. We cannot take the chance that Caliph could trace information back to him. We have to protect our man.'

"Now I threatened, and he told me the agent's code-name to protect both of us should we ever have to make contact. The code-name is 'Cactus Flower.'"

"That was all?" Peter asked, with evident disappointment.

"No, my control gave me another name. As a sop—and as a warning. The name they gave me was so close to Caliph as to be virtually the same. Again he warned me that he was giving me the name for my own protection."

"What was it?" Peter demanded eagerly.

"Your name," she said softly. "Stride."

Peter made an irritable gesture of dismissal. "My name is nonsensical. Why would I kidnap and mutilate my own daughter—and Cactus Flower. He might as well have said, 'Kentucky Fried Chicken.'"

"Now it's my turn to say I'm sorry."

Peter caught himself, realizing suddenly that he had been too quick to dismiss these scraps of information. He stood up and paced the deck of the Chris-Craft with choppy, agitated steps, frowning heavily. "Cactus Flower," he repeated. "Have you ever heard it before?"

"No," she shook her head.

"Since then?"

"No," again.

He searched his memory, trying for a sympathetic echo. There was none.

"All right." He accepted that as having no immediate value. "We'll just remember it for now. Let's come to my name—Peter Stride. What did you make of that?"

"It didn't mean anything then, except as a shock. Strangely enough, I did not immediately think of you, but I thought of confusion between the kidnapper and the victim."

"Stride?" he asked. "Peter Stride? I don't understand."

"No, well—Melissa-Jane is a Stride also."

"Yes, of course. They didn't give you the name Peter Stride then?"

"No. Just Stride."

"I see." Peter stopped in mid-pace as an idea struck him—and stared out thoughtfully to where the ocean met a blue horizon.

"But they gave me your full name later," she interrupted his thoughts.

"When?"

"After we received the news that Melissa-Jane had been rescued. Of course, I wanted to return to Paris immediately—to be with you. I was able to get onto a flight from Ben-Gurion Airport six hours after we heard the news. My heart was singing, Peter. Melissa-Jane was safe, and I was in love. I was going to be with you very soon. At the airport, while I was going through the security check before departure, the policewoman took me aside—to the security office. My control was waiting for me there. He had rushed out from Tel Aviv to catch me before I left for home, and he was very worried. They had just received an urgent message from Cactus Flower. General Peter Stride was now definitely Caliph-motivated, and would assassinate me at the first opportunity, he told me. And I laughed at him—but he was deadly serious. 'My dear Baroness, Cactus Flower is a first-class man. You must take this warning seriously,' he kept repeating."

Magda shrugged. "I still did not believe it, Peter. It was impossible. I loved you, and I knew you loved me—although perhaps you had not yet realized that yourself. It was crazy. But on the aircraft I had time to think. My control at Mossad has never been wrong before. Can you imagine my dilemma now—how dearly I wanted to be with you, and yet I was now terrified—not that you would kill me. That did not seem important—but that you would truly turn out to be Caliph. That was what really frightened me. You see, I had never loved a man before. I don't think I could have stood it."

She was quiet for a while, remembering the pain and confusion, and then she shook her head so that the thick fall of shimmering hair rustled around her shoulders.

"Once I reached Paris, my first concern was to learn that you and Melissa-Jane were safe at Abbots Yew, and then I could begin to try and find out how much substance there was in Cactus Flower's warning—but until I could decide on how safe it was, I could not take the chance of being alone with you. Every time you attempted to contact me, I had to deny you, and it felt as though some little part of me was dying."

She reached across and took his hand now, opened the fingers and bowed her head to kiss the palm and then hold it to her cheek as she went on.

"A hundred times I convinced myself that it could not be true, and I was on the point of going to you. Oh Peter—finally I could take it no longer. I decided to meet you at Orly that day and find out one way or the other, end the terrible uncertainty. I had the grey wolves with me, as you remember, and they had been warned to expect trouble. I didn't tell them to watch you," she explained quickly, as if trying to dispel any memory of disloyalty, "but if you had tried to get at me they would have—" She broke off, and let his hand fall away from her cheek. "The moment you walked into the private lounge at Orly, I saw it was true. I could sense it, there was an aura of death around you. It was the most frightening and devastating moment of my life, you looked like a different man—not the Peter Stride I knew—your whole face seemed to be altered and restructured by hatred and anger. I kissed you good-bye, because I knew we could never meet again." Remembering it her face darkened with sadness, as though a cloud shadow had passed over her. "I even thought that I had to protect myself by"—she gagged the words—"you were part of Caliph, you see, and it would have been the wise thing to do. I admit that I thought of it, Peter. Have you killed, before you could kill me—but it was only a thought, and it did not go farther than that. Instead I went on with the business of living, work has always been an opiate for me. If I work hard enough I can forget anything—but this time it didn't turn out that way. I've said it before, but it explains so much that I will say it again. I had never been in love before, Peter, and I could not turn it off. It tormented me, and I cherished doubts—about Cactus Flower's warning and what I had seen so clearly in the lounge at Orly Airport. It couldn't be, it just couldn't be true—I loved you and you loved me, and you just couldn't be plotting to kill me. I almost convinced myself of that."

She laughed curtly, but it had no humour in the sound, only the bitterness of disillusion.

"I came out here"—she made a gesture that embraced sea and sky and islands—"to be away from the temptation of going to you. A sanctuary where I could recover from my wounds and begin to get over you. But it didn't work, Peter. It was worse here. I had more time to think, to torture myself with wild speculation and grotesque theories. There was only one way. Finally I recognized that. I would bring you out here and give you the chance to kill me." She laughed again, and now there was the old husky warmth in it. "It was the most crazy thing I have ever done in my life—but thank God I did it."

"We went right to the very brink," Peter agreed.

"Peter, why didn't you ask me outright if I was Caliph?" she wanted to know.

"The same reason you didn't ask me outright if I was plotting to kill you."

"Yes," she agreed. "We were just caught up in the web that Caliph had spun for us. I have only one more question, Peter *chéri*. If I was Caliph, do you truly believe that I would have been so stupid as to give my telephone number at Rambouillet to the man who kidnapped Melissa-Jane, and instruct him to ring me for a friendly chat whenever he felt like it?"

Peter looked startled. "I thought—" he began, then stopped. "No, I didn't think. I wasn't thinking clearly at all. Of course, you wouldn't have done that—and yet, even the cleverest criminals make the most elementary mistakes."

"Not those who have been trained at the Odessa school," she reminded him, and seemed immediately to regret the words, for she went on quickly. "So there is my side of the story, Peter. I may have left something out—if you can think of anything, then ask me, darling, and I'll try to fill in any missing pieces."

And so they started once again at the very beginning, and went over the ground minutely, searching for anything they might have overlooked at the first telling of it, this time exhaustively re-examining each fact from every angle, both of them applying their trained minds to the full without being able to come up with more than they already had.

"One thing we must never let out of sight for a moment is the quality of the opposition." Peter summed it up as the sun began lowering itself towards the western horizon, its majestic progress flanked by cohorts of cumulo-nimbus cloud rising into towering anvil heads over the scattered islands, like silent nuclear explosions.

"There are layers upon layers, reasons behind reasons, the kidnapping of Melissa-Jane was not merely to force me to assassinate Kingston Parker, but you as well—the proverbial two birds—with a third bird to follow. If I had succeeded, I would have been hooked into Caliph for ever."

"Where do you and I go from here, Peter?" she asked, tacitly transferring ultimate decision-making to him.

"How about home, right now," he suggested. "Unless you fancy another night out here."

Peter found that his possessions had been discreetly moved from the guest bungalow to the owner's magnificent private quarters on the north tip of the island.

His toilet articles had been laid out in the mirrored master bathroom, which flanked that of the mistress. His clothing, all freshly cleaned and pressed, was in the master's dressing-room where there was one hundred and fifty-five feet of louvred hanging space—Peter paced it out and calculated it would take three hundred suits of clothing. There were specially designed swinging shelves for another three hundred shirts and racks for a hundred pairs of shoes though all were empty.

His light cotton suit looked as lonely as a single camel in the midst of the Sahara desert. His shoes had been burnished to a gloss that even his batman had never been able to achieve. Despite himself he searched the dressing-room swiftly for the signs of previous occupancy—and was ridiculously relieved to find none.

"I could learn to rough it like this," he told his reflection in the mirror as he combed the damp, darkly curling locks off his forehead.

The sitting-room off the suite was on three levels, and had been decorated with cane furniture and luxuriant tropical plants growing in ancient Greek wine amphoras or in rockeries that were incorporated into the flowing design of the room. The creepers and huge glossy leaves of the plants toned in artistically with jungle-patterned curtaining and the dense growth of exotic plants beyond the tall picture windows—yet the room was cool and inviting, although the sound of air-conditioning was covered by the twinkle of a waterfall down the cunningly contrived rock face that comprised one curved wall of the room. Tropical fish floated gracefully in the clear pools into which the waterfall spilled, and the perfume of growing flowers pervaded the room, and their blooms glowed in the subdued lighting.

One of the little golden Polynesian girls brought a tray of four tall frosted glasses for Peter to choose from. They were all filled with fruit and he could smell the sweet warm odour of rum mingled with the fruit. He guessed they would be almost lethal and asked for a whisky, then relented when the girl's eyes flooded with disappointment.

"I make them myself," she wailed.

"In that case—" He sipped while she waited anxiously.

"*Parfait!*" he exclaimed, and she giggled with gratification, and went off wriggling her bottom under the brief pareo like a happy puppy.

Magda came then in a chiffon dress so gossamer-light that it floated about her like a fine green sea mist, through which her limbs gleamed as the light caught them.

He felt the catch in his breathing as she came towards him, and he wondered if he would ever accustom himself to the impact of her beauty.

She took the glass from his hand and tasted it.

"Good," she said, and handed it back. But when the girl brought the tray she refused with a smile.

They moved about the room, Magda on his arm as she pointed out the rarer plants and fishes.

"I built this wing after Aaron's death," she told him, and he realized that she wanted him to know that it contained no memories of another man. It amused him that she should find that important—and then he remembered his own furtive search of the dressing-room for signs of a lover before him, and the amusement turned inward.

One wall of the private dining-room was a single sheet of armoured glass, beyond which the living jewels of coral fish drifted in subtly-lit sea caverns and the fronds of magnificent sea plants waved in gentle unseen currents.

Magda ordered the seating changed so they could be side by side in the low lovers' seat facing the aquarium.

"I do not like you to be far away any more," she explained, and she picked special titbits from the serving dishes for his plate.

"This is a speciality of Les Neuf Poissons. You will eat it nowhere else in the world." She selected small deep-sea crustaceans from a steaming creole sauce of spices and coconut cream, and at the end of the meal she peeled chilled grapes from Australia with those delicate fingers, using the long shell-pink nails with the precision of a skilled surgeon to remove the pips and then placing them between his lips with thumb and forefinger.

"You spoil me," he smiled.

"I never had a doll when I was a little girl," she explained, smiling.

A circular stone staircase led to the beach fifty feet below the dining-room and they left their shoes on the bottom step and walked bare-footed on the smooth, damp sand, compacted as hard as cement by the receding tide. The moon was a few days past full, and its reflection drew a pathway of yellow light to the horizon.

"Caliph must be made to believe that he has succeeded," Peter said abruptly, and she shivered against him.

"I wish we could forget Caliph for one night."

"We cannot afford to forget him for a moment."

"No, you are right. How do we make him believe that?"

"You have to die"—he felt her stiffen—"or at least appear to do so. It has to look as though I killed you."

"Tell me," she invited quietly.

"You told me that you have special arrangements for when you want to disappear."

"Yes, I do."

"How would you disappear from here if you had to do so?"

She thought for only a moment. "Pierre would fly me to Bora-Bora. I have friends there. Good friends. I would take the island airline to Tahiti-Faaa on another passport—and then a scheduled airline in the same name to California or New Zealand."

"You have other papers?" he demanded.

"Yes, of course." She sounded so surprised by the question that he expected her to ask, "Doesn't everybody?"

"Fine," he said. "And we'll arrange a suspicious accident here. A scuba diving accident, shark attack in deep water, no corpse."

"What is the point of all this, Peter?"

"If you are dead—Caliph is not going to make another attempt to have you killed."

"Good!" she agreed.

"So you stay officially dead until we flush Caliph out," Peter told her, and it sounded like an order but she did not demur as he went on. "And if I carry out Caliph's evident wishes by killing you, it's going to make me a very valuable asset. I will have proved myself, and so he will cherish me. It will give me another chance to get close to him. At least it will give me a chance to check out a few wild hunches."

"Don't let's make my death too convincing, my love. I am a great favourite of the police on Tahiti," she murmured. "I'd hate to have you end up under the guillotine at Tuarruru."

Peter woke before her and raised himself on one elbow over her to study her face, delighting to find new planes and angles to her high broad cheekbones, gloating in the velvety texture of her skin, so fine that the pores were indefinable from farther than a few inches. Then he transferred his attention to the curve of her eyelashes that interlocked into a thick dark palisade seeming to seal her eyelids perpetually in sleep—yet they sprang open suddenly, the huge black pools of her pupils shrinking rapidly as she focused, and for the first time he realized that the irises were not pure green but were flecked and shot through with gold and violet.

The surprise of finding him over her changed slowly to pleasure, and she stretched her arms out over her head and arched her back, the way a lazy panther does when it rouses itself. The satin sheet slid down to her waist and she prolonged the stretch a little longer than was necessary, a deliberate display of her body.

"Every other morning of my life that I woke without you there was wasted," she murmured huskily, and raised her arms still at full stretch to him, folding them gracefully around his neck, still holding her back arched so that the prominent wine-red nipples brushed lightly against the crisp black mat of curls that covered his own chest.

"Let's pretend this will last for ever," she whispered, with her lips an inch from his, and her breath was rich as an overblown rose, heavy with the smell of vital woman and rising passion; then her lips spread softly, warmly against his and she sucked his tongue deeply into her mouth, with a low moan of wanting—and the hard slim body began to work against his, the hands breaking from his neck and hunting down his spine, long curved nails pricking and goading him just short of pain. His own arousal was so swift and so brutally hard that she moaned again, and the tension went out of her body, it seemed to soften and spread like a wax figure held too close to the flame, her eyelids trembling closed and her thighs falling apart.

"So strong—" she whispered, deep in her throat and he reared up over her, feeling supreme, invincible.

"Peter, Peter," she cried. "Oh yes like that. Please like that." Both of them striving triumphantly for the moment of glory when each was able to lose self and become for a fleeting instant part of the godhead.

Long afterwards they lay side by side in the enormous bed, both of them stretched out flat upon their backs, not touching except for the fingers of one hand intertwined as their bodies had been.

"I will go away," she whispered, "because I have to, but not now. Not yet."

He did not reply, the effort was beyond him, and her own voice was languorous with a surfeit of pleasure.

"I will make a bargain with you. Give me three days more. Only three days, to be happy like this. For me it is the first time. I have never known this before, and it may be the last time—"

He tried to rouse himself to deny it, but she squeezed his fingers for silence and went on.

"It may be the last," she repeated. "And I want to have it all. Three days, in which we do not mention Caliph, in which we do not think of the blood and striving and suffering out there. If you give me that, I will do everything that you want me to do. Is it a bargain, Peter? Tell me we can have that."

"Yes. We can have that."

"Then tell me you love me again, I do not think I can hear you say it too often."

He said it often during those magic days, and she had spoken the truth, each time he told her she accepted with as much joy as the last time, and always each seemed to be within touching distance of the other.

Even when tearing side by side across the warm flat waters of the lagoon, leaning back with straight arms on the tow lines, skis hissing angrily and carving fiercely sparkling wings of water from the surface as they wove back and forth in a *pas de deux* across the streaming, creaming water, laughing together in the wind and the engine roar of the Chris-Craft, Hapiti the Polynesian boatman on the flying bridge looking back with a great white grin of sympathy for their joy.

Finning gently through mysterious blue and dappled depths, the only sound the wheezing suck and blow of their scuba valves and the soft clicking and the eternal echoing susurration that is the pulse beat of the ocean, holding hands as they sank down to the long abandoned hull of the Japanese aircraft carrier, now overgrown with a waving forest of sea growth and populated by a teeming fascinating multitude of beautiful and bizarre creatures.

Flying silently down the sheer steel cliff of the canted flight deck, which seemed to reach down into the very oceanic depths, so that there was the eerie fear of suddenly being deprived of support and falling down to where the surface light blued out in nothingness.

Pausing to peer through their glass face-plates into the still gaping wounds rent into the steel by aerial bombs and high explosive, and then entering through those cruel caverns cautiously as children into a haunted house and emerging victoriously with carrier nets of trophies, coins and cutlery, brass and porcelain.

Strolling on the secluded beaches of the outer islands, still hand in hand, naked in the sunlight.

Fishing the seething tide-race through the main channel at full spring tide, and shouting with excitement as the big golden amberjack came boiling up in the wake, bellies flashing like mirrors, to hit the dancing feather lures, and send the Penn reels screeching a wild protest, and the fibreglass rods nodding and kicking.

Out in the humbling silences of the unrestricted ocean, when even the smudge of the islands disappeared beyond the wave crests for minutes at a time, with only the creak and whisper of the rigging, the trembling pregnancy of the main sail, and the rustle as the twin hulls of the big Hobie cat knifed the tops off the swells.

Strolling the long curving beaches in the moonlight, searching for the heavenly bodies that so seldom show through the turbid skies of Europe—Orion the hunter and the Seven Sisters—exclaiming at the stranger constellations of this hemisphere governed by the great fixed cross in the southern heavens.

Each day beginning and ending in the special wonder and mystery of the circular bed, in loving that welded their bodies and their souls together each time more securely.

Then on the fourth day Peter woke to find her gone, and for a moment experienced an appalling sensation of total loss.

When she came back to him he did not recognize her for a breath of time.

Then he realized that she had cut away the long tresses of her hair, cropped it down short so that it curled close against her skull, like the petals of a dark flower. It had the effect of making her seem even taller. Her neck like the stem of the flower, longer, and the curve of the throat accentuated so that it became delicate and swan-like.

She saw his expression, and explained in a matter-of-fact tone, "I thought some change was necessary, if I am to leave under a new identity. It will grow again, if you want it that way."

She seemed to have changed completely herself, the languid amorous mood given way to the brisk businesslike efficiency of before. While they ate a last breakfast of sweet yellow papaya and the juice of freshly squeezed limes she explained her intentions, as she went swiftly through the buff envelope that her secretary had silently laid beside her plate.

There was a red Israeli diplomatic passport in the envelope.

"I will be using the name Ruth Levy"—and she picked up the thick booklet of airline tickets—"and I have decided to go back to Jerusalem. I have a house there. It's not in my name, and I do not think anybody else outside of Mossad is aware of it. It will be an ideal base, close to my control at Mossad. I will try to give you what support I can, try to get further information to assist you in the hunt."

She passed him a typed sheet of notepaper.

"That is a telephone number at Mossad where you can get a message to me. Use the name Ruth Levy."

He memorized the number while she went on talking, and then shredded the sheet of paper.

"I have modified the arrangements for my departure," she told him. "We will take the Chris-Craft across to Bora-Bora. It's only a hundred miles. I will radio ahead. My friends will meet me off the beach after dark."

They crept in through a narrow passage in the coral with all the lights on the Chris-Craft doused, Magda's boatman using only what was left of the waning moon and his own intimate knowledge of the islands to take her in.

"I wanted Hapiti to see me go ashore alive," she whispered quietly, leaning against Peter's chest to draw comfort from their last minutes together. "I did not exaggerate the danger you might be in if the local people thought what we want Caliph to think.

Hapiti will keep his mouth shut," she assured him, "and will back up your story of a shark attack, unless you order him to tell the truth."

"You think of everything."

"I have only just found you, monsieur," she chuckled. "I do not want to lose you yet. I have even decided to speak a word to the Chief of Police on Tahiti, when I pass through. He is an old friend. When you get back to Les Neuf Poissons, have my secretary radio Tahiti—"

She went on quietly, covering every detail of her arrangements, and he could find no omissions. She was interrupted by a soft hail from out of the darkness and Hapiti throttled the diesels back to idle. They drifted down closer to the loom of the island. A canoe bumped against the side, and Magda turned quickly in his arms, reaching up for his mouth with hers.

"Please be careful, Peter," was all that she said, and then she broke away and stepped down into the canoe as Hapiti handed down her single valise. The canoe pushed away immediately, and was lost. There was nothing to wave at, and Peter liked it better that way, but still he stared back over the stern into the night as the Chris-Craft groped blindly for the channel again.

There was a hollow feeling under his ribs, as though part of himself was missing; he tried to fill it with a memory of Magda that had amused him because it epitomized for him her quick and pragmatic mind.

"—When the news of your death hits the market, the bottom is going to drop out of Altmann stock." He had realized this halfway through their final discussion that morning. "I hadn't thought of that." He was troubled by the complication.

"I had," she smiled serenely. "I estimate it will lose a hundred francs a share within the first week after the news breaks."

"Doesn't that worry you?"

"Not really." She gave that sudden wicked grin. "I telexed a buying order to Zurich this morning. I expect to show a profit of not less than a hundred million francs when the stock bounces back." Again the mischievous flash of green eyes. "I do have to be recompensed for all this inconvenience, *tu ne penses pas?*"

And although he still smiled at the memory, the hollow place remained there inside him.

Pierre flew the Tahitian police out to Les Neuf Poissons in the Trislander, and there followed two days of questions and statements. Nearly every member of the community wished to make a statement to the police, there had seldom been such entertainment and excitement available on the islands.

Nearly all of the statements were glowing eulogies to "La Baronne" delivered to the accompaniment of lamentation and weeping. Only Hapiti had first-hand information, and he made the most of this position of importance, embroidering and gilding the tale. He was even able to give a positive identification of the shark as a "Dead White." The English name startled Peter until he remembered that the movie *Jaws* was in the island's cassette video library and was undoubtedly the source of the big boatman's inspiration. Hapiti went on to describe its fangs as long and sharp as cane knives, and to give a gruesome imitation of the sound they made as they closed on "La Baronne." Peter would willingly have gagged him to prevent those flights of imagination, which were not supported by Peter's own statement, but the police sergeant was greatly impressed and encouraged Hapiti to further acts of creation with cries of astonishment.

On the last evening there was a funeral feast on the beach for Magda. It was a moving ritual, and Peter found himself curiously affected when the women of the island, swaying and wailing at the water's edge, cast wreaths of frangipani blooms onto the tide to be carried out beyond the reef.

Peter flew back to Tahiti-Faaa with the police the following morning, and they stayed with him, flanking him discreetly, on the drive to the headquarters of gendarmerie in the town. However, his interview with the Chief of Police was brief and courteous. Clearly, Magda had been there before him; and if there was no actual exchange of winks and nudges, the commissioner's handshake of farewell was firm and friendly.

"Any friend of La Baronne is a friend here." And he used the present tense, then sent Peter back to the airport in an official car.

The UTA flight landed in California through that sulphurous eye-stinging layer of yellow air trapped between sea and mountains. Peter did not leave the airport, but after he had shaved and changed his shirt in the men's room he found a copy of the *Wall Street Journal* in the first-class Pan-Am Clipper lounge. It was dated the previous day, and the report of Magda Altmann's death was on page three. It was a full column, and Peter was surprised by the depth of the Altmann Industries' involvement in the American financial scene. The complex of holdings was listed, followed by a resumé of Baron Aaron Altmann's career and that of his widow. The cause of death as given by the Tahitian police was "Shark Attack" while scuba diving in the company of a friend—General Peter Stride. Peter was grimly satisfied that his name was mentioned. Caliph would read it, wherever he was, and draw the appropriate conclusion. Peter could expect something to happen now; he was not quite sure what, but he knew that he was being drawn closer to the centre like a fragment of iron to the magnet.

He managed to sleep for an hour, in one of the big armchairs, before the hostess roused him for the Pan-Am Polar flight to London's Heathrow.

He called Pat Stride, his sister-in-law, from Heathrow Airport. She was unaffectedly delighted to hear his voice.

"Steven is in Spain, but I am expecting him home tomorrow before lunch, that is, if his meetings go the way he wants them. They want to build a thirty-six-hole golf course at San Istaban"—Steven's companies owned a complex of tourist hotels on the Spanish coast—"and Steven had to go through the motions with the Spanish authorities. But, why don't you come down to Abbots Yew tonight? Alex and Priscilla are here, and there will be an amusing house party for the weekend." He could hear the sudden calculating tone in Pat's voice as she began instinctively to run through the short list of potential mates for Peter.

After he had accepted and hung up, he dialled the Cambridge number and was relieved that Cynthia's husband, George Barrow, answered.

"Give me a Bolshevik intellectual over a neurotic ex-wife any day," he thought as he greeted Melissa-Jane's stepfather warmly. Cynthia was at a meeting of the Faculty Wives Association, and Melissa-Jane was auditioning for a part in a production of Gilbert and Sullivan by the local drama society.

"How is she?" Peter wanted to know.

"I think she is well over it now, Peter. The hand is healed. She seems to have settled down." They spoke for a few minutes more, then ran out of conversation. The two women were all they had in common.

"Give Melissa-Jane my very best love," Peter told him, and

picked up a copy of *The Financial Times* from a news-stand on his way to the Avis desk. He hired a compact and while waiting for it to be delivered he searched swiftly through the newspaper for mention of Magda Altmann. It was on an inside page, clearly a follow-up article to a previous report of her death. There had been a severe reaction on the London and European stock exchanges—the hundred-franc drop in Altmann stock that Magda had anticipated had already been exceeded on the Bourse—and again there was a brief mention of his own name in a repetition of the circumstances of her death. He was satisfied with the publicity, and with Magda's judgement in buying back her own stock. Indeed, it all seemed to be going a little too smoothly. He became aware of the fateful prickle of apprehension down his spine, his own personal barometer of impending danger.

As always Abbots Yew was like coming home, and Pat met him on the gravel of the front drive, kissed him with sisterly affection and linked her arm through his to lead him into the gracious old house.

"Steven will be delighted," she promised him. "I expect he will telephone this evening. He always does when he is away."

There was a buff cable envelope propped on the bedside table of the guest room overlooking the stables that was always reserved for Peter. The message originated at Ben-Gurion Airport, Tel Aviv, and was a single word—the code he had arranged with Magda to let him know that she arrived safely and without complication. The message gave him a sharp pang of wanting, and he lay in a deep hot bath and thought about her, remembering small details of conversation and shared experience that suddenly were of inflated value.

While he towelled himself he regarded his image in the steamed mirror with a critical eye. He was lean and hard and burned dark as a desert Arab by the Pacific sun. He watched the play of muscle under the tanned skin as he moved, and he knew that he was as fit and as mentally prepared for action as he had ever been, glad that Magda was safely beyond the reach of Caliph's talons so that he could concentrate all his energies on what his instincts told him must be the final stage of the hunt.

He went through to his bedroom with the towel around his waist and stretched out on the bed to wait for the cocktail hour in Pat Stride's rigidly run household.

He wondered what made him so certain that this was the lead which would carry him to Caliph, it seemed so slim a chance and yet the certainty was like a steel thread, and the steel was in his heart.

That made him pause. Once again he went carefully over the changes which had taken place within him since his first exposure to Caliph's malignant influence; the fatal miasma of corruption that spread around Caliph like the poisonous mists from some evil swamp seemed to have engulfed Peter entirely.

He thought again of his execution of the blonde girl at Johannesburg what seemed like a thousand years before, but with mild surprise realized was months not years ago.

He thought of how he had been prepared to kill both Kingston Parker and Magda Altmann—and realized that contact with violence was brutalizing, capable of eroding the principles and convictions which he had believed inviolate after almost forty years of having lived with them.

If this was so, then after Caliph—if he succeeded in destroying him—what was there after Caliph? Would he ever be the same man again? Had he advanced too far beyond the frontiers of social behaviour and conscience? Would he ever go back? He wondered. Then he thought about Magda Altmann and realized she was his hope for the future, after Caliph there would be Magda.

These doubts were weakening, he told himself. There must be no distractions now, for once again he was in the arena with the adversary. No distraction, no doubts—only total concentration on the conflict ahead.

He stood up from the bed and began to dress.

Steven was delighted to have Peter at Abbots Yew again, as Pat had predicted.

He also was tanned from the short stay in Spain, but he had again put on weight, only a few pounds, but it would soon be a serious problem, good food and drink were two of the occupational hazards of success: the most evident but not the most dangerous temptations that face a man who has money enough to buy whatever idly engages his fancy.

Peter watched him covertly during the lunch, studying the handsome head which was so very much like his own, the same broad brow and straight aristocratic nose, and yet was so different in small but significant details, and it was not only Steven's thick dark moustache.

"All right, it's easy to be wise afterwards," Peter told himself, as he watched his twin brother. Seeing again the little marks, which only now seemed to have meaning. The narrower set of eyes, slightly too close together, so that even when he laughed that deep bluff guffaw of his they seemed still to retain a cold cruel light, the mouth that even in laughter was still too hard, too determined, the mouth of a man who would brook no check to his ambitions, no thwarting of his desires. Or am I imagining it now? Peter wondered. It was so easy to see what you looked for expectantly.

The conversation at lunch dwelt almost exclusively on the prospects for the flat-racing season which had opened at Doncaster the previous weekend, and Peter joined it knowledgeably; but as he chatted he was casting back along the years, to the incidents that might have troubled him more if he had not immediately submerged them under an instinctive and unquestioning loyalty to his twin brother.

There was Sandhurst when Steven had been sent down, and Peter had known unquestioningly that it was unjust. No Stride was capable of what Steven had been accused of, and he had not even had to discuss it with his brother. He had affirmed his loyalty with a handshake and a few embarrassed muttered words.

"Thank you, Peter. I'll never forget that," Steven had told him fervently, meeting Peter's gaze with steady clear eye.

Since then Steven's rise had been meteoric through the post-war years in which it seemed almost impossible for even the most able man to amass a great fortune, a man had to have special talents and take terrible risks to achieve what Steven had.

Now sitting at his brother's board, eating roast saddle of lamb and the first crisp white asparagus shoots of the season flown in from the Continent, Peter was at last covering forbidden ground, examining loyalties which until then had been unquestioned. Yet they were straws scattered by the winds of time, possibly without significance. Peter transferred his thoughts to the present.

"Stride," Magda's control at Mossad in Tel Aviv had said. Just the two names: "Cactus Flower" and "Stride." That was fact and not conjecture.

Down the length of the luncheon table Sir Steven Stride caught his brother's eye.

"Wine with you, my dear fellow." Steven lifted the glass of claret in the old salute.

"Enchanted, I'm sure." Peter gave the correct reply, a little ritual between them, a hangover from Sandhurst days, and Peter was surprised at the depth of his regret. Perhaps Caliph has not yet succeeded in corrupting me entirely, Peter thought, as he drank the toast.

After lunch there was another of their brotherly rituals. Steven signalled it with a jerk of the head and Peter nodded agreement. Peter's old army duffle coat was in the cupboard below the back staircase with his Wellingtons, and he and Steven changed into rough clothing sitting side by side on the monk's bench in the rear entrance hall as they had so often before.

Then Steven went through into the gunroom, took down a Purdey Royal shotgun from the rack, and thrust a handful of cartridges in his coat pocket.

"Damned vixen has a litter of cubs somewhere in the Bottoms, playing merry hell with the pheasant chicks," he explained as Peter asked a silent question. "It goes against the grain a bit to shoot a fox, but I must put a stop to her—haven't had a chance at her yet," and he led the way out of the back door through the orchard towards the stream.

It was almost a formal beating of the bounds, the leisurely circuit of the estate boundaries that the two brothers always made on Peter's first day at Abbots Yew, another old comfortable tradition which allowed them time to have each other's news and reaffirm the bond between them.

They sauntered along the river bank, side by side, moving into single file with Steven leading when the path narrowed and turned away from the stream and went up through the woods.

Steven was elated by the success of his visit to Spain, and he boasted of his achievements in obtaining another parcel of prime seafront property on which to build the new golf course and to extend the hotel by another five hundred rooms.

"Now's the time to buy. Mark my words, Peter—we are on the verge of another explosion."

"The cut-back in oil price is going to help, I'd expect," Peter agreed.

"That's not the half of it, old boy." Steven turned to glance back over his shoulder and he winked knowingly at Peter. "You can expect another five per cent cut in six months, take my word on it. The Arabs have come to their senses." Steven went on swiftly, picking out those types of industry which would benefit most dramatically from the reduction in crude prices, then selecting the leading companies in those sectors. "If you have a few pounds lying idle, that's where to put it." Steven's whole personality seemed to change when he spoke like this of power and great wealth. Then he came out from behind the façade of the English country squire which he was usually at such pains to cultivate; the glitter in his eyes was now undisguised and his bushy moustache bristled like the whiskers of some big dangerous predator.

He was still talking quickly and persuasively as they left the woods and began to cross the open fields towards the ruins of the Roman camp on the crest of the low hills.

"These people have still to be told what to do, you know. Those damned shop stewards up in Westminster may have thrown the Empire away, but we still have our responsibilities." Steven changed the Purdey shotgun from one arm to the other, carrying it in the crook of the arm, the gun broken open and the shining brass caps of the Eley Kynoch cartridges showing in the breeches. "Government only by those fit to govern." Steven enlarged on that for a few minutes.

Then suddenly Steven fell silent, almost as though he had suddenly decided that he had spoken too much, even to somebody as trusted as his own younger twin. Peter was silent also, trudging up the curve of the hill with his boots squelching in the soft damp earth. There was something completely unreal about the moment, walking over well-remembered ground in the beautiful mellow sunlight of an English spring afternoon with a man he had known from the day of his birth—and yet perhaps had never known at all.

It was not the first time that he had heard Steven talk like this, and yet perhaps it was the first time he had ever listened. He shivered and Steven glanced at him.

"Cold?"

"Goose walked over my grave," Peter explained, and Steven nodded as they clambered up the shallow earth bank that marked the perimeter of the Roman camp.

They stood on the lip under the branches of a lovely copper beech, resplendent in its new spring growth of russet.

Steven was breathing hard from the pull up the hill, that extra weight was already beginning to tell. There was a spot of high unhealthy colour in each cheek, and little blisters of sweat speckled his chin.

He closed the breech of the shotgun with a metallic clash, and leaned the weapon against the trunk of the copper beech as he struggled to regain his breath.

Peter moved across casually and propped his shoulder against the copper beech, but his thumbs were hooked into the lapels of the duffle coat, not thrust into pockets, and he was still in balance, weight slightly forward on the balls of his feet. Although he seemed to be entirely relaxed and at rest he was in fact coiled like a spring, poised on the brink of violent action—and the shotgun was within easy reach of his right hand.

He had seen that Steven had loaded with number four shot. At ten paces it would disembowel a man. The safety catch on the top of the pistol grip of the butt engaged automatically when the breech was opened and closed again, but the right thumb would instinctively slip the catch forward as the hand closed on the grip.

Steven took a silver cigarette case from the side pocket of his coat and tapped down a cigarette on the lid.

"Damned shame about Magda Altmann," he said gruffly, not meeting Peter's eyes.

"Yes," Peter agreed softly.

"Glad they handled it in a civilized fashion. Could have made it awkward for you, you know."

"I suppose they could have," Peter agreed.

"What about your job at Narmco?"

"I don't know yet. I will not know until I get back to Brussels."

"Well, my offer still stands, old boy. I could do with a bit of help. I really could. Somebody I could trust. You'd be doing me a favour."

"Damned decent of you, Steven."

"No, really, I mean it."

Steven lit the cigarette with a gold Dunhill lighter and inhaled with evident pleasure, and after a moment Peter asked him, "I hope you were not in a heavy position in Altmann stock. I see it has taken an awful tumble."

"Strange that." Steven shook his head. "Pulled out of Altmann's a few weeks ago, actually. Needed the money for San Istaban."

"Lucky," Peter murmured, or much more than luck. He wondered why Steven admitted the share transaction so readily. Of course, he realized, it would have been very substantial and therefore easily traced.

He studied his brother now, staring at him with a slight scowl of concentration. Was it possible? he asked himself. Could Steven really have master-minded something so complex, where ideology and self-interest and delusions of omnipotence seemed so inextricably snarled and entwined?

"What is it, old boy?" Steven asked, frowning slightly in sympathy.

"I was just thinking that the whole concept and execution has been incredible, Steven. I would never have suspected you were capable of it."

"I'm sorry, Peter. I don't understand. What are you talking about?"

"Caliph," Peter said softly.

It was there! Peter saw it instantly. The instant of utter stillness, like a startled jungle animal—but the flinch of the eyes, followed immediately by the effort of control.

The expression of Steven's face had not altered, the little frown of polite inquiry held perfectly, then turning slowly, deeper into puzzlement.

"I'm afraid you just lost me there, old chap."

It was superbly done. Despite himself Peter was impressed. There were depths to his brother which he had never suspected—but that was his own omission. No matter which way you looked at it, it took an extraordinary ability to achieve what Steven had achieved in less than twenty years, against the most appalling odds. No matter how he had done it, it was the working of a particular type of genius.

He was capable of running Caliph, Peter accepted the fact at last—and immediately had a focal point for the corroding hatred he had carried within him for so long.

"Your only mistake so far, Steven, was to let Aaron Altmann know your name," Peter went on quietly. "I suspect you did not then know that he was a Mossad agent, and that your name would go straight onto the Israeli intelligence computer. Nobody, nothing, can ever wipe it from the memory rolls, Steven. You are known."

Steven's eyes flickered down to the shotgun, it was instinctive, uncontrollable, the final confirmation if Peter needed one.

"No, Steven. That's not for you." Peter shook his head. "That's my work. You're fat and out of condition, and you have never had the training. You must stick to hiring others to do the actual killing. You wouldn't even get a hand on it."

Steven's eyes darted back to his brother's face. Still the expression on his face had not altered.

"I think you've gone out of your head, old boy."

Peter ignored it. "You of all people should know that I am capable of killing anybody. You have conditioned me to that."

"We are getting into an awful tangle now," Steven protested. "What on earth should you want to kill anybody for?"

"Steven, you are insulting both of us. I know. There is no point in going on with the act. We have to work out between us what we are going to do about it."

He had phrased it carefully, offering the chance of compromise. He saw the waver of doubt in Steven's eyes, the slight twist of his mouth, as he struggled to reach a decision.

"But please do not underestimate the danger you are in, Steven." As he spoke Peter produced an old worn pair of dark leather gloves from his pocket and began to pull them on. There was something infinitely menacing in that simple act, and again Steven's eyes were drawn irresistibly.

"Why are you doing that?" For the first time Steven's voice croaked slightly.

"I haven't yet touched the gun," Peter explained reasonably. "It has only your prints upon it."

"Christ, you'd never get away with it, Peter."

"Why, Steven? It is always dangerous to carry a loaded shotgun over muddy and uneven ground."

"You couldn't do it, not in cold blood." The edge of terror was in Steven's voice.

"Why not? You had no such qualms with Prince Hassied Abdel Hayek."

"I am your brother—he was only a bloody wog—" Steven choked it off, staring now at Peter with stricken eyes, the expression of his face beginning at last to crack and crumble as he realized that he had made the fateful admission.

Peter reached for the shotgun without taking his eyes from his brother's.

"Wait!" Steven cried. "Wait, Peter!"

"For what?"

"You've got to let me explain."

"All right, go ahead."

"You can't just say go ahead, like that. It's so complicated."

"All right, Steven. Let's start at the beginning—with Flight 070. Tell me why."

"We had to do it, Peter. Don't you see? There is over four billions of British investment in that country, another three billions of American money. It's the major world producer of gold and uranium, chrome and a dozen other strategic minerals. My God, Peter. Those ham-handed oafs in control now are on a suicide course. We had to take it away from them, and put in a controllable government. If we don't do that, the Reds will have it all within ten years—probably much less."

"You had an alternative government chosen?"

"Of course," Steven told him urgently, persuasively, watching the shotgun that Peter still held low across his hips. "It was planned in every detail. It took two years."

"All right." Peter nodded. "Tell me about the murder of Prince Hassied."

"It wasn't murder, for godsake man. It was absolutely essential. It was a matter of survival. They were destroying Western civilization with their childlike irresponsibility. Drunk with power, they were no longer amenable to reason, like spoiled children in a sweet-shop—we had to put a stop to it, or face a breakdown of the capitalist system. They have probably done irreparable damage to the prestige of the dollar, they have taken sterling hostage and hold it in daily jeopardy with the threat of withdrawing those astronomic balances from London. We had to bring them to their senses, and look how small a price. We can reduce the price of crude oil gradually to its 1970 level. We can restore sanity to the currencies of the Western world and secure real growth and prosperity for hundreds of millions of peoples—all at the cost of a single life."

"And anyway, he was only a bloody wog. Wasn't he?" Peter agreed reasonably.

"Look here, Peter. I said that, but I didn't mean it. You are being unreasonable."

"I will try not to be," Peter assured him mildly. "Tell me where it goes from here. Who do you bring under control next—the British Trade Union movement, perhaps?"

And Steven stared at him wordlessly for a moment.

"Damn it, Peter. That was a hell of a guess. But could you imagine if we had a five-year wage freeze, and no industrial action during that time. It's them or us, Peter. We could get back to being one of the major industrial powers of the Western world. Great Britain! We could be that again."

"You are very convincing, Steven," Peter acknowledged. "There are only a few details that worry me a little."

"What are they, Peter?"

"Why was it necessary to arrange the murder of Kingston Parker and Magda Altmann—"

Steven stared at him, his jaw unhinging slightly and the hard line of his mouth going slack with astonishment. "No," he shook his head. "That's not so."

"And why was it necessary to kill Baron Altmann, and torture him to death?"

"That was not my doing—all right, it was done. And I knew it was done—but I had nothing to do with it, Peter. Not the murder at least. Oh God, all right I knew it had to be done, but—" his voice trailed off, and he stared helplessly at Peter.

"From the beginning again, Steven. Let's hear it all—" Peter spoke almost gently.

"I cannot, Peter. You don't understand what might happen, what will happen if I tell you—"

Peter slid the safety catch off the Purdey shotgun. The click of the mechanism was unnaturally loud in the silence, and Steven Stride started and stepped back a pace, blinking at his brother, fastening all his attention on Peter's eyes.

"God," he whispered. "You would do it too."

"Tell me about Aaron Altmann."

"Can I have another cigarette?"

Peter nodded and Steven lit it with hands that trembled very slightly.

"You have to understand how it worked, before I can explain."

"Tell me how it worked," Peter invited.

"I was recruited—"

"Steven, don't lie to me—you are Caliph."

"No, God no, Peter. You have it all wrong," Steven cried. "It's a chain. I am only a link in Caliph's chain. I am not Caliph."

"You are a part of Caliph, then?"

"Only a link in the chain," Steven repeated vehemently.

"Tell me," Peter invited with a small movement of the shotgun barrel that drew Steven's eyes immediately.

"There is a man I have known a long time. We have worked together before. A man with greater wealth and influence than I have. It was not an immediate thing. It grew out of many discussions and conversations over a long time, years, in which we both voiced our concern with the way that power had shifted to blocks of persons unfit to wield it—"

"All right," Peter nodded grimly. "I understand your political and ideological sentiments. Leave them out of the account."

"Very well," Steven agreed. "Well, finally this man asked me if I would be prepared to join an association of Western world political and industrial leaders dedicated to restoring power to the hands of those fitted by training and upbringing to govern."

"Who was this man?"

"Peter, I cannot tell you."

"You have no choice," Peter told him, and there was a long moment as they locked eyes and wills; then Steven sighed in capitulation.

"It was ——." The name was that of a mining magnate who controlled most of the free world supply of nuclear fuel and gold and precious stones.

"So he is the one who would have been in control of the new South African Government with which you intended replacing the present regime in that country, if the taking of 070 had succeeded?" Peter demanded, and Steven nodded wordlessly.

"All right," Peter nodded. "Go on."

"He had been recruited as I was," Steven explained. "But I was never to know by whom. In my turn, I was to recruit another desirable member—but I would be the only one who knew who that was. It was how the security of the chain was to be maintained. Each link would know only the one above and below him, the man who had recruited him and the one whom he recruited in his turn—"

"Caliph?" Peter demanded. "What about Caliph?"

"Nobody knows who he is."

"Yet he must know who you are."

"Yes, of course."

"Then there must be some way for you to get a message to Caliph," Peter insisted. "For instance, when you recruit a new member, you must be able to pass on the information? When he wants something from you, he must be able to contact you."

"Yes."

"How?"

"Christ, Peter. It's more than my life is worth."

"We'll come back to it," said Peter impatiently. "Go on, tell me about Aaron Altmann."

"That was a disaster. I chose Aaron as the man I would recruit. He seemed exactly the kind of man we needed. I had known him for years. I knew he could be very tough when it was necessary. So I approached him. He seemed very eager at first, leading me on. Getting me to explain the way Caliph would work. I was delighted to have recruited such an important man. He intimated that he would contribute twenty-five million dollars to the funds of the association, so I passed a message to Caliph. I told him that I had almost succeeded in recruiting Baron Altmann—"

Steven stopped nervously, and dropped the stub of his cigarette onto the damp turf, grinding it out under his heel.

"What happened then?" Peter demanded.

"Caliph responded immediately. I was ordered to break off all contact with Aaron Altmann at once. I realized I must have chosen a potentially dangerous person. You tell me now he was Mossad. I did not know that—but Caliph must have known it. I did as I was told and dropped Aaron like a hot chestnut—and four days later he was abducted. I had nothing to do with it, Peter. I swear to you. I liked the man immensely. I admired him—"

"Yet he was abducted and horribly tortured. You must have known that Caliph had done it, and that you were responsible?"

"Yes." Steven said the word flatly, without evasion. Peter felt a small stir of admiration for that.

"They tortured him to find out if he had passed the information you had given him about Caliph to Mossad," Peter insisted.

"Yes. I expect so. I do not know."

"If the picture I have of Aaron Altmann was correct, they received no information from him."

"No. He was like that. They must have lost patience with him in the end—to do what they did to him. It was my first moment of disillusionment with Caliph," Steven muttered sombrely.

They were both silent now, until Peter burst out angrily, "My God, Steven, can't you see what a disgusting business you are mixed up in?" And Steven was mute. "Couldn't you see it?" Peter insisted, the anger raw in his voice. "Couldn't you realize it from the beginning?"

"Not at the beginning." Steven shook his head miserably. "It seemed a brilliant solution for all the diseases of the Western world—and then once I began, it was like being on board a speeding express train. It was just impossible to get off again."

"All right. So then you tried to have me assassinated on the Rambouillet road?"

"Good God, no." Steven was truly appalled. "You're my brother, good God—"

"Caliph did it to stop me getting close to Aaron's widow who was out to avenge him."

"I didn't know a thing about it, I swear to you. If Caliph did it, he knew better than to let me in on it." Steven was pleading now. "You must believe that."

Peter felt a softening of his resolve, but forced back the knowledge that this man was his brother, someone who had been very dear over a lifetime.

"What was your next operation for Caliph then?" He asked without allowing the softness to reach his voice.

"There wasn't—"

"Damn you, Steven, don't lie to me." Peter's voice cracked like a whiplash. "You knew about Prince Hassied Abdel Hayek!"

"All right. I arranged that. Caliph told me what to do, and I did it."

"Then you kidnapped Melissa-Jane and had her mutilated—"

"Oh God! No!" Steven's voice was a sob.

"—to force me to assassinate Kingston Parker—"

"No, Peter. No!"

"—and then to kill Magda Altmann—"

"Peter, I swear to you. Not Melissa-Jane. I love her like one of my own daughters. You must know that. I had no idea it was Caliph."

Steven was pleading wildly now.

"You have to believe me. I would never have allowed that to happen. That is too horrible."

Peter watched him with a steely merciless glint of blue in his eyes, cold and cutting as the edge of the executioner's blade.

"I will do anything to prove to you I had nothing to do with Melissa-Jane. Anything you say, Peter. I'll take any chance to prove it to you. I swear it to you."

Steven Stride's dismay and sincerity were beyond question. His face was drained of all colour and his lips were marble-white and trembling with the strength of his denial.

Peter handed the shotgun to his brother without a word. Startled, Steven held it for a moment at arm's length.

"You are in bad trouble, Steven," Peter said quietly. He knew that from now on he needed Steven's unreserved and whole-hearted commitment. He could not be forced to do what he must do at the point of a shotgun.

Steven recognized the gesture, and slowly lowered the gun. With his thumb he pushed across the breech-locking mechanism, and the weapon hinged open. He pulled the cartridges from the double eyes of the breeches and dropped them into the pocket of his shooting jacket.

"Let's get down to the house," Steven said, his voice still unsteady with the trauma of the last minutes. "I need a stiff whisky—"

There was a log fire burning in the deep walk-in fireplace of Steven's study. The portals were magnificently carved altar surrounds from a sixteenth-century German church, salvaged from the ruins of World War II Allied bombing and purchased by Steven from a Spanish dealer, after having been smuggled out through Switzerland.

Opposite the fireplace, bow windows with leaded panes and ancient wavy glass looked out over the rose garden. The other two walls housed Steven's collection of rare books, each boxed in its individual leather-bound container and lettered in gold leaf. The shelves reached from floor to the high moulded ceiling. It was a passion that the brothers shared.

Steven stood now in the fireplace with his back to the flames, one hand clasped in the small of his back, hoisting up the skirts of his tweed jacket to warm his backside. In the other hand he held a deep crystal tumbler, still half-filled with whisky, hardly diluted by the soda he had dashed into it from the syphon.

Steven still looked shaken and pale, and every few minutes he shivered uncontrollably, although the room was oppressively heated by the blazing fire and all the windows were closed tightly.

Peter sprawled in the brocade-upholstered Louis Quatorze chair across the room, his legs thrust out straight and crossed at the ankles, hands thrust deeply into his pockets, and his chin lowered on his chest in deep thought.

"How much was your contribution to Caliph's war-chest?" Peter asked abruptly.

"I was not in the same class as Aaron Altmann," Steven answered quietly. "I pledged five millions in sterling over five years."

"So we must imagine a network extending across all international boundaries. Powerful men in every country, each contributing enormous sums of money—and almost unlimited information and influence."

Steven nodded and took another swallow of his dark-toned whisky.

"There is no reason to believe that it was only one man in each country. There may be a dozen in England, another dozen in Western Germany, fifty in the United States—"

"It's possible," Steven agreed.

"So that Caliph could very easily have arranged the kidnapping of Melissa-Jane through another of his chain in this country."

"You must believe I had nothing to do with it, Peter."

Peter dismissed this new protestation impatiently, and went on thinking out loud.

"It is still possible that Caliph is a committee of the founder members—not one man at all."

"I don't think so"—Steven hesitated—"I had a very strong impression that it all was one man. I do not think a committee would be capable of such swift and determined action." He shook his head, trying to cast his mind back for the exact words which had formed his impressions. "You must remember that I have only discussed Caliph with one other person, the man who recruited me. However, you can be certain that we discussed it in depth and over an extended period. I was not about to put out five million on something that didn't satisfy me entirely. No, it was one man who would make the decision for all of us—but the decisions would be in the interest of all."

"Yet there was no guarantee that any individual member of the chain would be informed of every decision?"

"No. Of course not. That would have been madness. Security was the key to success."

"You could trust somebody you had never met, whose identity was hidden from you—you could trust him with vast sums of money, and the destiny of the world as we know it?"

Steven hesitated again as if seeking the right words. "Caliph has an aura that seems to envelope all of us. The man who recruited me"—Steven seemed reluctant to repeat the name again, proof to Peter of the influence that Caliph exerted—"is a man whose judgement I respect tremendously. He was convinced, and this helped to convince me."

"What do you think now?" Peter asked abruptly. "Are you still convinced?"

Steven drained the whisky glass, and then smoothed his moustache with a little nervous gesture.

"Come on, Steven," Peter encouraged him.

"I still think Caliph had the right idea," he said reluctantly. "The rules have changed, Peter. We were fighting for survival of the world as we know it. We were merely playing to the new morality—"

He crossed to the silver tray on the corner of his desk and refilled the whisky glass.

"Up to now we have had one hand tied behind our backs, while the Reds and the extreme left and the members of the Third World have had both hands to fight with and a dagger in each one. All Caliph did was to take off our shackles."

"What has made you change your mind then?" Peter asked.

"I'm not sure that I have changed my mind." Steven turned back to face him. "I still think it was the right idea—"

"But?" Peter insisted.

Steven shrugged. "The murder of Aaron Altmann, the mutilation of Melissa-Jane"—he hesitated—"other acts of which I suspect Caliph was the originator. They were not for the common good. They were merely to protect Caliph's personal safety, or to satisfy what I am beginning to believe is vaunted and unbridled lust for power." Steven shook his head again. "I believed Caliph to be noble and dedicated—but there is no nobility in some of the things he has done. He has acted like a common criminal. He has acted for personal advantage and glorification. I believe in the concept of Caliph—but I know now we have chosen the wrong man. He has been corrupted by the power that we placed in his hands."

Peter listened to him carefully, his head cocked to one side, his blue eyes clear and quietly searching.

"All right, Steven. So you discovered that Caliph is not a deity— but a man with a man's petty greed and self-interest."

"Yes, I suppose I did." Steven's handsome florid face was heavy with regret. "Caliph is not what I believed he might be."

"Do you accept now that he is evil—truly evil?"

"Yes, I accept that." Then, fiercely, "But God, how I wish Caliph had been what I believed he was at the beginning."

Peter could understand that, and he nodded.

"It was what this crazy world of ours needed," Steven went on bitterly. "We need somebody, a strong man to tell us what to do. I thought it was Caliph. I wanted it so badly to be him."

"So now, do you accept that Caliph was not that man?"

"Yes," said Steven simply. "But if there was a man like that, I would follow him again, unquestioningly."

"You said you would do anything to prove to me that you had nothing to do with Melissa-Jane—will you help me to destroy Caliph?"

"Yes." Steven did not hesitate.

"There will be great personal risk," Peter pointed out, and now Steven met his eyes steadily.

"I know that. I know Caliph better than you."

Peter found that his affection for his brother was now reinforced with admiration. Steven lacked very few of the manly virtues, he thought. He had strength and courage and brains, perhaps his major vice was that he had too much of each.

"What do you want me to do, Peter?"

"I want you to arrange a meeting with Caliph—face to face."

"Impossible." Steven dismissed it immediately.

"You said that you had means of getting a message to him?"

"Yes, but Caliph would never agree to a meeting."

"Steven, what is the single—the only weakness that Caliph has shown so far?"

"He has shown no weakness."

"Yes, he has," Peter denied.

"What is it?"

"He is obsessed with protecting his personal identity and safety," Peter pointed out. "As soon as that is threatened, he immediately reverts to abduction and torture and murder."

"That isn't a weakness," Steven pointed out, "it's a strength."

"If you can get a message to him—that his identity is in jeopardy. That somebody, an enemy, has penetrated his security screen and has managed to get close to him," Peter suggested, and Steven considered it long and carefully.

"He would react very strongly," Steven agreed. "But it would not take him very long to find out that I was lying. That would immediately discredit me, and as you said earlier I would be at grave risk for no good reason."

"It isn't a lie," Peter told him grimly. "There is a Mossad agent close to Caliph. Very close to him."

"How do you know that?" Steven asked sharply.

"I cannot tell you," Peter said. "But the information is ironclad. I even know the agent's code-name. I give you my word that the information is genuine."

"In that case"—Steven thought it out again—"Caliph would probably already be suspicious and would be prepared to accept my warning. However, all he would do would be to ask me to give him the name—pass it to him along his usual communications channel. That would be it."

"You would refuse to pass the information—except face to face. You will protest that the information is much too sensitive. You would protest that your personal safety was at stake. What would be his reaction?"

"I would expect him to put pressure on me to divulge the name—"

"If you resisted?"

"I suppose he would have to agree to a meeting. As you have pointed out, it is his major obsession. But, if he met me face to face, his identity would be revealed anyway."

"Think, Steven. You know how his mind works."

It took a few seconds, then Steven's expression changed, consternation twisting his lips as though he was in pain.

"Good God—of course. If I forced him to a face-to-face meeting, I would be highly unlikely to survive it."

"Exactly," Peter nodded. "If we baited it with something absolutely irresistible, Caliph would have to agree to meet you—but he would make arrangements to have you silenced immediately, before you had a chance to pass on his identity to anyone else."

"Hell, Peter, this is creepy. As you told me earlier today, I am fat and out of condition. I wouldn't be much of a match against Caliph."

"Caliph would take that into consideration when deciding whether to meet you or not," Peter agreed.

"It sounds like suicide," Steven persisted.

"You just signed on to be tough," Peter reminded him.

"Tough is one thing, stupid is another."

"You would be in no danger until you delivered the message. Caliph would not dare dispose of you until you delivered your message," Peter pointed out. "And I give you my word that I will never call on you to go to an assignation with Caliph."

"I can't ask for more than that, I suppose." Steven threw up his hands. "When do you want me to contact him?"

"How do you do it—the contact?"

"Advertisement in the Personal column," Steven told him, and Peter grinned with reluctant admiration. Neat, efficient and entirely untraceable.

"Do it as soon as you can," Peter instructed.

"Monday morning," Steven nodded, and went on studying his brother with a peculiarly intent expression.

"What is it, Steven?"

"I was just thinking. If only Caliph had been somebody like you, Peter."

"Me?" For the first time Peter was truly startled.

"The warrior king—utterly ruthless in the pursuit of the vision of justice and rightness and duty."

"I am not like that." Peter denied it.

"Yes, you are," Steven said positively. "You are the type of man that I hoped Caliph might be. The type of man we needed."

Peter had to presume that Caliph was watching him. After his murder of Baroness Altmann, Caliph's interest would be intense. Peter had to act predictably.

He caught the early Monday flight back to Brussels, and before midday was at his desk in Narmco headquarters. Here also he was the centre of much interest and power-play. Altmann Industries had lost its chief executive and there were strong undercurrents and court intrigues already afoot. Despite a number of subtle approaches, Peter stayed aloof from the struggle.

On Tuesday evening Peter picked up the newspaper from the news-stand in the Hilton lobby. Steven's contact request was in the small-ads section.

The children of Israel asked counsel of the Lord, saying, shall I go up again to battle?   Judges, 20:23.

The quotation that Caliph had chosen seemed to epitomize his view of himself. He saw himself as god-like, set high above his fellow men.

Steven had explained to Peter that Caliph took up to forty-eight hours to answer.

Steven would wait each day after the appearance of the personal announcement at his desk in his office suite in Leadenhall Street, from noon until twenty minutes past the hour. He would have no visitors nor appointments for that time, and he would make certain that his direct unlisted telephone line was unengaged to receive the incoming contact.

There was no contact that Wednesday, but Steven had not expected one. On the Thursday Steven paced restlessly up and down the antique silk Kirman carpet as he waited for the call. He was already wearing the jacket of his suit, and his bowler and rolled umbrella were on the corner of the ornate French ormolu desk that squatted like some benign monster beneath the windows which looked across the street at Lloyds Exchange.

Steven Stride was afraid. He acknowledged the fact with direct self-honesty. Intrigue was part of his existence, had been for nearly all of his life—but always the game had been played to certain rules. He knew he was entering a new jungle, a savage wilderness where those few rules ceased entirely to exist. He was going in over his head; Peter had pointed out to him that this was not his way, and he knew Peter was right. Peter was right, and Steven was afraid as he had never been in his life. Yet he knew that he was going ahead with it. He had heard that it was the mark of true courage—to be able to meet and acknowledge fear, and yet control it sufficiently to be able to go ahead and do what duty dictated must be done.

He did not feel like a brave man.

The telephone rang once, too loud, too shrill—and every nerve in his body jumped taut and he found himself frozen, paralysed with fear in the centre of the beautiful and precious carpet

The telephone rang again, the insistent double note sounded in his ears like the peal of doom, and he felt his bowels filled with the hot oily slime of fear, hardly to be contained.

The telephone rang the third time, and with an enormous effort he forced himself to make the three paces to his desk.

He lifted the telephone receiver, and heard the sharp chimes of the interference from the public telephone system.

"Stride," he said. His voice was strained, high and almost shrill, and he heard the drop of the coin.

The voice terrified him. It was an electronic drone, inhuman, without gender, without the timbre of living emotion, without either high or low notes.

"Aldgate and Leadenhall Street," said the voice.

Steven repeated the rendezvous and immediately the connection was broken.

Steven dropped the receiver onto its cradle and snatched up his bowler and umbrella as he hurried to the door.

His secretary looked up at him and smiled expectantly. She was a handsome grey-haired woman who had been with Steven for fifteen years.

"Sir?" She still called him that.

"I'm popping out for half an hour, May," Steven told her. "Look after the shop, there is a dear." And he stepped into his private elevator and rode down swiftly to the underground garage where his Rolls was kept, together with the private vehicles of his senior executives.

In the elevator mirror he checked the exact angle of his bowler, a slightly raffish tilt over the right eye, and rearranged the bloom of the crimson carnation in the buttonhole of the dark-blue Savile Row suit with its faint and elegant chalk stripe. It was important that he looked and acted entirely naturally during the next few minutes. His staff would remark on any departure from the normal.

In the garage he did not approach the maroon Rolls-Royce

which glowed in the subdued lighting like some precious gem. Instead he went towards the wicket gate in the steel roll-up garage door, and the doorman in his little glassed cubicle beside the door looked up from his football pools coupons, recognized the master and leaped to his feet.

"Afternoon, Guv."

"Good day, Harold. I won't be taking the car. Just stepping out for a few minutes."

He stepped over the threshold of the gate, into the street and turned left, down towards the junction of Leadenhall Street and Aldgate. He walked fast, without seeming to hurry. Caliph spaced his intervals very tight, to make it difficult for the subject to pass a message to a surveillance unit. Steven knew he had only minutes to get from his office to the call box on the corner. Caliph seemed to know exactly how long it would take him.

The telephone in the red-framed and glass call box started to ring when he was still twenty paces away. Steven ran the distance.

"Stride," he said, his voice slightly puffed with exertion, and immediately the coin dropped and the same electronic droning voice gave him the next contact point. It was the public call box at the High Street entrance to Aldgate tube station. Steven confirmed, but the voice troubled him deeply, it sounded like that of a robot from some science fiction movie. It would not have been so bad if he had felt human contact.

The two receiving stations, neither of which was predictable, and the distances between them, had been carefully calculated to make it only just possible to reach them in time, to make it impossible for the call to be traced while the line was still open. Caliph or his agent was clearly moving from one call box to the next in another part of the city. Tracing them even a minute after he had left would be of no possible use in trying to establish identity.

The voice distorter that Caliph was using was a simple device no bigger than a small pocket calculator. Peter had told Steven that it could be purchased from a number of firms specializing in electronic surveillance, security and countermeasure equipment. It cost less than fifty dollars, and so altered the human voice—phasing out all sound outside the middle range—that even the most sophisticated recording device would not be able to lift a usable voice print to compare with a computer bank memory. It would not even be able to determine whether the speaker was a man, a woman or a child.

Steven had an unusually clear path to the station, and found himself waiting outside the call box in the crowded entrance to the station while a young man in paint-speckled overalls, with long greasy blond hair, finished his conversation. Caliph's system allowed for prior use of the chosen public telephone, and as soon as the scruffy youth finished his leisurely chat, Steven pushed into the booth and made a show of consulting the directory.

The phone rang, and even though he was expecting it, Steven jumped with shock. He was perspiring now, with the walk and the tension, and his voice was ragged as he snatched the receiver.

"Stride," he gulped.

The coin dropped and Caliph's impersonal tones chilled him again.

"Yes?"

"I have a message."

"Yes?"

"There is danger for Caliph."

"Yes?"

"A government intelligence agency has put an agent close to him, close enough to be extremely dangerous."

"Say the source of your information."

"My brother, General Peter Stride." Peter had instructed him to tell the truth, as much as was possible.

"Say the government agency involved."

"Negative. The information is too sensitive. I must have assurance that Caliph receives it personally."

"Say the name or position of the enemy agent."

"Negative. For the same reasons."

Steven glanced at his gold Cartier tank watch with its black alligator strap. They had been speaking for fifteen seconds—he knew the contact would not last longer than thirty seconds. Caliph would not risk exposure beyond that time. He did not wait for the next question or instruction.

"I will pass the information only to Caliph, and I must be certain it is him, not one of his agents. I request a personal meeting."

"That is not possible," droned the inhuman voice.

"Then Caliph will be in great personal danger." Steven found courage to say it.

"I repeat, say the name and position of enemy agent."

Twenty-five seconds had passed.

"I say again, negative. You must arrange a face-to-face meeting for transfer of this information."

A single droplet of sweat broke from the hairline of Steven's temple and ran down his cheek. He felt as though he were suffocating in the claustrophic little telephone box.

"You will be contacted," droned the voice and the line clicked dead.

Steven took the white silk handkerchief from his top pocket and dabbed at his face. Then he carefully rearranged the scrap of silk in his pocket, not folded into neat spikes but with a deliberately casual drape.

He squared his shoulders, lifted his chin and left the booth. Now for the first time he felt like a brave man. It was a feeling he relished, and he stepped out boldly swinging the rolled umbrella with a small flourish at each pace.

Peter had been within call of the telephone all that week, during the hours of involvement with the series of Narmco projects which he had put in train before his departure for Tahiti, and which all seemed to be maturing simultaneously. There were meetings that began in the morning and lasted until evening, there were two separate day journeys, one to Oslo and another to Frankfurt, catching the early businessman's plane and back in the Narmco office before evening. Always he was within reach of a telephone and Steven Stride knew the number; even when he was in the NATO Officers Club gymnasium, sharpening his body to peak physical condition, or practising until after midnight in the underground pistol range until the 9-mm Cobra was an extension of his hands—either hand, left or right, equally capable of grouping the X circle at 50 metres, from any position, standing, kneeling or prone—always he was within reach of the telephone.

Peter felt like a prize fighter in training camp, concentrating all his attention on the preparations for the confrontation he knew lay ahead.

At last the weekend loomed, with the prospect of being boring and frustrating. He refused invitations to visit the country home of one of his Narmco colleagues, another to fly down to Paris for the Saturday racing—and he stayed alone in the Hilton suite, waiting for the call from Steven.

On Sunday morning he had all the papers sent up to his room, English and American and French—German which he could read better than he spoke, and even the Dutch and Italian papers which he could stumble through haltingly, missing every third word or so.

He went through them carefully, trying to find a hint of Caliph's activity. New abductions, hijackings or other acts which might give him a lead to some new Caliph-dominated pressures.

Italy was in a political uproar. The confusion so great that he could only guess at how much of it was from the left and how much from the right. There had been an assassination in Naples of five known members of the Terrorist Red Brigade, all five taken out neatly with a single grenade. The grenade type had been determined as standard NATO issue, and the execution had been in the kitchen of a Red Brigade safe apartment in a slum area of the city. The police had no leads. It sounded like Caliph. There was no reason to believe that his "chain" did not include prominent Italian businessmen. A millionaire Italian living in his own country had to be the earth's most endangered species after the blue whale, Peter thought wryly, and they might have called on Caliph to go on the offensive.

Peter finished the continental papers, and turned with relief to the English and American. It was a little before Sunday noon, and he wondered how he could live out the desolate hours until Monday morning. He was certain that there would be no reply to Steven's request for a meeting before then.

He started on the English-language newspapers, spinning them out to cover the blank time ahead.

The British Leyland Motor Company strike was in its fifteenth week—with no prospect of settlement. Now there was a case for Caliph, Peter smiled wryly, remembering his discussion with Steven. Knock a few heads together for their own good.

There was only one other item of interest in his morning's reading. The President of the United States had appointed a special negotiator in another attempt to find a solution to the Israeli occupation of the disputed territories in the Middle East. The man he had chosen was Dr. Kingston Parker, who was described as a personal friend of the President and one of the senior members of his inner circle of advisors, a man well thought of by all parties in the dispute, and an ideal choice for the difficult job. Again Peter found himself in agreement. Kingston Parker's energies and resources seemed bottomless.

Peter dropped the last paper and found himself facing a void of boredom that would extend through until the following day. There were three books he should read beside his bed, and the Hermes crocodile case was half-filled with Narmco material, yet he knew that he would not be able to concentrate—not with the prospect of the confrontation with Caliph overshadowing all else.

He went through into the mirrored bathroom of the suite, and found the package that he had purchased the previous day in the cosmetic section of Galéries Anspach, one of the city's largest departmental stores.

The wig was of good-quality human hair, not the obviously shiny nylon substitute. It was in his own natural colour, but much longer than Peter wore his hair. He arranged it carefully along his own hairline, and then set to work with a pair of scissors, trimming and tidying it. When he had it as close to his liking as possible, he began to tint the temples with Italian Boy hair silvering.

It took him most of the afternoon, for he was in no hurry, and he was critical of his own work. Every few minutes he consulted the snapshot which Melissa-Jane had taken with her new Polaroid camera, Peter's Christmas present to her, at Abbots Yew on New Year's Day. It was a good likeness of both the Stride brothers, Peter and Steven, standing full face and smiling indulgently at Melissa-Jane's command to do so.

It highlighted the resemblances of the two brothers, and also pointed out their physical differences. The natural hair colouring was identical but Steven's was fashionably longer, curling on his collar at the back, and appreciably greyer at the temples and streaked at the front.

Steven's face was heavier, with the first trace of jowls, and his colour was higher, perhaps the first ruddy warnings of heart malfunction or merely the banner of good living in his cheeks. Yet with the wig on his head, Peter's own face seemed much fuller.

Next Peter shaped the moustache, trimming it down into the infantry officer model that Steven favoured. There had been a good selection of artificial moustaches to choose from in the cosmetic section, amongst a display of artificial eyelashes and eyebrows, but none had been exactly right. Peter had to work on it carefully with the scissors, and then tint it with a little silver.

When he fastened it in place with the special adhesive gum, the result was quite startling. The moustache filled out his face even further, and of course the eyes of the twins were almost exactly the same shape and colour. Their noses were both straight and bony. Peter's mouth was a little more generous, and did not have the same hard relentless line of lip—but the moustache concealed much of that.

Peter stood back and examined himself in the full-length mirror. He and Steven were within a quarter of an inch in height, they had the same breadth of shoulder. Steven was heavier in the gut, and his neck was thickening, giving him a thrusting bull-like set to his head and shoulders. Peter altered his stance slightly. It worked. He doubted that anybody who did not know both of them intimately would be able to detect the substitution. There was no reason to believe that Caliph or any of his closest lieutenants would have seen either Steven or Peter in the flesh.

He spent an hour practising Steven's gait, watching himself in the mirror, trying to capture the buoyant cockiness of Steven's movements, searching for little personal mannerisms, the way Steven stood with both hands clasped under the skirts of his jacket; the way he brushed his moustache with one finger, from the parting under his nose—left and right.

Clothing was not a serious problem. Both brothers had used the same tailor since Sandhurst days, and Steven's dress habits were invariable and inviolable. Peter knew exactly what he would wear in any given situation.

Peter stripped off wig and moustache and repacked them carefully in their Galéries Anspach plastic packets, then buttoned them into one of the interior divisions of the Hermes case.

Next he removed the Cobra parabellum from another division. It was still in the chamois leather holster, and he bounced the familiar weight of the weapon in the palm of his hand. Reluctantly he decided he could not take it with him. The meeting would almost certainly be in England. The contact that Steven had had on Thursday had clearly originated in London. He had to believe the next contact would be in that same city. He could not take the chance of walking through British customs with a deadly weapon on his person. If he was stopped, there would be publicity. It would instantly alert Caliph. He would be able to get another weapon from Thor Command once he was in England. Colin Noble would supply him, just as soon as Peter explained the need, he was certain of that.

Peter went down and checked the Cobra pistol into the safe deposit box of the hotel reception office, and returned to his room to face the wearying and indefinite wait. It was one of a soldier's duties to which he had never entirely accustomed himself—he always hated the waiting.

However, he settled down to read Robert Asprey's *War in the Shadows*, that definitive tome on the history and practice of guerrilla warfare down the ages. He managed to lose himself sufficiently to be mildly surprised when he glanced at his watch and saw it was after eight o'clock. He ordered an omelette to be sent up by room service, and ten seconds after he replaced the receiver, the telephone rang. He thought it might be a query from the kitchen about his dinner order.

"Yes, what is it?" he demanded irritably.

"Peter?"

"Steven?"

"He has agreed to a meeting."

Peter felt his heart lunge wildly.

"When? Where?"

"I don't know. I have to fly to Orly tomorrow. There will be instructions for me at the airport."

Caliph covering and backtracking. Peter should have expected it. Desperately he cast his mind back to the layout of Orly Airport. He had to find a private place to meet Steven and make the change-over. He discarded swiftly the idea of meeting in one of the lounges or washrooms. That left one other location.

"What time will you be there?" Peter demanded.

"Cooks have got me onto the early flight. I'll be there at eleven-fifteen."

"I'll be there before you," Peter told him. He knew the Sabena timetable by heart, and all senior Narmco executives had special VIP cards which assured a seat on any flight.

"I will book a room at the Air Hotel on the fourth floor of Orly South terminal in your name," he told Steven now. "I'll wait in the lobby. Go directly to the reception desk and ask for your key.

I will check behind you to make certain you are not followed. Do not acknowledge me in any way. Have you got that, Steven?"

"Yes."

"Until tomorrow, then."

Peter broke the connection, and went through into the bathroom. He studied his own face in the mirror.

"Well, that takes care of getting a weapon from Thor." Caliph had not set the meeting in England. It was clear now that Paris was only a staging point, and that in his usual careful fashion Caliph would move the subject on from there—perhaps through one or more staging points, to the final rendezvous.

The subject would go in unarmed, and unsupported—and Peter was certain that afterwards Caliph would take his usual pains to ensure that the subject would be unable to carry back a report of the meeting.

I am drawing two cards inside for a straight flush, and Caliph is the dealer from a pack that he has had plenty of time to prepare, Peter thought coldly, but at least the waiting was over. He began to pack his toilet articles into the waterproof Gucci bag.

Sir Steven Stride marched into the lobby of Orly South Air Hotel at five minutes past noon, and Peter smiled to himself in self-congratulation. Steven was wearing a blue double-breasted blazer, white shirt and cricket-club tie, above grey woollen slacks and black English handmade shoes—none of your fancy Italian footwear for Steven.

It was Steven's standard informal dress, and Peter had only been wrong about the tie—he had guessed that it would be an I Zingari pattern. Peter himself wore a double-breaster and grey slacks under his trench coat and his shoes were black Barkers.

Steven's eyes flickered around the lobby, passing over Peter sitting in a far corner with a copy of *Le Monde*, then Steven moved authoritatively to the reception desk.

"My name is Stride, do you have a reservation for me?" Steven spoke slowly, in rich plummy tones, for very few of these damned people spoke English. The clerk checked swiftly, nodded, murmured a welcome and gave Steven the form and the key.

"Four One Six." Steven checked the number loudly enough for Peter to hear. Peter had been watching the entrance carefully; fortunately there had been very few guests entering the lobby during the few minutes since Steven's arrival, and none of those could possibly have been Caliph surveillance. Of course, if this was a staging point, as Peter was certain it was, then Caliph would have no reason to put surveillance on Steven—not until he got much closer to the ultimate destination.

Steven moved to the elevator with a porter carrying his single small valise, and Peter drifted across and joined the small cluster of guests waiting at the elevators.

He rode up shoulder to shoulder with Steven in the crowded elevator, neither of them acknowledging the other's existence, and when Steven and the porter left at the fourth stage Peter rode on up three floors, walked the length of the corridor and back, then took the descending elevator to Steven's floor.

Steven had left the door to 416 off the catch, and Peter pushed it open and slipped in without knocking.

"My dear boy." Steven was in his shirt sleeves. He had switched on the television, but now he turned down the sound volume and hurried to greet him with both affection and vast relief.

"No problems?" Peter asked.

"Like clockwork," Steven told him. "Would you like a drink? I got a bottle in the duty-free."

While he hunted for glasses in the bathroom, Peter checked the room swiftly. A view down towards the square functional buildings of the market that had replaced the picturesque Les Halles in central Paris, matching curtains and covers on the twin beds, television and radio sets, between the beds, modern soulless furniture —it was a room, that was the most and the least that could be said for it.

Steven carried in the glasses and handed one to Peter.

"Cheers!"

Peter tasted his whisky. It was too strong and the Parisian tap water tasted of chlorine. He put it aside.

"How is Caliph going to get instructions to you?"

"Got them already." Steven went to his blazer, hanging over the back of the chair, and found a long white envelope in the inside pocket. "This was left at the Air France Information Desk."

Peter took the envelope and as he split the flap he sank onto one of the armchairs. There were three items in the envelope.

A first-class Air France airline ticket, a voucher for a chauffeur-driven limousine and a hotel reservation voucher.

The air ticket could have been purchased for cash at any Air France outlet or agency, the limousine and hotel bookings could have been made equally anonymously. There was no possibility of a trace back from any of these documents.

Peter opened the Air France ticket and read the destination. Something began to crawl against his skin, like the loathsome touch of body vermin. He closed the ticket and checked the two vouchers; now the sick feeling of betrayal and evil spread through his entire body, numbing his fingertips and coating the back of his tongue with a bitter metallic taste like copper salts.

The air ticket was for this evening's flight from Orly to Ben-Gurion Airport in Israel, the hired-car voucher was good for a single journey from there to Jerusalem, the hotel voucher was for a room in the King David Hotel in that ancient and holy city.

"What is it, Peter?"

"Nothing," said Peter, only then aware that the sickness must have shown on his face. "Jerusalem," he went on. "Caliph wants you in Jerusalem."

There was one person in Jerusalem at that moment. Somebody who had been in his thoughts almost unceasingly since last he had embraced her in the darkness of Bora-Bora Island—so very long ago.

Caliph was in Jerusalem, and Magda Altmann was in Jerusalem —and the sickness was heavy in the pit of his stomach.

The deviousness of Caliph.

"No," he told himself firmly. "I have travelled that road already. It cannot be Magda."

The genius of Caliph, evil and effortless.

"It is possible." He had to admit it then. "With Caliph, anything is possible." Every time Caliph shook the dice box the numbers changed, different numbers, making different totals—but always completely plausible, always completely believable.

It was one of the basic proven theorems of his trade that a man, any man, was blinded and deafened and rendered senseless by love. Peter was in love, and he knew it.

"All right. So now I have to try and free my mind and think it all over again, as though I were not besotted."

"Peter, are you all right?" Steven demanded again, now with real concern. It was impossible to think with Steven hovering over him. He would have to put it aside.

"I am going to Jerusalem in your place," Peter said.

"Come again, old boy?"

"We are changing places—you and I."

"You won't get away with it." Steven shook his head decidedly. "Caliph will take you on the full toss."

Peter picked up his Hermes case and went through into the bathroom. He worked quickly with the wig and artificial moustache and then called, "Steven, come here."

They stood side by side and stared at themselves in the mirror.

"Good God!" Steven grunted. Peter altered his stance slightly, conforming more closely to his brother.

"That's incredible. Never knew you were such a good-looking blighter," Steven chuckled, and wagged his head wonderingly. Peter imitated the gesture perfectly.

"Damn it, Peter." The chuckle dried on Steven's lips. "That's enough. You're giving me the creeps."

Peter pulled the wig off his head. "It will work."

"Yes," Steven conceded. "It will work—but how the hell did you know I would be wearing a blazer and greys?"

"Trick of the trade," Peter told him. "Don't worry about it. Let's go through the paperwork now."

In the bedroom they laid out their personal documents in two piles, and went swiftly through them.

The passport photographs would pass readily enough.

"You have to shave your soup-strainer," Peter told him, and Steven stroked his moustache with one finger, left and right—lingeringly, regretfully.

"Is that absolutely necessary? I'd feel like I was walking around in public with no trousers on."

Peter took the slim gold ball-point from his inside pocket and a sheaf of hotel stationery from the drawer. He studied Steven's signature in the passport for a minute, and then dashed it off on the top sheet.

"No." He shook his head, and tried again. It was like Steven's walk, cocky and confident, the T was crossed with a flourishing sword stroke of the pen.

In sixty seconds he had it perfected.

"With that wig on your head you could walk into my bank any

day and sign for the whole damned bundle," Steven muttered uneasily. "Then go home and climb into bed with Pat."

"Now, *there* is an idea." Peter looked thoughtful.

"Don't joke about it," Steven pleaded.

"Who's joking?" Peter went through the credit cards, club membership cards, driver's licence and all the other clutter of civilized existence.

Steven's mastery of his brother's signature was not nearly as effective, but after twenty minutes' practice was just adequate for hotel registration purposes.

"Here is the address of a hotel on the left bank. Magnificent restaurant, and the management are very understanding if you should want to invite a young lady up to your room for a drink."

"Perish the thought." Steven looked smug at the prospect.

"It should only be for a few days, Steven. Just keep very low. Pay cash for everything. Keep clear of the George V or the Meurice, Le Doyen and Maxim's—all the places where they know you."

They went carefully over the last details of the exchange of identity, while Steven shaved off the moustache and anointed the bare patch tenderly with Eau de Sauvage.

"You'd better move now," Peter told him at last. "Wear this"— it was Peter's buff trench coat that would cover his blazer—"and let's change ties."

Steven was ready, and he stood rather awkwardly by the door, in the tightly fitting trenchcoat.

"Steven, can I ask you a question?" Peter did not know why he had to know now, it had been buried so deeply for so long, and yet at this moment it was deadly important to know.

"Of course, old boy." Steven seemed to welcome the postponement of the moment of parting.

"Sandhurst." Peter tried to keep the embarrassment out of his voice. "I never asked you before—but you didn't do it, did you, Steven?"

Steven met his eyes calmly, steadily. "No, Peter, I did not do it. My word on it."

Peter took his brother's proffered right hand and squeezed it hard. It was ridiculous to feel so relieved.

"I'm glad, Steven."

"Take care of yourself, old boy."

"I will," Peter nodded. "But if anything happens"—Peter hesitated—"Melissa-Jane—"

"Don't worry. I'll take care of it."

Why do Englishmen have such difficulty talking to each other, Peter wondered, let alone communicating affection and gratitude?

"Well, I'll be getting along then," said Steven.

"Take a guard on your middle stump, and don't be caught in the slips," Peter cautioned him with the old inanity.

"Count on it," said Steven, and went out into the passage, closing the door behind him firmly, leaving his brother to think about Jerusalem.

Only the name had changed from Lod to Ben-Gurion—otherwise the Arrivals Hall was as Peter remembered it. One of the few airports on the globe which has sufficient luggage trolleys, so that the passengers do not have to fight for possession.

In the Arrivals Hall there was a young Israeli driver with the name:

Sir Steven Stride

printed in white chalk on a schoolboy's black slate.

The driver wore a navy-blue cap with a black patent-leather peak. It was his only item of uniform, otherwise he was dressed in sandals and a white cotton shirt. His English had the usual strong American turn to it, and his attitude was casual and friendly—he might be driving the limousine today, but tomorrow he could be at the controls of a Centurion tank, and he was as good a man as his passenger any day.

"Shalom, Shalom," he greeted Peter. "Is that all your luggage?"

"Yes."

"Beserder. Let's go." He did not offer to push Peter's trolley, but chatted amicably as he led him out to the limousine.

It was a stretched-out 240 D Mercedes-Benz—almost brand new, lovingly polished—but somebody had painted a pair of squinting eyes on each side of the chrome three-pointed star on the boot of the vehicle.

They had hardly pulled out through the airport gates when one of the characteristic aromas of Israel filled the cab of the Mercedes—the smell of orange blossom from the citrus orchards that lined each side of the road.

For some reason the smell made Peter feel uneasy, a sensation of having missed something, of having neglected some vital aspect. He tried to think it all out again, from the beginning, but the driver kept up a running commentary as they pulled up the new double highway, over the hills through the pine forests towards Jerusalem, and the voice distracted him.

Peter wished he had kept the list that he had drawn up in the hotel room at Orly instead of destroying it. He tried to reconstruct it in his mind.

There were a dozen items on the plus side. The third was:

"Magda told me about Cactus Flower. Would she have done so if she was Caliph?"

And then directly opposite, in the "minus" column:

"If Magda is Caliph, then Cactus Flower does not exist. It was an invention for some undisclosed reason."

This was the item that pricked him like a burr in a woollen sock. He kept coming back to it. There was a link missing from the logic of it, and he tried to tease it loose. It was there just below the surface of his mind, and he knew instinctively that if he missed it, the consequences would be dire.

The driver kept chatting, turning to glance back at him every few minutes with a cheerful demand for recognition.

"That's right, isn't it?"

Peter grunted. The man was irritating him—the missing item was there, just beginning to surface. He could see the shape of it. Why had the smell of orange blossom worried him? The smell of flowers? Cactus flower? There was something there, something missing from the list.

"If Magda is not Caliph then—" Was that it? He was not certain.

"Will that be all right, then?" The driver was insisting again.

"I'm sorry—what was that?"

"I said, I had to drop a parcel off at my mother-in-law's," the driver explained again. "It's from my wife."

"Can't you do that on your way back?"

"I'm not going back tonight." The driver grinned winningly over his shoulder. "My mother-in-law lives right on our way. It won't take five minutes. I promised my wife I'd get it to her mother today."

"Oh, very well then," Peter snapped. There was something

about the man he did not like, and he had lost track of the item that had been worrying him.

He felt as though he was in a chess game with a vastly superior opponent, and he had overlooked a castle on an open file, or a knight in a position to fork simultaneous check on his king and queen.

"We turn off here," the driver explained, and swung off into a section of new apartment blocks, all of them built of the custard-yellow Jerusalem stone, row upon row of them, Israel's desperate attempt to house its new citizens. At this time of evening the streets were deserted as families gathered for the evening meal.

The driver jinked through the maze of identical-seeming streets with garrulous confidence and then braked and parked in front of one of the square, boxlike, yellow buildings.

"Two minutes," he promised, and jumped out of the Mercedes, scampered around to the rear and opened the boot. There was a scratching sound, a small bump and then the lid of the boot slammed and the driver came back into Peter's line of vision—carrying a brown paper parcel.

He grinned at Peter, with the ridiculous cap pushed onto the back of his head, mouthed another assurance through the closed window:

"Two minutes—" and went into the main door of the apartment.

Peter hoped he might be longer. The silence was precious. He closed his eyes, and concentrated.

"If Magda is not Caliph then—then—" There was the ticking sound of the engine cooling, or was it the dashboard clock? Peter thrust the sound to the back of his mind.

"Then—then Cactus Flower exists." Yes, that was it! "Cactus Flower exists, and if he exists he is close enough to Caliph to know of Sir Steven Stride's threat to expose him—"

Peter sat upright, rigid in his seat. He had believed that Steven Stride would be perfectly safe—until after the meeting with Caliph. That was the terrible mistake.

"Cactus Flower must stop Steven Stride reaching Caliph!" Yes, of course. Christ, how had he not seen it before. Cactus Flower was Mossad, and Peter was sitting in a street of Jerusalem—Mossad's front yard—dressed as Steven Stride.

"Christ!" He felt the certainty of mortal danger. "Cactus

Flower probably made the arrangements himself. If Magda Altmann is not Caliph, then I am walking right into Cactus Flower's sucker punch!"

The damned clock kept ticking, a sound as nerve-racking as a leaky faucet.

"I am in Cactus Flower's city—in Cactus Flower's limo—"

The ticking. Oh God! It was not coming from the dashboard. Peter turned his head. It was coming from *behind him*; from the boot which the driver had opened and in which he had moved something. Something that was now ticking away quietly.

Peter wrenched the door handle and hit the door with his shoulder, instinctively grabbing the Hermes case with his other hand.

They would have stripped out the metal partition between the boot and the back seat to allow the blast to cut through. There was probably only the leather upholstery between him and whatever was ticking. That was why he had heard it so clearly.

Time seemed to have slowed, so he was free to think it out as the seconds dropped as lingeringly as spilled honey.

Infernal machine, he thought. Why that ridiculously nineteenth-century term should occur to him now, he could not guess, a relic from the childhood days when he read *Boy's Own Paper*, perhaps.

He was out of the Mercedes now, almost losing his balance as his feet hit the unsurfaced and broken sidewalk.

It is probably plastic explosive with a clockwork timer on the detonator, he thought, as he started to run. What delay would they use? Thirty seconds? No, the driver had to get well away. He had said two minutes, said it twice—

The thoughts raced through his mind, but his legs seemed to be shackled, dragging against an enormous weight. Like trying to run waist deep in the sucking surf of a sandy beach.

"It will be two minutes, and he has been gone that long—"

Ten paces ahead of him there was a low wall that had been built as a flower box around the apartment block. It was knee high, a double brick wall with the cavity filled with dry yellow earth and precariously sustaining the life of a few wizened oleander bushes.

Peter dived head first over the wall, breaking his fall with shoulder and forearm, and rolling back hard under the protection of the low wall.

Above his head were the large windows of the ground-floor apartments. Lying on his side, peering up at them, Peter saw the reflection of the parked Mercedes as though in a mirror.

He covered his ears with the palms of both hands. The Mercedes was only fifty feet away. He watched it in the glass, his body braced, his mouth wide open to absorb blast shock in his sinuses.

The Mercedes erupted. It seemed to open quite sedately, like one of those time-lapse movies of a rose blooming. The shining metal spread and distorted like grotesque black petals, and bright white flame shot through it—that was all Peter saw, for the row of apartment windows disappeared, blown away in a million glittering shards by the blast wave, leaving the windows gaping like the toothless mouths of old decrepit men, and at the same moment the blast smashed into Peter.

Even though it was muted by the thick wall of the flower box, it crushed him, seemed to drive in his ribs, and the air whooshed from his lungs. The fearsome din of the explosion clamoured in his head, filling his skull with little bright chips of rainbow light.

He thought he must have lost consciousness for a moment, then there was the patter of falling debris raining down around him and something struck him a painful blow in the small of his back. It spurred him.

He dragged himself to his feet, struggling to refill his empty lungs. He knew he had to get away before the security forces arrived, or he could expect intensive interrogation which would certainly disclose the fact that he was not Sir Steven.

He started to run. The street was still deserted, although he could hear the beginning of the uproar which must follow. The cries of anguish and of fear.

He reached the corner and stopped running. He walked quickly to the next alley behind an apartment block. There were no street lights and he paused in the shadows. By now a dozen figures shouting questions and conjecture were hurrying towards the smoke and dust of the explosion.

Peter recovered his breath and dusted down his blazer and slacks, waiting until the confusion and shouting were at their peak. Then he walked quietly away.

On the main road he joined a short queue at the bus stop. The bus dropped him off in the Jaffa Road.

He found a café opposite the bus stop and went through into the men's room. He was unmarked, but pale and strained; his hands still shook from the shock of the blast as he combed his hair.

He went back into the café, found a corner seat and ordered falafel and pitta bread with coffee.

He sat there for half an hour, considering his next move.

"If Magda Altmann is not Caliph—" he repeated the conundrum which he had solved just in time to save his life.

"Magda Altmann is not Caliph!" He knew it then with utter certainty. Cactus Flower had tried to stop Sir Steven Stride reaching Caliph with his denunciation. Therefore Magda had told him the truth. His relief flooded his body with a great warm glow—and his first instinct was to telephone her at the Mossad number she had given him. Then he saw the danger. Cactus Flower was Mossad. He dared not go near her—not yet.

What must he do then? And he knew the answer without having to search for it. He must do what he had come to do. He must find Caliph, and the only fragile thread he had to follow was the trail that Caliph had laid for him.

He left the café and found a taxi at the rank on the corner.

"King David Hotel," Peter said, and sank back in the seat.

At least I know the danger of Cactus Flower now, he thought grimly. I won't walk into the next one blind.

Peter took one glance around the room that had been reserved for him. It was in the back of the hotel and across the road the tall bell tower of the Y.M.C.A. made a fine stance from which a sniper could command the two windows.

"I ordered a suite," Peter snapped at the reception clerk who had led him up.

"I'm sorry, Sir Steven." The man was immediately flustered. "There must have been a mistake."

Another glance around the room and Peter had noted half a dozen sites at which Cactus Flower might have laid another explosive charge to back up the one that had failed in the back of the Mercedes. He would prefer to spend a night in a pit full of cobras rather than accept the quarters that Cactus Flower had prepared for him.

Peter stepped back into the passage and fixed the clerk with his most imperious gaze. The man scampered and returned within five minutes—looking mightily relieved.

"We have one of our best suites for you."

Number 122 commanded a magnificent view across the valley to the Jaffa Gate in the wall of the Old City, and in the centre of this vista towered the Church of the Last Supper.

The gardens of the hotel were lush with lawns and tall graceful palms, children shrieked gleefully around the swimming pool while a cool light breeze broke the heat.

The suite abutted onto the long open terrace, and the moment he was alone, Peter lowered the heavy roller shutters across the terrace door. Cactus Flower could too easily send a man in that way. Then Peter stepped out onto the private balcony.

On the tall stone battlements of the French Consulate adjoining the gardens they were lowering the Tricolour against the flaming backdrop of the sunset. Peter watched it for a moment— then concentrated again on the security of the suite.

There was possible access from the room next door, an easy step across from window to balcony. Peter hesitated—then decided to leave the balcony unshuttered. He could not bring himself to accept the claustrophobic effect of a completely shuttered room.

Instead he drew the curtains and ordered a large whisky and soda from room service. He needed it. It had been a long hard day.

Then he stripped off tie and shirt, wig and moustache and washed away some of the tensions. He was towelling himself when there was a tap on the door.

"Damned quick service," he muttered, and clapped the wig on his head and stepped into the lounge, just as a key rattled in the lock and the door swung open. Peter lifted the towel and pretended to be still drying his face to cover the lack of moustache on his lip.

"Come in," he gruffed through the towel, and then froze in the doorway, and a vice seemed to close around his heart and restrict his breathing.

She wore a man's open-neck shirt, with patch pockets on the breasts, and khaki combat breeches hugged her narrow hips. The long legs were thrust into soft-soled canvas boots. Yet she carried herself with the same unforced chic as if she had been dressed in the height of Parisian fashion.

"Sir Steven." She closed the door swiftly behind her, and Peter saw her palm the slim metal pick with which she had turned the lock. "I'm Magda Altmann, we have met before. I have come to warn you that you are in very grave danger."

The abundant short curls formed a dark halo around her head, and her eyes were huge and green with concern.

"You must immediately leave this country. I have my private executive jet aircraft at an airfield near here—

Peter lowered the towel enough to allow himself to speak.

"Why are you telling me this?" he interrupted her brusquely. "And why should I believe you?"

He saw the quick roses of anger bloom in her cheeks.

"You are dabbling in things you do not understand."

"Why should you want to warn me?" Peter insisted.

"Because"—she hesitated and then went on sharply—"because you are Peter Stride's brother. For that reason and no other I would not want you killed."

Peter tossed the towel back into the bathroom and with the same movement pulled off the wig and dropped it onto the chair beside him.

"Peter!" Astonishment riveted her and she stared at him, the colour that anger had painted in her cheeks fled and her eyes turned a deep luminous green. He had forgotten once again how beautiful she was.

"Well, don't just stand there," he said, and she ran to him on those long, graceful legs and flung her arms around his neck.

They strained together silently, neither of them found words necessary for many minutes. Then she broke away.

"Peter, darling—I cannot stay long. I took a terrible chance coming here at all. They are watching the hotel and the girls on the switchboard are Mossad. That is why I could not telephone."

"Tell me everything you can," he ordered.

"All right, but hold me, chéri. I do not wish to waste a minute of this little time we have together."

She hid in the bathroom when the waiter brought the whisky, then joined Peter on the couch.

"Cactus Flower reported to control that Steven had requested a meeting with Caliph, and that he intended to denounce him. That was all I knew until yesterday—but I could build on that. First of all I was amazed that Steven was the subject of the first Cactus Flower report and not you, Peter—" She caressed the smooth hard brown muscle of his chest as she spoke. "It had never occurred to me, even when we discussed the fact that the report mentioned no Christian name."

"It didn't occur to me either, not until I'd already left Les Neuf Poissons."

"Then, of course, I guessed that you had taxed Steven with it, and told him the source of your information. It would have been a crazy thing to do—not your usual style, at all. But I thought that being your brother—" She trailed off.

"That is exactly what I did."

"Peter, we could still talk if we were on the bed," she murmured. "I have been without you for so long."

Her bare skin felt like hot satin, and they lay entwined with the hard smooth plain of her belly pressed to his. Her mouth was against his ear.

"Steven's request for a meeting went directly to Caliph through a channel other than Cactus Flower. He had no chance to head it off—"

"Who is Cactus Flower, have you found that out?"

"No." She shook her head. "I still do not know." And she raked her long fingernails lightly down across his belly.

"If you do that, I cannot think clearly," he protested.

"I am sorry." She brought her hand up to his cheek. "Anyway, Caliph instructed Cactus Flower to arrange the meeting with Steven. I did not know what arrangements were being made, until I saw Sir Steven's name on the immigration lists this evening. I was not particularly looking for his name, but as soon as I saw it I guessed what was happening. I guessed that Cactus Flower had enticed him here to make his interception easier. It took me three hours to find where Sir Steven would be staying."

They were both silent now, and she lowered her face and pressed it into the soft of his neck, sighing with happiness.

"Oh God, Peter. How I missed you."

"Listen, my darling. You must tell me everything else you have." Peter lifted her chin tenderly so he could see her face and her eyes came back into focus.

"Did you know that there was to be an assassination attempt on Steven?"

"No—but it was the logical step for Mossad to protect Cactus Flower."

"What else?"

"Nothing."

"You don't know if actual arrangements have been made for a meeting between Caliph and Steven?"

"No, I don't know," she admitted.

"You still have no indication at all of Caliph's identity?"

"No, none at all."

They were silent again, but now she propped herself on one elbow and watched his face as he spoke.

"Cactus Flower would have to make the arrangements for the meeting as Caliph instructed. He would not be able to take the chance of faking it—not with Caliph."

Magda nodded in silent agreement.

"Therefore, we have to believe that at this moment Caliph is close, very close."

"Yes." She nodded again, but reluctantly.

"That means that I have to go on impersonating Steven."

"Peter, no. They will kill you."

"They have already tried—" Peter told her grimly, and quietly outlined the destruction of the Mercedes. She touched the bruise in the small of his back where he had been struck by flying debris from the explosion.

"They won't let you get close to Caliph."

"They may have no choice," Peter told her. "Caliph is so concerned for his own safety—he is going to insist on the meeting."

"They will try and kill you again," she implored him.

"Perhaps, but I'm betting the meeting with Caliph is arranged to take place very soon. They won't have much opportunity to set up another elaborate trap like the Mercedes, and I'll be expecting it. I've got to go ahead with it, Magda."

"Oh Peter—" But he touched her lips, silencing the protest, and he was thinking aloud again.

"Let's suppose Mossad knew that I was not Steven Stride, that my real purpose was not to denounce Cactus Flower? What difference would that make to the thinking at Mossad?"

She considered that. "I'm not certain."

"If they knew it was Peter Stride impersonating Steven Stride," he insisted, "would that make them curious enough to let the meeting go ahead?"

"Peter, are you suggesting I turn in a report to my control at Mossad—?"

"Would you do that?"

"Sweet merciful God," she whispered. "I could be signing your death warrant, Peter, my darling."

"Or you could be saving my life."

"I don't know." She sat up erect in the bed and ran the fingers of both hands through the short dark curls, the lamplight glowed on her skin with a pale, smooth opalescence and the small fine breasts changed shape as she moved her arms. "Oh Peter, I don't know."

"It could be our only chance to ever get close to Caliph," he insisted, and the lovely face was racked with indecision. "Caliph believes I have killed you, he believes that I have transmitted a warning to him through my brother. He will have his guard as low as ever it will be. We will never have a chance again like this."

"I am so afraid for you, Peter. I am so afraid for myself without you—" She did not finish it, but pulled up her long naked legs and hugged her knees to her breast. It was a defensive foetal position.

"Will you do it?" he asked gently.

"You want me to tell my control your real identity, to tell him that I believe your real purpose is not to denounce Cactus Flower, but some other unknown."

"That is right."

She turned her head and looked at him.

"I will do it in exchange for your promise," she decided.

"What is that?"

"If I judge from my control at Mossad that you are still in danger, and that they still intend intercepting you before you reach Caliph—then I want your promise that you will abandon the attempt. That you will immediately go to where the Lear is waiting and that you will allow Pierre to fly you out of here to a safe place."

"You will be honest with me?" he asked. "You will judge Mossad's reaction fairly—and even if there is a half decent chance of my reaching Caliph, you will allow me to take that chance?"

She nodded, but he went on grimly, making certain of it.

"Swear it to me!"

"I would not try to prevent you—just as long as there is a chance of success."

"Swear it to me, Magda."

"On my love for you, I swear it," she said quietly, and he relaxed slightly.

"And I in turn swear to you that if there is no chance of meeting Caliph—I will leave on the Lear."

She turned against his chest, wrapping both her arms around his neck.

"Make love to me, Peter. Now! Quickly! I have to have that at least."

As she dressed she went over the arrangements for communicating.

"I cannot come through the switchboard here—I explained why," she told him as she laced the canvas boots. "You must stay here, in this room where I can reach you. If there is danger I will send someone to you. It will be somebody I trust. He will say simply. 'Magda sent me,' and you must go with him. He will take you to Pierre and the Lear jet."

She stood up and belted the khaki breeches around her narrow waist, crossing to the mirror to comb out the dark damp tangle of her curls.

"If you hear nothing from me, it will mean that I judge there is still a chance of reaching Caliph—" Then she paused and her expression altered. "Are you armed, Peter?" She was watching him in the mirror as she worked with her hair. He shook his head.

"I could get a weapon to you—a knife, a pistol?"

And again he shook his head. "They will search me before I am allowed near Caliph. If they find a weapon—" He did not have to finish it.

"You are right," she agreed.

She turned back to him from the mirror, buttoning the shirt over nipples of her breasts, which were still swollen and dusty red from their loving.

"It will all happen very quickly now, Peter. One way or the other it will be over by tomorrow night. I have a feeling here—" She touched herself between the small breasts that pushed out the cotton of her shirt. "Now kiss me. I have stayed too long already —for the safety of both of us."

Peter slept very little after Magda left him, even though he was very tired. A dozen times he started awake during the night with every nerve strung tightly, rigid and sweating in his bed.

He was up before first light, and ordered one of those strange Israeli breakfasts of salads and hard-boiled eggs with pale green centres to be sent up to his room.

Then he settled down once more to wait.

He waited the morning out, and when there had been no message from Magda by noon, the certainty increased that Mossad had decided not to prevent the meeting with Caliph. If there had been any doubt in Magda's mind, she would have sent for him. He had a light lunch sent up to the room.

The flat bright glare of noon gradually mellowed into warm butter yellow, the shadows crept out timidly from the foot of the palm trees in the garden as the sun wheeled across a sky of clear high aching blue, and still Peter waited.

When there was an hour left of daylight, the telephone rang again. It startled him, but he reached for it quickly.

"Good evening, Sir Steven. Your driver is here to fetch you," said the girl at the reception desk.

"Thank you. Please tell him I will be down directly," said Peter.

He was fully dressed, had been ready all that day to move immediately. He needed only to place the crocodile skin case in the cupboard and lock it, then he left the room and strode down the corridor to the elevators.

He had no way of knowing if he was going to meet Caliph, or if he was about to be spirited out of Israel in Magda's Lear jet.

"Your limousine is waiting outside," the pretty girl at the desk told him. "Have a nice evening."

"I hope so," Peter agreed. "Thank you."

The car was a small Japanese compact, and the driver was a woman, plump and grey-haired with a friendly, ugly face like Golda Meir.

He let himself into the back seat, and waited expectantly for the message, "Magda sent me."

Instead, the woman bade him "Shalom, Shalom" politely, started the engine, switched on the headlights and drove serenely out of the hotel grounds.

They swept sedately around the outer walls of the old city in the gathering dusk, and dropped down in the valley of Kidron. Glancing back Peter saw the elegant new buildings of the Jewish quarter rising above the tops of the walls.

When last he had been in Jerusalem that area had been a deserted ruin, deliberately devastated by the Arabs.

The resurrection of that holy quarter of Judaism seemed to epitomize the spirit of these extraordinary people, Peter thought.

It was a good conversational opening, and he remarked on the new development to his driver. She replied in Hebrew, clearly denying the ability to speak English. Peter tried her in French with the same result.

The lady has been ordered to keep her mouth tight shut, he decided.

The night came down upon them as they skirted the lower slopes of the Mount of Olives, and left the last straggling buildings of the Arab settlements. The lady driver settled down to a comfortable speed, and the road was almost deserted. It dropped gently down through a shallow valley, with the crests of a desolate desert landscape humped up each side of the wide metalled road.

The sky was empty of cloud or haze, and the stars were brighter white and clearer, as the last of the day faded from the western sky behind them.

The road had been well signposted, ever since they had left the city. Their direction was eastward towards the Jordan, the Dead Sea and Jericho—and twenty-five minutes after leaving the King David, Peter glimpsed in the headlights the signpost on the right-hand side of the road, declaring in English, Arabic and Hebrew that they were now descending below sea level into the valley of the Dead Sea.

Once again Peter attempted to engage the driver in conversation, but her reply was monosyllabic. Anyway, Peter decided, there was nothing she would be able to tell him. The car was from a hire company. There was a plastic nameplate fastened onto the dashboard giving the company's name, address and hire rates. All she would know was their final destination—and he would know that soon enough himself.

Peter made no further attempt to speak to her, but remained completely alert; without detectable movement he performed the pre-jump paratrooper exercises, pitting muscle against muscle so that his body would not stiffen with long inactivity but would be tuned to explode from stillness into instant violent action.

Ahead of them the warning signals of the crossroads caught the headlights, and the driver slowed and signalled the left turn. As the headlights caught the signpost, Peter saw that they had taken the Jericho road, turning away from the Dead Sea, and heading up the valley of the Jordan towards Galilee in the north.

Now the bull's horns of the new moon rose slowly over the harsh mountain peaks across the valley, and gave enough light to pick out small features in the dry blasted desert around them.

Again the driver slowed, this time for the town of Jericho itself, the oldest site of human communal habitation on this earth. For six thousand years men had lived here and their wastes had raised a mountainous tell hundreds of feet above the desert floor. Archaeologists had already excavated the collapsed walls that Joshua had brought crashing down with a blast of his ram's horns.

A hell of a trick. Peter grinned in the darkness. Better than the Nuke bomb.

Just before they reached the tell, the driver swung off the main road. She took the narrow secondary road between the clustered buildings—souvenir stalls, Arab cafés, antique dealers—and slowed for the twisting uneven surface.

They ground up onto higher dry hills in low gear, and at the crest the driver turned again onto a dirt track. Now fine talcum dust filled the interior and Peter sneezed once at the tickle of it.

Half a mile along the track a noticeboard stood on trestle legs, blocking the right of way.

"Military Zone," it proclaimed. "No access beyond this point."

The driver had to pull out onto the rocky verge to avoid the notice, and there were no sentries to enforce the printed order.

Quite suddenly Peter became aware of the great black cliff face that rose sheer into the starry night ahead of them—blotting out half the sky.

Something stirred in Peter's memory—the high cliffs above Jericho, looking out across the valley of the Dead Sea; of course, he remembered then—this was the scene of the temptation of Christ. How did Matthew record it? Peter cast for the exact quotation:

Again, the devil taketh him up into an exceeding high mountain, and sheweth him all the kingdoms of the world, and the glory of them—

Had Caliph deliberately chosen this place for its mystical association, was it all part of the quasi-religious image that Caliph had of himself?

He shall give his angels charge concerning thee: and in their hands they shall bear thee up—

Did Caliph truly see himself as the heir to ultimate power over all the kingdoms of the world—that power that the ancient chroniclers had referred to as "The Sixth Order of Angels"?

Peter felt his spirits quail in the face of such monumental madness, such immense and menacing vision, compared to which he felt insignificant and ineffectual. Fear fell over him like a gladiator's net, enmeshing his resolve, weakening him. He struggled with it silently, fighting himself clear of its mesh before it could render him helpless in Caliph's all-embracing power.

The driver stopped abruptly, turned in the seat and switched on the cab light. She studied him for a moment. Was there a touch of pity in her old and ugly face, Peter wondered?

"Here," she said gently.

Peter drew his wallet from the inner pocket of his blazer.

"No," she shook her head. "No, you owe nothing."

"*Toda raba,*" Peter thanked her in his fragmentary Hebrew, and opened the side door.

The desert air was still and cold, and there was the sagy smell of the low thorny scrub.

"Shalom," said the woman through the open window; then she swung the vehicle in a tight turn. The headlights swept the grove of date palms ahead of them, and then turned back towards the open desert. Slowly the small car pitched and wove along the track in the direction from which they had come.

Peter turned his back on it, allowing his eyes to become accustomed to the muted light of the yellow horned moon and the whiter light of the fat desert stars.

After a few minutes he picked his way carefully into the palm grove. There was the smell of smoke from a dung fire, and the fine blue mist of smoke hung amongst the trees.

Somewhere in the grove he heard a goat bleat plaintively, and then the high thin wail of a child—there must be a Bedouin encampment in the oasis. He moved towards it, and came abruptly into an opening surrounded by the palms. The earth had been churned by the hooves of many beasts, and Peter stumbled slightly in the loose footing and then caught his balance.

In the centre of the opening was the stone parapet which guarded a deep fresh-water well. There was a primitive windlass set above the parapet and another object which Peter could not immediately identify, dark and shapeless, crouching upon the parapet.

He went towards it cautiously, and felt his heart tumble within him as it moved.

It was a human figure, in some long voluminous robe that swept the sandy earth, so that it seemed to float towards him in the gloom.

The figure stopped five paces from him, and he saw that the head was covered by a monk's cowl of the same woollen cloth, so that the face was in a forbidding black hole beneath the cowl.

"Who are you?" Peter demanded, and his voice rasped in his own ears. The monk did not reply, but shook one hand free of the wide sleeve and beckoned to him to follow, then turned and glided away into the palm grove.

Peter went after him, and within a hundred yards was stepping out hard to keep the monk in sight. His light city shoes were not made for this heavy going, loose sand with scattered outcrops of shattered rock.

They left the palm grove and directly ahead of them, less than a quarter of a mile away, the cliff fell from the sky like a vast cascade of black stone.

The monk led him along a rough but well used footpath, and though Peter tried to narrow the distance between them, he found that he would have to break into a trot to do so—for although the monk appeared to be a broad and heavy man beneath the billowing robe, yet he moved lithely and lightly.

They reached the cliff, and the path zigzagged up it, at such a gradient that they had to lean forward into it. The surface was loose with shale and dry earth—becoming progressively steeper. Then underfoot the path was paved, the worn steps of solid rock.

On one hand the drop away into the valley was deeper always and the sheer cliff on the other seemed to lean out as though to press him over the edge.

Always the monk was ahead of him, tireless and quick, his feet silent on the worn steps, and there was no sound of labouring breath. Peter realized that a man of that stamina and bulk must be immensely powerful. He did not move as you might expect a man of God and prayer to move. There was the awareness and balance of a fighting man about him, the unconscious pride and force of the warrior. With Caliph nothing was ever as it seemed, he thought.

The higher they climbed, the more the moonlit panorama below them became increasingly magnificent, a soaring vista of desert and mountain with the great shield of the Dead Sea a brilliant beaten silver beneath the stars.

All the kingdoms of the world, and the glory of them, Peter thought.

They had not paused to rest once on the climb. How high was it, Peter wondered—a thousand feet, fifteen hundred perhaps? His own breathing was deep and steady; he was not yet fully extended, and the light sweat that dewed his forehead cooled in the night air.

Something nudged his memory, and he sniffed at the faintly perfumed aroma on the air. It was not steady, but he had caught it faintly once or twice during the climb.

Peter was plagued by the non-smoker's acute sense of smell. Perfumes and odours always had special significance for him—and this smell was important, but he could not quite place it now. It nagged at him, but then it was lost in a host of other more powerful odours—the smell of human beings in community. The smell of cooking smoke, of food and the underlying sickly taint of rotting garbage and primitive sewage disposal.

Somewhere long ago he had seen photographs of the ancient monastery built into the top of these spectacular cliffs, the caves and subterranean chambers honeycombing the crest of the rock face, and walls of hewn rock, built by men dead these thousand years.

Yet the memory of that faint aroma lingered with Peter, as they climbed the last hundred feet of that terrifying drop and came out suddenly against the stone tower and thick fortification, into which was set a heavy timber door twelve feet high and studded with iron bolts.

At their approach the door swung open. There was a narrow stone passageway ahead lit by a single storm lantern in a niche at the corner of the passageway.

As Peter stepped through the gate, two other figures closed on each side of him out of the darkness and he moved instinctively to defend himself, but checked the movement and stood quiescent with his hand half raised as they searched him with painstaking expertise for a weapon.

Both these men were dressed in single-piece combat suits, and they wore canvas paratrooper boots. Their heads were covered by coarse woollen scarves wound over mouth and nose so only their eyes showed. Each of them carried the ubiquitous Uzzi submachine guns, loaded and cocked and slung on shoulder straps.

At last they stood back satisfied, and the monk led Peter on through a maze of narrow passages. Somewhere there was the sound of monks at their devotions, the harsh chanting of the Greek Orthodox service. The sound of it, and the smoky cedarwood aroma of burning incense, became stronger, until the monk led Peter into a cavernous, dimly lit church nave hewn from the living rock of the cliff.

In the gloom the old Greek monks sat like long embalmed mummies in their tall wooden pews. Their time-worn faces were masked by the great black bushes of their beards. Only their eyes glittered, alive as the jewels and precious metals that gilded the ancient religious icons on the stone walls.

The reek of incense was overpowering, and the hoarse chant of the office missed not a single beat as Peter and the robed monk passed swiftly amongst them.

In the impenetrable shadows at the rear of the church, the monk seemed abruptly to disappear, but when Peter reached the spot he discovered that one of the carved pews had been swung aside to reveal a secret opening in the rock.

Peter went into it cautiously. It was lightless—but his feet found shallow stone steps, and he climbed a twisting stairway through the rock—counting the steps to five hundred, each step approximately six inches high.

Abruptly he stepped out into the cool desert night again. He was in a paved open courtyard, with the shining panoply of the stars overhead, the cliff rising straight ahead and a low stone parapet protecting the sheer drop into the valley behind him.

Peter realized that this must be one of the remotest and most easily defensible rendezvous that Caliph could have chosen—and there were more guards here.

Again they came forward, two of them, and searched him once again even more thoroughly than at the monastery gate.

While they worked Peter looked around him swiftly. The level courtyard was perched like an eagle's eyrie on the brink of the precipice, the parapet wall was five feet high. Across the courtyard were the oblong entrances to caves carved into the cliff face. They would probably be the retreats of the monks seeking solitude.

There were other men in the courtyard, wearing the same uniform with heads hidden by the Arab shawl headgear. Two of them were setting out flashlight beacons in the shape of a pyramid.

Peter realized they were beacons for an aircraft. Not any aircraft. Only one vehicle would be able to get into this precarious perch on the side of the precipice.

All right then, the beacons would serve to direct a helicopter down into the level paved courtyard.

One of the armed guards ended his body search by checking the buckle of Peter's belt, tugging it experimentally to make certain it was not the handle of a concealed blade.

He stood back and motioned Peter forward. Across the courtyard the big monk waited patiently at the entrance to one of the stone cells that opened onto the courtyard.

Peter stooped through the low entrance. The cell was dimly lit by a stinking kerosene lamp set in a stone niche above the narrow cot. There was a crude wooden table against one wall, a plain crucifix above it and no other ornamentation.

Hewn from the rock wall was a ledge which acted as a shelf for a dozen heavy battered leatherbound books and a few basic eating utensils. It was also a primitive seat.

The monk motioned him towards it, but himself remained standing by the entrance to the cell with his hands thrust into the wide sleeves of his cassock, his face turned away and still masked completely by the deep hood.

There was silence from the courtyard beyond the doorway. But it was an electric waiting silence.

Suddenly Peter was aware of the perfumed aroma again, here in the crude stone cell, and then with a small tingling shock he recognized it. The smell came from the monk.

Instantly, he knew who the big man in the monk's cowl was,

and the knowledge confused him utterly, for long stricken moments.

Then like the click of a well-oiled lock slipping home it all came together. He knew—oh God—he knew at last.

The aroma he had recognized was the faint trace of the perfumed smoke of expensive Dutch cheroots, and he stared fixedly at the big hooded monk.

Now there was a sound on the air, a faint flutter like moth's wings against the glass of the lantern, and the monk cocked his head slightly, listening intently.

Peter was balancing distances and times and odds in his head.

The monk, the five armed men in the courtyard, the approaching helicopter—

The monk was the most dangerous factor. Now that Peter knew who he was, he knew also that he was one of the most highly trained fighting men against whom he could ever match himself.

The five men in the yard—Peter blinked with sudden realization. *They would not be there any longer.* It was as simple as that. Caliph would never allow himself to be seen by any but his most trusted lieutenants, and by those about to die. The monk would have sent them away. They would be waiting close by, but it would take them time to get back into action.

There were only the monk and Caliph. For he knew that the dinning of rotor and engine was bringing Caliph in to the rendezvous. The helicopter sounded as though it were already directly overhead. The monk's attention was on it, Peter could see how he held his head under the cowl, he was off-guard for the first time.

Peter heard the sound of the spinning rotors change as the pilot altered pitch for the vertical descent into the tiny courtyard. The cell was lit through the doorway by the reflection of the helicopter's landing lights beating down into the courtyard with a relentless white glare.

Dust began to swirl from the down-draught of the rotors, smoked in pale wisps into the cell and the monk moved.

He stepped to the doorway, the empty dark hole in the cowl which was his face turned briefly away from Peter as he glanced out through the entrance of the cell.

It was the moment for which Peter had waited, his whole body charged, like the S in an adder's neck before it strikes. At the instant the monk turned his head away, Peter launched himself across the cell.

He had ten feet to go, and the thunder of the helicopter's engines covered all sound—yet still some instinct of the fighting man warned the huge man, and he spun into the arc of Peter's attack. The head under the cowl dropped defensively, so that Peter had to change his stroke. He could no longer go for the kill at the neck, and he chose the right shoulder for a crippling blow. His hand was stiff as a headman's blade and it slogged into the monk's shoulder between the neck and the humerus joint of the upper arm. Peter heard the collar bone break with a sharp brittle crack, high above even the roar of the helicopter's engines.

With his left hand Peter caught the monk's crippled arm at the elbow and yanked it up savagely, driving the one edge of shattered bone against the other so it grated harshly, twisting it so the bone shards were razor cutting edges in their own living flesh—and the monk screamed, doubling from the waist to try to relieve the intolerable agony.

Shock had paralysed him, the big powerful body went slack in Peter's grasp.

Peter used all his weight and the impetus of his rush to drive the monk's head into the doorjamb of the cell; skull met stone with a solid clunk and the big man dropped face down to the paved floor.

Peter rolled him swiftly and pulled up the skirts of his cassock. Under it the man wore paratrooper boots and the blue full-length overalls of Thor Command. On his webbing belt was the blue steel and chequered walnut butt of the Browning Hi-power pistol in its quick-release holster. Peter sprang it from its steel retaining clamp and cocked the pistol with a sweep of the left hand. It would be loaded with Velex explosives.

The woollen folds of the cowl had fallen back from Colin Noble's head, the wide generous mouth now hanging open slackly, the burned toffee eyes glazed with concussion, the big crooked prizefighter's nose—all the well-remembered features, once so dearly cherished in comradeship.

Blood was streaming from Colin's thick curling hairline, running down his forehead and under his ear—but he was still conscious.

Peter put the muzzle of the Browning against the bridge of his nose. The Velex bullet would cut the top off his skull. Peter had lost his wig in those desperate seconds, and he saw recognition spark in Colin's stunned eyes.

"Peter! No!" croaked Colin, desperately. "I'm Cactus Flower!"

The shock of it hit Peter solidly, and he released the pressure on the Browning's trigger. It held him for only a moment and then he turned and ducked through the low doorway leaving Colin sprawling on the stone floor of the cell.

The helicopter had settled into the courtyard. It was a five-seater Bell Jet Ranger, painted in the blue and gold colours of Thor Command—and on its side was the Thor emblem and the words:

THOR COMMUNICATIONS

There was a pilot still at the controls, and one other man who had already left the cabin of the machine and was coming towards the entrance of the cell.

Even though he was doubled over to avoid the swirling rotor blades, there was no mistaking the tall powerful frame. The high wind of the rotors tumbled the thick greying leonine curls about the noble head, and the landing lights lit him starkly like the central character in some Shakespearian tragedy a towering presence that transcended his mere physical stature.

Kingston Parker straightened as he came out from under the swinging rotor, and for an earth-stopping instant of time stared at Peter across the stone-paved courtyard.

Kingston Parker stood for that instant like an old lion brought to bay.

"Caliph!" Peter called harshly, and the last doubt was gone as Kingston Parker whirled, incredibly swiftly for such a big man. He had almost reached the cabin door of the Jet Ranger before Peter had the Browning up.

The first shot hit Parker in the back, and flung him forward through the open door, but the gun had thrown high and right. It was not a killing shot, Peter knew it, and now the helicopter was rising swiftly, turning on its own axis, rising out over the edge of the precipice.

Peter ran twenty feet and jumped to the parapet of the hewn stone wall. The Jet Ranger soared above him, its belly white and bloated like that of a man-eating shark, the landing lights blazing down, half dazzling Peter. It swung out over the edge of the cliff.

Peter took the Browning double-handed, shooting directly upwards, judging the exact position of the fuel tank in the rear of the fuselage, where it joined the long stalk-like tail—and he pumped the big heavy explosive shells out of the gun, the recoil pounding down his outflung arms and jolting into his shoulders.

He saw the Velex bullets biting into the thin metal skin of the underbelly, the tiny wink of each bullet as it burst, but still the machine reared away above him—and he had been counting his shots. The Browning was almost empty.

Eleven, twelve—then suddenly the sky above him filled with flame, and the great whooshing concussion of air jarred the stone under his feet.

The Jet Ranger turned over on her back, a bright bouquet of flame, the engine howling its death cry, and it toppled beyond the edge of the precipice and plunged, burning savagely, into the dark void below where Peter stood.

Peter began to turn back towards the courtyard, and he saw the armed men pouring in through the stone gateway.

They were Thor men, picked fighting men, men he had trained himself. There was one bullet left in the Browning. He knew he was not going to make it—but he made a try for the entrance to the stairway, his only escape route.

He ran along the top of the stone wall like a tightrope artist, and he snapped the single remaining bullet at the running men to distract them.

The crackle of passing shot dinned in his head, and he flinched and missed his footing. He began to fall, twisting sideways away from the edge of the precipice—but then the bullets thumped into his flesh.

He heard the bullets going into his body with the rubbery socking sound of a heavyweight boxer hitting the heavy punch bag, and then he was flung out over the wall into the bottomless night.

He expected to fall for ever, a thousand feet to the desert floor below, where already the helicopter was shooting a hundred-foot fountain of fire into the air to mark Caliph's funeral pyre.

There was a narrow ledge ten feet below the parapet where a thorny wreath of desert scrub had found a precarious hold. Peter fell into it, and the curved thorns hooked into his clothing and into his flesh.

He hung there over the drop, and his senses began to fade.

His last clear memory was Colin Noble's bull bellow of command to the five Thor guards.

"Cease fire! Don't shoot again!" And then the blackness filled Peter's head.

In the black swirl there were lucid moments, each disconnected from the other by eternities of pain and confused nightmare distortions of the mind.

He remembered being lifted up through the hatchway of an aircraft, lying in one of the light body-fitting Thor stretchers, strapped to it tightly, helpless as a newborn infant.

There was the memory of the inside cabin of Magda Altmann's Lear jet. He recognized the hand-painted decoration of the curved cabin roof. There were plasma bottles suspended above him, the whole blood was the beautiful ruby colour of fine claret in a crystal glass, and when he rolled his eyes downwards he saw the tubes connected to the thick bright needles driven into his arms—but he was terribly tired, an utter weariness that seemed to have bruised and crushed his soul—and he closed his eyes.

When he opened his eyes again, there was the roof of a long brightly lit corridor passing swiftly in front of his eyes. Gradually, he sensed the feeling of motion, and the scratchy squeak of the wheels of a stretcher. Quiet voices were speaking French, and the bottle of beautiful bright blood was held above him by long slim hands that he knew so well.

He rolled his head slightly and he saw Magda's beloved face swimming on the periphery of his vision.

"I love you," he said, but there was no sound and he realized that his lips had not moved. He could no longer support the weariness and he let his eyelids droop closed.

"How bad is it?" he heard Magda's voice speaking in that beautiful rippling French, and a man replied.

"One bullet is lying very close to the heart—we must remove it immediately."

Then the prick of something into his flesh searching for the vein, and the sudden musty taste of Pentothal on his tongue, followed by the abrupt singing plunge back into blackness.

He came back very slowly out of the dark, conscious first of the bandages that swathed his chest and restricted his breathing.

The next thing he was aware of was Magda Altmann, and how beautiful she was. It seemed that she must have been there all along while he was under. He watched the joy bloom in her face as she saw that he was conscious.

"Thank you," she whispered. "Thank you for coming back to me, my darling."

Then there was the room at La Pierre Bénite, with its high gilded ceilings and the view through the tall sash windows across the terraced lawns down to the lake. The trees along the edge of the water were in full leaf, and the very air seemed charged with spring and the promise of new life. Magda had filled the room with banks of flowers, and she was with him during most of each day.

"What happened when you walked back into the boardroom at Altmann Industries?" was one of the first questions he asked her.

"Consternation, *chéri*." She chuckled, that husky little laugh of hers. "They had already divided the spoils."

The visitor came when Peter had been at La Pierre Bénite for eight days, and was able to sit in one of the brocaded chairs by the window.

Magda was standing beside Peter's chair, ready to protect him from overexertion—physically or emotionally.

Colin Noble came into the room like a sheepish St. Bernard. His right arm was strapped and carried in a sling across his chest. He touched it with his good hand.

"If I'd known it was you—and not Sir Steven—I'd never have turned my back on you," he told Peter, and grinned placatingly.

Peter had stiffened, his face had transformed into a white rigid mask. Magda laid her hand upon his shoulder.

"Gently, Peter," she whispered.

"Tell me one thing," Peter hissed. "Did you arrange the kidnapping of Melissa-Jane?"

Colin shook his head. "My word on it. Parker used one of his other agents. I did not know it was going to happen."

Peter stared at him, hard and unforgiving.

"Only after we had recovered Melissa-Jane, only then I knew that Caliph had planned it. If I had known—I would never have let it happen. Caliph must have known that. That is why he did not make me do it." Colin was speaking quickly, urgently.

"What was Parker's object?" Peter's voice was still a vicious hiss.

"He had three separate objects. Firstly, to convince you that he was not Caliph. That's why his first order was to have you kill Parker himself. Of course, you never would have got near him. Then you were allowed to recover your daughter. It was Caliph himself who gave us O'Shaughnessy's name and where to find him. Then you were turned onto Magda Altmann—" Colin glanced at her apologetically. "Once you had killed her, you would have been bound to Caliph by guilt."

"When did you learn this?" Peter demanded.

"The day after we found Melissa-Jane. By then there was nothing I could do that would not expose me as Cactus Flower—all I could do was to pass a warning to Magda through Mossad."

"It's true, Peter," said Magda quietly.

Slowly the rigidity went out of Peter's shoulders.

"When did Caliph recruit you as his Chief Lieutenant?" he asked, his voice altered, softened.

"As soon as I took over Thor Command from you. He was never certain of you, Peter. That was why he opposed your appointment to head of Thor, and why he jumped at the first chance to have you fired. That was why he tried to have you killed on the Rambouillet road. Only after the attempt failed did he realize your potential value to him."

"Are the other Atlas unit commanders Caliph's lieutenants—Tanner at Mercury Command, Peterson at Diana?"

"All three of us. Yes!" Colin nodded, and there was a long silence.

"What else do you want to know, Peter?" Colin asked softly. "Are there any other questions?"

"Not now." Peter shook his head wearily. "There will be others later."

Colin looked up at Magda Altmann inquiringly. "Is he strong enough yet?" he asked. "Can I tell him the rest of it?"

She hesitated a moment. "Yes," she decided. "Tell him now."

"Atlas was to be the secret dagger in the sleeve of Western civilization—a civilization which has emasculated itself and abased itself before its enemies. For once we would be able to meet naked violence and piracy with raw force. Atlas is a chain of powerful men of many nations banded together, and Caliph was to be its executive chief. Atlas is the only agency which transcends all national boundaries, and has as its object the survival of Western society as we know it. Atlas still exists, its structure is complete—only Caliph is dead. He died in a most unfortunate air accident over the Jordan valley—but Atlas still exists. It has to go on, once that part which Caliph has perverted is rooted out. It is our hope for the future in a world gone mad."

Peter had never heard him speak so articulately, so persuasively.

"You know, of course, Peter, that you were the original choice to command Atlas. However, the wrong man superseded you—although nobody could know he was the wrong man at that time. Kingston Parker seemed to have all the qualities needed for the task—but there were hidden defects which only became apparent much later." Colin began enumerating them, holding up the fingers of his uninjured arm.

"Firstly, he lacked physical courage. He became obsessed with his own physical safety—grossly abusing his powers to protect himself.

"Secondly, he was a man of unsuspected and overbearing ambition, with an ungoverned lust for raw power. Atlas swiftly became the vehicle to carry him to glory. His first goal was the presidency of the United States. He was using Atlas to destroy his political opponents. Had he succeeded in achieving the presidency, no man can tell what his next goal would have been."

Colin dropped his hand and balled it into a fist.

"The decision to allow you to reach the rendezvous with Kingston Parker on the cliffs above Jericho was made by more than one man—in more than one country."

Colin grinned again, boyishly, disarmingly.

"I did not even know it was you. I believed it was Steven Stride, right up until the moment I turned my back on you!"

"Tell him," said Magda quietly. "Get it over with, Colin. He is still very weak."

"Yes," Colin agreed. "I'll do it now. Yesterday at noon, your appointment to succeed Doctor Kingston Parker as head of Atlas Command was secretly confirmed."

For Peter it was as though a door had at last opened, a door so long closed and locked, but through it now he could see his destiny stretching out ahead of him, clearly he could see it for the first time.

"You are the man best suited by nature and by training to fill the void which Kingston Parker has left."

Even through the weakness of his abused body, Peter could feel a deep well of strength and determination within himself which he had never before suspected. It was as though it had been reserved expressly for this time, for this task.

"Will you accept the command of Atlas?" Colin asked. "What answer must I take back with me?"

Magda's long fingers tightened on his shoulder, and they waited while he made his decision. It came almost immediately. There was no alternative open to him, Peter knew that—it was his fate.

"Yes," he said clearly. "Tell them I accept the responsibility."

It was a solemn moment. No one smiled or spoke for long seconds, and then,

"Caliph is dead," Magda whispered. "Long live Caliph."

Peter Stride raised his head to look at her, but his voice when he replied was so cold that it seemed to frost upon his lips.

"Never," he said, "call me that again, ever."

Magda made a small gesture of acquiescence, of total accord, then she stooped to kiss him on the mouth.

A NOTE ON THE AUTHOR

Wilbur Smith was born in Zambia in southern Africa and received his degree from Rhodes University. This is his thirteenth novel; among his other works are *A Sparrow Falls, The Eye of the Tiger, Eagle in the Sky, The Sunbird,* and, most recently, *Hungry as the Sea.* Mr. Smith lives with his wife in South Africa.